ONE SWEET KISS

"It's not here," Jane said. She turned toward the pines and laughed. "There it is! Stuck in one of the trees."

Thorpe rose from his knees and dusted off his buff breeches. The arrow had pierced the young trunk above the reach of her arms and Thorpe approached the tree and pulled the arrow from the ridged bark. He turned back to Jane. "A kiss for it?"

Jane stared at him in exasperation. "Keep it then!" she retorted. She would have moved away from him, but he caught her arm. "We can't be seen from here," he whispered. "One kiss, a brief kiss, nothing of passion, just a gentle touching of lips and I'll give it back to you. I don't want a trophy. I want you."

Jane wanted to slap his hand away, truly she did. So, what was it in the tenor of his voice, the deep resonance, that seemed to cause her to grow very still? She looked into his blue eyes and felt her heart begin hammering dangerously against her ribs. She could hardly breathe.

"You want me," he whispered. "One kiss? I'll only take one kiss, I promise you. Nothing more."

Jane saw the intense look in his eyes, saw his lips part and his head lean down toward her. A moment later, his lips were softly on hers, moist and gentle, a sensual delight that lifted her up high into the fragrant summer air . . .

Books by Valerie King

A DARING WAGER

A ROGUE'S MASQUERADE

RELUCTANT BRIDE

THE FANCIFUL HEIRESS

THE WILLFUL WIDOW

LOVE MATCH

CUPID'S TOUCH

A LADY'S GAMBIT

CAPTIVATED HEARTS

MY LADY VIXEN

THE ELUSIVE BRIDE

MERRY, MERRY MISCHIEF

VANQUISHED

BEWITCHING HEARTS

A SUMMER COURTSHIP

VIGNETTE

Published by Zebra Books

VIGNETTE

Valerie King

Zebra Books
Kensington Publishing Corp.

http://www.zebrabooks.com

ZEBRA BOOKS are published by

Kensington Publishing Corp.
850 Third Avenue
New York, NY 10022

First Printing: April, 1997
10 9 8 7 6 5 4 3 2 1

Printed in the United States of America

Now do take my advice, and write a play—if any incident happens, remember, it is better to have written a damned play, than no play at all . . .
—Frederic Reynolds

One

England, Derbyshire, 1817

Three acts and a farce.

His words came back to her.

Three acts and a farce.

Jane Ambergate pushed back pretty chintz curtains—a riot of blue and yellow flowers, green leaves, and a fluttering of red birds—in order to view the coachyard of the Peacock Inn. Lord Thorpe stood on the cobbles below, his feet planted apart as though he was on the deck of a ship of war.

Three acts and a farce.

These were the last words he had spoken to her a month ago, in June, at the very end of the London Season when he had again proposed that she succumb to the inevitable and become his mistress.

How much she hated him, the beast!

She recalled his words with a grimace that she was certain would add yet another unwanted wrinkle to her twenty-five-year-old complexion.

You and I aren't a great theatrical drama, he had insisted. *We are not three acts and a farce as most couples are. We're a vignette, beautiful but brief, quick flames that will come together then burn one another to cinders. Become my mistress, oh beautiful Jane. Forget Freddy and what would prove to be more farce than drama were the two of you to wed. Come with*

*me to Italy and the Mediterranean—a yacht, the constant sun-
shine, and more love than you've ever known.*

She had remembered how he had breathed his words into her
ear, promising delights she could only begin to imagine. She
had become dizzy, his tongue had traced the curve of her ear,
shivers had crept down her neck, her side, and had curled her
toes. Curled her toes! Even her toes had responded to his seductive ways.

The rogue!

The beast!

A kiss had followed.

Oh, why had she let him kiss her, barely hidden behind a
heavy forest-green velvet drape from an entire assemblage of
the *beau monde* in Lady Somercote's ballroom. She shouldn't
have slipped her arm about his neck. She shouldn't have encouraged him, but it was almost as though he had mesmerized
her. Was that his power, then, to cast the object of his flirtation
into a languid trance which the soundest reason couldn't defy?

Behind the drapes he had kissed her and not for the first
time, deeply and unrepentantly, until her body was aching for
him. Only Freddy's voice, calling to her from the hallway beyond, had saved her. She had come to her senses abruptly and
let her gloved hand give Thorpe a stinging slap across his
amused, handsome face.

The rogue!

The beast!

Only with the strongest effort was she able to shake off the
memory. Not that it did much good since Lord Thorpe was fully
visible to her from the upper-story window of her bedchamber.
He was standing by his flower-bedecked curricle, speaking to
Colonel Duffield. He held his beaver hat in his hand, slapping it
against his leg as he listened attentively to his friend. A moment
more and he suddenly broke into a roar of laughter, throwing his
head back and laughing like a commoner. Colonel Duffield was
an amusing man who could keep any drawing room alive with
a wealth of anecdotes he kept ready for every occasion.

Jane watched the men, wondering how she was to circumvent Thorpe's continuing his seduction of her. She was vulnerable to him, there was scarcely a female in London who was not, for Viscount Thorpe was an extremely handsome man. He possessed strong cheekbones, a slightly aquiline nose, sensual lips, and a firm jawline not softened in the least by the cleft of his chin. His eyes were stunning blue shards of glass that cut, seduced, or laughed at will. His brows were black, thick and arched. His hair was styled in Roman form, *a la Brutus,* in complete keeping with his strength of purpose and his determination to conquer the females to whom he gave dogged chase.

She was his object now. He had made that much clear to the entire *ton* at the outset of April. How it was he had finagled an invitation from her dear friend, Lady Somercote, she would never know, except that when he wished to be charming, none could surpass Lord Thorpe in the sweetness of his words, the perfection of his manners, or the beguiling resonance of his voice.

The rogue!

The beast!

She watched him, her anger at his presence in the small market town of Chadfield warring with her admiration of him. She wouldn't have been quite so susceptible to him had his beauty stopped with his face. How much easier it would have been and would be to deter his assaults if his body had been shriveled and uninteresting. Instead, he was like an Olympian god—as close to perfection as any man had ever been. He had a fine leg encased this morning in snug buckskin breeches, and his shapely calves were surrounded by perfectly constructed black leather top boots that gleamed in the July sunshine. He wore a dark blue coat of superfine molded to his broad shoulders and drawn to his narrow waist in a line so exquisite he might have been one of Michelangelo's statues come to life. His shirtpoints were moderate and held in rigid abeyance by a neatly tied neckcloth which other gentlemen copied and which had become known obscurely as *Thorpe's Revenge.* She thought the name had something to do with his having created the style in response to a challenge by Beau Brummell, but she had never been certain of it.

Whatever the case, he was all that any woman could want in a man. He was a Peer of the Realm and a man of fashion. He could do the pretty in a drawing room like none other. He was a strong, able dancer. He was handsome and wealthy. Only one thing was wanting to please the women of his acquaintance—in his ten years since his first London Season at the age of twenty-one, he had evinced not the smallest interest in taking a wife. He had had a dozen mistresses, several of whom had fought physically with him in public because of his notorious reputation for brutishly casting aside the ladies he conquered once he tired of them.

What a rogue!

What a beast of a man!

Unworthy of her notice or her interest!

Yet here she was, fixed by the window of her bedchamber at the Peacock Inn, staring down upon his handsome countenance like a schoolgirl and wondering what it would be like to make love to him.

At that moment, the flapping of his hat ceased suddenly and with a quick jerk he lifted his head and looked up at her. Good God! Could he read minds, as well?

She was caught, caught staring at him, caught lusting after him. She wanted to turn away with a lift of her chin but she wouldn't give him the satisfaction, not even when his smile grew crooked and lazy with understanding. Then he bowed, sardonically, a movement which caused Colonel Duffield to also look up at her. She narrowed her eyes slightly and inclined her head to them both. Then, with as much dignity as she could summon, she let the chintz curtain fall back into place.

Thomas Hathern, sixth viscount Lord Thorpe, chuckled softly as the chintz fell across the window and obscured his view of the widow Ambergate. His whole being was alive to her, a result of the hunt in which he was so contentedly engaged. He could not remember having enjoyed himself more even though Jane Ambergate had not yet fallen into his bed. The fact that she was proving difficult only enhanced the sensations he was experiencing, of vitality, of purpose, of intent. Every thought was fixed on possessing her, and by God he would before Lady Somercote's fortnight *fete* in Derbyshire was over.

At White's, his club in London—especially toward the end of the Season—the betting had increased with each passing sennight as to how soon he would break the widow to bridle. More than one of his friends had lost a small fortune because of his failure to achieve his object before the close of the Season in June. The odds changed again and again as the widow railed against his character, as she ignored his poetry, flowers, and jewel-boxes, as she resisted the kisses he stole from her. He had even become something of a laughing-stock, bested by an impoverished widow of insignificant connections who had been so foolish as to fall in love with an improvident Major of the Dragoon Guards, the 17th Lancers, who gambled away his fortune in the officers' tents on the Peninsula and in the Netherlands.

Thorpe could stand the nonsense, however. Let them laugh, he thought. Laugh all they would since he would be the one to taste of the widow's fruits and not any of them.

"Heard Linthwaite threatened to blow his brains out after losing his bet," the colonel offered, a half-smile on his lips.

"Linthwaite is a dimwitted nodcock," Thorpe responded indifferently. "Any man who would risk his fortune on a wager ought to set his pistol to his head and have done with it. Mark my words, whether he bets on my ability to get a lady into bed or not, he'll lose his fortune somehow. Such a man is almost determined on it."

The colonel shrugged his shoulders. "Can't help but think you may be right. Saw some of that in the Low Countries in '15. Watched a foot soldier stand up and cry out that Napoleon was a nearsighted frog and the next moment a six-pounder took his head right off."

Thorpe shook his head. He had nothing but disgust for a foolish man, and no sympathy at all.

The colonel took a confiding step toward Lord Thorpe. "So tell me, Thorpe, how did you manage to get an invitation from Lady Somercote? The *on dits* have it that she is pushing for a match between Waingrove and Mrs. Ambergate."

Lord Thorpe chuckled in a soft voice. "If I told all my secrets, the rest of you halflings would know how I work my wiles, and then where would I be?"

"You're as close-mouthed as Wellington!" the colonel cried.

Thorpe smiled crookedly. "You've never given me a finer compliment, Duffield. Thank you."

He watched the colonel's gaze shift from his face to an object just over his left shoulder. "You must excuse me," Duffield said quietly, his eyes narrowing. "You have your purposes and I have mine, and *she* has just climbed aboard her landau."

Thorpe turned as the colonel moved past him. He noted that Mrs. Newstead was settling herself into her rose and ribbon bedecked landau and was angling her parasol carefully in front of her against the strong July sunshine. The carriages were in line to travel eastward as soon as all the guests descended from their bedchambers. At eleven o'clock in the morning, the sun was Mrs. Newstead's enemy and not for the world would she risk the beauty of her complexion because of a stray sunbeam.

Faith, but she's pretty, he thought. She was a blonde piece of confection as tasty as she was avaricious. She had been his mistress last year and he would have been content to keep her longer, but she had gotten a bee in her bonnet about becoming his wife. What a fool she had been to suppose he would ever marry one of his mistresses. No, when he wed, his bride would be young, virginal, and trainable. He had almost resigned Mrs. Newstead to the limitations of her role when Mrs. Ambergate had appeared, her mourning clothes cast off, her beauty affixing his attention in a trice, her resistance to his advances, even at the outset, finalizing his intention of making her the next castle he meant to storm.

He watched Colonel Duffield climb the two steps of the carriage to take hold of Mrs. Newstead's small, gloved hand. Mrs. Newstead dimpled and demurred at something he was saying. She lowered her lashes, she smiled, she simpered. He knew her tricks, one and all. He watched her squeeze the colonel's hand before he bent to kiss her fingers, nearly falling into the landau as he did so.

Triumph was writ on every delicate blonde, peach, and blue-eyed feature. He understood something about her in that moment as he watched her in much amusement. She enjoyed the hunt as much as he did.

What was her game, though, he wondered.

They had parted on unusually amicable terms, a circumstance he found vaguely suspicious. But she had not upbraided him in public once since their separation, nor had she struck at him at a ball or at a masquerade as more than one of his former mistresses had done. No, Mrs. Newstead had far too much pride for that. But she had a reputation for connivery and cunning which had always sat a trifle uneasily with him. Of late, however, they seemed to have fallen into an easy friendship that appealed strongly to him and most of his suspicions had disappeared.

Whatever her present motives might be, however, when the door of the inn opened and Jane Ambergate stepped across the threshold and onto the dark stone cobbles of the innyard, Mrs. Newstead was entirely dismissed from his mind. For a long moment, he saw no one but Jane.

She was gowned in a costume that would have served any Cyprian well, he thought with a laugh. The decollete, charming to his eye, revealed at least one of the reasons he longed to take her to bed. Her breasts were full and ripe and utterly ill-concealed by her gauzy, white muslin gown. He would have wholly approved of her choice of attire had her purposes been to please him—which of course they were not. Regardless, her figure was perfection. The flowing fabric may have disguised her narrow waist and rounded hips, but he knew her figure well since he had held her in his arms frequently during the Season—mostly during

the waltz, but on more than one occasion he had stolen a kiss
from her.

He recalled their last kiss, shared from behind a pair of green
velvet drapes during a ball. He couldn't remember where they
had been, or much of what had happened afterward, but that
kiss, so electrified in quality, had stunned him in its intensity.
And Jane Ambergate had responded to him marvelously. He
could still recall the faint moan that had issued from her throat
as well as how scandalously she had leaned into him. Even now,
as he watched her, his body ached with the strong flow of
memories. He sighed. He wanted her badly.

She was beautiful, as well. He enjoyed simply looking at her.
She had large doe-eyes of a deep brown hue, fringed with thick
mahogany lashes. Her nose was straight and charming, her lips
of a rosy tinge were slightly bow-shaped and delightful for kissing. Her face was a perfect oval, her cheekbones high, her brows
carved in a soft arch over her large eyes.

A beautiful woman, indeed!

A luscious, softly curved, strong-willed, beautiful woman,
and very soon she would be his.

His gaze drifted to a young chit by the name of Henrietta
Hartworth who had emerged from the inn behind Jane and who
had linked arms with her.

Freddy Waingrove—the wealthy, honorable Frederick Waingrove—followed behind.

A lamb to the slaughter, he thought deliciously, as his gaze
settled on the tall young man. Perhaps he ought to warn him,
he pondered for half a second. But only half a second. He believed that simpletons of every order ought to be left to their
own devices as much as possible. That way they kept themselves
so occupied in their own stupidity that they rarely ever presented
a threat to his schemes.

Returning his gaze to Mrs. Ambergate, he noted that she was
scrutinizing in turn the line of coaches, curricles, landaus, and
gigs that stretched from the innyard and onto the High Street.
When she observed his own curricle, draped with mounds of

ivy and violet and gold ribbons, she let her gaze meet his. She was very careful, the widow Ambergate was. He liked that about her. She nodded civilly if not warmly. He returned her cool acknowledgement with a polite bow of his own, which he extended to Miss Hartworth and Mr. Waingrove.

Mr. Waingrove responded with a cold bow of his own. Some time in the past, toward the latter part of the Season, Mrs. Ambergate had informed Mr. Waingrove of a certain person—a gentleman, a *beast of a man*—who was taking liberties with her. Mr. Waingrove had foolishly tried to call him out. Fortunately, the encounter had been a private one and he had easily set aside Mr. Waingrove's accusations and his challenge.

Waingrove had tried to press him. "Then you will be known as a coward!" he had cried, his pale complexion dotted with pink patches. "For I shall tell everyone that you refused to meet me."

Lord Thorpe had eyed him contemptuously. "And if you dare to suggest any such thing to the *ton,* I shall go to Prinny myself and inform him that a certain man has chosen to flout the King's Law." Duelling had been outlawed for some time.

Waingrove had taken fright, just as Thorpe had meant him to. Later, he was certain the budding poet had thanked the stars for his refusal to pick up his gauntlet, for he would be dead by now as any simpleton would have known before trying to prove his honor on a duelling field with an opponent five times as accomplished with sword or pistol and in possession of a hundred times more bottom.

Thorpe had not hesitated to take Jane to task for having nearly cost her beau his life. To her credit, the widow had taken his rebuke to heart. She had blanched and nearly fallen into a swoon at the realization that her hints to a man of Freddy's stamp had had only one honorable effect—the challenge to a duel. Then, to his surprise, she had humbled herself—albeit for the first and last time in his acquaintance with her—and had thanked him sincerely for sparing the good and noble Mr. Waingrove. Of course, he would have been more gratified had he not suspected that her relief was due more to her hope of wedding Freddy's fortune than that her beau was spared the necessity of explaining to the heavenly host just how he had got himself killed.

As he watched Mr. Waingrove hand Mrs. Ambergate into her travelling chariot, as he watched Jane smile blindingly on the obtuse Mr. Waingrove, as he watched the pinched expression about Miss Hartworth's eyes, he turned away and smiled. How glad he was to be going to Challeston Hall, home of Lord and Lady Somercote, for their summer festivities. Endless amusements had already presented themselves, of plots and ploys, of wishings and yearnings, of love and of lust. Summer's bounty abounded in Derbyshire and in the fortnight festival Lady Somercote had planned for her guests.

He was ready. He had prepared himself for this day and for the following fortnight. He believed he would possess Mrs. Ambergate before the festivities had rung a final farewell. He would possess her and he would make her his next mistress.

As he mounted his curricle and settled his hat on his head, a troupe of musicians rounded the corner of the inn from the direction of the High Street and began playing their instruments. They were dressed in green clothes and wore mantles upon which had been stitched dozens of flowers, pine boughs, and ivy, a representation of summer which added to the joyous quality of the processional to Challeston Hall.

"The Joys of the Country" floated from their flutes, ancient lutes, and tambourines. Lord Thorpe laughed aloud. *The Joys of the Country,* indeed!

Jane heard Thorpe's laugh above the delightful sounds of the musicians and grimaced. She was placed fifth in the line of carriages and could see his hat through a mixture of windows, horses' heads, bouquets of flowers, and a rainbow of ribbons that floated from the coaches, gigs, and carriages in front of her. She found his laughter offensive, just as she found much about his lordship to be less than pleasing.

"So, what do you say, Mrs. Ambergate—Jane?"

Jane blinked and turned to look down at Freddy who was half perched on the carriage step and half on the ground as he leaned up toward her. She had been so distracted by Lord Thorpe's burst of laughter that she had failed to attend to her devoted swain. "I beg your pardon?" she queried softly, smiling sweetly upon him. "I fear the sunlight struck my eye and diverted my thoughts."

"But the sun is obscured by the roof of your coach, my pet," he corrected her gently.

Jane felt her smile grow stiff on her lips. "So it is," she responded more sweetly still. "Then I cannot imagine how it was that my mind began to run adrift. Pray, repeat your question, dearest one." She had persuaded him last week, while spending a few days at Mrs. Ullstree's home in Berkshire, to deepen his expressions of love for her by using pet endearments as well as her Christian name. If she was a little sickened by his perpetual use of his nicknames for her, she forebore her impatience and instead concentrated on his ten thousand a year.

At her command to repeat his question, he left the ground and seated himself on the carriage doorway and possessed himself of one of her hands. "I wish for a spiritual union, beloved Jane, more than life itself. I wish to be joined to you, to know your heart as only you know it. Tell me you wish for as much yourself."

His expression, so ardent, so hopeful, so covered in pink patches of anxiety, filled her with more joy than she had known in the past year of acute financial suffering.

Freddy wished for a union. He could mean only one thing of course—a union in which she would have preferred to wait to engage until their wedding night, but she had come to Derbyshire prepared to do whatever needed to be done in order to bring the wealthy, ethereal poet up to scratch.

She leaned toward him, trusting that the bodice of her gown, cut indecorously low, would engage his attention. She wore a gown of sheer muslin under which a somewhat immodest shift

of cambric hid only what was required to be hidden. But a skillful
bend of the waist could allow a gentleman a glimpse of his future.

She watched Freddy's gaze grow misty and his mouth fall
slightly agape as he caught sight of her charms. She pressed
his fingers and had the distinct satisfaction of watching him
swallow very hard. "My darling Freddy, I have longed to hear
you speak precisely these words—*a union*—for so many weeks
now that I am filled with joy at the expression of your wishes.
Of course I am willing to oblige you." She lowered her voice
and bent more closely toward him. "I will see that my key is
placed in your hands before the ball draws to a close tonight."

"Your key?" he murmured, blinking several times as he withdrew his gaze from the decollete of her gown and met her gaze.
"The key to your soul, of course. What a delightful metaphor,
my darling."

He was a remarkably attractive man, she thought, with his
golden hair swept forward about his temples and his brow, not
unlike Lord Thorpe's style.

But there, any similarity between the men ended. Freddy's
complexion was delicate and cherubic, his face oval, his lips thin
and rosy, his nose Patrician, his brow wide and sensitive. If ever
a poet was born and bred, Freddy Waingrove was that poet.

"A union, tonight," he whispered. His voice was hoarse as
he leaned toward her, almost as though he meant to place a
quite scandalous kiss on her lips. Immediately, she drew back.
She might be willing to let him into her bed tonight, but she
was entirely unwilling to risk her reputation merely because he
had determined he wanted a *spiritual union* with her.

He understood immediately. "I say!" he cried, shocked by
his own conduct. "Don't know what I was thinking! Never for
the life of me would I do harm to you or take that which was
not mine to possess, unless we were to be—"

Jane caught her breath. She waited. Her heart skipped several
beats. *Married!* Oh, Freddy, speak the words at last! Please!
Please! Open your mouth and speak the words! You can do it!
You can! *Unless we were to be married . . .*

He cleared his voice and looked away from her, his green-gold eyes taking on a distressed appearance. "That is . . . oh, I see that we are about to start! The musicians are filing toward the head of the procession and my Stanhope is second in line!" He turned toward her as he backed like a child out of her town chariot. "Tonight, my darling. Two sets at the ball?"

"Of course," Jane responded, smiling and trying with all her might to keep her severe disappointment from reaching her face before he was gone. As he slipped away, heading to the front of the line of carriages, she felt her spirits diminish in quick, painful stages.

Freddy had done it again. He had come to the brink of speaking of marriage to her, tottered on what appeared to be an ungovernable precipice for the tender spirit of the would-be poet, then fell back unable to bring himself to ask simply, "Jane, would you be my wife?"

Tears sprang to her eyes. She was glad to be in her closed town chariot so that she could allow some of her unhappiness to roll down her cheeks and fall to her lap. "Dear, hopeless Freddy," she murmured as she discreetly wiped her tears away. "Whatever am I to do with you?"

The question, posed in the silence of her coach, was soon forgotten as the processional to Challeston Hall began. The coaches in front of her began to move slowly forward. The musicians danced along beside the carriages, bowing to each guest as curricle, gig, and coach rolled down the King's Highway.

The small market town of Chadfield was situated on a gentle rise that descended to a golden stone bridge, bearing five arches, that crossed the River Hart. As Jane's postillion guided her chariot onto the cobbles of the High Street, an unobstructed view of Chadfield's primary geological attraction greeted her eyes— Wolfscar Ridge, a promontory of limestone that divided several miles of western Derbyshire and lent a wild, promising aspect to what was normally a calm, verdant series of gentle valleys and even gentler hills. A gorge allowed passage through the lower third of the ridge, but after that the villages of Bow Stones and Wirkwistle were separated by a route of more than eight miles even though, as the crow flies, they were but two miles apart since the ridge was otherwise narrow.

The sky above the easterly view of Wolfscar was an astonishing, cloudless blue, a sure sign that Lady Somercote's festivities would be smiled on by the heavens. The ridge was craggy but dotted with ash and oak until woods of pines and oak met the ridge near the valley's floor.

As her town chariot descended the decline toward the bridge, Jane saw that the village folk, undoubtedly having gathered from several of the surrounding smaller villages, as well as from Chadfield, had lined either side of the highway to cast flower petals and small fern leaves, ruffled off their fronds, at the carriages. Wooden whistles sounded along the way, tooted incessantly by mischievous boys. In the distance, she could hear music which the closer she drew to the bridge she realized was being performed by a string ensemble and a soprano, of beautiful voice, who sang a wistful popular ballad entitled, "The Poor Hindoo Girl."

By the time the wheels of Jane's coach rolled across the bridge and echoed off the water of the broad, swift-flowing River Hart, the full-voiced lady, gowned in a summery frock of lavender sprigged muslin, was performing, "My Mother Bids Me Bind My Hair."

Jane listened to the beautiful music, delighted in the sunshine glistening on the green grasses of the valley, and took great pleasure in the breeze that passed through her open windows. Children ran up to her windows and pelted her softly with rose petals until her lap, the seat on either side of her, as well as the floor of the carriage were covered in every shade of pink, yellow, deep burgundy, and white. She gathered up some of the petals and began herself to cast the flowers upon the heads of little girls, who wore wreaths of roses about long, curling locks. The girls squealed and scampered off, only to approach Mr. and Mrs. Ullstree's carriage behind Jane's.

She leaned her head out of her coach in the sheer joy of the moment, and waved at Henrietta and the Ullstrees who in turn waved back, their countenances also aglow with pleasure.

When the bridge was crossed and the rooftops of Ash Grange Farm came into view, the countryside opened up to another aspect no less pleasing than Wolfscar Ridge. Ten miles across, Windy Knowl graced the easterly horizon. The knoll rose in a soft curve and was cloaked in a thick pinewood that gave the rolling hill a bristled aspect. On the lower slopes of the hill was a herd of red deer, several score of which grazed along the flower dotted landscape. Lower still, and as the grade of the hill evened out to meet the valley floor, majestic Challeston Hall sparkled like a white diamond against the bright green of the grass and the dark forest of pine beyond.

The great house, of a light gray stone, was set in a park landscaped in the natural, picturesque design of Capability Brown. Scattered clumps of broad-based firs, towering beeches, and outcroppings of ancient oaks were mingled with lakes, stone bridges, and curved, graveled paths, lending the impression that nature alone had created the easy flow of the land. Except for the hedgerow surrounding the estate, dividing the lane and common lands from Lord Somercote's property, Challeston Hall looked as though it belonged to the valley and the valley to Challeston.

Farmlands, clumps of oaks, elms and pines, rooftops of barns, and the steeple of a far-off parish church dotted the outskirts of the estate. Jane thought of her husband's ill-tended, weed-infested property in Kent and shuddered.

Thoughts of Woodcock Hill Manor caused Jane to feel as though a cloud had suddenly moved swiftly over the countryside, dulling the sky, the pine-laden hills, and the white stone of Challeston. Poverty had robbed the manor of its beauty. The rainy English countryside lent itself to verdure and growth which was good for crops and bad for an estate that could not keep a staff of gardeners trimming the beeches, yews, hawthorns, blackthorns, and rhododendrons regularly. The manor was overgrown and seedy, not fit for a gentlewoman. But that hardly mattered since she would have to sell Woodcock Hill Manor at the end of July in order to keep from going to prison for her husband's debts.

At the end of July, she would have no home, no money, no jewelry, no furniture, no dowry, only the clothes on her back. She was worse than impoverished. She was destitute.

No one knew the truth, not even Lady Somercote.

Freddy Waingrove was her last hope.

With an effort born of months of training, she shook off the unhappy truths of her life, clasped her hands together tightly on her lap, and looked into the future. Somehow, she would overcome the poverty that snapped at her heels like a pack of hungry wolves. Somehow, she would keep the poorhouse at bay. Somehow, she would draw a proposal of marriage from Freddy's unwilling lips. Somehow.

She smiled.

Freddy had asked for a *spiritual union*. She knew him. She knew that once he was with her physically, he would be bound to her forever. He was not like Lord Thorpe who, once he possessed a woman, cast her aside like a worn-out greatcoat. Lord Thorpe had little respect or adoration for women. He took pleasure only in pursuing them, conquering them, and then treating them with punishing disrespect.

But Freddy! Freddy's love approached a form of worship. He had written her numerous sonnets and always his descriptions of her were exalted and high-minded. A physical love for Freddy would be nothing short of a spiritual union.

She found herself relaxing at these thoughts.

Tonight all would be settled.

She was sure of it!

When the carriages arrived at the front door of Challeston Hall, a squadron of footmen were waiting to escort the guests into the entrance where Lord and Lady Somercote awaited them. Jane stood on the threshold, behind Colonel Duffield and Mrs. Newstead, and let her gaze slowly rise toward the ceiling of the rotunda that formed the central roof of the entrance hall. She had the sense that she was in a cathedral, since the ceiling was enormously high and was painted in a dark midnight-blue over which the massive figures of biblical characters had been depicted—Adam and Eve, Moses, several kings, and finally a majestic Christ with a lamb at his feet. Intricate white stucco work framed the mural, below which three tiers of circular stairs spiraled downward, drawing her eye back to the entrance hall.

Some of the guests were already being taken to their rooms. She stepped forward and was greeted by Lady Somercote with a warm embrace.

"Welcome to Challeston, my dear Jane," the countess said. In a whisper, she added, "May all your dreams come true."

Jane felt a blush creep up her cheeks. Lady Somercote was her best ally in her pursuit of Freddy, but she was still uncomfortable being reminded of that pursuit.

Lady Somercote was a dignified woman of fifty years, her hair a lovely peppered gray. Her eyes were a light, smiling blue and her temperament was one of unruffled poise. She had a friendly disposition, enjoyed her duties as hostess more than any lady with whom Jane was acquainted, and once her loyalty was given, neither heaven nor hell would see it withdrawn.

Jane turned to greet her host, Lord Somercote, and suffered a shock. Gone was the powdered wig he habitually wore and in its place was a full head of thick hair dyed a flat black and styled in patrician wisps about his temples. "My lord," she breathed, hoping she did not betray in her manners the stupefaction she felt. "The country air seems to agree with you, for I have never seen you in better looks."

Lord Somercote beamed and his chest swelled with pride. He cast a brief, triumphant glance toward his wife, took Jane's hand, and with the aplomb of a dandy, placed a kiss on her fingers. Jane bit back the smile that cramped her cheeks. Lord Somercote looked absurd. She knew that he was speaking, that he was directing one of the servants to see to her comfort, but her senses were lost to everything except for that which she could see. He even looked thinner, and when she moved away from him and heard a strange creaking sound, she couldn't help but dart a glance toward him. He was bowing to Mrs. Ullstree and to Henrietta.

Good God! He was wearing a corset and his burgundy velvet coat was so tightly bound to his shoulders, arms, and back that she thought one more inch of bow and all the seams would pop. She withdrew her gaze abruptly, aware that she had begun staring at him. But the last thing she saw as she stepped around him and mounted the stairs nearly sent her into whoops. He was wearing a sash about his waist, like an officer, the fringe dangling almost to his knees.

She had never seen anything like it before! Had he become a dandy since the end of the Season? But why?

A half-hour later, Jane had perched herself on the edge of her bed and watched Lady Somercote anxiously. The countess was seated on a silk-damask chair of the palest, prettiest blue, near the doorway. She sat with one leg crossed over the other, the demi-train of her purple silk gown clinging to the carpet at her feet, one slippered foot bobbing nervously. Her elbow was on her knee and she tapped the fingertips of her right hand to her forehead. "I don't know how it happened—I don't know what happened! We were going along famously, the children were all wed and well established. I had just reached this glorious place in my life where I finally felt all my work was behind me and that I was now coming into my reward. Then, he dyed his hair!" At this point in her narrative, Lady Somercote lifted her head and eyed Jane in considerable bewilderment. "Jane!" she cried. "He dyed his hair! Tell me he does not look like a hideous crow!"

Jane was not certain how to comfort her good friend. "He—he appeared quite youthful, I thought," she offered tentatively.

At that, Lady Somercote rose abruptly from her chair. "Youthful!" she exclaimed. "Freddy is youthful. Even Thorpe is youthful. Somercote is—he's an old man, nearly sixty. I have never been more humiliated. He came down this morning—"

"This morning!" Jane cried, astonished. "Then you've had no warning, no time to adjust to the alteration in his appearance."

"Precisely so. And then there is *that woman!*"

Jane clasped her hands on her lap. She knew what Lady Somercote meant. "I didn't know she had been invited," Jane stated.

Lady Somercote began pacing. She started her nervous march at the ancient, carved wooden door, then wheeled her purple train about to march to the window, then back to the door. She rubbed her neck. "He was always faithful to me. Always. I didn't realize until now just how much his faithfulness meant to me. All those years when so many of his friends were conducting themselves in London with such disregard for their wives, spending their evenings at their clubs and in the arms of their mistresses, then using up the precious daylight hours in recovering from too much wine and the excesses of the Cyprian Corps. Never once did my dear Georgie stray. I suppose in some ways I felt superior." She stepped on her train, lifted her foot, and with a graceful sweep of her hand, moved the train out of the way, then continued her pacing. "Now look what has happened. And all because Mrs. Newstead decided she must have him. But why? Why my husband? Why couldn't she have set her sights on—on Mr. Ullstree?"

At that, Lady Somercote stopped in her tracks, met Jane's gaze, and both ladies burst out laughing. Mr. Ullstree, for all his worth, was a man of short stature, round cheerfulness, and a face that looked as though he had been made of pie dough and each feature shaped like a biscuit. Jane valued him as did any sensible woman. He was better than a good man, which made him a great man, and beloved by all who knew him. His character was above reproach, wisdom flowed from his mouth, and his wife, an extraordinarily beautiful woman, loved him infinitely.

Still, he was no Adonis and the thought of Mrs. Newstead casting sheep's eyes at him made Jane giggle more than once, even when poor Lady Somercote again took up her pacing.

"She is bent on having him, Jane," she said, nibbling on the side of her finger. She drew her finger back and stared at it strangely. "I've even begun that silly habit I had when I was a child and full of anxiety—chewing on my hand. What am I going to do? How am I going to keep Mrs. Newstead from his bed? I can see that he is determined on it."

"I still don't understand why you extended an invitation to her."

Lady Somercote reached the window which overlooked the gravel drive and the elegantly landscaped front grounds. She touched a fingertip to the glass and said, "He gave me no choice. If I didn't invite her, he wouldn't allow the *fete.*"

Jane was stunned. "He said as much?"

"Not precisely. Merely, that if she didn't come to Challeston, he would go to London."

Jane felt ill. "He is besotted!" she cried. "Is Mrs. Newstead a witch? How can she have bewitched him so?"

"There are some who have such gifts," Lady Somercote returned quietly.

Jane was caught up suddenly with the memory of Lord Thorpe kissing her behind the forest-green velvet drape. "Yes, some do," she murmured.

"What did you say?" the countess asked, turning back to Jane. "I didn't quite hear you."

"Nothing to signify," Jane said, sliding off the tall bed and crossing the room to stand beside her friend and hostess. Since the beginning of the Season, Lady Somercote had taken Jane under her wing. Her mother had been a good friend of the countess's many years ago, before she had died of the putrid sore throat when Jane was fifteen. The kindnesses with which Lady Somercote treated Jane now had resulted in not just a mother-daughter affection, but a real friendship in which the disparity in age seemed not to matter.

Jane slipped a comforting arm about Lady Somercote's waist. "You did right, though, by inviting Colonel Duffield, and if I were you, I would lay my concerns before him. He is quite an intelligent man and has been wanting to take Mrs. Newstead under his protection for some time. It is even gossiped that he wishes to marry her."

Lady Somercote let her hand fall away from the window and she turned around to eye Jane quizzically. "Are you certain of this?" she asked.

"Very much so. You have only to observe him a little today to see what his intentions, what his hopes, are. I am convinced he would make an exemplary ally."

"Jane, you give me hope. Now, if you'll excuse me and forgive me for deserting you, I think I ought to seek out the good colonel." She laughed as she crossed the room. "He is a charming man, a good man, though I must admit I hadn't understood until now precisely why he begged for an invitation to my *fete*. But why would he wish for a woman like Mrs. Newstead?" She was at the door, and her hand was on the brass handle as she posed the question.

Jane shrugged. "I don't understand men very well," she said. "Only look at the man with whom I tumbled in love and afterward married. Why did he gamble away his fortune and leave me ill-provided for?"

Lady Somercote released the handle and said apologetically, "Here I am, full of my own insignificant troubles when you are fixed so badly. But don't fret. I've arranged every meal so that Mr. Waingrove will be close at hand. Just do all that you've been doing and the future will secure itself. I'm sure of it."

Jane thought of what the night would hold for her in Freddy's arms and she was able to smile easily then to bid Lady Somercote to find the colonel at once.

Two

The long dining hall at Challeston was an impressive chamber some forty yards in length and housing a long mahogany table that could seat twenty-four people in a pinch. Tonight, Lady Somercote served twenty, including herself and her husband, eight house guests, and ten neighbors from the manor houses in the vicinity of Chadfield.

Jane looked up at the three massive chandeliers that drenched the table in a golden glow, then lowered her gaze to observe how beautifully the light reflected off the crystal goblets the countess had collected during the course of her lifetime. Silver service and a royal-blue trimmed plate sat in perfect symmetry to the edge of the table, the placement of the goblets and the position of each chair. White roses, mixed with blue columbine and trailing tendrils of ivy flowed from several large vases the length of the table.

The first course had been served and the second course was just beginning. The fare was excellent, of course. Lady Somercote was not to be surpassed by anyone. But Jane eyed each dish as it was offered to her with grave misgiving. Naturally, she accepted a small portion of them all, the lobster patties, thin slices of Yorkshire ham, stuffed pigeon, broccoli, asparagus, creams, jellies, and a variety of wines, but she had had her maid, Vangie, cinch her corset tightly beneath her breasts to make certain that her gown displayed her every beauty to perfection. The unfortunate result was that already she felt like the stuffed pigeon now being held beneath her nose for her inspection. She almost gagged as she nodded graciously to permit the footman to place a slice on her already burgeoning plate. Other than an unsteady appetite, however, she could not help but be gratified by the results of her careful toilette.

When she had descended the stairs wafting a soft, feathered fan over her features, Freddy's mouth had fallen agape. Just as it should have, she thought with pleasure.

Vangie had dressed her with intricate care. She had labored over her dark brown curls for over an hour until with curling tongs, hairpins, ribbons, and strings of pearls, she sported a ten-drilled rim of curls across her forehead, a smooth, braided chignon at the crown of her head, and a cascade of curls behind. The arrangement enhanced her delicate neck and sloped shoulders to perfection. She wore a string of pearls drawn toward the decollete of her gown by the weight of a silver locket. Her gown was of rose silk, slanted across her bosom and caught low on her shoulders with puffed sleeves. The bodice was trimmed with Brussels lace as were the sleeves and the hem. She wore pearl drops on her ears and had been liberal with her favorite perfume, oil of roses.

Her reflection in the mirror had prompted Vangie to sigh more than once. Jane recalled the moment she saw the transformation from travelling garb to balldress. She looked and felt like another woman entirely, not less so than because tonight she would be with Freddy and all her cares would at last disappear.

Later, at the bottom of the stairs, Freddy had forgotten all about Henrietta as he rushed forward to greet her. He had caught up her hand, his face aglow with worship and adoration. "Mrs. Ambergate," he had breathed. "Jane. You are a blazing candle in this dark, dark chamber."

Jane remembered having looked up at the chandelier in the entrance hall and bit her lip to keep from laughing. Over a hundred candles illuminated the foyer to a degree stronger than sunlight.

"How very sweet, Mr. Waingrove—Freddy." She had presented her gloved hand to him and he had caught it up in a passionate if awkward kiss. After giving expression to his strong sentiments he took up her arm and would not release it until he had escorted her to the drawing room where most of the guests had already assembled and had seen her comfortably settled on a chair of forest-green velvet.

"You have forgotten Miss Hartworth," she reminded him gently.

Freddy had gasped and hurried to find the hapless young woman. While he went in search of her, Jane had been introduced to many of the surrounding neighbors by Lord Somercote, whose bright black hair was still being stared at and remarked over by one and all. For the opening festivities, the guests' attire approached court-dress. The men wore only white—tail coats, waistcoats, satin breeches, stockings, and buckled shoes. The effect was summery and elegant. The ladies, of course, wore what pleased them, so long as the fabrics were the most expensive and finest to be found in the London shops and made up with the artistry only French dressmakers can achieve. Jewels glittered in the scattered candlelight of the dark green chamber, fans fluttered, snuff was passed round, and once Freddy returned with Miss Hartworth on his arm, he attended to them both in gentlemanly turns.

To wit, therefore, all was in readiness.

Jane had never known such sublimity as the moment had offered. The beauty of the assemblage was a balm to her soul, a reminder that not all the world lived on the edge of poverty as she had while she was married. She basked in each expensive perfection and over and over again turned to smile at Freddy and to assure him with her expressions and dimplings that she belonged to him.

Just before dinner, however, Freddy had appeared to be experiencing some pain. When she walked into the dining room, her arm lightly on his, she asked him quietly if all was well.

"Why yes, indeed!" he had stammered. "Every now and again, I feel a trifle queasy."

"Freddy, might I suggest you seek the advice of a physician, for it seems to me that more often than not you have the headache. Or am I mistaken?"

He had smiled, almost nervously at her. "You are not mistaken, though I trust your opinion of me will not now suffer because of my imperfect health."

"Why would it?" she had responded. "I admire your mind and your good heart above all else. We are none of us afterall, perfect in our bodies."

Now why had it been she wondered, that at that very moment, Lord Thorpe had passed in front of her, casting her a quizzical glance before chuckling, then moving away?

She knew his thoughts, the beast! She knew his opinion of Freddy—that she would eat him for breakfast if ever they married. And Thorpe—well, his body was perfection!

But she hadn't let Thorpe ruin the moment and she had turned her energies instead toward trying to make Freddy more comfortable throughout dinner.

He sat on her right and the owner of nearby Longcliffe Hall, Sir William Hazelwood, sat on her left. In turns, she attended to both men, taking a glass of wine with each of them as the moment decreed, enjoying listening to Sir William's county gossip—the well-dressings were not to be missed, especially the rather scandalous pose of an Adam and Eve at the village of Bow Stones—and recommending every medicinal treatment for the headache she could think of to poor Freddy.

While she was finishing the second course, she leaned close to her swain and gently touched his arm. "I hope your pains will not affect our *union*," she offered in a whisper.

Freddy turned and smiled adoringly at her. "Not in the least. In some ways, when I am experiencing such discomfort, I find that the spirituality of any moment can be considerably heightened."

Freddy had such an unusual way of looking at life that Jane did not know whether to be scandalized by what he had said or utterly mystified. How could the pain of the headache possibly enhance the lovemaking act? Whenever she had the headache, she screamed if anyone touched her.

Well, afterall, Freddy was poetical and perhaps he simply saw the universe in reverse. She turned back to Sir William and learned more about the traditional Derbyshire well-dressings which had been a custom of the county for many centuries. A viewing of the local well-dressings was to be part of Lady Somercote's festivities, so Jane listened to Sir William's discourse on the subject with great interest. According to tradition, the Derbyshire folk custom of dressing the local village wells with large clay tablatures pressed with flowers, seeds, and leaves to create biblical scenes, had begun centuries earlier as a thanksgiving for the pure limestone springs which had preserved the villagers from the Black Death.

Jane thought it a lovely sentiment and looked forward to viewing the well-dressings during the course of the festivities.

When at last dinner drew to a close, the ball commenced in which Lady Somercote officially welcomed her guests to a fortnight of beauty and delights such as only the summer and Derbyshire could possibly provide.

Jane danced gleefully until her feet and legs ached, then she danced some more. Once Freddy had gone down a few sets, his headache seemed to vanish and Jane was assured that the evening would not be sacrificed to his discomfort. She was happier than she could remember being in a long time. All was proceeding to the best of conclusions, her life was finally coming to a place of agreeable order, and nothing was going to happen that might possibly disrupt her enjoyment of her most triumphant moment.

She danced and sipped several iced cups of champagne. Again she danced, feeling giddy with life and hope and the pleasures of a ball.

Not even when Lord Thorpe claimed her for the waltz and began whirling her about the prettily decorated ballroom would she allow that anything could go wrong. She felt content in his arms, and soon quite dizzy—perhaps she had had one too many cups of champagne—as he turned her and turned her again. He was a strong, athletic dancer and she gave herself, for the first time, to a complete enjoyment of his abilities. She had no need for reserved conduct with him tonight. Tonight all would be settled between herself and Freddy, and Thorpe would no longer be a threat once her betrothal was announced.

But how much she delighted in Thorpe's expertise on the ballroom floor!

She was herself a rather physical woman. She loved to ride, to practice her archery daily, to play at billiards, to drive her phaeton around the country lanes in Kent.

"You are a fool, Mrs. Ambergate," Thorpe breathed into her ear as he turned her again. The music from the orchestra—some thirty musicians plying their instruments in all—flowed over her as she moved in rhythmic circles within the safety of his arms.

"A fool?" Jane countered archly, smiling and happy. "And why is that?"

"Because you are wasting your efforts on a simpleton—a boy of a man who is unworthy of you."

"Unworthy of me?" Jane cried, feeling giddy and thinking Lord Thorpe was the simpleton. "I? Unworthy of that great man? He is a gifted poet, if you must know, and one day he will be as admired as Byron and that new fellow, John Keats. Mark my words, you silly man!"

"How much champagne have you had to drink, Mrs. Ambergate?" he asked, eying her askance.

She smiled and giggled. "Not enough. Tonight I am celebrating."

He turned her and turned her again, drawing her scandalously close to him. "What are you celebrating, my pretty Jane?"

"I can tell you only that I know that very soon Freddy is going to ask me to marry him."

Thorpe frowned. "You're not serious?"

"But I am. He has spoken of a spiritual union and he is not one to speak lightly of such matters." She used Freddy's metaphor and believed that Lord Thorpe, being such an obtuse and beastly man would not possibly comprehend the underlying meaning of the words.

"Spiritual union?" he queried, a frown between his brows.

"Yes, tonight—that is, I mean I suppose you could say that tonight we are joining in a spiritual way. We are of a mind in so many things, you can have no idea."

Lord Thorpe, much to her surprise, fell silent. Jane was gleefully delighted. Let him wallow in his disappointment and despair. He would not have his widow afterall, many of his friends would lose their bets at White's, and she would enjoy every moment of her triumph from the second it became known she was to become the next Mrs. Waingrove.

Lord Thorpe was nonplussed for a long moment as he continued to waltz Jane Ambergate about the ballroom floor. She felt heavenly in his arms and her beauty was having an exhilarating effect on his senses. He had danced with her before, many times, but never like this. She felt so alive in his arms as though she was on the brink of experiencing nothing short of a joyous rebirth. He had a strong sense that were he to make love to her right now, in her present state of mind, it would be an event he would hold in the highest regard the remainder of his days.

The awareness of her extraordinary exhilaration prompted him to seek an understanding of what was going forward. From all that he had been able to determine during the course of the Season, as he skillfully listened to the conversations of others, then discreetly posed a question here and a question there, poor Freddy Waingrove was completely torn in his sentiments toward the beautiful Jane Ambergate. He loved her, but he frequently developed a nervous disorder, or a tic, or the headache when he was with her. Yet when he would return to her, he knew such sublime sensations as to cause him to fall into a fit of poetical musings and declarations. One moment he was madly in love with her. The next moment he declared she brought a madness out of him.

Why then was Jane convinced he was so close to offering for her?

After the waltz, he left Jane in the care of Mr. Marehay, the owner of a tidy property and manor house near the market town of Chadfield called Rowgreave Court. While they went down the complicated quadrille, while he noted that Jane missed many of the required turns and passes because of the champagne, while he delighted in the sound of her laughter as the attentive and jovial Mr. Marehay directed her to her proper places, he began his investigation.

When he hinted to Mr. Waingrove that *spiritual union* was a fine sentiment and that he wished he could achieve a more exalted approach to life, Mr. Waingrove at first proved resistant to speaking on the subject. But with a deftness born of practice, Lord Thorpe coaxed Freddy to expound on his philosophies. In order for a marriage to enjoy every prosperity, there must first be a spiritual union before a physical one. Spirituality, fineness of thought, of being, of words, of books, of companionship, these were the hallmarks of a truly noble and blessed marriage.

Freddy droned on and on.

Lord Thorpe listened with feigned attentiveness as he watched Jane move with grace and physical ease. There was so little that was spiritual about Jane, at least in the sense Freddy described, yet she had spoken of a *spiritual union* that was to occur tonight.

"So tell me," Lord Thorpe said, interrupting the genius's diatribe. "Can such a union take place in one night?"

"Never," Freddy responded firmly.

"Hmm," Lord Thorpe answered. "I have taken up far too much of your time. I see that Miss Hartworth is lacking a partner and is looking in your direction."

"Eh?" he cried. "Poor little thing. I should go dance with her, shouldn't I?"

Lord Thorpe restrained his amusement. "Yes, you most definitely should. I wonder what Miss Hartworth would think of the concept of *spiritual union*. From what little conversation I have had with her, I should think she would be intrigued by such a notion."

"You do?" Freddy queried. "I say, I rather think you may be right on that head." He then eyed Lord Thorpe strangely. "You're not such a bad fellow, are you?"

"I fear Mrs. Ambergate would disagree with you."

"Well, she is a female afterall," the poet responded cryptically, as he bowed slightly to Thorpe then made a quick, awkward progress toward Miss Hartworth.

Lord Thorpe quickly left the ballroom. He had a hunch about precisely what Jane's concept of a *spiritual union* might entail and he wasn't about to let the moment pass. He swiftly ascended the stairs, stole into her bedchamber, then rang for her maid.

Vangie was shocked when she scratched on the door, and he opened it and drew her swiftly inside. "Whatever are you doing, m'lord?" she asked.

"So tell me," he said, standing over the maid and intimidating her by placing his hands on her shoulders. "What has your mistress planned tonight? Tell me, Vangie, or I'll see to it that Lady Somercote learns of a certain footman with whom you've been dallying since you arrived."

Vangie gasped, blanched, and sank down onto the light blue silk-damask chair by the door. "You wouldn't," she whimpered.

"Wouldn't I just. Only tell me what is going forward tonight and I will allow you to continue your tryst in secret."

A moment later, Thorpe left Jane's room and went directly to Freddy's. Beneath a counterpane of gold satin, he found a brass key tied up with a violet ribbon and a missive addressed to Mr. Waingrove in Jane's script. He pocketed both and left the room.

To his surprise, he found Colonel Duffield in the hallway. "Missed my chamber," Thorpe said, chuckling.

"The devil you did," Duffield responded as he passed by him.

Thorpe went to his chamber and closed the door. He quickly opened the missive and read the brief note. *My dearest Freddy, you cannot imagine my delight at your suggestion of a union between us. I have left the key of which we spoke earlier today. I long to share my love with you. Yours, most faithfully, J. A.*

"Good God!" he breathed, partly in disgust at Jane's complete lack of knowledge of her "lover," and partly in the excitement at the thought of just how he meant to make use of the violet beribboned brass key.

Jane lay in her bed, enjoying the feel of the fine linen against her skin. She had debated for over half an hour whether to wear a modest nightdress or whether to leave off the unnecessary shift. In the end, she had chosen the latter because tonight she meant to ensure that Freddy would propose to her long before morning's light.

The bedcurtains were drawn securely about the bed. The moment between them would be utterly private. A single candle was lit on the nightstand beside the bed and she had pushed back the bedcurtain where it met the wall sufficiently to cast a glow upon her pillows. Her long brown hair was spread out on the embroidered cases and she had showered rose petals all over the bed. The fragrance was heady and combined with the champagne she had imbibed throughout the evening; her whole body was lit with a pleasant glow. She had known some pleasure with her husband, as infrequently as he had been at home with her during their five-year marriage, so she had no fear of the event about to transpire.

If only she loved Freddy, she thought wistfully. Yet she had loved Edward and he had proved to be so unstable that she had come to believe love was a fable that existed only in sonnets and plays, songs and myths. Reality was so different from the girlhood fantasies she and her friends had enjoyed that at twenty-five all she wanted from a marriage was the security that had been denied to her for the several years of her first marriage.

She closed her eyes and began to feel very sleepy. The champagne was having its effect afterall . . .

Freddy, she murmured as she drifted away into a delightful place of slumber.

The next moment she awoke in darkness to the sensation of a man in her bed. She gasped and would have cried out in her confusion but his hand was suddenly on her mouth. She awoke sufficiently to remember that Freddy was supposed to come to her.

She cooed his name. "Freddy, my darling." But he placed a finger on her lips, an indication he wanted no speech, nor did he speak. Just as well, she thought languidly as his fingers began tracing the line of her cheek and her jaw and her ear. She was too sleepy, her mind too dulled by wine, to speak and wanted only to give herself to him in dutiful response to his wishes.

How would a poet make love she wondered distractedly as she felt his tongue begin tracing the curve of her ear. Just like Thorpe, she thought with a laugh. His breath was now hot in her ear. He breathed so purposefully and the sensation was so wonderful that she moaned her delight and reached over to touch and stroke his arm. How muscular he was. She had not thought Freddy would be quite so strong. Of course he did like to ride. No, wait a minute. Freddy didn't like to ride, but Thorpe did. Thorpe loved to ride and to drive his horses pell-mell through the streets, even in London.

But this wasn't Thorpe, this was Freddy! Why had she drunk so much champagne!

Whoever the man with her was, she thought stupidly, she loved his breath and the sweet kisses he placed along her cheek and down her neck. A spattering of gooseflesh rippled down her side. She caught his scent which reminded her forcefully of Thorpe's shaving soap. How very odd to think such dissimilar men would use the same brand of soap.

He kissed her deeply and purposefully, his hands touching her gently. She drew in a long slow breath, enjoying the stroke of his hands over her curves. She overlaid his hand with her own, dragging her fingers along his arm. She heard him groan faintly, a sound that pleased her.

"I want a quiver full of children, my love," she whispered. The kiss that followed startled her for it was insistent and demanding. How quickly her whole body seemed to respond to his kiss. She again wrapped her arms about him. He held her so close to him that she could hardly breathe. Wildly, he kissed her until she felt that her body was on fire.

Her mind began to drift to magical places of warmth and safety. Each kiss he placed on her lips she returned with a kiss to match his own ardor. With each touch she offered a touch of her own. Unable to help herself, her mind became consumed with Thorpe. Deep within her heart she pretended that the man beneath the tips of her fingers and pressing his lips to hers was a man with demanding blue eyes and hair the color of a raven. She became lost in that magical place, her body responding to his as though she had been with him a thousand times. His kiss drew her time and again more deeply into herself and into the pleasure spiraling ever upward within her.

When he joined her the magic remained, clinging to her mind and to her body as though her life had always been this way. The rhythm of his love for her matched the strong beatings of her heart—the hopes of her life taking wing with each roll of his hips against hers.

She was saving herself and the children she would one day bear. She was at peace with herself.

Thorpe couldn't believe what was happening.

In his wildest dreams, he would not have conceived of Jane Ambergate responding to him—or was she responding to *Freddy?*—with such abandon, such sweet, marvelous sensuality. He had been pursuing her for so long, longing for her, that for him the pleasure was acute, almost to the point of painfulness. He let the pulse of his hips carry him out of himself. He felt free and alive, wonderfully alive as Jane moaned. He kissed her more deeply. She wrapped her arms tightly about him, the closeness of her body a soothing balm to the tension rising within him. As he moved over her and felt her back arch, he carefully guided her toward oblivion. She gave a cry that he silenced by placing his hand over her mouth, then equally his own need ripped through him in a long, wondrous wave of ecstasy.

Jane felt him shudder as he collapsed against her. She was stunned by how satiated she felt and the sensation prompted her to cling to him wishing that the moment would never end. She felt so safe and so at peace with the world and with the struggles of her life. She wanted to feel this way forever.

The moment could not last long, however. He stretched himself out beside her and held her fast for a long moment. Then, placing a farewell kiss on her neck and whispering for her to meet him at the yew maze at eleven o'clock on the morrow, he left her bed.

Jane wanted to call him back, to keep him beside her through the night, but she was too worn out to do more than make a protesting groan as the door clicked shut and the key turned in the lock.

Dear, dear Freddy. She breathed deeply, satisfied beyond words and content to know that in this moment she had secured her future. She would experience great happiness as Freddy's wife. Her thoughts began to drift to a place of dreaminess and bliss. She was moving through the halls of Swan Court, Freddy's home in Shropshire. Cherubic children bounded about her knees, a dozen of them.

A few exhausted, drowsy, satiated moments more and she was sound asleep.

Lord Thorpe bathed and dressed for bed, yet did not immediately seek his pillow. For a long time, he sat on the edge of his bed, his bare feet flat on the blacks and reds of the Aubusson carpet of his bedchamber. He was stunned, stunned by what he had done to Jane, stunned that she had let him, stunned that instead of feeling victorious in this moment, he felt sickened with regret.

Triumph had lasted until she had said, *I want a quiver full of children*. Somehow, her words, so innocently spoken, had changed everything for him, the way he viewed her, the way he saw what he was doing, even his desire for her instead of diminishing had only sharpened to a point of painful need, a need to touch her again, to have her respond to him, *to him,* to his touch, to his lovemaking.

Good God what was happening to him? He had seduced women before, this one should be no different, but for some reason she was. Yet, why? Perhaps because she had resisted him for so long and perhaps because he had taken her without her knowledge. That was something he had never done before—tricked a female. The strange thing was, he didn't feel guilty about it, at least not precisely. His conscience was not what was bothering him. It was something else, something he couldn't quite grasp, something beyond the edges of his reasoning.

Fatigue rolled over him suddenly. The day had been a long one—the processional from Chadfield, the dinner, the Opening Ball and then making love to Jane. He was dog-tired, he realized with a laugh. He threw back the counterpane of red silk and climbed between welcome sheets. What would happen tomorrow, he wondered.

He smiled as he drifted off. He could hardly wait.

The next morning, Jane awoke to an oddly drizzly sky. She pushed back her pale blue silk bed-hangings in order to enjoy the gray light flooding the chamber through the window. She sighed at the sounds of the rain. She didn't care whether it was raining, snowing, or hailing. She didn't care in the least. Nothing could dispel the way she felt right now—her sense of sunny peacefulness and contentment. Her body felt relaxed in a way it had not been for a long, long time. If ever, she thought with a start.

She giggled as she propped herself up on her pillows and recounted the night with glee. Her long, dark brown hair hung about her shoulders. She hadn't even bothered to put on her mobcap or her nightclothes, for that matter. She reached for her embroidered linen nightgown, hanging askew about the bottom bedpost, and quickly slipped it over her head. It wouldn't do for Vangie to discover her unclothed, though of the moment she felt as though she hardly cared about anything, even her modesty. Her thoughts were fixed sublimely on all that had happened last night.

When Freddy had finished with her and left her bed, she had been in too languid a state to do anything except fall deeply asleep.

Freddy, she murmured.

She blinked as she watched the rain spatter against the window in a light flurry. Summer storms never lasted long.

She sighed. She was to meet Freddy at the yew maze at eleven and the yew maze would be wet. But that didn't matter. All that mattered was that she see her lover again as quickly as possible, that she tell him how wonderful he had been last night, and that his ardor would prompt him to drop to his knee and beg for her hand in marriage.

She breathed a sigh of the deepest joy. They would be married, he would give her a dozen children, children she longed for with every particle of her soul and her spirit. She hadn't realized how much she wanted a family until she had told him as much last night.

A quiver full of children.

She had blurted out the words without thinking. Freddy had never spoken of whether he had wanted children or not, but his response to her words, the intensity of his kisses, had made his wishes clear.

The pleasure he had given her!

She was still in a dumbfounded state. How had Freddy been able to love her so expertly when he trembled every time he took her hand in his? He had kissed her once during the Season, clumsily, and afterward with so many apologies that she had felt chagrined. If Freddy was so afraid of kissing her how could he possibly make love to her? But last night he had proved her fears completely unfounded. Freddy was all she needed, all any woman needed, she thought wickedly.

Tonight. He would come to her again tonight. Those would be the first words she would speak to him in the yew maze. She would tell him to keep her key, she would insist he come to her every night during the festivities if he wished for it, she would hear his professions of love, she would accept his hand in marriage.

After a time, she unlocked her door and rang for her maid, then climbed back onto the large, four-poster bed. Glancing at the clock on the mantel, she saw that the hour was half past nine. Plenty of time to prepare herself to meet Freddy again.

Vangie arrived, her face oddly pinched with concern as she slipped into the bedchamber and dropped a nervous curtsy. "Yes, ma'am? Will you be having chocolate as usual?"

Jane smiled at her maid. "Yes, but I also want some eggs, bread, and brambleberry or apricot jelly, oh, and bacon if you please. Also, I want a bath—a very hot bath—and set the curling tongs to heating because I am meeting Mr. Waingrove at eleven."

She was surprised that her maid did not move a fraction of an inch for a long moment, but stood blinking at her quite strangely. Vangie was a pretty young lady, quite tall with large hazel eyes and a smattering of faint freckles across her nose. She wore a black bombazine gown over which she sported a lace apron. A white linen cap, trimmed with lace, covered her black curls. "Mr. Waingrove?" she queried in a faint voice.

"Well, yes, Vangie," she responded, a frown now creasing her brow. "Whatever is the matter? You've grown quite pale. Are you feeling well?"

Vangie gave her head a quick shake. "It's just that—well, I thought—that is—last night—"

"You are making no sense," Jane said, scooting up in bed. "Are you certain you didn't eat spoiled meat yesterday or perhaps you've a touch of the ague?"

Vangie bit her lower lip and dropped her gaze to the floor.

"I—I confess I didn't sleep well, ma'am. Forgive me. I'll tend to your needs at once!" She hurried from the chamber to give her orders to a waiting lower maid, then moved to the fireplace to strike the tinderbox and set the coals to blazing in order that the curling tongs might be made ready.

Jane tried to prompt further information from her maid. She did not want her abigail to suffer needlessly. But after a few minutes, she could see that Vangie's color had returned to her cheeks and once she saw Jane settled into her bath, her spirits had returned to normal.

The hot water, laced with oil of roses, seeped into her every muscle. She relaxed for a long time, until her breakfast arrived. She donned her shift and a thick robe of maroon velvet and sat in a comfortable chair by the window to enjoy her meal. The rain was lessening every minute, leaving a clear view of the swans gliding about one of the small lakes beyond the drive. A beautiful, ancient fir tree stood majestically beside the lake.

A breeze rattled the window and the shower stopped almost at the same time. A blue sky began to peek through in the distance. Jane knew that by eleven, the sun might already be shining on the yew maze.

Every time she thought of the maze and her assignation with Freddy at eleven o'clock, a flow of joy and contentment swept through her. No one should be allowed to be so happy, she thought with a smile. Something startled the swans and with a stretch of their necks and a furious paddling of hidden feet they shot toward the stone footbridge which traversed the lake. She loved to watch the graceful creatures and wondered what had frightened them.

A chill went through her, something tugged at her memory, something about last night, the scent she had smelled—of Thorpe's shaving soap. She would never have believed the two men could share anything in common, even shaving soap. But then the whole experience had been so utterly extraordinary that her mind and heart were still whirling about dizzily.

How happy she was to be at Challeston and to have made

the decision to permit a union. Whatever had frightened the swans no longer seemed to be a threat as they moved slowly from beneath the light gray stone bridge.

Her meal complete, Jane said, "I should like to wear the cherry frock, the chip hat, and carry a wicker cutting basket which you will probably need to secure from the kitchens. Lady Somercote informed me yesterday that I was free to roam her flower beds at will and to cut whichever flowers appealed to me." She sighed, "And please dress my hair a little differently this morning. What do you think of long ringlets over one shoulder?"

"Very charming," Vangie responded uneasily.

Jane seated herself at her dressing table with its fine gilt mirror and met her maid's surprised gaze in the reflection of the looking-glass. "What is it?"

"I was just thinking of the cherry frock, ma'am," she responded with a crease between her brows. "Will you be wanting a chemisette?"

Jane giggled. "Of course not." The gown was cut very low, and with the use of her corset she would achieve precisely the effect she wished for. She intended to leave nothing to chance when she met Freddy in the yew maze. Besides, after last night, she was convinced he would be pleased with her gown.

An hour later, Jane twirled in front of the long looking-glass near the fireplace. The gown, made of an Indian cotton and block-printed in a cheerful pattern of cherries and dark green stems and leaves, was caught up high at the waist with scarcely three inches separating the bodice from the tight waistline. Even Vangie, setting aside her concern for her mistress's modesty, could not keep from clapping her hands in approval. "So charming!" she cried. "When he next sees you he will tumble in love with you if he has not already. Indeed, what man could resist you in such a pretty gown—especially such a man!"

Such a man! Jane wondered a little at her maid's choice of words but then dismissed them. Freddy undoubtedly seemed like a wondrous creature to all the female servants.

She curtsied playfully. "Thank you," she simpered, which

only made Vangie laugh. Her abigail was two years younger than she, but they were separated in station by centuries. Vangie laughed again, but Jane watched as her expression suddenly fell and her brow crinkled.

"What is it, Vangie?" Jane asked, ceasing her antics in front of the mirror. "I vow ever since you entered my chamber this morning you've been behaving curiously. At first I thought you were ill but now I can see that you are not. What is amiss, then? You may tell me."

"It is just that—you don't seem angry about last night at all? Have you perchance changed your mind about Mr. Waingrove?"

Jane felt her cheeks grow warm with embarrassment. "Of course not. But how could you have known about—about last night, I mean?"

Vangie fluttered her hands. "I don't—I guess I supposed because—well, I did see you enter Mr. Waingrove's bedchamber with your key and a missive," she finished lamely, her cheeks a dark crimson.

Jane couldn't continue the conversation. She was far too mortified by it. She had never given herself to a man before without benefit of marriage, and her conduct was wholly improper. It was one thing to secretly do things, but another to have the secrets brought to light. She found Vangie's allusion to her lovemaking with Freddy therefore quite painful.

At the same time, another thought struck her. Why would Vangie confront her with it? And why was she so distressed? It was not as though affairs were uncommon among the *beau monde*. She also realized that her maid had never commented on her conduct before. And what had she meant by having perchance changed her mind about Mr. Waingrove?

She began to feel uneasy, just as she had earlier when she had watched the swans dart beneath the bridge. Something in her memory nagged at her, warning her that some mischief was afoot. But no matter how thoroughly she searched through every thought, she could find nothing out of the ordinary except that she had given herself rather wantonly to a man she meant to marry.

"Perhaps we ought to forget all about this," Jane said at last, quietly turning away from her maid and pretending to adjust the red satin ribbons beneath her left ear. She didn't want obscure and inexplicable worries to mar in any way the joy she was feeling, so she set her mind to the yew maze and to the future. "Well, then!" she added cheerfully in an attempt to get over the uncomfortable moment lightly. "I have some flowers to pick."

Three

Lord Thorpe waited in the center of the yew maze, the tails of his brown coat of superfine damp from having brushed against the thick hedges as he made his way through the maze. He had awakened with a slight headache, a circumstance which did not surprise him since he had not slept very well. He slipped a hand into the pocket of his coat and felt Jane's key trapped snugly within. His fingers touched the smooth violet silk of the ribbon so prettily tied about the end of the key and he let go of a heavy sigh.

He shook his head and set one booted foot on the stone bench situated on the south end of the central, grassy square. He looked down at his gleaming, gold-tasselled Hessians dotted with droplets of water. Why were his spirits so heavy? He ought to be *aux anges* after last night. Instead he felt like the devil!

When he had finally awakened at eight o'clock this morning, his mind had been besieged with thoughts of Jane which not even two strong cups of coffee and a hearty breakfast had served to allay. He could think of nothing else but Jane, of his history with her since her arrival in London last April, of the strength of his initial attraction to her when he had first caught sight of her driving with Lady Somercote in Hyde Park, of her beauty, of her exquisite body.

He could recall every detail of that first meeting. She had worn a violet silk bonnet, trimmed with a delicate lace below the brim and a spray of lilies of the valley in a circlet about the crown. She had been a vision, her dark brown hair dangling in delicate curls beside her cheeks, her expression open and forthright, her brown eyes seductive and compelling. When he had looked into her eyes, steadily and purposefully, there was no wavering, no simpering, only a faint expression of surprise as she blinked at him.

From that moment, he had wanted her.

The next day, he had informed Mrs. Newstead that he was through with her fussings and frettings, that he had believed she understood they would never marry, and that he would not be moved to alter his decision were she to fall into a decline, or a fit of hysterics, or strike him in public! She was his mistress no longer.

Fortunately, Mrs. Newstead had accepted his decision with good grace and had instead become his friend and to some degree his confidant.

Jane had then become his object, especially when at their next meeting she lifted a single haughty brow to him upon his greeting and offered him two fingers.

Clearly she had been informed of his reputation.

Two cold fingers.

She couldn't have known that this small act was for him like a gauntlet thrown at his feet even though more than one lady of his acquaintance had previously employed such artifice in hopes of gaining his notice. No, Jane's was not a naturally conniving nature. Instead, she had exacted his interest by the mere fact that besides being quite lovely, she had made it clear he would get none of her.

None of her.

Except that she had been wrong and last night he had had all of her. He felt a rush of pure physical pleasure flow through him with a kind of electric quality that again surprised him. The air crackled and glanced off his skin, his brown coat, his buff breeches, his gleaming Hessians. He glanced up at the sky, but the clouds were breaking up so he could not suppose that what he was feeling might be a precursor to a lightning strike.

He laughed at himself and at what he was feeling and experiencing. In some ways, he felt as though he had never made love to a woman before. Jane was the first—certainly the first like this, and the first he had taken without her knowledge of who he was.

But the more he considered this, the more he was convinced she knew damn well who it was that had climbed into her bed. She can't have believed even for a second that Freddy Waingrove would have made love to her as he did.

He had watched Freddy around Jane. The budding poet could hardly bring her fingers to his lips without trembling. Surely Jane could not truly have believed it was Freddy who had made love to her?

His thoughts grew very still as images of the night before began to sweep through his mind. His whole body became quiet and pensive as inwardly he watched the entire event.

Jane.

She had been wild and loving, intense and very physical. She had spoken of children. She had not objected to anything he had done to her.

Jane.

A strange liquid sensation enveloped his heart, warming his body.

Jane.

Good God, what was happening to him. He couldn't be falling in love with her.

No. Impossible. Not love.

Lust. Luscious, full, ripe, abundant lust. And more than he had ever known.

Still, he grappled with the heaviness that weighed his heart. Was he regretting having tricked her? Not precisely. Then what the devil was causing him so much distress? He shook his head. He didn't understand what had snagged him.

He shrugged. Maybe he feared that she might be angry with him for what he had done, even if she had enjoyed the delights of love. Perhaps he ought to humbly beg her pardon before offering her a *carte blanche*. Yes, that's what he would do and then he would elucidate all the ways he would provide for her in the future. He knew of her extreme financial difficulties and a year or two as his mistress would set her up for life. He would tell her as much, and she would get more from him than any of his previous mistresses. He was nothing, if not generous with those who came under his protection.

Then tonight, he would arrange to come to her bed again. The mere thought of it sent another electric thrill rushing through him.

Jane spoke at length with the butler before proceeding to the maze. He had politely given her the information she sought— the key to the intricately patterned labyrinth. Not for her to amble down a dozen wrong passages, ruining her pretty gown of red cherries and deep green leaves, before finally reaching the center of the maze. She had not labored over her appearance only to have her skirts so dampened by the wet yews that she would be unsightly to receive the proposal of the man she was determined to love, the man who had the night before made love to her so beautifully.

Therefore she slowly made her way down each dewy corridor. Memories of the night before still sang in her heart.

Freddy.

Dear, dear Freddy.

At last she reached the opening to the center. Freddy was waiting for her with his boot planted on the stone bench.

"My darling," she called to him as she stepped through the arched opening. She opened her arms wide, the flat wicker cutting basket sliding a little down her arm. But the exhilaration she was feeling evaporated instantly at the sight of the man before her. "You!" she cried, lowering her arms and catching the basket at the handle before it slid to the ground. "What are you doing here? I suppose you have frightened Freddy away. What did you do? Stare him down with that stupidly ferocious eye of yours? Where is he, Lord Thorpe? How long ago did you see him? A half-hour, a quarter-hour? Why are you here?"

She watched a hard expression overtake the viscount's face. "He hasn't been here," Thorpe responded coldly. "Were you expecting him?"

"Well, of course I was expecting him," she responded. "Though that is hardly any of your concern."

His gaze swept over her bonnet, the decollete of her gown, and the pretty cherries and leaves of the fabric. A slow, knowing, and familiarly wicked smile replaced his former coldness. "Take me, Jane," he said seductively, sliding his boot off the stone bench. "Freddy's not here, I am, and it is clear to me you had something more interesting in mind than just a little harmless flirtation."

Jane felt a warmth rise on her neck and her cheeks. "You are insufferable!" she cried, despising him for turning her affection for Freddy into something low and sordid. She turned on her heel.

"One moment!" he called to her. "I have something of yours I feel I ought to return to you."

She should have ignored him, instead his words culled forth all her former nagging worries that something was not as it should be. She turned back to him, eying him warily. "Something of mine?" she queried, her mouth suddenly dry. "Did I misplace a glove or a kerchief?"

He shook his head. "Not a glove or a kerchief, but it is something violet in color. Are you missing anything in particular, that you can recall, of a hue between purple and a deep, dark pink?"

Jane frowned. "No, not that I know of." What was he about? And why did he stare at her as though she hadn't a yard of Indian cotton covering her limbs? Or was this just some silly ploy to keep her talking that he might try to take another kiss from her? She straightened her shoulders and smiled. He could take nothing from her now. Since last night, she belonged completely to Freddy. He wouldn't dare even try to kiss her once it became known she was betrothed to Freddy Waingrove. "Well, do you mean to return my property to me? Or do you intend to keep ogling me in that ridiculous manner of yours?"

She watched him slip his hand into his pocket. A moment later, he withdrew something both gold and shiny and violet, just as he had said. She frowned as he shook out the object and she watched a key drop then dangle at the end of a violet ribbon—a brass key, a long, heavy, door key.

The key to her bedchamber?

"What is the meaning of this?" she asked quietly. She felt oddly stunned as though he had struck a numbing blow across her cheek. All her worries seemed to become focused completely on the sight of the key, glittering in the July sunshine as he swung it gently back and forth, back and forth.

"Your key, madame. I felt obliged to return it to you this morning as a point of civility and as a way of expressing my deepest appreciation."

"How did you get it?" she asked stupidly. "Did you take it from Freddy?" She didn't understand what had happened. She didn't even care she was revealing to him that she had lent her bedchamber key to Freddy and therefore she had given him the right to come to her bed.

He slowly approached her. She tore her gaze from the sight of the key dangling from the violet ribbon and met his gaze. How odd he looked, how cruel the smile on his lips and in his eyes.

"Have you—have you hurt Freddy?" she asked, frightened suddenly. "How did you get my key? Why do you look at me in that terrible manner?"

He laughed harshly. "Stubble it, Mrs. Ambergate—Jane. I ought to be permitted to call you Jane from now on. Besides, you can't make me believe you actually thought Freddy Waingrove was with you last night when he can hardly look you in the eye without trembling. Don't play the widgeon with me."

"I don't know what you're talking about," she whispered. He was very close to her. Panic rose in her chest as she recalled the night, how more than once she had thought of Thorpe. She blinked rapidly. If only she could recall the night clearly, but she had taken far more champagne then she was used to. "You will need to be more precise," she said, breathing in shallow gasps.

"You know what I'm talking about. Search your recollections of last night and you'll understand exactly what I'm saying to you."

She eyed him contemptuously. "You can't mean what I think you mean. You've tricked me somehow. You've discovered Freddy came to me and—and—" She broke off, swallowing hard.

He just stared at her, that horrible, cruel, knowing stare.

"It's not possible," she whispered.

He caught her arm as she took a step backward. He held her tightly. She felt the need to run away. Tears had already begun biting at her eyes. "It's very possible," he said. "I forced your maid to tell me what was going forward last night. You were far too confident at the ball, far too happy, and your demeanor intrigued me. Vangie directed me to Mr. Waingrove's bedchamber. The rest, if you'll allow yourself to believe it, you know, once I found the key beneath the pillow and your missive."

Jane felt ill. She placed a hand over her mouth. Thorpe had made love to her, not Freddy. All her plans disintegrated in that moment. She was lost. Utterly and completely lost.

"Oh, don't look so downcast," he said, stroking her cheek gently with his finger. "If I'm not much mistaken, you enjoyed yourself prodigiously last night, and I am fully prepared to take you into my bed tonight. We can do everything we did last night and a little more. You'll never be unhappy with me, Jane, I promise you that much. I know how to please a woman. And as for your lack of funds, I can take care of you. I am a very wealthy man, afterall. And isn't that what you've been after all these months? Why settle for a mouse of a man when you can have me?"

Jane looked up at him, some of her nausea passing. She was still so shocked, stunned, and aggrieved by what had happened that she really didn't know where to begin. "I had thought you bad," she said at last, her voice strangely calm. "But I had never believed you could be so cruel. You're a reprobate, my lord. Perhaps my pursuit of Mr. Waingrove has not been noble, but at least I am honest with my prey. My motives may be impure, but in the end Freddy will have my loyalty if not my heart, and the children of my body, if God so wills it. But what precisely were you giving to me besides the fleeting pleasures of physical intercourse?"

He narrowed his icy blue eyes at her. "So you think it enough to chase after a man's fortune and extend him so kindly your 'loyalty' and the 'children of your body.' How very much like a woman to think this way. Do Freddy Waingrove a favor—become his mistress, present him with a by-blow or two, take his money, and be done with it. But don't prate about your virtue when I know you have none. If I thought for a moment you could love Freddy Waingrove, maybe I wouldn't care. But right now, I tell you you'll ruin his life if you continue down this path and drag him to the altar. And if you think I'll stand by and do nothing, you're greatly mistaken."

She heard his words, but more so the bitterness behind them. He saw her as his equal in the worst way, and she was disgusted by it. What did he know of her difficulties anyway? Nothing. Lord Thorpe was one of those creatures who saw only what he wanted and would say or do anything to achieve his ends.

"You deceived me," she said at last. "And I despise you for it."

"I could believe that, had you not enjoyed yourself so much last night. Confess the truth, Mrs. Ambergate. You thought of me last night even though you insist you believed you were with Freddy. I was in your mind when I was making love to you, not Waingrove. Tell me at least that much." His hand was still roughly on her arm.

"Of course I thought of you," she said quietly. "I've wanted you from the first day—you remember, don't you?—in Hyde Park. Thorpe, you looked at me and I thought the heavens had come down and sprinkled me with magic. I felt as though you'd somehow climbed into my soul. I even dreamed about you that night. I wondered if I could love you, or if you could love me. Then I learned about Mrs. Newstead and, and the others. Maybe I'm wrong in my hope of becoming Freddy's wife, but I know one thing—I'll never become your mistress, to be used up for a time, then cast aside. I have no respect for you, Lord Thorpe, just as you apparently have none for me. Now give me my key and if you ever come to my bedchamber again, don't expect me to keep silent about it."

"This isn't the end," he said, his blue eyes taunting. "Before the fortnight is over, you'll be my mistress."

"Before the fortnight is over, I'll be betrothed to Freddy Waingrove," she returned with a slight lift of her chin. He released her arm, a challenging smile on his face as he lifted the key and handed it to her. She took it, turned on her heel, and left.

Thorpe let Jane go and he returned to the bench where as before he placed a booted foot on the smooth gray stone. For a long moment, he stared at the gold tassel dangling from the V of his boot. He reviewed all that had been said between him and Jane Ambergate. Now, more than ever, especially since she had had the audacity to hold herself above him, he was determined to seduce her, to break her, to interfere and disrupt her pursuit of Waingrove. He had thirteen days left in which to complete his objective. He chuckled to himself. Thirteen days, and he meant to enjoy every last one of them.

His heart began to thrum in his neck and in his chest as he thought of her and her strong spirit. He understood now that he had believed she would fall into his arms once she realized he had been in her bed last night. The fact that she hadn't only increased his desire to possess her, body and soul. He shivered with the thrill of it, the exhilaration of the chase. But what to do next? How to get under her skin again? She would be tougher than before, yet more vulnerable if he was any judge of women—and he was.

When he left the yew maze, he encountered Mrs. Newstead

who had just emerged from the expansive flower garden to the north of the maze.

"What were you doing in there?" she cried gaily. "I didn't know you enjoyed mazes, or did some hapless wench fail to keep her assignation with you?"

Sophia Newstead was shorter than Jane by a little. She wore a pale yellow patterned gown of Indian calico trimmed about the hem with three rows of cornflower-blue ruffles. Her straw chip hat was tied with a matching blue bow beneath her chin and a trio of luscious blonde ringlets dangled charmingly beside each cheek. The dark shade of the ribbons enhanced her blue eyes and for a brief moment he felt all his former enchantment of her flow over him. She was lively, quick-witted, and lovely in a doll-like manner. Her nose was small, her cheeks dimpled, her lips a delicate rose which he supposed had been deepened through a judicious use of her rouge pot. He felt a sudden desire to take her in his arms and kiss her as he used to do. But quick on the heels of this impulse was his memory of several of her tantrums when she had broached the subject of turning their relationship into a marriage. His desire faded swiftly. She was not worth the fits she threw.

"What a lovely picture you present this morning, Sophia," he said, carefully avoiding her question. "Quite beautiful in fact. I would say Derbyshire agrees with you."

She curtsied and smiled, then took his arm. "You must do the pretty with me, Thorpe, and take me for a turn about the flower garden." She drew him back toward the gate from which she had just emerged. He didn't hesitate to accompany her.

"If it pleases you," he said gallantly.

"Of course it pleases me," she responded sweetly. "I am always happiest when I am with you. Besides, you will love the garden. Every flower imaginable is present since the rows cover more than half an acre, which explains why the house is full of bouquets in every corner of every room. I am told by my abigail that several maids work on the arrangements constantly to keep the house fragrant and pleasing to the eye. What a marvel of industry Lady Somercote is. She quite puts me to shame." She paused for a moment, then looked up at him askance. "But you haven't told me about your recent flirtation, for I will not believe you were in Somercote's maze merely for the pleasure of getting wet from dripping yew branches. Who were you meeting there? Come, now! Confess all, or I shall begin torturing you."

He placed a dramatic hand against his chest. "You strike fear in my heart with such a threat."

She giggled and pinched his arm. "You are being quite absurd."

He lifted the latch to the garden and opened the gate. "I shan't tell you," he said, giving the door a light shove.

"Odious man," she responded, simpering, dimpling, and smiling.

He laughed at her tricks and allowed her to precede him into the vast garden. Sophia was right. Every bloom imaginable was present including camellias, violets, roses, peonies, carnations, pansies, irises, primula, and clematis, all arranged to bring delight to the soul. In the center of the garden were several closely clipped topiaries, amusingly representative of a monstrous teapot and a teacup and saucer, the cup of which was large enough to hold a small child. At the far end of the garden were several purposeful lopsided beehives arranged in a row, each hive bearing a large, weathered, coiled basket for a hat.

He felt his spirits soften in the presence of the homey, fragrant garden. His shoulders relaxed as they moved along the easternmost path that led in a wide circle about the garden. He sighed deeply and drew in the sweet country air. Some of his former tensions at having argued with the widow Ambergate began to subside. A peaceful sensation drifted over him. He was glad to be in the country, to be at Challeston, even to be with Sophia.

"We are such excellent friends now," Sophia said softly. "Surely you trust me enough to reveal with whom you had what undoubtedly was a pleasant tryst?" She looked up at him, smiling in a childlike manner up into his face. "Oh, no. Now what is that frown for? Your tryst wasn't pleasant?"

He chuckled slightly. Sophia had always been skilled at determining the meaning of frowns, scowls, smirks, lifted brows, and pinched lips. She was being no less skilled now.

"You are far too perceptive of the moment for your own good. As it happens, I was in the maze with Mrs. Ambergate."

They had ambled halfway down the garden when she stopped and stared at him. She clucked her tongue. "Oh, but you do intrigue me now. Of course I should have suspected it was she with whom you had enjoyed a *tête-à-tête,* but do you tell me that you did not *enjoy* your flirtation with her?"

"In part," he said. Now how had it come about that she had finagled Jane's name from him and why the deuce did he feel almost compelled to confide in her. "We argued, as it happens. She seems to feel that there is a great difference between a woman setting her cap for a man in order to gain the security of his fortune, and a man—such as myself—pursuing a lady to make her his mistress while promising to provide her with the same manner of security." He let his gaze drift over the flower garden, again smelling deeply the fragrance of roses and sweet peas. "Quite absurd, isn't it?"

When she didn't at first respond, he looked down at her and saw that she had turned her face away from him and was looking back down the garden. He thought perhaps something was wrong and posed his question again, "Don't you think her argument an absurd one?"

Mrs. Newstead turned back to look at him and blinked rapidly several times. "Yes, of course I do," she responded cheerfully. "I do beg your pardon, I, I was caught for a moment wondering just how the topiaries were clipped into these amazing shapes."

Thorpe glanced at the topiaries. "They are extraordinary," he said.

"Indeed."

He glanced down at her but her face was obscured by the brim of her chip hat. He could have sworn there was a strangely hard edge to her voice.

She continued her progress up the path and he followed obe-

diently in tow, her arm still wrapped about his. "So you argued
with Mrs. Ambergate in the yew maze. I must say, Thorpe, for a
man who has known so many women—and that, so intimately—I
do not think you have conducted your flirtation with Mrs. Ambergate at all properly. If you are not careful, you will lose her
entirely. She is not to be won by your usual seductions—"

"You are absolutely right," he blurted out, cutting her off.
His chest swelled with pride and pleasure as he recalled events
of the night before.

Again she stopped their progress. "What is it you are not
telling me?" she demanded. "I know that look of yours. You've
a mighty secret and I only wonder just how I am to get you to
open your budget."

He merely smiled at her and continued down the path. If she
glanced up at him several times, he remained mute so as not to
reveal the truth of what happened between him and Jane Ambergate.

"As I was saying," she murmured, leaning close to him.
"You'll not win Mrs. Ambergate through your usual methods.
She is set on having Mr. Waingrove. Of course, my own opinion
is that you'll never have Mrs. Ambergate. She despises you.
She'll never be your mistress and you'll never know her in bed.
With all your several charms, she will choose marriage to that
sapskull Waingrove before she ever becomes either your lover
or your mistress."

Thorpe looked down at her and said, "You're wrong. Already,
you are mistaken."

"I knew it," she snapped triumphantly. "You've bedded her,
haven't you? Admit it, oh, wicked one. Only tell me, how did
you manage it!"

"Why do I feel as though I've been duped this time?"

"Because you have. You forget that I know you extremely
well and I can see by the gleam in your eye and by the way you
have been swelling your chest since having emerged from the
yew maze that your masculine pride is soaring. Only how did

you do it, for I would have taken an oath that she would never have permitted you into her bed."

He couldn't resist telling her the rest. He had triumphed and he wanted the world to know it. He had triumphed because of Jane's lust for Freddy Waingrove's fortune and he didn't care that her own foibles had cost her the very thing she had been withholding from him for the past several months.

He then told Sophia of having forced Vangie's hand by threatening to expose her and of having stolen the key from Waingrove's room during the ball.

"You didn't!" Mrs. Newstead breathed ecstatically. "Oh, but you are wicked—my lovely Thorpe. Such a naughty man."

He could tell by the lascivious expression on her face that she wished to hear more, in particular the details of the night's events, but there he drew the line. "I never once told a soul about the pleasures I shared with you, so pray don't expect me to begin revealing anything about Mrs. Ambergate."

She pouted and moaned her disappointment, then cuddled his arm more closely. "I still think we ought to have been married," she murmured. Her fragrance, of lavender mingled with a touch of roses, greeted his senses.

"We should have slain one another at the end of the first day, my dear," he responded, smiling down at her.

"Perhaps," she said quietly. "Well, you have told me of your conquest so I shall tell you of mine—or nearly so. Duffield has offered for me."

"Indeed," he responded.

"You needn't sound so shocked," Sophia retorted. "Not everyone is as hateful of the married state as you."

"You are betrothed then?" he asked.

"No," she said succinctly. "I can't bear Colonel Duffield. He is clumsy, he is not as expert at kissing as you are, and he is not in the least handsome."

"You're not still hoping that you and I—?"

"Until you are wed, I shall hope, not that I believe I have even a remote chance of succeeding, but when one has created a dream, very often the dream proves reluctant to depart. Do you intend to offer for Mrs. Ambergate?"

He snorted his disgust. "Heavens, no."

"What do you mean to do then?"

"I shall make her my mistress, of course."

"She'll never agree!" Mrs. Newstead cried. "You duped her, Thorpe, you didn't win her heart. She is not like the rest of us, willing to be at your beck and call because we can't seem to help ourselves. Jane Ambergate, though I despise her completely, has a will greater than even your own."

"You are mistaken," he said evenly.

"And you are an arrogant fool! I tell you it can't be done and I'm willing to wager on it."

He turned to look down at her and watched as she bent over a border of pansies and picked a purple, velvety flower. "A wager?" he asked, intrigued. "A bit of gaming might enhance the pleasure of the pursuit."

She chuckled. "How well I know you but believe me this wager will not be a child's bet—in fact, I intend to see you stake it all." She looked up at him as she held the pansy to her cheek and let the soft petals brush against her delectable complexion. Her face was shaded from the sun by her chip hat, her blue eyes were sparkling, and her even teeth peeped from between her pretty, smiling, rouged lips.

"What do you have in mind, minx?"

"I'll wager that you can't make her your mistress before the fortnight is out. If you lose the wager and fail to get Mrs. Ambergate to agree to live with you outside of wedlock, then you'll have to marry me."

"And if I succeed?" he queried.

"If you succeed," she paused for a moment, grimacing slightly, "I'll marry Colonel Duffield."

A broad smile spread over Thorpe's face. "You've a wager, my little minx, but if I were you I would be planning to purchase my brideclothes. Derby is a large enough city with certainly enough dressmakers to see the job done."

"You've an excellent notion, there," she responded with a challenging light in her eye, "But it won't be because I shall become Mrs. Colonel Duffield."

The twang and whistle of the bowstring and arrow as Jane let yet another feathered missile fly was like a soothing ointment on her singed sensibilities. The center of the target, fixed fifteen yards away, bore an invisible image, dead center, of Thorpe's frequently amused face.

"The devil take it!" she murmured beneath her breath as the arrow missed the center by a hair. Freddy stood a few feet from her and cheered every arrow that hit the target, so much so that her nerves were even further chafed by his enthusiasm.

The sun was shining fully now on the gently landscaped grounds about Challeston Hall. She stood in the shade of a stately beech tree. She had originally taken her arrows and her target out to the south lawn in order to relieve some of her anger and frustration by practicing one of her favorite sports. She wanted solitude, time to think, time to regain her composure.

After having been confronted with the truly horrifying truth that Lord Thorpe, without her knowledge, had had his way with her last night, she had known an internal chaos and turbulence of no mean order. She needed time alone, time apart from her own schemes with regard to Freddy Waingrove, time to relax, to think, to ponder, to plan.

She had gone to her bedchamber to fetch her archery equipment and had contemplated changing her hat and gown. But the pretty cotton dress patterned with cherries was comfortable and the chip hat, with its broad brim, adequate protection against the bright sunshine. She chose therefore, to slip a modest lace fichu into the decollete of her gown and obscure the seductive neckline.

Solitude and the release of physical exertion was what she had sought and intended. But as she had quit her bedchamber, Freddy had happened to find her, and the moment he caught sight of the target and her bow and arrows, his demeanor took on a glow of excitement. "I shall come with you, my dearest Jane, if you don't mind overly much? To see you firing your arrows one after the other so puts me in mind of the goddess Artemis that I am always inspired to create verse afterward. You can have no idea. Do you object?"

She thought him ridiculous with his countenance shining and his gold-green eyes sparkling. "Please yourself," she had responded quietly, wanting him to take up her hint that just this once she would like to be left alone.

"Oh, thank you," he gushed. "I won't be a moment. I must gather up my writing desk, pens, paper, and inkpot, and I shall be with you anon."

Anon. Good God! Freddy could be so ridiculous.

"I'll be on the *north* lawn," she had lied. When he disappeared down the hall, away from the stairs leading to the entrance hall, she stayed in the hall only long enough to make certain he didn't perceive that she had no intention of waiting for him. Nor did she have the smallest intention of practicing her archery on the north lawn.

Despite her tactics, he found her, though quite out of breath. "Jane," he called to her in a playful voice, his writing desk slung awkwardly beneath his arm. "I don't like to correct you, but this is the south lawn."

Jane feigned surprise and turned about in a circle, glancing at Windy Knowl, then twirling to face Wolfscar Ridge. "So it is," she exclaimed, wondering if he would catch the facetious note to her voice. He didn't.

"You poor females haven't the smallest sense of direction. But never fear, that is why God created them 'male and female' so that we could guide and protect."

Freddy couldn't guide himself out of an empty ewe's udder, Jane thought vindictively.

She recalled now precisely the feeling that had overcome her in that moment. She had known the strongest impulse to tear into him, to give him a verbal lashing he would not soon forget, or at the very least to explain what he apparently could not perceive on his own—that she wished him anywhere but with her.

Now, however, as she let her last arrow fly, and he trotted over to the target to retrieve her arrows like a good English spaniel, she found that much of her agitation with him, and even with Thorpe, was dimming. She wondered again at all that had happened. As Freddy carefully began removing each of eight arrows, her mind fell backward to the night before when she had received Thorpe into her bed, into her body, and even to some degree into her soul.

A terrible sadness and frustration again came over her. She felt horribly violated but at the same time, when she recalled how much pleasure she had received from Thorpe, inevitably a strange warmth would flow over her. She had to admit to herself that some of the sadness she felt was in knowing that she would never enjoy such pleasure again, thoughts of course which served only to make her feel lustful, guilty, and ashamed of herself.

She glanced at Freddy who was now running toward her in his awkward way. He had grass stains on his knee breeches where he had fallen twice in running to fetch her arrows. How could she have ever thought for a moment that Freddy was making love to her last night? Was Thorpe right in accusing her of knowing full well that it was he who had been with her and not Freddy Waingrove?

She forced herself to remember the night in as many vivid details as she could, but her mind had been foggy with sleep and with more wine than she normally imbibed. All that she could put together with any cohesion was that for some strange reason—and perhaps now not so strange at all—she had kept imagining Thorpe was loving her.

"What is it, precious Jane?" Freddy asked.

Jane blinked and saw that he was standing in front of her, a sheen of perspiration on his brow from his exercise, his blonde hair sticking unattractively to his forehead The day, though it had begun with a shower, was now proving to be humid and quite warm. She took the arrows from him but did not at first address his question. "Freddy," she said at last, an odd thought striking her. "I believe I owe you an apology."

"No, no, how is that possible?" he demurred. "How could you owe me any such thing?"

"Well, for one thing, I failed to get my key to you last night." She watched him, she wanted to see his reaction. For the first time since having met with Thorpe in the yew maze she realized Freddy had seemed utterly oblivious to the fact that she had failed—although through Thorpe's cunning—to get her key to him.

His brow furrowed, his eyes crinkled at the corners, his lips drew together in a bemused frown. He shook his head in bewilderment. "What do you mean, your key?"

"You remember, don't you, the key that would allow for our *union?*" she suggested hopefully. She had been with Freddy for over an hour and he hadn't made even the smallest suggestion about her bedchamber key. He hadn't asked about it, or hinted, or expressed even the mildest disappointment.

He smiled brightly. "Oh, that," he responded. "You mustn't reproach yourself. Afterall, the ball kept us both so occupied that I daresay we wouldn't have had time to properly become one with our thoughts and spiritual ideals anyway. I suppose you might say that a ball is hardly a place to consummate the soulful essence of such a joining." He was blushing, yet for all the pink patches on his face, she now understood to a nicety that they were not speaking of the same thing.

"And just where ought we to 'consummate' such a joining?" she prompted hopefully, curious as to precisely what he would say.

She watched him swallow. "I believe a natural setting would be quite exquisite. Perhaps while meandering through the pine wood yonder, or I hear there is a warm spring not far from Challeston—Oak Cloud Spring I believe it is called—or perhaps beside the quiet pools to be found deep within the local caverns. There is such a cavern near the River Hart, I believe."

Jane tilted her head and watched him speculatively. He might be adverse to a complete physical union, but she rather suspected that when he thought of such places, he was also imagining that the measure of privacy these locations would afford would also allow for a little discreet hugging.

Smiling inwardly, she decided to put her swain to the test. "Darling, Freddy," she breathed. "When we are alone at these places, would you kiss me? For I confess that I have been wishing for it ever so much." She lowered her gaze modestly. "In fact, I would wish for it even now, if you are of a mind." She leaned toward him, returning her gaze to his and letting him know by the slight parting of her lips that she was ready and willing.

He blinked rapidly and she knew that he wanted to oblige her. He took a quick, awkward step toward her, his hands outstretched. She tried to move her arrows and her bow out of the way in time to receive his curious assault, but his hand became tangled in the bowstring. His natural nervousness when he was around her arose and before long, his whole arm was caught in her bow, three of the arrows had fallen to the grass, and the rest became tangled up in the string since Jane's hand was caught between the bowstring and his burgundy coatsleeve, as well.

She started to laugh. Poor Freddy bore the frightened expression of a child who was about to panic. "Gently, Freddy!" she commanded him. "Gently!" again she cried, more sharply still.

He froze, staring at the long bow as though it had attacked him.

"Do you know how many times this has happened to me?" she queried in a soft voice, aware she had to reassure him quickly or he would likely faint. "A dozen times. Sometimes I think each arrow has a mind of its own and the bowstring directs them all randomly."

"Truly?" he asked hopefully, his brow riddled with anxiety.

She nodded as she slowly eased her hand from beneath the pressure of the bowstring against his coat, then disengaged each arrow, one after the other, letting them all fall to the ground. "If you will just relax your shoulder—?"

In slow stages he did, and Jane was able to slip the bow off of him. She thought she heard him whimper with relief and her heart went out to him. Poor Freddy Waingrove. He was a mass of sensibilities, all ready to rise and devour him when he least wished for it. "Did the bow hurt you?" she asked. She cast her bow aside and began gently touching his arm and shoulder. "There or there?" she asked.

He shook his head. "That was quite silly, wasn't it?" he suggested, embarrassed.

"Not by half," she answered seriously. "I promise you, I've suffered more than once at the hands of my bowstring." She paused and caressed his cheek with her hand. "You've been so kind for the past half-hour or so, fetching my arrows so that I might enjoy my archery. You are very good to me besides being one of the handsomest gentlemen of my acquaintance. Has any lady ever told you as much before?" She looked into his eyes and sidled close to him. He blinked, he swallowed nervously, and an expression of anticipation lit up his face.

"You are everything I want in a woman," he murmured, leaning toward her. His nervousness seemed to dissipate. He was going to kiss her, perhaps a real kiss this time, and afterward she would suggest a walk in the woods or a trip to the warm springs or perhaps to the caverns. He was so close . . .

"Jane," he murmured, his lips barely a breath away. "I've wanted for so long—"

"Hallo!" a sweet, female voice intruded from behind, yet some distance away.

Freddy leaped away from Jane as though a coal had burned his lips. He stumbled and fell backward. Jane turned to watch as Henrietta Hartworth waved to her. Beside her was Thorpe, his arm supporting hers lightly. She groaned inwardly as Freddy regained his feet.

Thorpe again—always appearing when he was least wanted. He had undoubtedly come in search of her since a familiar amused expression was on his face. But the closer he drew the angrier she became. Freddy struggled to his feet, then quickly began briskly dusting off his breeches as though he'd fallen into a pile of dirt.

Without waiting for either Miss Hartworth or Thorpe to reach her before she continued her archery, Jane quickly picked up her bow and her arrows and stuffed the arrows into the green velvet quiver on her back. She turned toward her target, again mentally envisioned Thorpe's face dead center, and let an arrow fly.

Bull's eye!

Miss Hartworth exclaimed, "How very accurate! You are to be congratulated, Mrs. Ambergate. I know of no one who can ply the bowstring as you do."

"Yes!" Thorpe cried, though in his voice Jane heard a sardonic quality that was akin to fingernails on a board of slate. "Unequalled skill! I've never seen a target pierced so neatly before."

Miss Hartworth was exchanging pleasantries with Freddy and Lord Thorpe had drawn close to her. Her anger boiled to the surface of her sensibilities, burning her soul and setting fire to her tongue. She wanted to come the crab with him more than anything, but not for such a reason would she expose herself to Freddy and thereby diminish her chances of winning his hand in marriage.

She glanced at Thorpe and narrowed her eyes at him. He was a damnable man. *I've never seen a target pierced so neatly before.* She knew very well he was referring to his conquest of last night.

The rogue!

The beast!

"I couldn't have missed that shot," she stated, watching him closely as he regarded the target and feigned his admiration. "I was picturing your nose, and look how I hit the mark to perfection."

He turned to hold her gaze firmly. "As I hit mine, and I have no regrets. Do you?"

She withdrew another arrow. Her hands were trembling with rage. She hated Lord Thorpe, hated him with a passion. If it was the last thing she did, she would serve him some injury, do him some harm. She took several deep breaths and brought her temper to heel. She let another arrow fly and, because of her overwrought state, she was not surprised that the arrow struck the target far to the right, nearly missing the board entirely.

She heard him cluck his tongue. "Not even close," he murmured. "What a shame. And the first one so true to the mark."

She drew another arrow and another, letting each fly in quick succession. She wanted to silence his voice by concentrating on the twang and whistle of her arrows and bowstring. When all eight were stuck in the target, Freddy ran to retrieve them.

"I'll bet if you stood in the sunlight you couldn't hit the target," he suggested.

Jane eyed him with great hostility but was ready to meet any challenge he wanted to present to her. "Move the target near the rhododendron shrubs!" she called to Freddy, who promptly obeyed, then returned the arrows to her.

Jane moved out of the shade of the tree, as did the whole party, Henrietta and Freddy standing behind her and Thorpe beside her. The next eight arrows were even closer to the center than the last.

"Very good," Thorpe said. "I see you hit my nose completely with one arrow and grazed a nostril with another."

Jane was still too angry to be amused.

Freddy collected the arrows and Thorpe offered his next challenge. "Thirty yards," he said. "You'll miss the target at least three times."

How provoking he could be! "I'll not miss it once," she returned confidently.

And she didn't.

He continued his challenges and one by one Jane met them, lifting her chin each time and watching his expression change from one of amused playfulness to, in the end, as she nailed the target dead center at two hundred feet, one of true admiration.

"I'd like to see what you could do blindfolded," he said seriously.

"Indeed?" she asked, surprised.

"You have mastered your skill so completely, that I wouldn't wonder that you could do it blindfolded."

Jane was intrigued. "Have you a kerchief?" she asked. Now, how had it happened that her anger had disappeared?

He slipped his hand into his pocket and withdrew a neatly pressed square. "I think this will work, but you will have to remove your chip hat."

Without the smallest hesitation and because she was deeply curious as to what she actually could do blindfolded, she quickly untied the red silk ribbons and promptly cast aside her bonnet. But before she could tie the kerchief about her head she heard Miss Hartworth murmur something incoherent.

Jane realized in the excitement of meeting Thorpe's challenges that she had forgotten all about Freddy and Henrietta. Turning around toward them, she saw that Henrietta had a hand to her forehead.

"I am sorry," she said apologetically. "But I never could abide the sun overly much. Pray, excuse me. I must return to the house."

"Hetty, I'm sorry!" Jane cried. "I forgot. You should have at least remained in the shade."

Henrietta smiled faintly. "I wanted to see you shoot your arrows. You really are marvelous." She then turned quickly about, her complexion pale, and began walking toward the house.

Freddy watched her with great concern, then glanced back at Jane. "I should go with her," he said, when Henrietta stumbled slightly. Hetty and Freddy had been acquaintances since childhood and he always had one eye to her comfort. "Lend her my arm—don't you think?"

He was asking permission and Jane waved him away. "Yes, do go," she said. Henrietta was a gentlewoman in every sense of the word, including her inability to do anything that wasn't gentle. She could not go for long walks, or hike about even the smallest grade of hills, or dance for much above an hour in the course of an evening.

As Jane watched her accept Freddy's arm gratefully and lean

heavily against him, she found herself feeling vexed and guilty. "Perhaps we should all go," Jane said, frowning slightly. Hetty was clearly unwell.

More than anything, however, she wanted to see just what she could accomplish blindfolded. She looked back at the target longingly.

"No you don't," Thorpe said. "Miss Hartworth is in excellent hands, for whatever else Freddy might be, he is a skilled nursemaid. But I'll not let you use Miss Hartworth as an excuse to get out of my challenge. Besides, if I don't miss my guess, you want to be blindfolded to see just how well you can perform."

He seemed to understand her, too well, perhaps.

She sighed. "Yes, I do." She let him tie the kerchief about her brown curls. He stationed himself behind her and with his hands on her arms, pointed her as best he could toward the target. "See what you can do," he murmured into her ear. Despite her wish otherwise, his breath on her ear caused a spattering of gooseflesh to travel down her side and she caught her breath. Again, she was reminded of last night.

Using every power of concentration, however, she let go of such useless thoughts and instead focused her mind on the target. She took in a deep breath, drew back the arrow and the bowstring as one, and between heartbeats, let the arrow fly. Twang. Whistle. A faint thud in the distance.

She had hit the target!

She let out a cry and whipped the kerchief from about her eyes. "Not bad by half!" she cried, turning to face Thorpe joyfully.

"No," he smiled softly. "Not bad by half. Try again?"

She nodded vigorously. He again tied the kerchief about her eyes and over and over she fired away at the target, missing only once, when at the last moment he tweaked her elbow. She railed at him for this inconsiderate joke, but he wouldn't allow her to be overly serious. Besides, he was impressed and that pleased her, oddly enough.

"There, you see?" he said. "I was right. You've mastered

your sport so keenly that you can do it blindfolded. Just as I've mastered mine. It was very dark last night, if you recall—though I wasn't exactly blindfolded."

Jane felt a blush creep up her cheeks. She held the knotted kerchief in one hand, her bow in the other. Her quiver was empty as she looked up at him. "Must you be so crude?" she queried.

"Yes," he responded flatly, his lips a serious line, but a light of amusement danced in his eyes.

A chuckle escaped Jane's throat. "You are a beast of a man, you know that, don't you?"

"Yes," he responded again.

Jane couldn't help it. Lord Thorpe might be many things, but at least he had no pretenses. Besides, she was enjoying herself hugely which had not been the case earlier when Freddy had fetched for her and applauded her every move.

She set off after her arrows and he came with her.

"I think the arrow, whose course I so unkindly interrupted, went off into the rhododendrons. I'll find it for you."

Jane went to the target and took some pleasure in removing each missile. Not one had come within even an inch of the outer edge of the circle, she realized with glee, as she returned each to the soft quiver on her back.

"I can't find it!" Thorpe called to her. He was behind a hedge of rhododendrons which presented a summery mass of purple flowers to her eye. Next to the rhododendrons was a group of young conifers and the air was redolent with the fragrance of pine.

Jane took off the quiver which she now realized had given a slight ache to her shoulder. "I'll help," she returned. She rounded the shrubs and saw that he was gingerly searching through the branches. His breeches had pine needles and purple flowers fixed to the knees, and his hat was at his side also collecting debris. For fifteen minutes, they searched the shrubs and finally Jane gave up. "It's not here," she said. She turned toward the pines and laughed. "There it is! Stuck in one of the trees."

Thorpe rose from his knees and dusted off his buff breeches.

The arrow had pierced the young trunk above the reach of her arms and Thorpe approached the tree and pulled the arrow from the ridged bark. He turned back to her. "A kiss for it?" he asked in a low voice.

Jane stared at him in exasperation. "Keep it then!" she retorted.

"A trophy of last night's romp?" he challenged her.

"You rascal. Stop it. You've been a most agreeable companion for the past half-hour. Don't spoil it now."

She would have moved away from him but he caught her arm. "We can't be seen from here," he whispered. "One kiss, a brief kiss, nothing of passion, just a gentle touching of lips and I'll give it back to you. I don't want a trophy. I want you."

Jane wanted to slap his hand away, truly she did. So, what was it in the tenor of his voice, the deep resonance, that seemed to cause her to grow very still like a small animal caught in a trap? She looked into his blue eyes and felt her heart begin hammering dangerously against her ribs. She could hardly breathe.

"You want me," he whispered. "One kiss? I'll only take one kiss, I promise you. Nothing more." All the while he spoke, he lowered the arrow he still held in his hand to the delicate lace fichu covering the decollete of her gown. He slipped the head of the arrow into the lace. Slowly and quite seductively, he began withdrawing the lace from the bodice of her cherry-print gown.

Jane felt the lace sliding across her bare skin, a sensation that sent a ripple of desire shivering deep into her abdomen. She saw the intense look in his eyes, she saw his lips part and his head lean down toward her. A moment later, his lips were softly on hers, moist and gentle, a sensual delight that lifted her up high into the fragrant summer air. The scent of pine was heavily on her. His kiss was warm and inviting. Desire, liquid and fiery, rolled over her in a powerful, delicious wave.

He stopped kissing her. He drew back and looked deeply into her eyes. "There, you see? You may trust me. One kiss only." His gaze raked the decollete of her gown. "I want more, of course. From the moment I first saw you I have wanted more.

I have wanted all that you could give me." She was breathing hard, he was too close, his voice too rich and seductive, his eyes too devouring. She wanted him, badly. She wanted him now.

He lifted a hand, his fingers moved above, but not touching, the exposed skin of her breasts. He held her as though he was a skilled sorcerer. He lifted his hand close to her cheeks, her eyes, her lips, but still he didn't touch her.

"You see. You may trust me. I asked only for a kiss. I took only a kiss."

What he said was true, essentially. But the rest was untrue. He had taken much more than a kiss, though he had not touched her. He had taken her will and bent it to his own. For of the moment, she wanted nothing more than to have his hands upon her.

"You're so beautiful, Jane," he whispered, his breath lightly on her hair. "But I'm going to leave you now, even though I want to do a great deal more than kiss you. I'll see you at dinner."

He stepped away from her and with a slight bow handed her the lost arrow, which now held her lace fichu dangling from the tip. He then skirted the rhododendrons and would have been gone from sight shortly had she not stayed him.

"Thorpe!" she called to him, her senses still very much heightened as her mind slowly returned to order. She watched him pause, an amused smile on his lips.

"Yes?" he queried, so very sure of himself.

"I want a husband and a home I can call my own," she said simply. The smile on his face dimmed and a different light in his eye, almost of concern, brought a troubled expression to his face. She continued, "I want a quiver full of children, as well. Like all women do."

He held her gaze for a long moment, then shook his head. "Not all women," he responded at last. "I'll see you at dinner— and after."

Four

Jane dressed with great care for dinner and for the selection of the vignette partners which would take place later in the evening. Lady Somercote's fortnight festival always included, as the height of her entertainment, the performance of a series of vignettes acted out by couples chosen by chance from cards selected at random from a silver bowl. The players were given a theme and each couple was directed to create and perform a brief vignette—or scene as from a play—based on that theme.

Jane was looking forward to this particular aspect of the party because secretly at heart she thought she might have enjoyed a life on the stage had she not been born the daughter of a baronet. The excitement, the pleasure of taking on a different role for each play, the thrill of bringing a character to life by gesture, voice, and performance—these activities appealed enormously to her.

Perhaps that was what she was doing anyway, she thought with a smile as she left her bedchamber to make her descent to the forest-green drawing room. She was acting out a role in order to capture a husband for herself—but not just any husband. This time, she wanted a good man, who disliked gaming as Freddy did, and who would undoubtedly be faithful to her for the duration.

She had not selected Freddy as her object lightly. Once she had arrived in London, she had carefully examined every prospective suitor to whom Lady Somercote introduced her. Many were eligible candidates but in the end, Freddy had won her because he possessed so many fine qualities. If he seemed to lack a certain strength of will, she was not concerned. His wealth was large enough to overcome such a character deficiency, a trait she was convinced was not necessary for the sustenance of a growing family.

Besides, she was very fond of him, even if he was something of a nodcock.

As for Thorpe and his seductive conduct with her among the pines and rhododendrons, she had taken some time to reflect on what had happened and determined that she would be wise not to allow herself to be alone with his lordship again. She only fell into mischief with him when their solitary state permitted him the liberty to behave however he wished to behave.

With all her objectives in proper order once more, she knew herself prepared to meet either of the gentlemen in question. When she passed through the fine gold and green antechamber that preceded the drawing room and finally entered the receiving room where Lady Somercote and her guests had gathered, she knew herself to be gowned and groomed immaculately, an effort designed solely to continue her assault on Freddy's heart, an effort she knew would please him because he possessed the eye of an artist.

Her dark brown hair was pinned in a chignon atop her head with a lovely fringe of delicate curls just touching her forehead. Vangie had wound a thin band of gold ribbon through her chignon. She wore a gown of gold silk, trimmed with exquisite white lace drawn up ruff-like at the back of her neck and descending to a pretty decollete at the front of her bodice. Her sleeves were slightly puffed at the shoulders but brought to a tight fit about each arm halfway to the elbow and edged with small point lace. Three pearl buttons arranged vertically at the side of each sleeve provided just the right accent.

The skirt of the gold gown sported an elegant, flowing demi-train, also edged with lace. Her slippers were of white silk embroidered with gold thread and Henrietta, upon first seeing her,

said she looked very regal, like the Empress Josephine, Bona-
parte's ill-fated first wife. Freddy likened her to Juno and Lord
Somercote, touching his hair at the temples, nodded his agreement. Jane could not immediately remove her gaze from Lord
Somercote since his black hair glimmered beneath the light of
the chamber's fully lit chandelier. He had not been ungenerous
in his use of Macassar oil. Now he looked like a glossy crow—
poor man!

She bit her lip to keep from laughing outright as she moved
into the chamber.

Thorpe, standing across the room and sipping a glass of
sherry, inclined his head as his gaze swept over her. He was
engaged in conversation with Mrs. Ullstree and did not make
the smallest move to leave her. Jane was pleased that he remained politely beside the older woman regardless of his
avowed intentions of seducing her. Freddy, on the other hand,
exhibited a wretched lapse in manners, since in his eagerness
to be with her, he deserted his hostess, Lady Somercote, leaving
her standing by herself. He crossed the room to take up her
hand and placed an awkward kiss on her gloved fingers. She
debated for a moment whether or not to reprimand her swain
for his rudeness. In the end, however, she withheld her disap-
proval, believing that though a wife might have excellent effect,
a widow who was still in effect a mere object of pursuit, could
quite possibly explode her chances of a happy outcome if she
became a nag. She chose, therefore, to be cautious rather than
instructive and allowed him to take her in to dinner.

Dinner was uneventful except that a growing anticipation for
the event to follow had set a buzz flowing around the table, not
less so when Lady Somercote rose and elucidated her selection
of the theme to be employed in the creation of the vignettes.

The theme was love and marriage.

Jane felt her heart leap at the words, wondering if her friend
had deliberately chosen the theme in order to advance her own
cause. Whatever the case, she glanced at Freddy, again seated
beside her, and hoped desperately that Fate would allow her to

become partners with him. She would then have no doubt of her success in bringing the reluctant Freddy Waingrove up to scratch.

The vignettes could reflect the happiest parts of love and marriage, or the darkest parts of unfulfilled hopes and expectations—whatever appealed most to the couples as they prepared their scenes together.

But uppermost in everyone's mind was who was to partner whom. Naturally, each lady would be paired with a gentleman, which could only enhance the final result of the collaboration between the partners. "For what could be duller," Lady Somercote had cried, "than two men discussing the beauty of marriage?"

The entire table had erupted into a shout of laughter. There wasn't a man present who hadn't been chastised at one time or another during the course of his life for his lack of interest in the subject. Besides, love and marriage can only be of true interest between a man and a woman.

By the time the elegant dinner was concluded, spirits were high as the assemblage moved back into the green drawing room and Lady Somercote brought forward her silver bowl in which had been placed five cards. On each of the cards was written the name of one or the other of her gentlemen guests.

"Miss Hartworth, will you come forward and select your partner for the vignettes? Henrietta, a slip of a girl and painfully shy by nature, did not like being the first, but she bore her part well, holding her head high and moving with petite grace to the bowl. In a childlike way, she placed a hand over her eyes as she paused for a moment, then dipped her free, gloved hand into the bowl. She withdrew a card, took a deep breath, and handed it to Lady Somercote without having stolen so much as a peek at the name inscribed thereon.

The countess stood several inches over Henrietta giving the young lady an even more youthful and diminutive aspect than ever.

"Mr. Waingrove," Lady Somercote stated in her lovely, contralto voice. "You are to partner Miss Hartworth." Jane knew

a quick, intense disappointment which she kept hidden behind
a smiling demeanor. Of course it was silly to think that she
could get her wish when she had a one in five chance of Freddy
becoming her partner. Still, she knew what the opportunity
could have meant to her and that loss rankled.

She then watched as a deep blush suddenly suffused Henrietta's face. The poor girl immediately lowered her gaze and
resumed her seat beside Mrs. Ullstree on a sofa of dark green
velvet.

Poor Henrietta, Jane thought. She is too meek to be in company and certainly will have a great deal of difficulty performing her vignette. She decided therefore that it was a wonderful
thing that Freddy was to have charge of her. He was always
tender with Hetty and she would need a great deal of tenderness
now in order to get through the creation and performance of a
theatrical vignette. How terrible it would have been had Henrietta been partnered with either Thorpe or Duffield or even
Lord Somercote, for that matter. These men would have chewed
her up for breakfast without having realized once they had mistaken her for their bacon.

Lady Somercote's voice interrupted her flow of thoughts.
"And now, Mrs. Newstead, will you oblige us?"

Mrs. Newstead, gowned to perfection in a clinging white
muslin with ruffles about the hem, pearl ear-drops dangling
from each perfect lobe, and her breasts displayed to advantage
from a tightly drawn corset, moved gracefully to the bowl. Jane
noted that Lady Somercote's polite smile seemed a little stiff
as she held the bowl toward the widow.

Mrs. Newstead, dimpling and smiling at Thorpe and then
Colonel Duffield and even Lord Somercote, made the assemblage laugh by also placing a hand over her eyes, mocking poor
Henrietta. Jane couldn't laugh, nor could Lady Somercote as
the widow selected a card. She handed the card to her hostess
who held her composure tightly in check as she read her husband's name.

Jane could not keep her gaze from flying to the earl's face, nor could she deny that he was infinitely pleased as he stroked his black locks and ogled the widow.

"I hope I will not disappoint you," Mrs. Newstead said pointedly, addressing and curtsying to her new partner.

"You could never disappoint anyone, madame," he said, rising to bow in response. "I daresay we shall create the best vignette of them all. See if we won't!"

Though Mrs. Newstead obviously was ready to give an equally flirtatious response, her words died on her tongue as Lady Somercote quickly moved the selection process forward. "Mrs. Ambergate, will you choose?"

Jane approached the bowl, but only as she realized that three gentlemen remained and one of them was Lord Thorpe did she comprehend the amount of danger she was in. The actors would be practicing in solitude as often as was required to complete the brief dramas, and what she particularly did not want to enjoy with Lord Thorpe was even a minute's solitude. She looked at the cards and felt her heartbeat quicken. One chance in three. She would either know safety or despair. What would it be?

She turned her head away and bid Lady Somercote stir up the remaining cards. She then dipped her hand in the bowl and picked up the card on the top.

"Lord Thorpe," Lady Somercote stated.

Jane forced her complexion to remain even. She would give no one the satisfaction of seeing a single emotion from her. She turned and curtsied to Thorpe, who, because he was standing by the white stone fireplace, and all the players were in front of him and therefore could not see his face, winked at her.

The rogue!

The beast!

She quickly returned to her seat as Lady Somercote begged Mrs. Ullstree to draw her partner—she would either be performing with her own husband or with Colonel Duffield, and as chance would have it she was happy to have chosen Colonel Duffield. "For though I adore my spouse," and here she smiled sweetly on her husband, "I live too many months of the year with him and he with me to want to write a vignette about the joys of marriage—or even the despairs, for that matter." Because her demeanor was kindness itself, a chuckle ran through the crowd and no one was surprised when Mr. Ullstree rose from his seat and greeted his wife with a kiss on her cheek before she sat down again.

Lady Somercote lifted the last card and said, "It is my pleasure, Mr. Ullstree, to have you as my partner."

"And I, you, m'lady," he responded with pretty dignity.

Each couple was then given several sheets of paper, ink pots, and pens, and told to come back in an hour with the gist of the idea for their vignettes to be presented to the others. The purpose was to make certain that enough variety was being created in order to keep the final presentation of the vignettes as pleasing as possible.

Thorpe and Jane were directed to the sword-room, a place Jane thought was entirely appropriate given the nature of their relationship. She moved to the round inlaid table in the center of the chamber upon which sat a heavy, spiked steel ball mounted on a carved wooden holder. She set the paper on the table and Thorpe followed suit, placing the silver tray, pens, and filigreed ink pot next to the paper.

"This settles it then," he said, as he glanced at each of four high-panelled walls on which were displayed armament from many centuries past. "We must design a vignette that discusses to perfection the struggle of man with woman."

"Of woman with man," Jane retorted, correcting him with a lift of her chin.

He smiled.

She moved to the fireplace, an ancient hearth whose stone was of a different texture and color than the rest of the house. A tidy log fire burned brightly within. "Look at this," she said. "What does this mean, this enormous fireplace and these old, yellowish stones?"

"A kind of limestone," he said, moving to stand beside her. "This must be the core of a more ancient house, kept by Lord

Somercote's father when he had Challeston built—or rebuilt it, that is."

"It's lovely though the inside of the fireplace is blackened with age and use, of course. I wonder how old it is?"

Thorpe turned around and viewed the walls again and the windows that overlooked the back formal gardens and the yew maze in the distance. The display of weapons reached to the ceiling on every wall. "Or how old some of these lances and swords are. Look at that mace and that broadsword—perhaps it saw the Crusades—"

"The War of the Roses—?" Jane suggested.

He moved to stand next to her. "The Duke of Normandy's crossing of the English Channel?"

She looked up at him. "Aren't we a romantic pair," she said with a smile. "Supplying places and people to swords and stones."

She shouldn't have said such a friendly thing to him, for he took it as an invitation. "We could be a pair," he suggested, turning to her and slipping a quick arm about her waist. "You look lovely tonight, Jane. Freddy spoke of Juno but he was wrong. All of the volumes I've read speak of Aphrodite as the true reigning goddess—"

"Thorpe, please," Jane said, placing a hand on his chest. She didn't want the moment to go further. "We have less than an hour to come up with something dignified for our part in the play. If you begin kissing me—"

"If I begin kissing you, I won't stop," he breathed, leaning toward her.

She purposefully stepped on his foot, dipped, and slid under his arm. He laughed but caught her easily about the waist again, this time with both hands, and turned her to face him. He held her slightly away from him and kneaded her waist. Jane placed her hands on his. She found the sensation exhilarating. Suddenly, he squeezed her so tightly that she nearly lost her breath.

Why did she want to fall into his arms?

"No," she whispered. "The vignette is the thing."

He smiled, looking deeply into her eyes. "It is," he whispered in return.

She recalled to mind what he had told her during the Season—that they were a vignette, a brief flame, and she pushed his hands down and away from her. "I've just thought of something. Why don't we begin our scene with that horrible thing you said to me at the end of last Season. Do you remember? Something like, 'we are not three acts, but a vignette'—"

"Three acts and a farce," he corrected her. A smile suffused his face. "You're right. We should begin there."

He moved quickly to the table, lifted the lid of the inkpot, and bent over to begin scribbling.

"The whole of it shall be an argument," Jane said, beginning to pace behind him. "What you want from me and what I want from, if not you, then from any man in a passionate context."

He had one hand flat on the table as he wrote. He was slightly bent over. He looked up at her, his eyes narrowed. "A husband, children?" he queried quietly.

"Precisely so," she said, her hands clasped in front of her.

The air between them grew oddly still. Her mind was free of thoughts as she watched him. He turned to fix his gaze on the deadly spiked ball nearby, his pen was silent, his whole body, even bent as it was, seemed to be poised, waiting, but for what?

Finally, he laid the pen down and faced her. "I will make you this promise," he said. "I won't take you again, unless you ask me to."

Jane felt his words flow over her like a river of warm water. She was touched, deeply touched. She knew he was sincere. She felt he had handed her his sword and empowered her to use it at will.

"Thank you," she murmured. "That is the kindest thing you've ever done for me. Thorpe, I want you to understand something. I do want you. You know that. You know that my reticence is not a matter of not longing for you, for your physical self, but rather that the end of it is entirely repugnant to me. I can't abide the thought of becoming your mistress. What would follow? Would I then take another man into my bed and then another? I won't do it. But I want you to know that I am very grateful for what you have just said to me. You've proven yourself a friend."

He lifted a hand. "You didn't let me finish," he said, words that brought her gratitude drawing up shortly. He continued, "I have a condition."

Though she believed he had been sincere somehow she knew his condition would be impossible to meet. "And what would that be?" she asked, coolly.

"That you give up this madness about Waingrove."

Jane turned abruptly away from him and moved to stand beside the fireplace watching orange, red, and yellow flames dance along the burning logs. Her heart sank all over again. He would never understand her or her situation. She heard his footsteps as he moved to stand just behind her.

"There is no difference in my book," he breathed urgently, the heat of his words burning her neck. "Whether Mrs. Newstead accepts my protection or whether you accept Waingrove's hand in marriage—there is no difference. Can't you see that?"

She lowered her gaze to the ancient peg and grooved floor. "At least my object is different—"

"It is the same—a man's protection for your womb."

"How can you speak so?" she cried.

"There is no difference and the reason I'm not married is I have yet to meet a lady who I respect and admire, who sees a difference."

She shook her head and turned to face him, eying him squarely. "It is not so simple. You don't understand. You can't possibly understand what it is to be a woman in these modern times. Our choices are so limited, while yours—Thorpe, you can do anything you wish to do, you can accomplish any whim you set your mind to. You could navigate all the oceans of the world if you wished for it." She paused and took a deep breath. He was very close. He could have kissed her if he wanted to, but there was no desire between them now, only the argument.

She held his gaze firmly. "Do you know what my choices are? Tell me what you would have me choose and what my prospects of having a home would be then? Woodcock Hill is mortgaged to the moneylenders. At the end of this month, I have no home. Edward used up my dowry. I have nothing, only the mediocre education granted me by an inferior governess who greatly enjoyed a bottle of port every evening. Shall I follow in her profession and become a governess—"

"Sell your jewels—!" he urged her.

Jane laughed in despair and set her forehead on his shoulder. "You are too naive, or have the *on dits* not quite relayed my circumstances in their entirety?" She drew back, smiling, yet feeling only despair. "I am destitute. Need I be plainer?"

"Then if you must sell yourself, sell yourself to me," he pleaded, sliding his hands about her waist again, then drawing her close to him. His breath became a whisper on her ear and her neck. "I will secure your future. Whatever you need, whatever you want, I can give all to you."

The nearness of him and his strength was strangely comforting. She knew an impulse to slip her arms about his back and to acquiesce. She would know safety in his embrace. In his offer of protection, she knew she would want for nothing. Did he know how much he tempted her?

"That's the rub," she said, bringing herself to order and pulling away from him. "What I want is a passel of children. I always have. When nothing came of my marriage, when I proved childless, I was never more dismayed. If I could have at least had one or two babes to call my own, to carry about in my arms, to ease the pain of having wedded a gamester, then I could have been content. But there were no children with Edward, and I want a family. Would you then have me bear my babes out of wedlock? Is that what you are suggesting to me?"

He seemed stunned by her speech. "What of your family?"

"I have none," she said. "Well, I have a brother who resides in India. He is a lieutenant with the army there—the East India Company. But my mother passed away ten years ago, when I was but fifteen. Papa—" Tears bit her eyes at the recollection of so many sad and painful memories. She swallowed and regained her composure. "My father perished from consumption when I was still in the schoolroom."

"I'm sorry," he said softly. "No cousins, aunts, uncles?"

She shook her head. She touched the corner of her eye to keep a tear from trickling down her cheek. She gestured broadly with her hand and forced a laugh. "Don't repine on my behalf! I didn't mean to sound complaining or aggrieved by my lot. Heaven knows I've enjoyed a degree of comfort despite my losses that most will never know in this lifetime. Speaking of these things has only put me in mind of people I loved and who I miss dreadfully on occasion, even after all these years. Even Edward, for all his faults, was an agreeable companion." She smiled wistfully and moved to the window overlooking the vast formal garden. Scattered Chinese lanterns lit the square, hedged beds in a dim but romantic glow. "When he would come back from a campaign—mind we had not seen one another in months, sometimes years—he would sit with me for hours, twirling my long curls about his fingers and reading to me from his or my favorite books. He loved poetry, does that seem odd?" She glanced at him over her shoulder and saw that he was watching her with a curious light in his blue eyes.

"A little," he responded quietly, a familiar, crooked smile on his lips.

"It was odd—this great big soldier, reading poetry and coddling me. I adored every moment of it. I hated the poverty, of course, and his gaming. But Edward loved me." She fell silent recalling her husband and dwelling on the best of her memories of him. The many arguments she had endured about his gaming habits she had long since relegated to the back of her mind along with the memory of hearing of his death and quickly afterward the sum of his debts.

Thorpe's voice intruded. "But if you'd had children," he said, addressing an entirely different aspect of the discussion at hand, "what would you have done then? Major Ambergate would have died and you would have been left in the same condition, only with babes to support, as well."

Jane shrugged. "I daresay I would have married my neighbor, Mr. Leybourne. He lived retired near Woodcock Hill. He had been engaged in trade most of his life and he was very fond of me. He offered for me shortly after Edward's demise. A good-hearted soul. In fact." Here she turned back to him. "I almost accepted his offer anyway. I was on the brink of doing so, when Lady Somercote wrote to me and extended her support of me."

"So you came to London to make your fortune—or rather to acquire the fortune of one of your suitors."

She nodded. "Not less so than many younger sons who seek the large dowries of their wives to enhance their annual incomes."

He narrowed his gaze at her. "So just what was the dowry you brought to your marriage?"

"The question is impertinent," she said, lifting a brow, but not feeling in the least offended. She liked Thorpe and had he not been in such a determined, lascivious pursuit of her, she rather thought they would have become the very best of friends instead of unsteady enemies.

"Tell me anyway," he commanded her.

She hesitated, but only for a moment. "Twenty thousand."

His mouth dropped agape. "I begin to understand a little of your lack of compunction in pursuing Waingrove. You feel you've been cheated."

She frowned at his remark. "No," she responded slowly. "I don't think that's true. My only thought, during all this time, has been that I've had to suffer because of my husband's atrocious addiction to every form of gaming and that I no longer want to suffer."

"You want the ease then, of Waingrove's fortune and you want that more than your self-respect?"

"If that is how you choose to see the situation, then yes I want the ease his fortune can bring to me more than I want my self-respect. But I disagree with your views. This isn't a matter of self-respect, but of survival and common sense. Of what use will I be to my children if I can't put food in their mouths or see to their futures with even a modicum of success?"

"You've not accepted your lot," he stated.

She smiled faintly. "And you judge far too harshly because you are well shod."

He appeared stung by her last comment. "My condition remains," he stated. "I ask you, then, will you give up your pursuit of Mr. Waingrove?"

She shook her head. "I can't," she answered simply. "You want me to be a paragon, and I refuse to take on that mantle. I will make Freddy a good wife, loyal and helpful. He will lack for nothing. I will manage his home with meticulous care. I will raise his children to respect him and to love him."

"You are still selling yourself."

"If you choose to see it that way, then I can't change your opinions. Have it as you will."

"Then I tell you plainly, Mrs. Ambergate, I am not done with you."

"Please yourself, m'lord," she responded coolly. "You always do. As for the vignette, write what you will. I am done with your scrutiny of my character. I am returning to my bedchamber. You may tell my hostess that I've the headache."

He bowed to her and she left the sword room. Her head was aching, but not less so her heart.

On the following day, while descending the elegant circular staircase in anticipation of seeing the local Derbyshire well-dressings, Jane received Henrietta's unnecessary apologies.

"I am so very sorry!" Henrietta cried, slipping her small hand into Jane's. "Never was a fate more cruelly decided than this one. You, to endure Lord Thorpe's company and at the same time to be denied Mr. Waingrove's attentions! I shouldn't have drawn his name. It's all my fault. If only I hadn't covered my eyes."

Jane was stunned and paused their progress down the stairs.

Earlier, she had found Henrietta pacing the end of the hall near
her bedchamber door, deeply distressed. Her friend had been
waiting to speak to her and to confess her horrible misdeeds,
but never would she have suspected that Henrietta somehow
faulted herself for having won Freddy as a partner in the drawing the night before.

"Hetty, you make too much of it!" Jane cried as she took
another step down the stairs. "You sound as though you orchestrated the drawing of the vignette partners yourself, which I
know you did not."

"Oh, I didn't!" she cried. "I promise you I didn't. I wouldn't
do such a wretched thing! But I fear I have ruined your chances
of bringing Fr—that is, Mr. Waingrove—up to scratch. You
should have been his partner. Perhaps we could switch?"

Jane gave her hand a squeeze. "Don't be such a goose. You
and Freddy have been friends for so long that I can't think of
anyone I would rather have him partner than you." She watched
Henrietta blush a fiery crimson and felt an irritation rise within
her. Miss Hartworth could be a goose and a ninnyhammer and
she was being both now. She was also a young lady with a sweet
temperament and a heart of spun gold. If only she would cure
herself of falling into the blushes whenever she was complimented, reassured, or merely addressed!

She was a slight young lady, thin of frame and of face. She
might have been beautiful had she not been so frail. Her hair
was a pretty auburn and her dove-like complexion enhanced
her fragile appearance. Her eyes were an exquisite hazel, the
precise color of her eyes changing dramatically with each shift
of light, a fact Freddy commented on frequently and which he
had enshrined in one of his numerous sonnets: "To the Orbs of
a Lovely Little Lady." *Orbs* always put Jane in mind of swiftly
spinning planets and she had been hard-pressed to keep from
laughing when Freddy had read the poem to her.

Henrietta wore a modest gown of small block-patterned green
squares on a pale yellow Indian cotton, a shade that cast her small
face into the background of her gown. Over her auburn curls,

she wore a straw poke bonnet trimmed with green ribbons. She looked most unhappily like a country dowd—poor thing!

Jane had learned one thing from her mother—to dress to the nines no matter what the occasion. Having known the agenda of the fortnight festivities far in advance, she had taken her list of events to Lady Somercote's dressmaker in New Bond Street at the end of June and had spent a sennight working with that imaginative French dressmaker in creating every *ensemble* she had brought with her to Derbyshire. The results had been superb.

For the well-dressings, she wore a summery gown, long in the sleeve for protection against the sunshine, of the finest muslin gauze. The fabric had been stitched carefully to include a thousand infinitesimal gathers about the Empire waistline in order to give the appearance of a delicate cloud when she walked. She wore a bustle high at the back which forced the muslin to float behind her, an effect enhanced by the long cut of the fabric at the hem. About the hem, three rows of meticulous ruffles, each an inch in height, surrounded the skirt lending the precise weight to keep the gown from blowing away at the first sign of a breeze. Beneath the gown, a shift of white silk kept the muslin gliding easily about her legs.

She carried a matching parasol and wore a bonnet of tightly gathered white muslin, over which a net veil passed just below her dark brown eyes. White lace gloves, pearl ear-drops and white silk slippers completed her toilette.

"Don't trouble yourself a moment more," she assured Henrietta as she set them both to moving down the circular stairs again. The entrance hall was alive with footmen and guests all proceeding in and out of doors in preparation for the drive to view the many wells, dressed for the annual summer ceremonies. Through the open doors, she could see at least two of the five landaus, hired specifically to accommodate the procession. The low, open carriage was a perfect vehicle for the event and Lady Somercote had taken great pains to find five for the pleasure of her guests.

"But you don't understand," Henrietta said in a quiet, disturbing voice as they reached the entrance hall floor. "Yesterday, during your archery practice, I all but stole him away from you. And then, last night, you had to go off with Thorpe and . . . and Freddy, I mean, Mr. Waingrove and I—"

Jane took Hetty's arm and locked it firmly about hers. "You worry far too much. As for yesterday, I was grateful Freddy was close by to see you returned to the house."

"He was overset," she remarked.

"He cares about you."

"I don't mean that," Hetty said. "I think he had had a little more sun than was good for him. By the time we reached the morning room and sent for a little lemonade for me, he was quite ill. He would never say anything to you—he doesn't like to distress you—but he had a violent headache. Do you think it was the sunshine?"

Jane was startled by what Henrietta had just revealed to her. "You were right in one thing—he said nothing to me. I am sorry to hear he was so ill."

"Don't fret, Jane. I took care of him. I saw him removed to his bedchamber and kept cold compresses on his forehead. They seemed to ease his discomfort. I read to him and wrote a letter to his mother on his behalf. By five o'clock he was better and of course you saw him at dinner." Henrietta smiled softly. "He was perfectly cured!"

Jane didn't know what to say, and had it been anyone other than Henrietta she would have been stunned and distressed that her friend had spent the afternoon in her beau's bedchamber. "I shall have to speak with him," she said. "I only wish I had known about his illness."

"I know," Hetty breathed. "That is why I had to speak with you. Had you been able to sit with him all afternoon I feel assured you might have won his affections at last. But he refused—adamantly so—to have you brought to him. I'm so sorry, Jane! I tried. Indeed, I did!"

"Stuff and nonsense," Jane murmured kindly when Hetty's hazel eyes filled with tears. She felt mildly irritated with the young lady and though she doubted anything she might say would reassure Henrietta, she again adjured her not to give the occasion the smallest thought, then got rid of the sensitive young lady by directing her gently to the last carriage in the row of five landaus.

Mouthing a final apology, Henrietta obediently crossed the gravel drive to her carriage.

Each lady was to take up a place in one of the carriages and would remain in that carriage throughout the viewing of four wells in four different nearby villages. After the viewing of each well, the gentlemen would move to the next carriage back, the gentleman in the last carriage moving to the front landau, and so on. This way a variety of conversation and companionship would ensue, the object of all of Lady Somercote's entertainments.

Jane was placed fourth in line, with Lady Somercote leading, Mrs. Ullstree next and Mrs. Newstead third. Henrietta, the youngest, was last. The gentlemen were placed initially with their vignette partners and would rotate from there. Jane was not surprised therefore to find Lord Thorpe leaning negligently against the low door of their landau, his arms folded across his chest. His expression was familiar, the lazy smile, the slight cock of his head, his blue eyes penetrating and cool.

What a rogue!

What a beast!

She inclined her head to him, then moved past him to greet Freddy and to inquire after his health.

Freddy, who had been helping Henrietta to get situated in the landau, looked up in surprise at her greeting. "Jane!" he cried. His gold-green eyes took in her gown at a glance and his complexion became instantly patched with red splotches. "How exquisite you are, my pretty dove! I've never seen a gown so radiant, so reflective of the sun's glory, so stately yet with an air of funning."

An air of funning.

Jane felt a familiar irritation rise within her, not unlike that which she experienced earlier while speaking with Henrietta. Why couldn't he just say, *Hallo,* instead of dousing her with a horribly fulsome compliment. "Thank you, Freddy," she responded, lowering her gaze and simpering as she had seen Mrs. Newstead simper times out of mind.

She placed her gloved hand on the top of the low door and for this small effort was rewarded with his gloved hand smacked atop hers. *Gently, Freddy,* her mind cried inwardly. He fondled her hand and leaned forward in his seat, forgetting Henrietta's presence entirely. He whispered, "I look forward with great intensity to the moment that we drive together at the end of the day. Do you as well, my love?"

Jane lifted her gaze to meet his. The expression on his face was ardent and hope rose swiftly within her. "Very much so," she whispered. "Dear, Freddy." His face became suffused with color as he smiled.

She then bid him lean back in his seat and tell her about his illness of yesterday.

"I had not meant to worry you," he said earnestly. "But thank you for asking. I believe it started when I was fetching your arrows. After that, I began to feel quite peculiar. You know how that little throbbing begins just at the temple and proceeds in minute stages toward the nape of my . . ."

Jane settled in for the long listen, pasted a smile on her face, and wondered how she could have played the idiot so completely as to have actually asked to be told the details of his sufferings. Freddy was long on suffering. They were like his compliments—wretchedly fulsome and unnecessary.

Thorpe had heard and seen enough to set him chuckling beneath his breath. Jane was a fool and she had brought her present misery down on her own head. So she thought she would enjoy even a day's happiness being married to such a creature.

Well, then, if she achieved her ambition he felt certain she would atone for her wicked pursuit of the man simply by having to be with him day in and day out once they were wed.

"Aren't we full of mirth today," Mrs. Newstead's voice intruded on his happy thoughts.

"And aren't we full of mischief," he countered. Mrs. Newstead, her blonde ringlets in a riot of curls that peeped charmingly from beneath the brim of her apricot silk bonnet, was a summery vision. She wore a matching gown, over which a silk apron was gathered up at the sides and pinned to the waist with apricot silk rosettes. Her short white silk gloves, her puffed sleeves, and her white silk parasol gave her the appearance of a fashionable shepherdess. He continued, "Has his lordship expressed his admiration of you?"

Mrs. Newstead let out a trill of laughter, as familiar to him as the fit of his hands about her narrow waist. "Does he like my apron, do you mean?" she queried, her blue eyes dancing with pleasure. "Very much so. He said I looked like one of the undermaids. I think he rather fancied the image."

Thorpe narrowed his eyes at her. "He has never left the fold before," he suggested tentatively.

"There is always a first time."

"His wife is your hostess."

Mrs. Newstead shrugged and smiled. "So tell me," she said, giving their conversation a quick turn. "How goes our wager? Which man will I be wedding come Monday next?"

Thorpe glanced toward Jane whose expression was fraught with fatigue as she nodded every now and again at something or other Freddy was saying to her. The budding poet was quite animated about his subject but he could see Jane was bored to tears. Thorpe chuckled. "Our wager prospers, at least from my point of view, and now that I think on it I am convinced you will enjoy being Mrs. Colonel Duffield."

"You are too confident, my lord," she said, feigning a haughty countenance. "You are bound for a fall, mark my words." Then with a twirl of her pretty white parasol she turned and strolled away.

He watched her go, thinking he wanted to find some way of preventing her from conquering Lord Somercote but not precisely understanding why.

Lord Somercote approached him next, stroking lightly the black bristly hair above his ear. "Pretty little thing, isn't she?" he asked in a low voice. Lord Somercote was a tall man, slightly taller than Lord Thorpe. He cleared his throat as he spoke, his gray eyes fixed to Mrs. Newstead's swaying form as she approached the Ullstrees and began chatting lightly with them.

"A neat little Bird of Paradise," he responded, coming immediately to the point.

Lord Somercote cleared his throat again and cast a nervous glance toward Thorpe. "That obvious, eh?"

"Your designs? Or hers?" Thorpe queried casually.

"I say, Thorpe," Lord Somercote said, a sudden frown between his brows. "A bit presumptuous, what?"

"Didn't mean to offend you, m'lord," he said easily. "I was only commenting on the subject you brought forward. Do you wish for my opinion?"

Somercote seemed disconcerted by his directness and at first didn't respond. His gaze shifted uneasily to his wife who had joined the Ullstrees and Mrs. Newstead, then back to Thorpe. "Always thought you enjoyed her."

"Cost me a pretty penny, though, but more to the point, I didn't have much else to lose. I'm not married," he responded, again with a directness that caused Lord Somercote to grind his teeth and shortly afterward to stalk away.

Lady Somercote soon left the little group and made her way to Thorpe's carriage. She exchanged a few commonplaces with him then asked beneath her breath, "Whatever did you say to him? He's as mad as fire."

"Sorry, m'lady. Between gentlemen."

Lady Somercote eyed him curiously. "Humph," she responded softly. "You spoke to him of Mrs. Newstead and he did not take your remarks kindly."

"He did not," Thorpe responded.

Lady Somercote smiled and moved to the third coach at which Mrs. Newstead had just arrived. She then said something to the widow which caused the delicate peach beauty to lift her chin.

Colonel Duffield, who had been standing near enough to have overheard the exchange, strolled up to Thorpe, barely able to repress a grin.

"What did she say?" Thorpe asked beneath his breath.

"Told her to take her claws off her husband if she knew what was good for her."

Thorpe did not try to suppress his amusement. He laughed aloud which drew the attention of much of the party toward him. Duffield made a fist and punched him affectionately on his arm. He then moved to join Mrs. Newstead, leaning over the low door of the carriage in order to continue his own private campaign.

Mrs. Ullstree, ever one to enjoy a variety of people, began her own progress down the rows of carriages, pausing to greet Colonel Duffield and to comment on the pretty apricot silk of Mrs. Newstead's gown before arriving to greet Lord Thorpe.

She was a handsome woman, in her late forties if Thorpe guessed correctly. He knew she had been a great beauty in her day and had married one of the ugliest men available. She had raised seven children, seen carefully to the ways of her household, and had somehow managed to preserve her dignity and still enjoyed a soft-toned version of her beauty. He was always slightly awed in her presence, a fact that seemed to please her as he bowed over her hand.

"I should kiss your fingers, madame, if I didn't think you would likely give me a set down."

"And I would," she responded with a warm smile. "How do you go on, Lord Thorpe? You are as handsome as ever and still so very much unattached. Do you know what a sore trial you are to us poor females?"

He responded to both her questions, beginning with the former. "I am very well, quite content, as it happens, but as for your second query, I don't know what you mean?"

"An unattached male, worth no less than ten thousand a year and handsome in the bargain, is a form of torment you perform almost ritualistically upon our young maidens year after year and upon your mistresses as well if I am not mistaken."

He knew he should be offended but he wasn't. He respected Mrs. Ullstree too much for that. "How then am I to make amends?"

"Get yourself married, and your sins will be forgiven, one and all."

"But what you suggest is impossible. I have found no one—" He couldn't finish the sentence in light of the disapproving expression on her face.

Mrs. Ullstree lifted a brow. "Worthy?" she suggested.

He decided to be honest with her and nodded. "I find most of the ladies I meet in the course of a Season to be avaricious, their designs more exclusively on my pocketbook than on my heart. But tell me about you. I've always been curious. Your marriage seems to me to have been one of the mysteries of the age. You have always struck me as deeply content and your husband equally so. Explain your happiness to me." He felt embarrassed suddenly, realizing that given her beauty she must have wed Mr. Ullstree for reasons similar to the ones about which he had just complained.

Mrs. Ullstree smiled. "I married an ugly man with a lot of money. I decided early on to take no chances. I believe he was so grateful to get me that therein lies the root of our continued contentment."

Thorpe was shocked and drew his brows together in a serious frown. Never would he have believed she would have held, and certainly not admitted to, such wretched ambitions and designs. He opened his mouth to speak, but she cut him off.

"My lord, don't even think of moralizing with me. I know you wish to but I won't allow it. You are far too romantic in your notions for your own good. You expect perfection in a woman while you are, at the very same time, stealing the virtue of one woman after another. Thank God women are generally of a more practical turn than men—though I daresay it is because we have to be. We have our children to consider, and of what use is it to love and to be impoverished only to watch our children starve and suffer needlessly? Trust me when I say that the moment a woman hears her child crying out its suffering, love flies straight out the window. Think on what I've said. I feel you've a good heart, but you're greatly misguided."

Mrs. Ullstree walked away and he was left to wonder in amazement at what she had said to him—especially since Jane had told him something similar the night before. He eyed Mrs. Ullstree narrowly as she greeted Jane, Freddy, and Miss Hartworth. Perhaps she had been funning with him, presenting notions she in no way truly believed. Whatever the case, her words had unsettled him, no less so than because he held her in high esteem. He watched her return to her husband and take his hand in a gesture of affection and he wondered about their relationship once more. Had she married him for his fortune? Was her husband truly content in spite of it? Whatever the case, Mr. Ullstree presented the appearance of a man who was indeed very happily wed.

Lady Somercote began encouraging her guests to take their places. Mrs. Ullstree and Colonel Duffield climbed aboard the second carriage while Lady Somercote and Mr. Ullstree took the first. Lord Somercote joined Mrs. Newstead, and they sat at a polite distance from one another. The transactions of the morning seemed to have had some effect on them. Perhaps. Or perhaps they were merely being discreet.

Thorpe waited for Jane to join him but she was still listening intently to her swain.

When the butler finally approached Jane to inform her that the carriages were ready to start, she cast him such a look of gratitude that Thorpe again laughed aloud. He suspected the rest of the day would be filled with much amusement, not less so than when Jane approached him, lifted her white muslin skirts, and cast him a darkling look. "Must you laugh like a farm laborer at a haying?"

Again Thorpe laughed which only brought an even more reproachful expression to her face.

"You're so pretty," he said. "Especially when you are wearing the look of a long-suffering wife, or wife-to-be, who has had to listen to her husband recount his ailments, or do I much mistake your recent conversation with Mr. Waingrove?"

Jane huffed and grimaced as she settled her voluminous skirts into the phaeton. "Oh do stubble it, Thorpe!" she cried as the train of landaus began to move forward. "I am out of temper and you shall feel the brunt of it unless you are very kind to me for the next hour or so."

He placed his hand gently over hers. "I shall be kindness itself," he remarked, giving her hand a squeeze.

He could see her temper rise all over again as she picked up his hand with her free hand and cast it back at him. He laughed again, a cool northerly breeze suddenly wafting over the carriages, and sat back prepared to enjoy the day.

Five

Jane sat beside Lord Thorpe, her heart full of gloomy thoughts. The viscount had struck her to the core with his curt comment about Freddy's ails. She had done her duty. She had listened to him patiently. Well, she had sort of listened to him. She had even wondered at Henrietta's frequent interjections about each turn of his health during the long afternoon of his sufferings.

But by the time the butler had relieved her of her station beside Freddy's landau, she was so fatigued with his complainings and moanings that she found herself actually looking forward to being with Lord Thorpe. Realizing that he was a better companion for her than Freddy disheartened her in the extreme.

Ever since her argument with Thorpe the evening before, she had been reviewing his criticism of her ambitions over and over. She had examined her mind and her heart, her marriage to Edward, her mother's life, her father's life, the rules governing her society. She had placed Thorpe's position under the candlelight of as much honest scrutiny as she could emotionally afford, and she had had to admit to herself that his arguments were not without merit.

However, she was no longer a chit of eighteen, able to embrace every virtue blindly. To be as Thorpe wished her to be, an impoverished but high-minded widow, was not something at five and twenty that she could accept graciously.

The blessings of life, promised to her in some vague teaching about always being good and true and virtuous, had not come to her in her first marriage. Instead, she had been ruined financially and her choices severely limited. Thorpe had chosen to judge her for choosing to pursue a husband she thought suitable for a woman of her age and her station in society. But Thorpe had a fortune of his own, and every whim of which he so much as conceived, was his for the taking. What did he know of poverty? What would his thoughts be were he to consider becoming, say, a tutor for the rest of his life, enslaved to the sons of other men, travelling down the road of existence, from one family to the next, never having a family of his own, never knowing love, and enjoying only two afternoons per week to himself?

She glanced at him now. He had leaned his head against the squabs, removed his hat, and was letting the sunshine beat upon his handsome face.

"You don't look like much of a tutor," she said.

He turned his head and lifted his brows. "What?" he asked. "Did I hear you correctly? What do you mean, I don't look like a tutor?"

"I was just wondering what you would do if you suddenly lost your fortune," she said with a slight shrug of her shoulders and a twirl of her parasol.

At that he slapped his hat back on his head and sat up. He turned toward her, sliding one of his booted legs behind hers. She didn't flinch. "I would never lose my fortune," he said firmly. "Only a fool would do that."

"And I married a fool."

"Yes, you did."

"And I must pay the piper."

"Yes, but which piper do you intend to pay, or do you intend to regale me with how delightful Mr. Waingrove is and how you are sure if you married him the pair of you would know a bliss unbounded."

Jane could not be offended, not today, not after having had to listen to how many drops of laudanum Freddy was able to consume without falling asleep, not with the pretty July sunshine casting the entire verdant countryside into a glow, not with the carriage rocking her and soothing her as it rumbled toward the first of four Derbyshire well-dressings.

She smiled. "I promise to keep silent about Freddy, if you will promise to keep your opinions about my choice of future in your pocket."

She glanced at him, a half-smile on her lips. He smiled in return, meeting her gaze fully. She didn't speak, nor did he, as a silent understanding passed between them. This time, he took her hand and she didn't protest. She found the gesture comforting. She sensed that even though he disapproved he understood, and that knowledge eased away a great many of her tensions.

"So who designed your gown, pretty Jane?" he asked.

She smiled. "It is lovely, isn't it?"

"Very."

She answered his question. "Lady Somercote's dressmaker in New Bond Street. She calls herself Madame Babette. Quite a silly appellation, I thought, but oh, the skill of her eye and her fingers."

Gently he began to drift his fingers over hers, a movement that was so languid and soft as to not exist. Again, she was comforted. She turned away from him and let her gaze drift over the countryside. All the while he touched her.

The carriages were heading east, to the village of Knowlwood on the far side of Windy Knowl. The land flattened out to permit the growth of several hundred acres of corn. The line of landaus stretched out to keep the fine dirt of the country lanes from rising too quickly and covering the occupants of the later carriages in dust.

She felt Thorpe's booted leg move ever so slowly along the length of her calves. She should tell him to stop, especially since a spattering of gooseflesh moved up her legs in a wave of pleasure and desire. He shouldn't be touching her in such a familiar and sensual manner.

She looked back at him and shook her head once slowly. But he didn't stop and she was beginning to find it difficult to breathe. He slid his hand, gloved in York tan, from her wrist to her waist and began making circles on her stomach and along her arm. She could barely breathe now as the intimacy of his touch filled her with desire.

"Let me come to you tonight," he whispered, his deep resonant voice rushing over her. "I want you, Jane. I want you in my bed and unless I am mistaken, you are desiring the same thing. Let me come to you."

She placed her hand on his and stopped the torturous circles. She shook her head. "No, I can't. I won't."

"But you want to." His voice was low and insistent.

"I've already told you it's not a matter of what I want or what I long for."

"Just once," he pressed her. "Just tonight. Forget about Freddy, about everything tonight. Forget about Edward and your dowry, everything you've lost. Let me make some of it up to you."

Jane wanted to say yes, though she didn't understand why, except that because of his earlier treachery she already knew what it would be like to be with him, to have him loving her, to feel him inside her, to be one with him.

Why was she being tormented?

She closed her eyes, and summoning every ounce of strength, she picked up his hand and placed the offending, torturing article away from her.

He chuckled. "As you will," he responded.

They did not speak again until the landau stopped near the Parish Church of St. Michael in front of which the village well had existed for six centuries and had been adorned by an annual well-dressing for nearly as many years.

"How appropriate, I think," Thorpe said as he assisted Jane in alighting from the carriage and drew her near the unusual creation of seeds, berries, flowers, and leaves. "Adam and Eve."

Jane leaned close to him and, under her breath, said, "But it is you, this time, who is tempting the woman with your apples of promise, m'lord. I wonder what punishment the Lord God will assign to you because of your seductions?"

She didn't give him a chance to respond but instead moved to stand by Lady Somercote who was gesturing for her to attend to her. The countess soon drew her apart.

"I have been thinking," she said quietly, "about something Colonel Duffield told me and I wish for your advice."

"My advice?" Jane asked, shocked.

"Hush. Not so loud." In an altered voice, she pointed to an arched trellis leading to a garden. "Jane," she cried for all to hear. "Do come with me to see the roses and what else lies in the garden beyond." Within a few minutes, they were in a secluded garden, strewn with pansies and hollyhock, roses and columbine, all spreading out in an unruly fashion in response to the summer's rich sunlight and frequent showers.

"I can't conceive of how I could possibly advise you," Jane murmured, afraid her voice might carry. "Or why you would seek my advice."

"I shall tell you. The colonel has suggested that I trick my husband, play a sort of prank on him. Since George seems to be enamored of Mrs. Newstead, Colonel Duffield thinks I ought to come to his bed, but not as myself. Well, that is, that I should approach his bedchamber as, as—"

Lady Somercote's cheeks turned a rosy color that nearly matched the fuschia-colored silk of her bonnet. She could not seem to finish Colonel Duffield's suggestion. "It is most improper!" she said at last. "Quite wicked."

Jane bit her lip. "Not as Mrs. Newstead!" she cried.

Lady Somercote tilted her head and nodded.

"Oh, dear!" Jane felt a blush creep up her cheek as she was put yet again in mind of her first night at Challeston when Thorpe had duped her, pretending to be Freddy. How curious that the colonel would have suggested something so similar to Lady Somercote. "Quite scandalous!"

"Indeed. I fear I blushed to the roots of my hair when he told me, even worse than now, and he painstakingly changed the subject—such a good man! However, later, the more I thought on it, especially since my husband was so good as to inform me that *dear Mrs. Newstead* is such *a delightfully charming creature—*"

"He cannot possibly have said as much to you," Jane cried, her heart ached for her friend.

Lady Somercote clasped her hands tightly together. "Those were the words of my husband only this morning as he watched her descend the stairs! How could he have said so to me! To me! Does he think I'm an idiot! Does he believe I do not know what he is about! And that ridiculous corset! Every time he moves, he creaks and groans. I am mortified for him, yet he doesn't seem to notice what a spectacle he's making of himself!"

"And his hair," Jane suggested, her lips twitching.

Lady Somercote met her gaze and the two ladies burst out laughing together. "Isn't it awful!"

"Horrid!"

"And he thinks Mrs. Newstead is in love with him!"

"He doesn't know her. He can't know her."

"I believe Thorpe may have warned him against her."

Jane wasn't sure she had heard correctly. "What do you mean?"

"I mean that earlier, my husband sidled up to Thorpe, just after Mrs. Newstead had left Thorpe's company, and exchanged a few words with him. The way my husband's eye followed Mrs. Newstead's form, I couldn't help but feel that he was speaking to Thorpe of his former mistress—oh, it is too appalling for words. Men can be such beasts! Anyway, afterward I could see that George was quite unsettled and even avoided speaking with Mrs. Newstead. When I asked Thorpe about it at first he said, 'Between gentlemen.' But when I suggested that he had said something of Mrs. Newstead that George did not take kindly, he responded that in effect George had, indeed, been less than pleased with his remarks concerning his former mistress. I vow I was never more gratified."

Jane was stunned. Perhaps she shouldn't have been, but she was. "You think he supported you against Mrs. Newstead?"

Lady Somercote nodded in quick succession. "I believe he did. Why do you seem so shocked?"

"Thorpe is such a rogue. I would have supposed he would have encouraged your husband rather than spoken against the lady."

Lady Somercote eyed her curiously for a long moment. "What an odd opinion you have of Lord Thorpe," she said. "He is not so bad as you think."

Jane lifted a brow. "He is far worse than you know!"

Lady Somercote opened her mouth to speak but for a moment was far too stunned to do so. "Jane!" she cried, her eyes opening wide. "What has happened? Tell me. I know that expression on your face. You've a secret!"

Jane felt a blush suffuse her cheeks. "I can't speak of it," she said and immediately brushed past her hostess. If she remained with Lady Somercote, she feared she would tell her all.

But Lady Somercote was not to be set aside so easily. She quickly caught Jane's arm and gently bid her stop. "What has he done?"

Jane debated telling Lady Somercote everything, but she couldn't. She didn't know if it was because she was humiliated by the fact that she had made love to one man while believing she was making love to another, or whether it was her discomfort in speaking of the subject anyway or whether it was because of some quirky, misguided loyalty to Thorpe. "I can't tell you," she said somberly. "It's a very private matter and would be of no use were it brought to light."

Lady Somercote could only lift her brows and wonder.

"I don't mean to offend you or put you off," Jane added hastily. "I would tell you if I thought it wise or best, but it is not." She then glanced back at the travellers and saw that many of the guests were staring at them and whispering. She urged Lady Somercote to continue the voyage through the countryside.

Lady Somercote slipped an arm about Jane's waist and Jane

returned the compliment. They passed through the rose-bedecked arch and walked slowly back to the village well. "So tell me what you think," the countess said. "Ought I to trick my husband?"

Jane smiled. "What harm could it do? He belongs to you, doesn't he?"

Lady Somercote gave her a squeeze. "Thank you. That is what I thought, but I needed to hear you say as much."

Once the ladies took up their places in their respective carriages, the gentlemen rotated and Jane found Lord Somercote beside her. Except for the uniform color of his black hair, he appeared dashing in the July morning light. He wore a coat of dark gray superfine, embroidered with a subtle black stitching on the lapels. Light gray pantaloons fit his trim legs. Hessians clothed his shapely calves and if his corset creaked with each turn of his head, Jane ignored it.

She complimented him on his coat, her remarks causing his chest to swell slightly. He was a good-hearted man—if a trifle misguided at the present—and she had always thought of him as a father-figure in her life. While they travelled west toward the small market town of Chadfield and again passed down the lane separating two fields of tall corn, she asked him his opinion of Lord Thorpe.

A slight frown of perplexity appeared between his brows. "He does not withhold his opinion, that is for sure," the earl said, his lips compressed. "And he seems to have a strident opinion on every subject."

Jane smiled. "That he does. I was about to venture the same observation. But tell me, do you admire him—as a man, as a gentleman, I mean?"

His gaze was fixed on Wolfscar Ridge which was now plainly visible since Windy Knowl had been rounded again and left behind. The Ridge, dotted with ash and oak, gleamed in the rising sunlight. To the right of the carriage, Challeston Hall was now fully under the sun's beneficence.

The frown remained as Somercote pondered her question and

finally said. "I suppose I do. He is so much younger that I think of him as I do my sons, and one does not always remember that one's children are adults and worthy of mature scrutiny and critique. Do I admire Thorpe? I'm not sure how to answer you." He glanced at Jane. "Why do you ask?"

Jane twirled her white muslin parasol and gave her head a shake. "He is in many respects an enigma to me. I have been trying to make him out ever since I first met him in April. He has been assiduous in his attentions to me."

Lord Somercote smiled crookedly. "A pursuit of which the entire *ton* is acutely aware."

"One would have to be a simpleton not to have noticed as much," she continued. "It is rare for a man to fix his attention on a lady and his conduct fail to attract remark." She watched a faint blush rise on his cheeks and she realized, though she had not meant for her words to have any other meaning, he was thinking of his own interest in Mrs. Newstead. She ignored his faint discomfiture and pressed him, "But what is your opinion? Is Thorpe truly as wicked as I believe him to be?"

Lord Somercote cleared his throat and she had the sense that he was casting off his mantle of hunter and replacing it with a cloak of fatherly responsibility. "You certainly shouldn't let him press you to do anything against your own convictions. He is a favorite among the ladies and I know for a fact he's had to fend off the assaults of more than one woman bent on possessing him—or his title, or his fortune, or whatever it is they're after of the moment. And believe me, I've known a great many such females in my day and they are not easily managed. To my knowledge, however, he's never seduced an innocent if that is what you fear. Of course, I should like to see him settled but I certainly can understand his reluctance in marrying any female."

"Neither of you seem to have a great deal of trust in the female sex."

"It is not a matter of trust," he said simply. "I don't mean to malign your sex, but more often than not a lady wishes for a man's fortune rather than the man himself. It is the way of our world, so you won't hear me make judgments on that score, but if it is possible, when it comes to marriage, a man ought to be valued for himself and not the number of groats in his pocket."

Jane sighed and turned to view Wolfscar Ridge. She found her spirits depressed by all that the earl had said to her since he had ingenuously confirmed Thorpe's opinions. And her own, if the truth be known. She didn't want to marry anyone merely for what he could give her. But she was being forced down that path by a number of circumstances that had been completely outside of her control. Her only comfort was that she knew that once she was committed to Freddy she would make a good wife.

"You were very fortunate in your choice of bride, then," she said. "Lady Somercote has so frequently told me of her devotion to you, of how violently she tumbled in love with you at Vauxhall Gardens so many years ago, that you must be immensely gratified at so much good fortune. One hears constantly of this or that marriage not being a love match and yet you got what you wanted—a lady completely, utterly in love with you."

Lord Somercote's frown deepened on his brow. "We were more blessed than most," he murmured, shifting uneasily in his seat. His corset creaked and groaned.

Jane turned toward him eagerly, forgetting his pursuit of Mrs. Newstead. "I have never asked you this before," she said quickly. "And you may tell me to go to the devil if you wish, but did you fall in love with her at Vauxhall, as well?"

He appeared startled as he turned to look at her. "Well," he drawled. Again he cleared his throat, shifted in his seat, again the corset cried out to be released from its duties.

Lord Somercote did not answer right away, but Jane could tell that he was pondering her question. In easy stages, his expression began to lighten and a soft glow entered his gray eyes.

When he spoke, his tone was reverent as he called for the past. "She wore a cherry-striped gown over wide paniers, a red brocade spencer, and Moroccan slippers. Her hair was powdered and built high as was the fashion so many years ago. My face was powdered as well and I wore a patch near my mouth. A real

Macaroni! I'm surprised when I think she actually encouraged my advances that night! What a stripling I was. But she was so pretty and lively. Yes, I tumbled hard that night." He fell into a reverie and was only brought out of it as the wheels of the landau struck the stones of the bridge while crossing the River Hart. "You've taken me back three decades," he said laughing. "And not an unpleasant journey, I might add." The landau began its ascent to Chadfield, the horses straining in harness.

After that, however, his brow grew furrowed and a heaviness settled into his jaw. More than once he pulled on his black, oily hair.

Jane felt that to have said more would have been an unkindness. She could see that her words, though innocently asked, had caused a certain amount of guilt to overtake her companion.

In Chadfield, at the Church of St. Andrew, another well was viewed, this time the local foliage, seeds, berries, and blooms, had been pressed into a slab of soft mud in which they dried, creating the image of an ark and a rainbow. Another biblical theme.

Afterward, a nuncheon was enjoyed at the Peacock Inn, an event that flowed with wine and brought everyone's laughter and good will rising to the surface. Colonel Duffield presented several riddles and anecdotes which kept everyone in stitches, especially Mr. Ullstree whose laughter rose to a sharp pitch— almost the cry of a whooping crane—at the peak of his mirth.

Once the nuncheon was concluded, and the ladies had regained their landaus for the next trip to the village of Bow Stones, west of Wolfscar Ridge, the gentlemen rotated and Jane found herself in the delightful company of the colonel. When he complimented her on her toilette and insisted that her costume was by far the most delightful, Jane shook a finger at him.

"You cannot fool me, Colonel," she said, with a teasing half-smile. "Those words have already been spoken today, I am convinced of it. At least two times, if I do not mistake the matter, and twice more again before the excursion is over."

He threw up his hands with a laugh. "You've found me out, my dear Mrs. Ambergate."

Jane chuckled. "You are a very good man," she said easily.

He cast a surprised glance at her. "Do you think so?" He queried, not displeased.

"You only wish everyone to think you are wicked but I know the truth."

"You do?"

She nodded. "A man who conducts himself with such civility and good will cannot be so very wicked as he pretends."

"Mrs. Newstead says that I am a boor and a conceited oaf."

"Mrs. Newstead knows you mean to spoil all her schemes."

A discerning light came into his dark eyes. "You seem to know as much, as well. Am I that obvious in my intentions?"

Jane considered his question. "No," she answered slowly. "In fact, I'm not sure what it is you want from these fortnight festivities, though I have been told you wish to be married."

His gaze became fixed on the landau in front of them, which was now some distance ahead as before to keep the dust of the lanes from choking the carriages behind. "The truth is, I'm not certain myself anymore. But what of you?" he asked abruptly, giving the subject a hard turn. "Mr. Waingrove is proving a reluctant suitor. Have you set your sights on a new conquest yet?"

Jane was both startled and confused, startled that he would be so forthright about her pursuit of Freddy and confused as to whom he might be referring. "You can't mean Thorpe," she said, deciding not to demure and make a protest about her hopes to make Freddy her husband.

"Why not?" he asked, a wry smile on his lips.

"Because Thorpe does not have marriage in mind," she responded as forthrightly as he.

"Ah," the colonel murmured. "Are you sure?"

Jane stared at him as though he had gone mad. Then she laughed. "You cannot be serious!" she cried. "Thorpe has all but told me that there isn't a lady worthy of his hand. He wants a female so virtuous as to be enshrined in a holy temple but at the same time, since he does not believe such a lady can exist, he treats all the females of his acquaintance as being one step away from belonging to the Cyprian Corps."

"If you hope to wed him," he said, again startling her, "then you must realize that a man with a title and a fortune cannot be treated like other men. They are so used to pursuit apart from their characters that they have lost the ability to judge accurately. To win Thorpe, all you must do is convince him of your virtue."

Jane was entirely taken aback by what Duffield was saying to her, by the fact that he would even suggest she ought to consider Thorpe as an eligible *partis,* by the fact that he would speak of such things to her, and by the fact that he couldn't know she had no virtue to speak of where he was concerned. "It is too late for that," she murmured.

"You must redefine *virtue* then," he offered helpfully.

She looked at him as though wondering if he was an Englishman. "The Church of England has already laid out the parameters on that score," she responded, lifting a brow.

"But the Church of England does not live in your shoes, now does it?"

Jane was both intrigued and unsettled so she wasn't sure, when the wheels of the carriage struck the cobbled streets of the small village of Bow Stones, whether to be grateful the journey was over or not. Colonel Duffield handed her down from the carriage and offering his arm to escort her to the well outside the Church of St. Stephen, whispered, "Do think on what I've said. I believe you and Thorpe are a match. You are certainly his equal, in every possible way except in fortune."

Since they were met by Mrs. Newstead and Mr. Ullstree at that moment, the conversation was let drop.

The well at Bow Stones was dressed with a portrait of Christ holding a child on his knee. The intricacy of the workmanship drew all of Lady Somercote's guests toward the creation. An artist must have overseen the work since the tenderness between the child and the Christ was a tangible thing. Jane felt sudden longings sweep over her. She had been without a family for a very long time.

She glanced at Thorpe, who was attending to Lady Somercote, and wondered about all that the colonel had said to her. Were they a match? Could she love such a man? Could he love her? She frowned slightly. Whenever she was with him, he easily took command of her physically, a circumstance that never failed to puzzle her. Yet, this wasn't love. She knew as much.

So, the question remained, could she love Lord Thorpe?

Could she truly *love* him?

She was struck suddenly by how Lady Somercote, Colonel Duffield, and Lord Somercote each responded to the viscount. Each had expressed nothing short of respect for him. She watched him look directly at Lady Somercote as he spoke to her. His gaze never wavered for a moment, his attention was fixed on the lady at hand.

She realized he was always this way, no matter who he was with. His attention would be fixed on the lady at his side as if she was the only person in the world in that moment. Nor was his attitude a matter of flirtation, for he was not flirting with Lady Somercote. Indeed, he was listening intently to something she was saying as though the subject between them was serious. When she noticed that Lady Somercote shot an anxious glance toward her husband several times, she suspected that her conversation with Thorpe was revolving around the hapless earl.

Was he advising her, she wondered. The thought of Thorpe advising anyone was such a novel concept that she began to see him through new eyes. Instead of the devil who was on her heels nine minutes out of ten, she saw a dignified man who cared about his friends. A strange emotion flowed through her, of sudden interest, of heightened desire. Her face grew flushed, she could feel the warmth on her cheeks.

Lady Somercote said something to Thorpe, then walked away to join Mrs. Ullstree and Henrietta. Perhaps on instinct, his gaze was drawn to her. Their eyes met. She found herself smiling shyly. He seemed a little startled and a questioning expression entered his blue eyes. He made as if to move toward her but Mrs. Ullstree called to him and his purpose was diverted.

Jane was relieved. He was a man of perception and in this moment she knew herself to be utterly vulnerable to him. She watched him attend now to Mrs. Ullstree. He bowed politely. As he began answering a series of questions she posed to him while at the same time gesturing to the Christ and Child well-dressing, never once did he look back at her, though she felt certain he wished to.

After a moment, Mr. Ullstree, his eyes sparkling, approached her. "Admiring the artistry?" he queried.

She looked at him directly, for they were of a height. Mr. Ullstree besides being unhandsome, was also a short man. "Why, yes," she murmured, turning to gaze fully at the well-dressing. She wondered if he had watched her staring at Thorpe. "I am amazed at the detail of these dressings and the emotions they can evoke. How ever do you think the artist managed to capture such an affectionate expression between child and Lord?"

He clucked his tongue at her. "You've mistaken me, madame," he said teasingly, shaking his shaggy locks. Mr. Ullstree sported a head of thick and frizzy dark brown hair so that frequently he looked like a brown bear. "I saw you admiring the other work of art." He cast a single, penetrating glance toward Thorpe.

Jane swallowed and spent the next several seconds keeping a flush of embarrassment from suffusing her face. "Oh," she murmured when her sensibilities were partially under control. "I was staring at him, wasn't I?"

"You were, but not without cause. I've even caught m'wife ogling Lord Thorpe, so you are certainly forgiven."

Mr. Ullstree had a charming way of expressing himself and Jane couldn't find it in her heart to be either offended or embarrassed any longer. "He's a very handsome man," she agreed.

"Come, let me escort you to your landau. We are about to depart and I am to be your next companion."

Jane smiled at him and allowed him to lead her to the landau. Shortly afterward, the rest of the party followed suit and before long the train of carriages was again rolling down the cobbles and onto the King's Highway.

For several miles, the party travelled north since Wolfscar Ridge jutted out of the landscape and prevented an easterly track. Mr. Ullstree carried on a comfortable conversation for the three-mile trek north, and when an adjoining highway carried the landaus east, Jane found herself posing a question that had been on the tip of her tongue for the last two miles. "Mr. Ullstree, forgive my impertinence, but would you answer a question for me about, well, about your marriage. I have observed that you and your wife are two of the happiest people among the *beau monde,* yet with less reason than many. To what do you attribute the success of your marriage? Please tell me to stubble it if I give offence."

Mr. Ullstree smiled. "I am not in the least offended and will happily tell you the truth. I married a beautiful woman and every day I pretend I'm grateful she married an ugly man."

She saw the twinkle in his eye. "Do be serious."

He nodded. "As you wish. The fact is, we don't brangle in public," he stated.

This was not the response she was looking for. She wanted knowledge and understanding, not just a practical recounting of their marital compromises. "Yes, but many do not argue while in society. Is there nothing more?"

He thought for a moment, or at least pretended to. "We don't brangle in private, at least not before nuncheon."

Jane couldn't keep a chuckle from her voice. Still, she wanted to hear his wisdom and found herself growing impatient. "Come, sir, surely you can counsel a widow better than this."

"She let's me drink my port alone."

Jane saw the playful expression on his pudgy face along with the twitch of his lips, so she frowned at him.

He sighed and she hoped he would finally take up her hint and give her the advice she sought. Instead, he said, "I let her go to Bath for a fortnight each August without complaining."

Jane gave him her severest expression, then tried a little honey. "Please?" she asked as sweetly as she could.

He scowled, but still she saw that he would not be serious. "I am always polite to her mother."

"All right, all right, I concede. You do not wish to tell me your secrets. Very well, but I take it unkindly in you."

"Madame," he responded, placing a shocked hand against his chest. "Again you've misunderstood me. These are the secrets, this is my wisdom. You believe it must be a complicated business, contentment in a marriage, but I tell you it's simple. Respect and consideration, no two people in any relationship need more than this." He paused then added, "Except for a little kissing in the yew maze now and again."

She couldn't keep from laughing outright. He had such a funny face that when he was at his charming best he took on the visage of a gnome, a delightfully friendly gnome. "I see what you are trying to tell me and I will take it to heart. I suppose you may be right."

Later, at Wirkwistle, Jane was viewing the well-dressing with Mr. Ullstree when Freddy moved to stand beside her. She was a little unsettled by the sight of the crucified Christ because there seemed to be an inordinately striking resemblance between the image of the Christ and Freddy. She blinked at her beau beside her and then back to the Christ. "What do you think?" she asked.

Freddy, who had not been viewing the well-dressing but had been looking at her with an enrapt expression, whispered, "We are to travel the last part of the journey together. We will be alone for a time. I confess I have been anticipating this moment for the past hour with every beat of my heart."

Jane, who felt certain Henrietta had overheard his professions of eagerness, cleared her throat and directed his gaze to the well-dressing.

Freddy took up her hint directly and turned to behold the portrait composed of berries, seeds, nuts, flowers, and leaves.

He stared at it for a long moment, then cried, "That's my mother!"

Several of the guests gasped.

He hurriedly explained. "I don't mean it's my mother, but the face, the eyes, the chin, it looks just like her!"

"And like you!" Henrietta chimed.

Freddy's brows rose. "Good God, you've the right of it! Well, I've never seen anything so extraordinary. I've got the goose-flesh all over my arms! I must say, I don't think I care for it, though—it's quite unsettling."

Jane was a little startled to hear Thorpe's voice in a whisper behind her. "Appropriate," he murmured. "Lamb to the slaughter." She snapped around to glare at him since she knew precisely what he meant by such a remark. But he merely lifted a brow as though daring her to prove him wrong.

"Oh, it's beautiful!" Henrietta breathed, drawing Jane's attention back to the well-dressing and to Freddy. Hetty turned to look at Freddy over her left shoulder. Her soft hazel eyes were glowing as she continued, "You should feel honored, Fr—er, Mr. Waingrove, truly."

Freddy's expression lightened. "I suppose you're right," he said, adjusting his emotions.

"Of course she is," Jane agreed, laying her hand on Freddy's shoulder. This gesture forced him to turn to look at her. The deep furrow in his brow eased up in quick stages. He glanced from Jane to Henrietta. "How fortunate I am to have two such kind ladies among my acquaintance."

Jane smiled at him and glanced toward Henrietta prepared to smile at her, as well, but for some reason Henrietta did not meet her gaze. Her glow had disappeared and she returned her attention to the well-dressing. Jane thought she looked almost sad. But why, she wondered. Perhaps she was just tired, a thought which prompted her to slide her hand down Freddy's shoulder and take his arm. "My dear, I confess I find myself fatigued after the day's exertion. Would you mind terribly escorting me to our carriage?" In truth, she was hardly tired at all and had found the excursion pleasantly exhilarating, especially after having enjoyed hearing both Colonel Duffield's and Mr. Ullstree's intriguing opinions. But she knew Freddy well and that feigning a little fatigue would spark his attentiveness.

"Of course you are, dearest one," he murmured, gazing adoringly down into her face. He blinked at her and his complexion took on a familiar blotchy appearance. He turned them both away from the well-dressing and escorted her to the waiting landau. The remainder of the guests stayed to observe the odd coincidence of Freddy's resemblance to the unhappy crucifixion image, but not for long. The afternoon was on the wane and besides dressing for dinner, then enjoying another of Lady Somercote's fine feasts for the evening meal, the partners would be expected to practice their vignettes again.

On the drive back to Challeston Hall, with the sun at her back, Jane slipped her hand in Freddy's and had the comfort and encouragement of having him receive it without protest. A mile before reaching the lane to Challeston, another lane, leading to the northeast, appeared.

"Where does that lead?" Jane queried.

"Oh," Freddy remarked with a smile. "That is the road to Oxslip, a little hamlet beyond Windy Knowl. I believe the warm springs are to be found there—Oak Grove Spring, aptly named because it is situated near a grove of oaks."

"Does the spring remain the same temperature all year?"

"Precisely so." Freddy's gaze was fixed down the lane. "Just beyond that rise—there, you can see the tips of the trees, so at variance from the pines coming off Windy Knowl. Such beautiful country hereabouts. I should like to write a poem . . ." She heard the tenor of his voice change and she knew that very soon he would engage in one of his poetic fits.

"Perhaps we ought to go to the spring tomorrow, just you and I," she posed hopefully.

He looked back at her, his brows lifted in surprise, his expression pleased. "I could take my lap desk—"

"I could request a nuncheon packed up in a wicker basket—"

"It would be lovely!" he cried. "Ever since we arrived here I have wanted to spend some time alone with you. But somehow it seems the opportunity has continued to elude me."

"We must make every effort to correct that," she said, pressing his hand and smiling sweetly at him. Purposefully she found herself affecting the expression Henrietta wore when she looked at Freddy.

She watched her swain take a deep, halting breath. "Oh, Jane," he murmured, struggling for air. "I—I am so in love with you. There, I've said it! Oh, I know I've said it before but each time I speak the words, they come forth anew, reborn, a—a, oh, just look how I search for the right expression. You've done that to me. You've addled my brain, dear, dear Jane." He chuckled. "That rhymes, you know." Jane felt slightly ill, especially when his gaze clouded and his lips moved over the words again, *You've addled my brain, dear, dear Jane,* as though they needed to be memorized.

Jane took a deep breath and in spite of a sudden wish to do just the opposite, she scooted closer to him, knowing that she was for once actually making progress. "Have I addled you?" she asked, drawing his attention back to her.

"You know you have," he responded hoarsely. She watched his chest rise and fall quickly as he struggled for breath. "My darling, Jane, how I do love you. I have from the first, so very much. And, and I have wanted to ask you something these many weeks and more." He paused and moaned softly. "Would you . . . that is, do you think . . ."

He broke off suddenly and pressed a hand to his temple.

Say the words, her mind commanded him. *Oh, Freddy, please just open your mouth and speak!*

"What is it?" she asked, gently touching his temple. Her heart was beating rapidly. He was so close to offering for her. "What did you want to say? What were you saying?"

"Forgive me," he said, wincing. "I can't, that is, I'm sorry. I fear I've a little of the headache again."

"Perhaps you've had too much sunshine," she offered, her

heart sinking as the carriage rolled by the juncture to Oak Cloud Spring.

"Yes, that must be it. Too much sun."

Jane patted his hand but she felt a strong irritation begin to rise within her. Why did Freddy have to have so many headaches and why did they frequently arise the moment he was preparing to become a man and seize his future in his hands?

She then felt tremendous guilt at her uncharitable thoughts. Freddy did not have her constitution, but should she blame him for that? Of course not! How ungenerous that would be. Besides, she had many more days left in which to bring him to heel, and tomorrow he would take her to Oak Cloud Spring, a place of seclusion in which he might put pen to paper and she might ply him with enough food and wine to extract a proposal of marriage from him.

After dinner that evening, Jane stood with her hands on her hips in the sword room, near the round inlaid table, and glared at Lord Thorpe. "So you think it proper that we perform a vignette that reflects our every thought on this subject?" she asked, still angry. He had concluded that their vignette would succeed above all the rest were they to speak their minds honestly, each of them, about why they were distressed with the other's opinions.

"Why not?" he asked. "What are you afraid of? That the rest will judge you? You've already been judged, as have I, a dozen times over—by the way we style our hair, or don our clothes, or give voice to an inappropriate remark at precisely the wrong moment. Why not present our arguments to the other guests?"

Jane wasn't certain but she suspected that she was afraid Freddy would disapprove.

"I wouldn't concern yourself about Mr. Waingrove," he said, reading her mind.

"What?" she shot back. How could he have known her thoughts?

"You are as easily read to me as any of the books in Somercote's library. I know your mind, I understand how you think." He smiled crookedly. "For frequently, we think very much alike. Were I in your shoes I would be fearing that such an exposure of sentiment might set him against me. But I don't believe you are such a coward as that."

"You can be so very provoking," she responded. But she wasn't angry. She knew he was right. "Very well," she acquiesced. "I suppose in the end if I will know any happiness with Mr. Waingrove, he will need to know my thoughts and opinions anyway."

"Just so," Thorpe commented. His blue eyes ware sparkling, he was reveling in his victory. She took up an Empire chair beside the table and Thorpe joined her by drawing forward a second one from near the doorway. For the next hour, they ruined sheet after sheet in trying to put their little drama on paper. Thorpe requested a bottle of Madeira and two glasses. Jane accepted one from him, but would allow herself no more, nor did Thorpe imbibe more than a second one himself, she noted approvingly.

The wine allowed Jane to sit back in her chair, to let her mind wander as she took small sips. Her gaze moved from mace to broadsword, to fencing sword, to armory, to bows, to arrows. "What if we performed the vignette with swords," she suggested suddenly. "And used the blades and the points as a metaphor."

Thorpe smiled, leaning back in his chair and eying her wonderingly. "What a beautiful idea," he said. He set his glass, halffull, on the table, moved to the wall opposite the windows, and removed two fencing swords. "Come," he called to her, offering her one of the swords. She accepted it and took up her position opposite him, her left arm held aloft and arched over her head.

He narrowed his blue eyes. "Who taught you?" he asked.

"My father, a little. I begged him until he nearly ran me through first before agreeing to my pleas."

"I should have known you were a stubborn child," he said, laughing as he assumed his position.

After a moment, steel met steel in a lovely rasping and scraping sound that caused Jane's heart to jump with excitement. She had not fenced in a long time, although she realized almost immediately that her gown of purple silk was an encumbrance to the quick movements of her feet. Still she kept up with Thorpe even as he increased the pace until they were both laughing and his eyes were bright with excitement. The contest thrilled her. Of course in this case there was no question that he was better at the whole of it than she, but it didn't matter. She was good enough to keep up with him and strong enough to keep her sword in her hand though four times he tried to disarm her.

She leaped and eventually took to holding her skirts in one hand so that she could better move about the panelled wood floor. Once she pinked his arm and he gasped. She laughed at him, jumped away, and kept her sword aloft. Again metal clinked, rasped, and scraped.

Her skirts, however, finally got caught in her footwork and she stumbled backward, her blade flew out of her hand, sliding across the floor, and Thorpe stood over her holding his sword to the well of her neck. She was breathing hard and laughing.

"You're mine," he said. "I've beaten you in battle and I'm taking you as my reward."

She took the blade in her gloved hand and shoved it away. "Never," she said, laughing, still lying prone on the floor. He dropped to his knees beside her. The next moment his mouth covered hers in a hard, demanding salute as he stretched out partially on top of her.

Jane tried to protest but he had the advantage of her physically. He kept her arms pinned with his hands. His hips and chest kept her from moving away from him. Besides, before very long his kiss became warm and sensual and she lost all interest in fending him off.

The wine and the exercise were warm in her veins. Her heart was still beating strongly from the excitement of the swordplay and she found very soon that her arms were wrapped tightly about his neck. He thrilled her, everything about him seemed to resonate with her own desires, desires she kept hidden even from herself. She felt his hand on her breast, teasing her, inviting her, coaxing her. She didn't tell him to stop. Her breath came in short gasps. The moment was too exhilarating, too unexpected. She knew what would happen next, especially when she felt his hand drawing up the hem of her skirts.

"No," she murmured, but he kissed her hotly and for a long moment as he stroked her legs she again lost all desire to push him away.

"Become my mistress, Jane," he whispered, so deeply into her ear that she gasped with the pleasure of it. His fingertips moved lightly, seductively over her legs until she could hardly breathe. "I'll give you everything you need, everything. You know I will."

She wanted to say yes. Every part of her body was begging her to acquiesce. Almost the words formed on her lips, especially when he traced the curves of her ear with his tongue.

"Become my mistress and you will know more of this." He drove his tongue into her ear and her abdomen drew up into a coil of pleasure. His hand began roaming her inner thighs. A few moments more . . .

"No," she protested at last. "I can't do it."

The passion that had taken such strong hold of her began to ebb quickly away. She couldn't become his mistress. She would not permit herself to fall into the misery of that trap.

When he tried to kiss her again, she turned her face away. "No," she murmured.

His entire body grew still and for a long, tense moment, he remained where he was. Then in slow stages he let her skirt back down to her ankle and began to slide off of her. When he had gained his feet, he reached down and assisted her to rise as well.

When she was facing him, he looked at her wonderingly. "So you mean to have him, then, even when you so eagerly fall into my arms."

"I am ambivalent, but only because you're here and because, well, because I enjoy your company as much as I do." He seemed surprised by her remark. "But I will marry Freddy, if he wishes for it. We will remove to his home and I shall never see you again. The matter is simple in essentials, afterall."

He cast his gaze toward the floor, but took up her hand in his. He fondled her fingers and finally smiled at her. "I still intend to take you to Fairfield Hall once we are finished here." Fairfield was his home in Kent.

She shook her head. "Will you never give up?"

"Only if you actually walk down the aisle. I suppose then I will have to leave off my pursuit of you. But not until then, Jane. I swear it."

"I am duly warned," she answered with another smile.

He suddenly grabbed her up in his arms. "You're too pretty for words and when you smile like that, it's all hallow with me." He was kissing her before she could again protest, not that it mattered, for she wouldn't have repulsed him. She knew that once she, too, walked down the aisle, she would never allow another man to kiss her. Once her vows were spoken, they were utterly and completely sacred. So, he kissed her until it pained him to continue. Then he walked away, returning both swords to the wall and resuming his seat. He filled his glass to the brim and in one quick gulp finished the whole of it. Afterward, he took up a pen and began scratching.

"Will you refuse me again," he spoke aloud as he wrote.

He looked up at her, waiting for a response.

"Yes," she called to him. He quickly scratched the word on the paper. She continued slowly, *"But not for the reason you think. I cannot accept your terms. No matter how tempting. I must choose for the children I hope to one day bear."*

He sighed deeply as he traced her words in dark ink.

Six

On the following morning, Jane requested from the house-keeper a tidy basket of victuals to take on her trip with Freddy to Oak Cloud Spring. She had her maid dress her hair with great care, arranging it in long dark brown ringlets at the back of her head and in a knot at the crown in order to support a charming half-bonnet of apricot muslin over white silk. The bonnet sat forward on her head and over the shallow brim a narrow fringe of white point-lace framed her face to perfection. Her Empire gown was of apricot muslin over a soft white cambric. The muslin was trimmed to a scalloped three-quarter length in order to expose the pretty white fabric beneath. She wore pearl ear-drops and a necklet of pearls. On her feet, she sported slippers of apricot silk, on her hands, a pair of silk gloves, and over her bonnet she held a silk parasol to match the slippers and gown.

She met Freddy at the bottom of the stairs, feeling assured and happy not only about their forthcoming picnic but also by the manner in which she had left Thorpe on the night before. She had found that in the end she wanted to be safe from the possible consequences of becoming his mistress more than she longed for the fulfillment of his embraces. For that reason, she was able to greet Freddy with a warm smile and a dainty twirl of her parasol as she reached the entrance hall floor.

"How handsome you are today, Mr. Waingrove," she said brightly.

He blinked at her, bowing over her hand. He kissed her fingers lightly, pressed her hand, then quickly let go of her. "Jane, you're the most beautiful lady I know," he responded, sounding breathlessly overcome. "So charming—your hair, so delightfully arranged. I fear, however—that is, I'm very sorry, but I can't go with you today—it, it wouldn't be seemly."

Jane looked up at him and frowned slightly. "What do you mean, you can't go, that it wouldn't be seemly?" She heard footsteps coming from the direction of the drawing room. "Wait, don't speak just yet," she murmured. She quickly took hold of his arm and guided him the opposite way. They walked down the long gallery off the entrance hall and passed into the grand music room.

The round, high-ceilinged chamber was of a delicate yellow-gold and a deep royal blue, a combination repeated in the patterns of the domed ceiling, in the blue velvet and gold-fringed drapes flanking several tall windows, and in the geometric designs of the large, round carpet. A gilt harp, a harpsichord, and a pianoforte of a highly polished rosewood formed a trio in the center of the carpet about which were placed cozy gatherings of black lacquer Empire chairs covered in a blue fabric matching the drapes. An adjoining antechamber connected the music room to the south wing of the mansion.

The chamber was stately, far too stately Jane thought for trying to bring her *beau* to heel, but there was little she could do about that. "Why have you decided that you can't go with me?" she asked calmly.

He ran a hasty hand through his blonde hair. "You and I are become very good friends, indeed, more than friends. For that reason, my affection for you rises up within me on occasion frequently to the point that I find my sensibilities tend to overtake me. I fear—that is—I don't want to harm you or to disrupt the beauty of what I believe to be our budding love for one another." He turned to face her, "We would be alone together for an hour, perhaps two," he continued, almost panic-stricken. "Sometimes when I am with you I find that my heart races with, with my mounting desire to know you better, to, to kiss you, to do that which is not seemly. Jane, I won't have it. I simply don't trust myself to, to be alone with you today."

Jane lowered the parasol from her shoulder and closed it with a soft snap. She took a quiet step toward him and in an even, gentle voice asked, "Are you saying that you sometimes feel overcome with a wish to kiss me?"

He nodded and she watched him swallow visibly.

She smiled, tenderly and sweetly. She could see that he was ready to bolt. He was six feet away from her. She took another step toward him. "But I see nothing wrong with stealing a kiss or two—especially." And here she lowered her lashes, striving for a modesty and a reticence she in no way felt. "Especially since we are so fond of one another."

"Jane," he breathed. She knew that he had taken two steps toward her.

Excellent.

"Freddy," she murmured, lifting her face to him so that she was able to view him just below the point-lace fringe of her bonnet.

He stood with his lips parted for a long, breathless moment. She knew what was happening. He was poised on the cliff again. He wanted her. She saw it in his eyes, in his hands which were drawn up into tight knots of desire, in the way his entire body strained toward her. "Jane," he breathed again. "My dearest Jane."

She lifted the brim just a little more and, letting her parasol fall to the floor, she extended her arms to him. "Freddy," she called to him.

He almost let himself fall off the cliff. He took a half-step, he leaned a little more as though pushing against the wind, he opened his arms, as well. Then with a strangled cry, he turned away from her, racing for the open door.

Jane was dumbfounded as the door slammed shut between herself and her beloved. She couldn't believe Freddy had actually ran from her. What was wrong with him?

"Henhearted gudgeon!" a masculine voice called scornfully from behind her.

Jane whirled around, facing the antechamber that joined the music room to the south wing of the house. "Thorpe!" she cried, panic seizing her first, then outrage. "How long have you been there! Oh, how could you? Did you hear and see all?"

"You didn't check to see if you were at liberty to conduct a flirtation in secrecy, now did you? Perhaps I ought to give you a lesson or two."

"Odious man!" she retorted.

"Don't be so hard on Frederick—"

"I was referring to you," she snapped.

He donned a hurt expression she knew to be wholly theatrical in design. "Odious? You've cut me to the quick. I'll never heal from such a terrible wound."

"I should have run you through with a sword last night when I had the chance."

At that he smiled and began walking lazily toward her. "Yes, you should have," he agreed. He wore riding gear, a blue coat fitting his broad shoulders to perfection, a neckcloth tied in immaculate folds, and buckskin breeches that clung to his strong athletic legs. His well-made top-boots were dusty from the dry summer lanes. "As for my odious conduct in eavesdropping, the fact is I've been out riding and when I'm done I always pass through the music room after leaving the stables." He gestured toward the south-easterly windows.

Jane glanced out the window and saw that the stables were indeed visible from the chamber. She also saw that her low phaeton was making its way to the front of the mansion. She was deeply disappointed and in her disappointment she did not want to stand about and argue with Thorpe. "I must go," she said with a long-suffering sigh. "My carriage is being brought round even as we speak."

"Where are you going?" he asked. "Maybe I should accompany you."

"I intend to tool about the countryside a bit. I've not handled the ribbons for over a sennight and I'm missing it."

He let his gaze rake her gown, her pearl ear-drops, and the parasol lying on the floor. "So Waingrove refused to go with you because he doesn't trust himself, eh? What a fool."

Jane rolled her eyes. She was out of patience with Freddy and she did not possess the composure necessary to properly set aside all of Thorpe's nasty remarks. "He could not attend to me because of sentiments so fine you could hardly appreciate a one of them. So, if that is being foolish, then Mr. Waingrove can be as foolish as he wishes. You might learn something from him."

He narrowed his eyes. "What fustian. I know this much. If I'd promised to take a lady out on a drive, I'd not recant at the last minute regardless of the delicacy of my feelings."

Jane wouldn't listen to another word, especially since generally he made sense when he argued with her about anything. "Good-day, m'lord. I'm sure I won't see you until later this evening when we will again attack our vignette."

She turned and walked toward the door but he quickly caught up with her. "One moment, Jane," he said, his lips twitching. "Are you sure you wouldn't like me to go with you, just to keep you company today? You seem awfully blue-deviled."

She again rolled her eyes. "You'd only end up trying to kiss me again, and given the state of my nerves of the moment, I'd probably plant you a facer for your effort. So, I would advise you to take your flirtations and yourself off. Let me alone today, that I might work my own way out of the sullens."

He smiled and bowed to her, letting her pass.

She was grateful he did. At least he had come to comprehend her sentiments correctly—she was in no way prepared to be congenial, and especially not with him, since Freddy's inability to restrain his emotions had cost her an entire afternoon's effort.

No, what she wanted of the moment was to handle the ribbons, to drive along the quiet country lanes with the wind blow-

ing in her face as the wheels of her phaeton rolled as quickly
along as the horses would take them.

Thorpe watched her walk quickly but with great dignity down
the long hallway leading to the entrance hall. He certainly admired her spirit. She was obviously disappointed that her *beau*
had failed her so miserably and there was even a part of him
that knew an impulse to hunt Freddy Waingrove down and call
him to book for his incivility toward a lady. Forget his sensibilities! Damne, where were his manners?

At the same time, he realized nothing could be more foolish
since, as he watched the pretty blue phaeton make its way slowly
past window after window of the elegant music room, an opportunity of unequalled possibilities was currently presenting
itself right beneath his nose. If he was careful, he could make
more progress this afternoon in his own schemes than he could
in a dozen wranglings in the sword room while creating and
practicing the vignette with the delectable Mrs. Ambergate.

Instead of following in Jane's wake, therefore, he turned on
his heel and retraced his steps. Time to try out another of Lord
Somercote's fine geldings. The earl had an excellent stable, and
Thorpe hoped to put a number of his hacks through their paces
before the fortnight was spent.

After returning her parasol to her bedchamber and retrieving
her leather driving gloves, Jane mounted Lady Somercote's
phaeton. A footman strapped a large wicker hamper of food,
dinner service, and champagne to the boot of the carriage and
afterward informed her the basket was secured. When the postillion turned the reins over to her and she bid him return to the
stables instead of hopping up behind, she ignored the surprised
lift of his eyebrows and with a smart slap of the reins, set the
beautiful pair of chestnuts in motion. If Freddy would desert
her, then she would enjoy her picnic by herself.

Blast the man!

As the horses and carriage picked up speed, Jane felt some of her irritability and sullenness begin to vanish. She loved driving and knew that after a half-hour or more her nerves would be calmer and she could then set her mind to figuring out what next she ought to do with her reluctant swain. Poor Freddy. Poor hopeless, useless Freddy.

Lady Somercote's phaeton turned out to be a delightfully sprung vehicle. The color of the body was a delicate robin's egg-blue, accented on the doors in a beautiful ivory scroll-work—a lady's carriage, to be sure. The chestnuts were elegant steppers and before long, she found herself easing the horses and the phaeton onto the lane heading south east toward Oak Cloud Spring. She let them stretch their legs for a time, but once a mile mark had been passed, she lifted the reins, gave a hard slap on their flanks, and at the same time let go of a firm shout.

The geldings did not mistake her command, they immediately lengthened their strides and within seconds the phaeton was bowling down the winding lane at a spanking pace. The lane followed Glapwich Stream and was relatively free of small holes and more dangerous pits. Only occasionally did the wheels of the phaeton bounce through a rut. Other than that, the drive was exactly what she needed since she could give her horses their head.

When she reached the turn-off to the warm springs, she drew the horses to a complete stop, wondering if she ought to continue the delightful excursion, or enjoy a nuncheon by herself at the spring.

With a smile, she chose the latter.

Oak Cloud Spring was situated near Glapwich Stream and a grove of ancient pollarded oak trees. The spring itself was nestled in a thick copse of grasses, wild roses, privet, elder, and ash.

When Jane brought her horses to a standstill near the banks of the spring, a breeze whipped through the tops of the ash trees, making a sound that sent a shiver of delight spinning through her. The sky was a cloudless, deep blue above the tops of the trees. The smell of roses floated up and around the horses and phaeton.

She watched her horses stamp their hooves and she knew she needed to tend to them. She untied her bonnet and settled it on the seat next to her. The frilly apricot silk and lace confection would only be in the way as she wrestled with the harness.

Once she had the horses hobbled and the heavy harness removed, she whisked bunches of grass from the thick carpet all around her and began rubbing each of them down. While she was thus employed, a deep, masculine voice intruded.

"Well met, Mrs. Ambergate! But what a surprise to find you here!" Jane whirled around, stunned by the sound of Thorpe's voice. She hadn't even heard him approach. He was some twenty feet away, astride one of Somercote's beautiful black coverhacks, smiling down at her with a familiar, crooked smile twisting his lips.

So he had followed her!

The rogue!

The beast!

She sighed and threw up her hands. "I suppose it will be of no use to tell you to go away."

He shook his head. "No use at all." He leaned forward slightly and easily slid his leg off the saddle and jumped lightly to the ground.

He shouldn't be so athletically graceful, she thought distractedly. "I've come to see the spring," she explained. "And to, to enjoy a quiet nuncheon."

"A perfectly delightful outing," he responded, a warm, provocative smile on his lips. A wave of gooseflesh travelled down her neck, arm, and side. She knew what he was thinking, his thoughts could not be clearer were he to stand atop the closest tor and shout them into the surrounding countryside.

He picked up the reins of his horse, drew the gelding forward, and tied him to a nearby shrub. He, too, picked up a few handfuls of grass and rubbed away the sheen of sweat from his glossy black coat.

She watched this considerate ministration and knew she should leave. She should put her pretty chestnuts back in harness, tie her bonnet atop her curls, and drive pell-mell back to Challeston Hall before Thorpe so much as spoke another word to her. Instead, once he had finished with his horse, she gestured toward the large wicker basket with a sweep of her hand and said, "Well, if you must torment me, at least bring along the food. I haven't eaten since breakfast and I'm starved. Presumably you are the same." She lifted her chin and began removing her gloves in quick jerks.

He drew near her and caught up her chin in his hand. "Anything for you, my beautiful Jane?" As she met his gaze, the blue of his eyes seemed to cut straight through her soul, a strange vibration running the length of her at the mere touch of his fingers. She drew in a deep breath, wishing she did not respond to him so readily. Her instinct was to run, but her feet refused to budge. Instead, she smiled up at him, a faint expression that caused his gaze to descend to her lips. How serious he appeared suddenly, serious and intent. He leaned toward her and placed a gentle kiss on her lips—a warm, sensual touch that caused her abdomen to tighten ominously. When he drew back from her and released her chin, she saw that his eyes were heavy with desire. She had no doubt then of what the afternoon would hold.

"You should get the food now," she reminded him breathlessly.

He nodded slowly and equally as slowly moved toward the low phaeton to retrieve the basket.

Seven

When Jane passed through the narrow aperture of roses and privet leading into Oak Cloud Spring, she felt as though she was passing through a mist. Behind her lay the world she grappled with every day in all of its coarse demands, truths, and compromises.

But here, with vapors rising off the deep blue waters of a pool emanating from a spring that remained even in temperature all year round, she thought that perhaps just this once she might be Guinevere entering Camelot. Just once. Just once she would forget what was real and painfully true, and she would give herself over to the complete fantasy of the moment that life could be perfect, simple, and wonderful.

Thorpe led the way, settling the basket near the spring. When she moved to assist him in preparing the nuncheon, he refused to allow her to lift a finger. Instead, he removed a plaid woollen blanket from the basket, spread it out carefully on the grass, then in quick stages scattered dishes, cutlery, and Cook's delicacies on the blanket. He bid her take up a seat opposite him, opened a bottle of champagne, and poured her a glass. He toasted her with a smile, "To my beautiful Jane."

She sipped the champagne, delighting in the bubbles that tickled her nose, and let her cares drift from her with each ensuing sip.

When a meal of cold pheasant, artichoke hearts, and thick

chunks of buttered bread had been enjoyed along with the champagne, Jane turned to eye the steaming water with some longing.

The spring formed the pool from a hot, bubbling river that rose from deep within the earth. Since Oak Cloud Spring was at a slightly higher elevation than Glapwich Stream, the warm waters tumbled at the far end of the pool down a series of stepstone waterfalls joining the stream some thirty yards away. Surrounding the stream was verdant growth, thick grasses, yellow, pink, and burgundy roses, even a spray of brambleberries had found its way into the hedge surrounding the spring.

The fruit, in varying stages of ripeness, beckoned Jane from Thorpe's side.

"Brambleberries," she cried, rising from the blanket. "And heavy on the vine. What a perfect dessert, for they appear to be ready for the picking."

"They do, indeed," Thorpe commented, his voice deeply resonant.

Jane paused in her steps for a flickering moment. She understood precisely what he meant. She knew her former instinct to run. Instead, she took a deep breath and moved to the vine where she began to pluck the dark violet fruit from its prickly stems. She slipped one then two then three into her mouth. The sweet but tart flavor caused her to close her eyes and lick her lips more than once as she savored summer's bounty.

Thorpe joined her. When she opened her eyes he was smiling down at her. "I will have to thank Freddy for this day," he murmured and before she could protest, he took her in his arms and kissed her fully on her lips.

She gasped, parting her lips slightly. His tongue touched hers, the flavor of the ripe fruit flowing within her mouth as he gently searched her. She leaned into him, the mist of Camelot surrounding her fully. Gone were all thoughts of Freddy and of her future. She felt only the length of Thorpe's body as he pressed himself more tightly against her, his tongue rimming the inside of her lips.

His hands glided over her back, shaping her buttocks, then

returned to squeeze her waist. Desire flowed through her veins. She slipped her arms about his neck and held him close to her, parting her lips even further, permitting Thorpe to invade her more completely still. She heard him groan and the sound of his deep, masculine voice brought her stomach into a tight coil of longing.

He drew back from her slightly to kiss her cheeks and her ear. "Swim with me," he murmured. "Be one with me in the water."

Jane felt weak and helpless as he turned her in his arms and began unbottoning her gown. She did not protest, nor did she even want to.

Within a few minutes, he was leading her to the water's edge, his own clothes shed, and assisting her to enter the steaming pond. Once submerged to her neck, she easily slid into his arms. He groaned as he held her against him, his hands playing magically over her breasts, her waist, her back, her buttocks. A minute more and he parted her thighs, entering her.

The mist began to fill Jane's mind more fully. She felt lost in a wonderland of sensation and rising desire. The ancient rhythms that had always belonged to man, drove her ever upward until she was clinging to his back, his shoulders, his neck, and begging for release. He kissed her neck, teasing her. He kissed her lips, taunting her. He drove his tongue into her mouth and the mist spiraled ever upward until stars exploded in her head.

He followed quickly after, holding her roughly, plunging into her wildly, until his passion was spent.

She clung to him and tears began to flow down her cheeks, but she wasn't certain why. The joining had been intensely wondrous and passionate. But it was over.

Life moved in forward stages as unstoppable as the roll of the waves along the seashores. Already Jane could see that the mist had begun to evaporate even though she hadn't spoken. The sunshine glinted on the water, she eased an arm from about his neck and let her hand gently glide across the surface of the pond. The ripples caused the sunlight to break up into a thousand pieces, gleaming golden beams that shattered the mist.

In a quiet voice, she said, "This changes nothing, Thorpe, you must know that."

He didn't answer her for a long moment. "You mean you intend to continue your pursuit of Waingrove?" he asked, his voice stunningly calm.

"Yes," she replied, drifting away from him.

She floated on her back and from the corner of her eye saw him rise from the pond. He dressed himself slowly, gathered up the leftover food, plates, and cutlery, packed the basket carefully, and carted it toward the carriage.

Jane quit the steaming spring only when she heard the hoof-beats of his horse gallop madly away.

Later that night, in the sword room, Jane stood with her arms folded across her chest, glaring down at Lord Thorpe. He was seated seven feet away from her, in a black-lacquered Empire chair, a leg settled casually at the ankle on his opposite leg. He was still very angry with her and because of it, she was angry, too.

"Why don't we start at the beginning," she suggested, letting one of her arms leave its protective place against her chest for a brief moment as she gestured to the pages in a neat pile on the round table. Thorpe's chair was near the table and he lifted a hand to tap the spiked ball as he continued to return her glare.

He narrowed his eyes, pursed his lips, and grabbed the stack of papers. *"Three acts and a farce,"* he read, grinding his teeth. "Well, we've had at least one act, now, haven't we, or was it the farce?"

"Quit being so theatrical, Thorpe," she snapped. "We made love—and shouldn't have—that's all. Nothing's changed."

His nostrils flared as he glanced down at the vignette. He breathed deeply, again grinding his teeth. Once more, he tapped the spiked ball with his fingers. "Everything's changed," he growled. "Everything. Why can't you see that?"

"What do you intend to tell me now?" she asked, tapping her fingers against her arm in counterpoint to his own restless fingers. "Do you intend to tell me that before Oak Cloud Spring you didn't love me and now you do? Do you intend to tell me that before you had your way with me, I was free to choose what was best for my life but now I'm not? Do you intend to tell me that since we made love, you own me and I must become your mistress because that is what *you* want?"

He threw the papers on the floor. A childish gesture, perhaps, but he was clearly enraged. "What I want is for you not to play the hypocrite in this situation? What you are doing is wrong—"

"And what you are doing, I suppose, is perfectly within the bounds of proper moral conduct on all counts?"

"More than you."

"Spoken like a man with so much wealth he can't possibly comprehend the difficulties of anyone else."

"I just can't believe that you intend to go through with it."

"I do. I made a mistake today, that's all."

He leaned forward, letting his ankle slide off his knee so that both feet were planted on the floor in front of him. He stared at the vignette scattered about on the floor.

Thorpe didn't know why he was mad as fire, but he was. He was as angry with himself, though, as he was with her. Why had he assumed that once he took her again, she would comply with his desire to make her his mistress? Good God, if nothing more, his assumption could be viewed as the worst sort of male arrogance. He stood up, then bent over to pick up the pages. He felt very confused.

The whole day had been a long string of tantalizing hopes for him, only to end in crushing disappointment, a disappointment so severe that he had begun to question just why he felt as though she had poured coals over his heart when she had told him, yet again, even after an exquisite experience at Oak Cloud Spring, that she was still intent on pursuing Waingrove.

He knew of course that Mrs. Newstead was waiting in the wings for the final outcome and perhaps there was part of him that had been hoping he could tell her all was settled between himself and Mrs. Ambergate, but that formed only the smallest part of his sentiments, a negligible part, really. What had somehow come to chafe him was the fact that Jane was proving to be such a stubborn, calculating hypocrite. How could she even think of pursuing Freddy now, now when she had deliberately forfeited her virtue to another man?

But that wasn't the only thing that was bothering him. Earlier, after supper, before the vignetters had broken up to compose and practice their scenes, Jane had persuaded Freddy to take a walk in the lantern-lit formal gardens with her. He had been so consumed with jealousy at that point that he had stolen to the sword room, which overlooked the garden, and had secretly observed their *tête-à-tête*.

Freddy had stumbled and bumbled his way along, but then, just before they had returned to the house, he had taken Jane into his arms and kissed her, a very long, passionate kiss. When he released her, the expression on her face had stunned him, for not only had she seemed surprised but infinitely pleased. Only then had he truly come to understand that she had no intention of giving up Freddy Waingrove—Oak Cloud Spring or not. And Frederick Waingrove, it would seem, had finally come to his senses about the beauty who had chosen him to settle her future.

A match made in hell, if ever one was.

He was in a temper. He knew as much. He knew he was of no use to Jane tonight, at least with regard to their vignette. Therefore, when he had retrieved all the papers, he handed them to her and bid her good-night. It would seem this time, he had the headache and would she please make his excuses to their hostess, he intended to seek his bed.

Jane watched him go, feeling numb. What a fool she had been today. How could she have let her lusts and her desires for Thorpe not only complicate her relationship with him but also threaten her schemes where Freddy was concerned. What a ninnyhammer she had been today. The strangest part of all was that she felt as though she had betrayed not Freddy, but Thorpe. How absurd to think that she had any loyalty to him whatsoever given the nature of his intentions toward her! Absurd and ridiculous.

But as the door closed behind the man with whom she had made the most pleasurable love she had ever known, she knew a despair greater than anything before. But what else could she have done when he had been teasing her for so many days, when he had already stolen her virtue the night he took the key from beneath Freddy's pillow, and when he had followed her to the spring? She tried to picture Freddy loving her as Thorpe did, but she could only chuckle. Freddy was like a puppy, while Thorpe was like, well, he was like a thoroughbred stallion.

She moved to the black Empire chair and sat down still holding the vignette in her hands. In the three days they had been composing and working out the swordsplay of their vignette, they had made little progress. In only a week they would be called upon to entertain the other guests with a well-constructed scene reflecting thoughts on love and marriage.

Oh, blast, she thought, tears rushing to her eyes. Why was this happening to her? Why had Thorpe come along, all masculine, physical, and demanding to so completely cut up her peace and to so neatly thrust a spoke into the wheel of her perfectly arranged schemes. She settled her hand on her forehead and let several tears fall to the top paper. Her tears smudged the words, *Three Acts,* much she cared.

Almost, when she had seen Thorpe for the first time after their lovemaking at the spring, she had known an impulse to cast in her lot with him. She had been descending the stairs, holding the skirts of her elegant robin's egg-blue silk gown in hand, and he had been waiting at the bottom of the stairs, ostensibly she thought, to see her. She had met his gaze, she had looked deeply into his blue eyes and for a long, long moment felt as though she was falling into the sky. He never smiled, he just looked at her with an expression of wonder on his face, at least she had thought it was something like wonder.

But Freddy had appeared shortly after, exuberant in his praise of her light blue gown and the single white ostrich feather in her hair. She had taken Freddy's arm. She had left Thorpe standing alone at the foot of the stairs.

When Freddy had actually taken her into the gardens after dinner and apologized for not having attended her to Oak Cloud Spring, saying that he had behaved both foolishly and without consideration for her feelings, she had been amazed. But when he had actually taken her in his arms and kissed her, Thorpe was all but forgotten. She decided her fate then and there. Freddy would be her husband and the father of her children. Whatever fantasies she had been holding in her mind about Thorpe were immediately cast aside.

But now, after having seen the torture in Thorpe's mind, her doubts began pummeling her sensibilities once again. Who was he really? What was his significance in her life? Was he truly a creature of worth as Colonel Duffield and Lady Somercote believed him to be?

Confusion reigned. Her practical decision to pursue Freddy was at war with what she could now see was not only a passion for Lord Thorpe but also a mounting affection for him, as well.

As she glanced at the pages of the vignette, she couldn't help but wonder precisely what *Act Two* would bring.

Saturday night, the ballroom thrummed with gently stomping feet. Chairs, upholstered in royal-blue velvet sat back to back twelve in a row on each side. The orchestra was playing Mozart's *Allegro* in G Major and twenty-five guests were parading about the chairs in a quick circle, waiting breathlessly for the music to stop. When the conductor would raise his baton abruptly and the notes would cease, one guest would be left without a chair, thus eliminated from the game.

Overhead, three chandeliers, blazing with lit candles, presided over the magical game and what was proving to be a lively masquerade ball. Dressed as Cleopatra, her mask still tied tightly about her head but beneath her straight, black wig, Jane watched, waited, and listened. Forgotten were all her troubles—her need to be betrothed to Freddy before the fortnight *fete* ended and her unending wish that Thorpe had never entered her life.

The music strode forward boldly, laughter resounded through the ballroom in which fifty costumed guests were watching the game, and Jane touched every other blue velvet chair as she made her way about the chairs.

The music stopped.

The shrieking began.

The vying for chairs commenced.

More shrieking, exclaiming, and sliding of feet.

Dear Mr. Ullstree, wearing the traditional garb of the court jester—tri-cornered, violet velvet hat with bells at each point, black tights, and a violet and black doublet—exclaimed his disappointment at having Henrietta steal a chair from him. He good-humoredly took up her hand and kissed it, which sent Henrietta's cheeks firing up to a brilliant crimson below her half-mask of white silk embroidered with seed pearls. She was gowned in a flowing pink silk cloud and bore small wings of stiff tulle on her back. Her light brown hair was a mass of ethereal ringlets over her head and cascaded in a delicate wave down her back. She had never appeared to such advantage before, Jane thought. She seemed to be enjoying the game and moved with a spritely lightness of foot that enhanced her fairy's costume.

Lord Somercote removed a chair, though he still remained in the game. The music began again. Mozart's genius again filled the ballroom. The players began to move swiftly about the chairs, twenty-three remaining. A hum of anticipation, of excited groanings and tensions, flowed about the circle. Feet stomped and slid. Jane continued to touch every other blue chair as she moved relentlessly among the flow of revellers.

The music stopped.

Squealing and laughter rose to the chandeliers.

A scrambling and sliding ensued.

Poor Mrs. Newstead, her cumbersome, powdered wig falling slightly askew, found herself on the lap of Colonel Duffield and bereft of a chair. She was laughing however, a vision with her powdered face and a small black patch near her left eye. The colonel slipped an arm about her waist and tickled her. He was dressed as Moses, wearing a loose gown of brown linen and over his head a covering of orange and brown striped silk bound at the forehead with a knit brown band tied at the back of his head. A black beard completed his costume. Jane was scandalized by his conduct, but Mrs. Newstead—apparently quite ticklish—merely squealed and laughed loudly until the colonel released her. She wore wide paniers over which an exquisite gown of layers and layers of gold lace had been draped and, in the process of being tickled, she exposed more of her white stockinged and gartered legs than most men would witness in the course of their lifetimes. She was the most beautiful 'Marie Antoinette' Jane had ever seen.

Mrs. Newstead pouted as she marched away from the players, but no one was sorry to see her go, since her paniers had effectively ousted at least half a dozen players before her.

Another chair was withdrawn.

The music began again.

The spectators clapped faster and faster which forced the orchestra to increase the tempo of Mozart's *Allegro*.

A swell of groans began to mount all about the players and around the perimeter of the ballroom. Jane touched the chairs, her heart beat erratically in her breast, she loved the competition of it all. She wanted to win.

The music stopped.

Scrambling and wailing followed.

Jane slid into a chair, and found the heavy leather belting of Thorpe's costume biting into her lap. He tried to secure the chair next to him but he only ended up landing squarely on

Mrs. Ullstree's lap. The ladies had ousted him effectively from
the game. Mrs. Ullstree wore the intriguing and colorful silks
of an East Indian princess. Thorpe was wearing the revealing
uniform of a Roman soldier, his thighs and legs bare except for
the leather about his calves. He backed away from both ladies,
bowed—though only very slightly for modesty's sake—and
moved with smiling good grace to join the spectators about the
edge of the ballroom floor. Jane watched him, thinking he, too,
appeared to advantage in his choice of costume. His muscled
thighs, covered with masculine hair, brought forcefully to mind
Oak Cloud Spring. Jane felt desire coil up into a tight spring
just below her heart. The mere thought of having made love to
him in the warm waters of the spring never failed to flood her
entire body with a tingling sensation.

She blinked and looked away from him. She didn't want him
to see, even for the briefest second, that he had the smallest
effect on her. He may have been piqued with her the night of
their joining at Oak Cloud Spring, but the very next day he had
begun assaulting her vulnerable sensibilities yet again. She had
been somewhat successful at turning aside his renewed flirtations because she had reaffirmed within her own heart her intention of marrying Freddy. Yet whenever Thorpe was near, her
mind inevitably returned to Oak Cloud Spring and almost as
frequently to their joining on the first night of the festivities.

Never in her life had her thoughts been so wicked as when
Thorpe came within view! He had but to smile at her, or wink,
or lift an amused brow, and desire for him flowed through every
vein of her body. How glad she would be when all was settled
between herself and Freddy and when she left Challeston Hall
so that she would no longer be tempted by Lord Thorpe.

Her attention was drawn swiftly away from her hopeless
thoughts, when Lord Somercote whisked another chair away
from the diminishing rows and rejoined the circle of players.

The music recommenced.

The flow of the revellers again resounded on the polished,
planked wood floor of the ballroom.

Mozart's tune shimmered against the blazing crystal overhead and magic spilled over the masqueraders once more.

The music stopped. Shrieking and exclamations poured in a rising wave from one player to the next.

Jane found a seat and glanced round to see who the next victim would be. Struggles ensued. The chairs filled up. Lord Somercote, wearing Shakespeare's pointed black beard, moustache, and a burgundy velvet coat with the word Bard embroidered in black letters on one lapel, remained standing. He was a fairly handsome poet and playwright, but his long legs, encased in black tights were a little thin of muscle and made him resemble something of a crow. He bowed politely to his wife who had won the last chair from him. But instead of moving quickly away, his gaze was caught by the sight of his wife. Apparently he had not observed her costume previously.

Lady Somercote wore the garb of a lovely shepherdess in a blonde, curling wig. Her gown of aqua silk over a white linen undergown was quite short, revealing well-turned ankles. The bodice was laced up the front, cut daringly low, with only a narrow ruffle of white lace peeping from the laces to conceal her charms. Lord Somercote, as he bowed to his wife a second time, blinked at her in astonishment as he dropped his gaze to her bosom. His brow rose and an odd blush crept up his neck. In a daze, he cleared his throat and removed another chair.

Mozart again lit up the ballroom, this time faster still.

The players began to trot in a dizzying circle.

The music ceased abruptly.

Jane scrambled for a chair and found one.

Freddy was left standing. His pale complexion was dotted with pink patches below his black half-mask. He didn't wear a costume—one of only three men who had not seen fit to engage in the playful nature of the masquerade ball. He had told Jane earlier that he could simply not bring himself to don the robes of another character, that somewhere within the integrity of his soul he knew that to become what he was not would be to break apart his essential spiritual unity.

Jane grimaced as she watched him and recalled his arguments.

What fustian, she thought not for the first time. She had concluded he had merely been too lazy to create a costume for the ball and cloaked his apathy in philosophical rubbish.

She was irritated with him. Again.

Thorpe was glad he had been eliminated from the game, for now he was able to observe Jane at his leisure and without the least fear of being caught staring at her. She was a vision of strength and femininity in her costume as Cleopatra. Her gown was of an exquisite red silk in a long tunic over white linen. Her lovely figure was defined by a roping of gold braid over the red shimmering fabric that began beneath her full breasts and crisscrossed over her abdomen to encircle her waist. She wore a breastplate of sorts of gold silk, padded and stitched to resemble a coil of metal bands. A tiara of brass wound in the shape of an asp was settled in a ring over a straight black wig cropped Egyptian-style at the shoulders. Matching gold coils on both wrists completed a costume that was exotic, powerful, and had the effect of pulling Thorpe's mind back to Oak Cloud Spring and even further back to the first night at Challeston when he had tricked her.

All his senses were fully heightened as he watched Jane in round after round of the lively musical chairs. She moved with grace, tension, and quickness as the music stopped, as she fought for a chair. He saw her red, embroidered silk slippers and several times her well-turned ankles. The music would start and she would touch every other blue chair as though making the chairs her own as she moved around and around the back-to-back rows. A powerful feeling rose in his chest as he watched her. She was enjoying the heat of the game, the competition, the quest for the prize.

They were a lot alike, he realized with a start and the realization spread in a warm heat through his stomach and into his

loins. He wanted to kiss her again, to hold her in his arms, to
feel her full, ripe body pressed against his. He shook his head,
slightly bemused. How was it he could still desire her so much
when he disapproved so strongly of her intention to marry
Freddy Waingrove in spite of her involvements with him? He
had seen her true character and could not respect her, no matter
how much she argued that she would do all she could to make
Waingrove a good wife. What fustian!

Prior to Oak Cloud Spring he had been able to forgive her
for setting her cap for the would-be poet. But after he had made
love to her at the spring, he could only view her intention of
wedding Freddy Waingrove as the worst kind of hypocrisy.
There was only one place Jane Ambergate belonged—in his
bed and nowhere else, not until he was done with her.

This last thought brought him up short, as another round of
musical chairs came and went. Only thirteen players remained
and still Jane was one of them.

Until he was done with her. He felt an odd heat burn his
neck. Herein was the truth with which Jane kept herself separated from him. She knew fully well that when she became his
mistress, an ending was as sure as the beginning and it was
always the same—he used the ladies up and then cast them
aside, just as Jane had said, as she had always said.

Suddenly her hypocrisy did not seem so brutal. What alter-
native had he offered her anyway? A brief spate of love and
sensual pleasure that would sour as surely as the sun rose and
set? Love, even congenial affection, dwindled, faded, and died
without the marriage vows and legitimate children to sustain
the day-to-day branglings.

The music began. The music stopped. The hurried footsteps
commenced. The squealing replaced the music. Jane's eyes were
lit with an unearthly excitement.

How very much she loved the chase. He recalled her fervor
when plying her bow and arrow. He remembered her delight as
she slapped the horses' flanks with the reins and set them to
flying down the lane toward the Peak District. He saw her now,

energetic, vitalized by a silly game. He knew what she was feeling. He felt the same way during a fox hunt, or while riding and taking a fence at neck-or-nothing speed, or when his fists were raised in trained boxing style as he pitted his cunning against the great Jackson in his London boxing salon.

His chest swelled with pride as he watched her. A roll of pleasure moved through him, leaving behind a hum in every limb. His abdomen tightened. Desire to be placed securely between her thighs sent a bolt of passion ripping through him. He found it hard to breathe.

Only six chairs remained. The music stopped. He closed a fist. Find a chair, his mind commanded her. She did. She was laughing now, her brown eyes sparkling.

Four more times the music sparked and ceased. Four more times Jane ousted a player.

Only two remained now—Colonel Duffield in his Moses garb and Jane as an enchanting Cleopatra. The crowd in the ballroom pressed close so that the orchestra could not see what was happening. Thorpe held some of the crowd back. Lady Somercote called out for the orchestra to begin. Mozart invaded the crackling air. The lonely blue chair mocked the last two players. Jane was near the seat, still the music played. One note, one step, another note, another step. The colonel was moving close to the chair, Jane was reluctant to give up the front side of the seat.

The music stopped. They were the same distance from the chair. Each slid with athletic grace toward the seat, they arrived at the same time, their hips bumped, both pressed each other, their eyes locked in fierce competition. Jane struggled to keep her part of the chair. The colonel was by far the stronger. He could push her off. Thorpe watched in fascination as Jane slid her arm behind him. A moment later, the colonel cried out, leaned forward, laughed, and Jane effectively pushed him off the seat. He fell with a plop to the floor.

Thorpe blinked. Cleopatra had tickled Moses off the mountain.

The entire assemblage burst into laughter and applause. Colonel Duffield rose quickly and took Jane's proffered hand. His eyes were full of laughter as he bent over her hand and placed a generous kiss on her fingers. He then lifted her to her feet, the orchestra commenced Mozart's *Allegro* one last time, and Colonel Duffield led Jane about the ballroom, holding her hand aloft in a victorious march. She laughed and blew kisses to the crowd. Her antics caused a round of enthusiastic applause to erupt in a rolling wave through the masqueraders. Thorpe found himself grinning broadly, clapping hard and steadily, as she pranced proudly about the ballroom.

Congratulations flowed. Merriment reigned. Thorpe's discontent with both his conduct and hers seemed to evaporate with the very simple thought that he wished to be with her, to dance with her, to enjoy the pleasure of her company.

Jane received the adulation of the crowd with a delight that sent her spirits soaring. She felt at home at Challeston, not only with Lady Somercote's fortnight guests but with the numerous additional revellers from the surrounding countryside. She could not remember enjoying herself so much in a long, long time.

She looked for Freddy, but could not see him in the many faces that offered their congratulations then moved on to seek partners for the forthcoming waltz. Oh, the waltz. Freddy had to dance the waltz with her; she had been saving it most especially for him. Her campaign had been proceeding to a nicety ever since he had finally broken down and kissed her in the garden outside the sword room. He had kissed her twice since then and his professions of affection were growing more tender. Even his complexion did not become quite so dotted with red patches as before. Somehow he was becoming accustomed to showing his affection for her.

But as she scanned the ballroom, she came to realize he was not there. She wondered if he had even witnessed her victory.

She knew a disappointment that flowed in a long quick stream clear to her toes. Why couldn't he have remained in the ballroom at least long enough to offer his praise for her skillful maneuvering of the chairs?

In the end, she had to move away from the ballroom floor where several couples were already taking up their places for the waltz. Her disappointment mounted, replacing the euphoria of the moment.

"Where is your swain?" a familiar resonant voice sounded from behind her.

A spattering of gooseflesh popped all over her neck as Thorpe's breath touched her skin. "Oh," she murmured, turning around to face him. "If you are referring to Fr—that is, to Mr. Waingrove, I'm not sure."

"He left shortly after you began your victory march. He had a hand to his temple and Miss Hartworth was attending him. I believe he has developed one of his infamous headaches."

Jane wanted to detect a sarcastic note in his voice, but she couldn't find one. In fact, she didn't quite understand the expression on his face either, for a certain kindness, almost an admiration, had entered his blue eyes.

But that was impossible. She knew how he felt about her pursuit of Freddy, especially since Oak Cloud Spring.

She shook her head, unwilling to trust him, the black wig moving in a strange, languorous manner over her shoulders. "What do you want, Thorpe?" she asked baldly. "If you mean to upbraid me again, I warn you now I won't tolerate a word of complaint from you. Already, you've come the crab with me more often than I have found comfortable and if you think I shall merely—"

"Whoa!" he cried, lifting a hand playfully. "I've come only to beg you to dance with me."

She eyed him suspiciously. "You plan to take me to task once we are locked together on the ballroom floor. You know I won't desert you and cause a scandal, so I can only suppose that once

I am held captive by the waltz, you intend to force your arguments on me again. But I promise you—"

"I want only a dance," he murmured, taking a step toward her. "I promise I won't speak a single disparaging word to you about anything."

She swallowed hard. She felt her heart constrict lightly in her chest. If only he wouldn't look at her in just that manner as though he wished to devour her.

"I believe you," she whispered.

Jane let her gaze drop to his lips. Somehow the very air between them was shifting and changing right before her. She didn't understand exactly what was happening or why her breathing was suddenly becoming very light and quick, or why a dizziness was assailing her. It was almost as though his thoughts were pummelling her mind and her heart and filling her with questions, with wonderings and with a sudden, powerful desire for the Roman soldier in front of her. He wore a helmet to which was attached an intricate trail of blue feathers that flowed over his left shoulder. She licked her lips slightly and reached up to touch the feathers. They were soft beneath her fingers.

He caught her hand. "Dance with me, Jane."

She nodded, feeling so strange that she couldn't have uttered a single word of protest had she wanted to.

He led her out for the waltz, the orchestra struck the first note, and Jane felt as though with the first step she was moving back to Camelot, or perhaps back a little further when England was dotted with Roman villas and Hadrian's Wall was just being built. Her hand about his back touched the smooth dark brown leather of his costume. Her heart constricted again, then swelled with each turn of the dance. Why did he make her feel this way, she wondered for the hundredth time.

"You were marvelous tonight," he murmured huskily. "I was never more glad than when you and Mrs. Ullstree ousted me from the game, for then I was able to watch you unhindered."

"You were watching me?" she queried breathlessly.

He smiled crookedly. "I was watching you and remembering the two times we've been together——"

"Oh," Jane whispered, a rush of pleasure flowing over her. The dance took a turn, he shifted his hand slightly and drew her more closely to him. "You shouldn't. You shouldn't be speaking of such things." Her voice sounded helpless and faint.

"I want to speak of what has happened between us," he murmured. "Of what it was like to kiss you, to hold you in my arms, to move within you."

Jane felt a blush overtake her cheeks. At the same time, her knees began to feel wobbly. "Please, Thorpe," she whispered, desire flowing over her abdomen and down her thighs. "This won't do. It isn't seemly."

"I don't give a fig for what's *seemly,*" he retorted deeply into her ear. "All I care about is making certain that you know how much I love being with you and how much your liveliness and sense of fun and gig please me."

Jane sighed deeply. His words were seducing her. She could feel the tension in his body. She looked into his eyes. How powerfully connected to him she felt, in ways she couldn't explain. "I will confess that I haven't enjoyed myself so much in years. When I lived in Kent, I was notorious for my enthusiasm for all the seasonal events—I danced round the maypole, I never missed the haymaking in the summertime, and whenever anyone would get up a maying, even if it was the height of July or August, I was the first to dance the Scottish reel down the canvas tent floor. I understand when you say you don't give a fig for what's seemly. Dancing about the maypole is just so much deuced fun!"

She recalled that that was how Edward had first seen her and fallen in love with her. She had been dancing round the maypole, flowers bunched in her hair in almost a comical fashion, her gown of white muslin trailing with ribbons in a rainbow of colors. He had made certain he was introduced to her father and the rest resulted in a marriage that was wonderful and unsteady all at the same time.

Thorpe smiled at her. "I wish I had known you then," he murmured, "when you were just a chit out of the schoolroom. I wish I could have danced round the maypole with you."

She smiled and laughed and it seemed to her that all the tension between them suddenly evaporated. A camaraderie was born in that moment, a friendship based on similar delights. She felt her heart warm to him and she couldn't keep a grin from her face.

"What a pretty Cleopatra you are," he said.

"And I won't tell you what a devilishly handsome Roman soldier you make since I'm sure it would swell your head and then your helmet would likely burst."

He chuckled, twirled her, and moved her in his habitually graceful manner about the ballroom floor.

When all the guests had left for their homes or retired to their rooms, Lady Somercote held Jane back from ascending the stairs and instead drew her into the forest-green drawing room. "I have been wanting to speak with you all evening, Jane," she murmured, glancing nervously toward the open doorway leading to the entrance hall. She was clearly afraid of being overheard. "For I have at last formed a plan, but we must act at once for I overheard my husband speaking to that wicked woman, begging her to come to his bedchamber tomorrow night."

Jane was shocked but not surprised. "Oh, dear," she murmured.

"Precisely so."

"I'll do whatever you ask of me," she assured her worried but determined hostess.

Eight

The next morning, which was Sunday, Jane remained in her bedchamber instead of attending services in Lord Somercote's chapel. She was on a mission for her hostess in response to Lady Somercote's pleas of the night before.

Upon awakening, Jane had professed a terrible headache, which Vangie helped her feign by making a fuss belowstairs while searching for ambergris to burn in Jane's little china house. She also demanded laudanum for her mistress, lavender water, a stack of bathing cloths, and a basin of cold water.

Vangie would do whatever she had to do to cure her poor, suffering mistress of the headache.

The staff was properly concerned and Lady Somercote insisted on remaining with her invalided guest instead of attending services. Prayers would be said for poor Jane Ambergate.

Once Vangie was able to confirm, however, that all the guests were in the chapel and that Mrs. Newstead's abigail was flirting with one of the stableboys, both Jane and Lady Somercote stole into the widow's bedchamber.

War was war.

"We are very wicked," Jane whispered to her as she took one last long peek down the empty hallway, then closed the door.

"I shan't let a matter of ethics keep me from averting that woman's hideous designs on my vulnerable husband."

Jane turned around to find Lady Somercote already moving purposefully toward her guest's wardrobe—a smaller chamber attached to the elegant bedroom decorated *en suite* in peach silks and accented with dark green tassels, cording, and pretty silk-damask pillows. The violet silk skirts of her ladyship's gown rustled as she swept into the dressing room.

Turning the key in the lock of the bedchamber door, Jane followed quickly behind. When she passed into the dressing room she found Lady Somercote holding up Mrs. Newstead's enormous white powdered wig and half-mask of gold silk trimmed with a small edging of rose-colored lace. "This is all I need," she said. "My abigail located the Marie Antoinette gown in the laundry. Apparently, she spilled a glass of Madeira on the skirts. My maid thinks she can steal the gown without anyone the wiser. Besides, Mrs. Newstead will have no use of it until she leaves and her abigail shall be told that we are working on the lace in stages in order to remove the wine stain."

Jane smiled. "So, what do you plan to do with the costume, then?" She watched a faint pink blush tinge her hostess's cheeks.

"Why, I shall become Marie Antoinette, of course."

"Oh, my," Jane murmured, her eyes opening wide at the suggestiveness of Lady Somercote's remark. "But will he not know his own wife?"

Lady Somercote smiled and simpered, she tossed her head and squealed. She sounded just like Mrs. Newstead. "I have been practicing for days," she explained when Jane blinked at her.

"Won't he know your voice?" she pressed.

"But, madame," Lady Somercote said, speaking in a high, French accent, "why should he, when I am but a poor French woman destined *pour la guillotine?*"

Jane clapped her hands. "You speak delightfully. I don't wonder that you couldn't have enjoyed a turn on the stage. Lord Somercote will be delighted."

The ladies giggled together and afterward returned to their respective bedchambers.

* * *

Jane made a full recovery by that evening, though she had disliked kicking her heels in her bedchamber for the entire afternoon. She disliked even more entering company when she smelled so strongly of ambergris, but there was nothing for it if she hoped to keep everyone's suspicions at bay. When she joined her fellow guests for cards after dinner was concluded, she was congratulated on her return to good health, and several times she found she had to subdue the high spirits she felt in light of the fact that she was supposed to have been ill the entire day.

Most of the guests were gathered in the formal green drawing room about two card tables. Mrs. Ullstree was playing piquet and cribbage with Lord Thorpe while Freddy, Colonel Duffield, Mrs. Newstead, and Lord Somercote were playing whist. Jane took a seat on a sofa some distance from the fireplace in order to help Henrietta wind a ball of yarn. Mr. Ullstree, a book open on his lap and a half-finished glass of port at his elbow, was seated in a chair by the fire snoring gently. His wife was close by and every now and then gently prodded him to wake him up. He always awoke congenially, nodded, and smiled. He would take another sip of wine, read a paragraph or two, and again doze off, only to begin rumbling the air once more. He was forgiven by the assemblage because he was ordinarily the most civil of men and because he was beloved.

Lady Somercote was occupied on some business with her housekeeper—or so it was reported, though Jane rather thought she was tending to the details of just how and when she was to steal into her husband's bedchamber later that night in the guise of the widow Newstead dressed as Marie Antoinette. A riddle within a riddle. She glanced at Lord Somercote and wondered if he would know the difference between the women.

She smiled, chuckled, and dipped her hand once more. She had a skein of blue-green angora stretched from hand to hand, held out in front of her. Hetty was winding the yarn into a tidy ball. Even in such elegant surroundings, where the guests were expected only to amuse themselves, Henrietta could not repress her homey occupations, the urge to make some useful employment of her time. Jane had agreed to assist her, and was rather contented since she was still pretending to have just recovered from a violent headache.

"I am glad you were able to perform this task for me," Henrietta said, not looking at Jane.

Now that Jane thought on it, Hetty had scarcely looked at her above once or twice since she arrived in the drawing room. It was almost as though she was avoiding her gaze. Had Henrietta actually schemed to have a few moments alone with her?

The thin, waifish young woman continued, "For I have been wanting to speak with you for some time." Laughter erupted from the whist table and Hetty glanced nervously over her shoulder, then whispered, "I hope we cannot be heard."

"Secrets?" Jane queried with a half-smile. The fact was, she was a little startled that Henrietta looked both guilty and nervous all at once.

"Yes—er, no. That is, not precisely." Henrietta's gaze flittered up to hers, then flittered down to the growing ball of blue-green yarn. "You see, Fr—that is, Mr. Waingrove asked me to speak with you."

Jane blinked at her friend. Once, then twice. "Did I hear you correctly, Hetty? Mr. Waingrove asked you to speak with me? About what? What can he possibly have you say to me that he cannot say himself?"

Hetty dropped the ball into her lap. Her expression collapsed into a mass of dismay. "You are offended. I told him you would be. I told him that he ought to address you himself, but he would have none of it. He trembled at the thought and he was certain that if you heard his gentle rebuke from my lips that you would not then fly into the boughs or fall into a fit of the sullens. Of course I told him you would do neither such thing, but he pressed me, saying that he knew how females generally responded. He said his mother was always coming the crab and could scarcely be brought down from her high ropes whenever she was offended. What else could I do, Jane, but oblige him? He was very distraught."

Jane strove to keep her mounting temper in check. She didn't know which sentiment to experience first—outrage that Freddy felt in need of rebuking her about anything, or fury that Hetty would speak to her as though she, too, was convinced she was in need of a scolding.

Taking a deep breath, she decided to find out what manner of indiscretion or incivility or odious conduct she had committed. "What is his complaint?" she asked simply.

Hetty leaned forward confidentially and Jane felt her temper rise another notch. "Mr. Waingrove thought—and I couldn't help but agree with him—that you rather made a spectacle of yourself last night."

Jane drew in a small gasp. Her temper rose yet another notch. She pushed the yarn off her arms as though trying to rid herself of vermin. "What do you mean?"

Hetty breathed what seemed to be a sigh of relief. "I knew you would not be adverse to hearing a gentle criticism of your conduct. I told Mr. Waingrove as much a dozen times last night, but he wouldn't listen to me. We paced the long gallery until three o'clock in the morning. He held my hand tightly and even shed tears over his misery. So you can see that a proper response to my hints is precisely what's needed to bring yourself back into his good graces."

Jane chuckled softly, not because she found amusement in anything Hetty was saying, but because she was utterly dumbfounded. She couldn't believe what was being said to her. Did Hetty realize that she was confessing to having spent several hours alone, unchaperoned, with a man? Jane shook her head, trying to clear her thoughts in order to address the issue at hand. "So what you are saying is that you were alone with Mr. Waingrove for several hours."

"Well, yes, I confess I was. But I was only acting as his

guardian angel, at least that is what he called me. He was woefully overset, poor man."

Jane nodded, wondering suddenly if Henrietta had designs on Freddy herself. But this notion she cast aside as ridiculous. Henrietta was incapable of having designs on anyone or anything. She was neither capable of deceit nor of cunning. With that thought, her temper subsided a little. "So, pray, Miss Guardian Angel, in what way precisely did I make such a spectacle of myself as to have given Freddy a disgust of me?"

"Oh, you did not give him a disgust. At least not precisely. He was merely revolted by your blowing kisses and waving to those who congratulated you upon winning that rather silly game of musical chairs."

Jane was stunned that her somewhat theatrical parading about the ballroom had disturbed Freddy. "Revolted, you say?"

Hetty nodded vigorously and smiled shyly. "But only, I think, because I know that he hopes to make you his wife one day. I believe he was distressed because of his close connection to you. Were you not of such importance to his future, I daresay he would have believed your conduct to have been merely unguarded."

Jane let out a deep sigh. "I suppose then," she murmured, more to herself than to Hetty, "that when we are married, Freddy will expect me to conduct myself with greater discretion and modesty."

"Of course," Hetty responded enthusiastically, her face wreathed in smiles. "He said as much last night. Oh, I knew you would understand right away. Freddy speaks often of how he wishes to make you his wife, but that he can't seem to find the courage to do so. And last night, when he was again talking to me of the violence of his feelings for you, I couldn't help but offer my services in trying to bring a better understanding between you."

"Will you also accompany us on our honeymoon journey?" Jane asked facetiously.

Hetty laughed and blushed. "Well of course not. I expect that

We'd Like to Invite You to Subscribe to Zebra's Regency Romance Book Club and Give You a Gift of 4 Free Books as Your Introduction! (Worth $18.49!)

I f you're a Regency lover, imagine the joy of getting 4 FREE Zebra Regency Romances and then the chance to have these lovely stories delivered to your home each month at the lowest prices available! Well, that's our offer to you and here's how you benefit by becoming a Zebra Home Subscription Service subscriber:

- 4 FREE Introductory Regency Romances are delivered to your doorstep
- 4 BRAND NEW Regencies are then delivered each month (usually before they're available in bookstores)
- Subscribers save almost $4.00 every month
- Home delivery is always FREE
- You also receive a FREE monthly newsletter, *Zebra/Pinnacle Romance News* which features author profiles, contests, subscriber benefits, book previews and more
- No risks or obligations...in other words you can cancel whenever you wish with no questions asked

Join the thousands of readers who enjoy the savings and convenience offered to Regency Romance subscribers. After your initial introductory shipment, you receive 4 brand-new Zebra Regency Romances each month to examine for 10 days. Then, if you decide to keep the books, you'll pay the preferred subscriber's price of just $3.65 per title. That's only $14.60 for all 4 books and there's never an extra charge for shipping and handling.

It's a no-lose proposition, so return the FREE BOOK CERTIFICATE today!

AN
$18.49
VALUE....
FREE!

*No
obligation
to buy
anything,
ever!*

ZEBRA HOME SUBSCRIPTION SERVICE, INC.

120 BRIGHTON ROAD

P.O. BOX 5214

CLIFTON, NEW JERSEY 07015-5214

once you learn to conform yourself better to Mr. Waingrove's strict but honorable dictums on how his wife must conduct herself, you will get along perfectly well and will need no one to intervene as I have tonight."

"You are all sweetness and generosity," Jane said, amazed at her friend. She did not know whether to admire Hetty's ingenuous beliefs or despise her for them. Henrietta clearly thought Freddy to be a paragon of sorts.

"Shall I tell Freddy, then, that you are utterly ashamed of your conduct last night?"

"Please do," she responded flatly. "Though I trust you to properly embellish my sentiments so that he will be assured of my humbled state."

Hetty laid a hand over Jane's. "You may trust me indeed to see this little rift in your love repaired." Then Hetty winked and smiled.

Jane glanced over at the whist table and saw that Freddy's gold-green eyes were just barely visible over the rim of his cards and that he was staring at her horror-stricken. Jane was so appalled and disgusted by the whole situation that the only thing she could do was hide her anger by placing a hand over her face and pretending to stroke her forehead as though in great pain. Afterward she picked up the yarn and replaced it on each hand. Hetty began to wind the blue-green yarn about the ball again.

Jane turned the subject by asking how Mrs. Hartworth fared, if her gout had improved, and if the new spectacles the doctor had provided for her were permitting her to read the scriptures again. "Oh, yes, indeed," Hetty exclaimed. "Her toe is not nearly so swollen and she sent me a letter recently in which she had copied several intriguing verses from I Kings. She spoke of her new spectacles as a miracle and I couldn't help but think that my prayers had been answered in the most—"

Jane heard no more. She couldn't bear to listen to Hetty's ramblings about her mother's health and had only introduced the subject in order to leave the one that had made her as mad as fire. The skein of yarn about her arms was growing thinner with each passing second. She could hardly wait till the task was complete, for she suddenly realized that though she had pretended to have the headache earlier, in fact she now had one.

On the following morning, Jane wore a summery frock of patterned Indian calico block-printed with tiny blue flowers. Over her dark brown curls, she wore a simple straw poke bonnet bearing a long spray of bluebells all about the crown. She wore white lace gloves and a modest matching lace fichu to protect her bosom against the summer sun. Draped over her elbows she carried an elegant shawl of the finest pale yellow cashmere. Freddy had been enchanted with her costume which she had modeled on those Henrietta had worn during the course of the fortnight event. She knew the effect to be charming, but the truth was she disliked the image she had seen reflected in the looking-glass that morning. It was far too proprietous for her tastes.

Jane walked with Freddy along the lake in front of the mansion. Several white swans were gliding over the smooth waters beneath the shade of an enormous, ancient fir tree. Small white feathers dotted the grass surrounding the lake. She held his arm and sighed. He was speaking in his melodious voice, but she was only partly listening. He was reviewing in detail every feeling he had possessed from the moment he had seen her win the musical chairs of two night's before, how he had been dismayed that she had not permitted Colonel Duffield to win, how horrified he had been that she had won so dishonorably by tickling one of Wellington's finest officers, how embarrassed he had been when she had actually beamed her delight in winning at all, and finally how truly mortified for her he had been when she had exposed herself so thoroughly by marching about in a circle on the poor colonel's arm and throwing kisses to the applauding, vulgar masses. He could only conclude that such immodest conduct had erupted from having imbibed more champagne than she ought to have.

Jane had hardly had any champagne at all and she thought Freddy was being absurd. But she didn't say so. She didn't say anything. She walked meekly by his side, her heart as heavy as stone. She believed he took her silence as acquiescence to his strictures on her conduct.

Freddy's harangue and her sullens were broken up abruptly by a sudden whoop and a shout. From the south, the sounds of quick, hard hoofbeats ripped through the peaceful stillness of the day. She turned to see Thorpe pressing one of Somercote's geldings to lengthen his stride. Behind Thorpe on another of the earl's fine horses, Colonel Duffield slapped his riding crop against his gelding's flanks.

A race!

Jane's heart suddenly came alive and she felt it beat as though for the first time in hours. She looked up at Freddy who had paled at the sight of Thorpe riding his horse neck-or-nothing. Freddy scowled, shook his head, and clucked his tongue. "What a pair of inconsiderate fellows," he murmured as Thorpe shot by.

Jane, however, caught Thorpe's eye and saw reflected in the blue depths an amused, knowing, and quite insufferable expression indicating he knew very well he was enjoying himself and she was not.

The beast!

The rogue!

At the same time, she couldn't help but smile at him and return a nod that meant she acknowledged his hit. He grinned and disappeared down the road.

"Now whatever did he mean by leering at you in that odious manner?" Freddy cried. "I vow if I had half his ability with either sword or pistol—"

He broke off as Colonel Duffield reached them. But instead of shooting past, the colonel drew up his mount with a quick jerk. Dirt clods flew all around them as his horse reared up, then planted his hooves firmly in the dark brown earth by the fir tree. "Mrs. Ambergate, Thorpe tells me you have a beautiful seat. You ought to join us. We're having a bit of fun as you can see."

Jane felt her heart lurch and every sense fire up at the very idea of mounting one of Somercote's geldings and giving her horse his head.

Duffield held his hand down to Jane. "Come—Waingrove won't mind. I'll ride you back to the stables and have you mounted in a trice."

"I'm not suitably gowned," she said, swallowing hard and letting her gaze rove the horse's black, sweating coat hungrily. She wanted more than anything to oblige him. Her heart began beating in strong, steady beats against her ribs. She loved to ride. She loved the thrill of a horse beneath her, of his hooves pounding into the dirt, his sides heaving. There was no greater exhilaration.

He barked at her. "Come! Now!" He shook his hand toward her. "Don't be a simpleton! You know you want to come!"

Jane couldn't resist. She released Freddy's arm and ran toward the outstretched arm. She'd been raised around horses from the time she was out of leading strings, and with one easy jump, Colonel Duffield caught her about the waist, she caught the pummel of the horse, and between the two of them she dragged herself onto his lap sitting side-saddle.

"Jane!" Freddy called after her.

"I can't help it, Freddy!" she called back as the colonel spurred his horse forward then turned him around toward the stables. "I love to ride!"

She matched Duffield's bounce and set herself easily into the rhythm of the horse's stride. Within less than a minute, they had returned to the stables. Jane paced in uneasy anticipation for the groom to saddle her a fine, spirited gelding. He had first wanted to give her a piebald mare of mild temperament but she had only to move down the row of stalls to find the horse she wanted. He had a devilish gleam in his eye, reared up when the groom approached him, and she couldn't help but think he reminded her of Lord Thorpe.

She laughed as the groom handed her the reins, offered her his cupped hands, and threw her tidily into the saddle. The horse went through his antics for a minute or two, shying, shaking, even kicking a little. But she loved horses. She patted his neck, kept a tight hand on the reins, and let him know with every ounce of her being that she loved him just the way he was and that if he would only cut her a little slack, she'd give him the best ride of his life.

She felt the colonel's eyes on her and when she glanced at him, he nodded approvingly. She nodded in return, smiled, and gave her horse a solid kick. Without a preamble, the gelding darted away from the stables. Jane laughed aloud, holding her reins together, leaning forward slightly and lowering her head. What did she care if her gown exposed half her legs to the knees! She loved to ride.

She waved at Freddy as she flew past him. His expression was horrified but she rather thought he ought to know some of the truth about her if he was indeed considering asking her to become his wife.

She followed the path that Thorpe had taken which led toward Windy Knowl, the deer herd, and the pine woods. She reached the first gate and opened it, shooing the colonel through, then passing through herself. The colonel closed the gate and they hurried on past several shy deer who scattered away from them as they thundered by and on up the dirt riding trail that caught the northernmost slope of the hill.

The sunlight dappled the trail through the thinning edge of the forest. The smell of pine was richly in the air. Jane kept her horse moving at a tidy pace, letting him run when the path opened up, pulling him only as little as she needed to when the path turned. Windy Knowl dropped off to the east. The path opened up into a narrow valley through which a branch of Glapwich Stream wended its way. In the middle of the valley, on the far side of the stream, Thorpe sat on his horse, waiting undoubtedly for Colonel Duffield. He was looking off to the west, and glancing in the direction of his gaze, Jane saw that he had a clear, excellent view of Wolfscar Tor.

He shifted his head toward them as they approached, then straightened his shoulders when he saw that she was riding with Duffield.

He laughed aloud, grinning broadly at the sight of her. His voice reached her even from across the valley. He understood her so well.

Once she picked her way across the stream and drew near enough to hear him, he cried out, "You're not even in riding gear. What the devil are you doing?"

"It's all Colonel Duffield's fault!" she called back. "He enticed me and I couldn't restrain myself." She glanced back at Duffield and smiled at him. Duffield, however, was at that moment exchanging a rather piercing look with Thorpe. Jane wondered if the men had planned this.

She was certain of it when Duffield said, "You owe me a guinea, Thorpe!"

Thorpe shook his head. "I'm in awe of you. I still don't know how you managed it."

Duffield glanced at Jane and said. "I wagered him I could get you to come with us. He said nothing would tear you away from Freddy Waingrove because you were in love with him. I told him he was a baconbrained idiot."

Jane glanced back at Thorpe and then at Duffield. "Men!" she uttered with mock disgust. But before either of the gentlemen in attendance could begin to argue with her succinct appraisal of the general character of their gender, she gave her lively horse a kick, told him he needed to make up for the men near him, and sped past Thorpe before he knew what she was about.

Jane rode for miles in a broad circuit around Windy Knowl. She had ruined her lace gloves, but she didn't care. Her slippers were coming apart at the seams, but they had never fit quite right. Her skirts and stockings, where her ankles were exposed, were muddy from the numerous streams the gelding pounded through on their journey through the countryside.

As they met the lane connecting the villages of Chadfield and Knowlwood and the long stretch of cornfields came into view, only then did Jane begin to tire. She slowed her horse's pace and both men finally drew abreast.

"Thorpe was right, Mrs. Ambergate. You've an excellent seat," Colonel Duffield said, trotting his horse gently beside her own.

"Thank you, Colonel. And thank you for persuading me to join you."

He chuckled. "You didn't protest very loudly, m'dear," he said, not unkindly.

Jane laughed with him. "I suppose it was Thorpe's fault, however." She glanced toward the viscount, who caught her eye and smiled knowingly at her. "He gave me that look of his that said he meant to have a great deal of fun and gig and that he knew I would be missing out entirely. What else could I do but pick up his gauntlet?"

"That is certainly Thorpe's way," the colonel responded, looking at the viscount over Jane's head and chuckling again. "He is forever taunting all of us."

The wondrous welcome fatigue of riding hard for a couple of hours began to slip through Jane's veins in slow, easy stages. She felt relaxed and at peace with the world. A hard ride was precisely what she had needed after having to listen to Freddy's astonishing criticisms of her conduct at the masquerade. Even now, as glimmerings of his speeches began to come back to her, the very thought of them sent a drenching shower on her spirits so much so that she had to blink several times to snap herself back to her place of contentment.

Goodness, she thought. Whatever would he be like as a husband? But this hapless thought was more than she could bear. She instantly nudged her horse into a canter and again she was pounding down the lane.

"Jane!" the colonel called after her. "We can't keep up!"

Jane laughed, forcing her blue-devils away, and before long her horse was galloping hard down the straight of the lane.

Jane returned to her bedchamber following her ride, seeking solitude and a little rest before the usual round of evening events began. Dinner, and socializing afterwards, besides the extra time needed to labor over the vignettes, would be enough to tax her already worn sensibilities. But in her current distress over Freddy's harangue, she knew she needed time alone—to think, to recover her spirits, to decide how to address her swain's rigid ideals and notions.

A nuncheon served in her bedchamber, a hot bath, and an hour reading from an intriguing novel called *Pride and Prejudice,* had given her what she required most—perspective. By the time she was ready to dress for dinner, she was more confident about what she needed to do. She sat at her dressing table ready for her abigail's ministrations.

Vangie shaped her long brown locks in a myriad of curls down her back through a steady application of one of several curling tongs heated on a bed of coals. When her hair had cooled, and the curls were set, Vangie brushed her locks carefully then pulled her hair high to the crown of her head. With the placement of three white drooping ostrich feathers behind, her face was framed with a mass of delightful, ethereal curls. She was enchanted with the way her coiffure looked but she was convinced Freddy would not be so delighted.

Understanding as much, she felt in her heart that her plans were slipping away from her. Over the past few weeks, and more especially the past few days, she had come to understand Freddy Waingrove far better than she had expected to. He was a great deal more sensitive than she had at first supposed. He was given to flights of fancy, to imagining fears that set his head to throbbing, and to an excess of sensibility that rivaled even Mrs. Bennett, a character in the very novel she had been reading earlier that day.

When she had first set her cap for Frederick Waingrove, she had known him only as a tall, handsome man, of excellent for-

tune, of perfect civility, and of great poetic genius. He had sin-
gled her out from the first, before she had decided he would
make a worthy husband and good father for her children. He
had sought her in every drawing room, ballroom, and assembly
room she had graced. Several of her friends had congratulated
her on the match. Lady Somercote had given her blessing. What
more could have been wanting?

Except for respect and love, she thought. She sighed, gazing
down at her hands while Vangie tucked, tugged, and otherwise
arranged her half-robe of silk stripes in pale green and pale pink
which formed a demi-train behind. Beneath the gown was an
underdress of ivory silk. The half-robe was clasped at the bosom.
A tiny point lace edged the low decollete of the bodice and the
hems of each delicately puffed sleeve. She wore a necklet of
emeralds and matching emeralds on each ear—paste, of course,
but still quite beautiful. Long ivory silk gloves and an elegant
shawl of matching Brussels lace completed a toilette as regal as
any ensemble that had graced London during the recent Season.

Respect and love, Jane thought as she regarded her image in
the long looking-glass. She fluttered open her fan of white feathers and shaded her lips and her nose so that only her eyes were
visible. No, Freddy would not like her *ensemble* but Thorpe
would. Thorpe would approve heartily of her expensive eye for
color, for fabric, for style. Freddy liked only that which expressed
simplicity. A white muslin gown suited his notion of what was
acceptable in even the most fastidious drawing room. While she
was fond of silk and even of satin and tulle on occasion.

Whatever was she going to do?

Jane glanced at the clock on her mantel and was a little surprised that she was a full hour beforetimes. She recalled that
sherry was always served in the library for anyone wishing for
an aperatif before dinner. Since she knew she had a mission of
sorts to accomplish this evening, she decided to venture to the
library. She descended the circular staircase and found her heart
quailing a little. She didn't want to speak with Freddy, to confront him about what she felt to be their mounting differences;

she didn't want to force an ending when she had no other re-
spectable course before her except that of becoming his wife.

Still, what must be done, must be done, she thought firmly,
lifting her head high and squaring her shoulders. The library
door was open and she walked in wondering if she might be
alone for a time.

But in this she was mistaken, for a man was already waiting
in the library. She smiled, relief flooding her. It was only Thorpe
and since she knew he would approve of her appearance, she
found herself relaxing in quick stages as she entered the tall,
lofty chamber.

The library was on the first floor of the mansion and sat on
the corner which faced the north and westerly vistas. None of
the red deer could be seen from the several windows, but the
late light of the afternoon streamed into the gold chamber,
flooding the warm wooden planked floor with a welcoming
glow. The numerous books, smelling wondrously of leather,
were arranged along deepset walls and shelves in protection
against stray sunbeams. A variety of tables glistening with bees-
wax and supporting at least five summery flower arrangements
were scattered throughout the august chamber. Long, gold velvet drapes hung to the sides of each of six tall windows. Above
each set of drapes, brass rods decorated with eagles supported
heavily fringed ivory velvet valances. Settees and comfortable
chairs in leathers and in gold velvet with an occasional Empire
chair covered in striped gold and ivory silk were arranged in
comfortable groupings throughout. In a recess between book-
shelves a charming decanter of sherry had been placed along-
side a dozen small glass stemmed goblets.

Thorpe rose from his chair near the north window and folded
up a copy of the *Times* setting it on a table next to the chair
upon which sat his own glass of wine. "Well met, Mrs. Ambergate? May I pour you a glass of sherry?"

"Very formal, my lord Thorpe," she returned, feeling at ease.
"And yes, indeed, you may."

He smiled. His face was sun-bronzed from the long ride they

had enjoyed together earlier. A sense of peace attended him as he moved across the chamber.

She joined him by the recessed wall and queried, "You are no longer angry with me?"

"What? For setting your horse to galloping when I didn't have an ounce of strength left in me to keep up with you?"

She chuckled as he poured her a glass of the nut-colored wine and handed it to her. She lowered her voice as she said, "I wasn't thinking of that, at all."

"Ah," he murmured, comprehending her. "You mean, am I angry that after making love to you, you rejected me?"

"I hardly rejected you," she said, meeting his gaze and feeling a familiar dizzy sensation flow over her. "I rejected what you were offering."

"I was offering myself," he stated.

She had the sense he liked talking about what had happened between them. "Whatever the particulars," she continued softly, "I am only glad that you got over your initial burst of rage so quickly. For a moment, that first night, I thought you were intent on exacting a pound of flesh because of my choices."

He chuckled out loud. "Come sit with me. My sherry is over here."

She followed him across the chamber. She was finding it quite agreeable to be alone with him.

"And may I say that you are elegantly gowned tonight. But then, you always are. I admire that in you, especially given your circumstances."

"But I have done so with a design, so do you still admire me?"

She sat down in one of the gold and ivory striped Empire chairs. He asked if she wished for a footstool and she did. She was much struck by this attention to her comfort as he brought the footstool forward and placed it beneath her feet.

She settled her slippers nicely on the low needlepoint stool, her heels settling on a kitten playing with yarn. He remained by her feet for a long moment and, looking up at her, began tracing his finger over her right ankle.

Jane caught her breath and glanced quickly toward the open doorway at the far end of the chamber. No one was there. She glanced back at Thorpe and stayed him by leaning forward and taking hold of his wrist. "Do not," she commanded him. "Have you gone mad?"

But he circled her hand quickly with a turn of his wrist and caught her fingers in a firm grasp. With his free hand he continued to trace his finger along her ankle. She felt his touch through her fine silk stocking. His finger circled to the back of her ankle and his palm was suddenly on her calf and moving in a long, languorous slide up her leg.

She drew in a pained breath for she felt as though her soul and her body had just caught fire. Oh, what Thorpe could do to her with a mere touch of his hand, a look of his eye, or a word uttered in his deep, resonant voice. She leaned back in her chair, her gaze never once wavering from his. She let him touch her leg. He slipped his finger beneath her garter and gave it a gentle tug. He smiled crookedly.

Then he stopped, quite suddenly, as quickly as he had begun, drawing her skirts back down about her ankles. He rose to stand over her, taking her hand in his. He looked down at her, holding her gaze again. "My dear, beautiful Jane," he whispered. "I want you so much that I ache just looking at you. I have from the first. And even though we've been together twice, I feel as though every time I look at you, or touch you, or hear you speak it is the first time all over again. Won't you reconsider my offer? Come to Europe with me. We'll make love every day, we'll go riding, you can teach me some of your archery skills, I can improve your fencing techniques, perhaps we could even write a play together."

Jane squeezed his hand tightly, the same way his words were serving to squeeze her heart. She knew the most outrageous impulse to say yes, not because she wanted to do all the things he had suggested but because she wanted to be with him.

She shook her head and he released her hand reluctantly, then resumed his seat.

From the corner of her eye Jane saw that Lady Somercote was entering the library. She turned and smiled at her good friend but noticed at once that something had happened, for the countess had a peculiar light in her blue eyes and walked on an unusually quick step. She wore an elegant Empire gown of white silk embroidered with gold thread, a gold silk shawl draped charmingly over her elbows, and in her hair several bands of gold in decreasing sizes had captured her peppered black hair in the traditional Greek manner. She looked as though she had just emerged from between the covers of *la Belle Assemblee*.

Thorpe rose to greet her, taking a gold silk glove in his hand and placing a friendly salute on her fingers. She smiled and tried to appear at ease, but there was a spriteliness to her manner, as she asked Thorpe how he was enjoying her husband's stables, that brought a quizzical expression to his eye as he answered her question.

"But you will have to excuse me," the countess said after listening distractedly to Thorpe. "For I fear I must steal Mrs. Ambergate from your side. You will forgive me, won't you?"

He nodded to her. "Of course."

Lady Somercote gestured for Jane to rise from her chair in so hurried a movement that Jane was now certain something untoward had occurred. Her own heart began to thrum gently against her ribs in a staccato of anticipation. News of last night's adventure, no doubt. Had Somercote discovered her charade?

Once they were in the hallway, Jane took Lady Somercote's arm and gave her a squeeze. "Do tell me what is going forward," she cried. "Though I believe I can guess and the news is good, is it not?"

"The news," Lady Somercote returned, "Is remarkable. Truly remarkable. Only, only I can't speak with you here. We must go somewhere to be private—the flower garden, I think."

Jane did not speak as the countess led her to the back of the house, onto the terrace, through a hedge, and into the fragrant

gardens. At the far end, the five coiled basket beehives, which
sat at homespun angles and from which honey was collected
daily, buzzed with activity. Jane picked up her demi-train and
again took up Lady Somercote's arm. She leaned into her in
order to hear her quietly spoken secrets.

"He never once suspected 'twas I who had come to his bedchamber," she said breathlessly, leaning her head near Jane's.
"He kept mumbling Mrs. Newstead's name—"

"And you didn't mind?" Jane cried, astonished.

She paused. "Do you want to know the truth?"

Jane looked at her, caught her gaze, and nodded her head
briskly. She was feeling very wicked of the moment.

"I wouldn't confess this to anyone else, but I rather found
the whole of it enormously exciting. There I was, pretending to
be Mrs. Newstead and dressed as Marie Antoinette. I was speaking with a French accent and he didn't suspect in the slightest
that he was kissing his wife! Really, it was extraordinary, though
I must say I took great pains not to do anything that might have
seemed familiar. And, and George—my goodness!—he was so
ardent in his expressions, his voice so full-throated and seductive and Jane, he did things he has never done before!"

Jane felt a blush creep up her cheeks. She bit her lip. She
waited to hear more, both fascinated and embarrassed at the
same time.

Lady Somercote continued, "I won't trespass on your sense
of modesty by revealing more except to say that had I known
such bliss was possible, I should have hired a dozen costumes
many years ago and kept them close at hand. So if you ask me
was I angry that he called me his darling Sophia, I'm afraid I
will have to tell you a firm, 'No.' What do you think of that?"

They were nearing the beehives and since Jane had a healthy
fear of the stinging creatures, she turned her hostess about and
encouraged her back toward the house by again taking her arm
and guiding her forward. "I don't know what to say," she said,
giving her dark brown curls a shake, "except perhaps to congratulate you. Were you never afraid of discovery?"

"A single candle burned on the chest of drawers across the room and I insisted the drapes be drawn about the bed. He did not demure and I never once removed my corset."

The images these details brought forward in Jane's mind caused a new blush to rise on her cheeks. She pressed an ivory silk gloved hand to her burning face and sighed. "I am so very happy for you. But what will happen when he learns he has been tricked?"

Lady Somercote trilled her laughter. "I don't intend to tell him, at least not right away. And besides, in my French accent last night I begged him not to address me on the following day about our romantic adventure."

"And he agreed?"

The countess nodded. "Of course, you should have seen how he ogled Mrs. Newstead at nuncheon. I only wish you had been there to see and to share in my secret for I nearly burst out laughing a dozen times and poor Mrs. Newstead kept nodding to him and smiling and finally frowning for he kept winking at her. I was never more delightfully amused in my entire existence."

"A just punishment for the pair of them," Jane pronounced.

"Indeed. But there is something you can do for me tonight."

Jane wondered what on earth her ladyship had in mind. "I will do whatever you ask of me."

A slow, devilish smile spread over the countess's face. "I want to borrow your Cleopatra costume and tomorrow, at some point during the canal ride and *al fresco* picnic, I want you to make it known that your costume is missing and cannot be found, that even your maid, Vangie, searched everywhere but could not locate the gown, the mask, or the black wig."

Jane giggled. "How very *risque*."

"Indeed," Lady Somercote responded on a happy sigh.

Nine

When Jane returned from the gardens with Lady Somercote's arm wrapped in a friendly manner about her own, she found Freddy pacing the light gray stone of the terrace. She learned quickly that he had been waiting for her, that he had something of a private nature he wished to say to her. He asked if Lady Somercote would be willing to relinquish Jane's arm that he might take it up and guide her through the yew maze.

Lady Somercote glanced toward Jane, smiled, and winked surreptitiously before turning to Freddy and acquiescing with a slight curtsy. Freddy, caught off guard by the countess's playful manner, jerked slightly as he received Jane's hand from her ladyship.

Lady Somercote bid them enjoy the yew maze which she then informed them was always at its most charming in the fading sunbeams of the late afternoon light. She then adjusted her gold silk shawl, twirled about in a happy circle, and tripped lightly into the house.

Jane, who had let down her demi-train of pale pink and green striped silk, again picked it up and allowed Freddy to guide her decorously down the three wide steps of the terrace. The yew maze was set at a distance from the terrace, just beyond a broad expanse of carefully groomed gardens in the French style of the mid-eighteenth century. Pathways of parquetried stone steps intermingled with flowerbeds, each of which were borded by low tight hedges and trimmed immaculately. A rose tree, bearing ivory-colored roses, stood rigidly in the center of each flower-bed. Every rose tree was surrounded by colorful pansies and purple allysum. The effect was uniform, and quite lovely in the measured manner of gardens before Capability Brown demanded a less structured approach to landscaping.

Lady Somercote had insisted that this last remnant of the previous gardens remain. Mr. Brown had found her insistence trying but had had to acquiesce in light of the fact that she had planted each tree lovingly with the help of her children many, many years ago.

Jane held the silk of her demi-train in her gloved hand and walked slowly beside her swain. She wondered what he would now say to her. Several times during her restful afternoon she had debated whether or not she ought to apologize for having abandoned him by the lake when she had taken up Colonel Duffield's irresistible offer of a horseback ride. But each time she had considered offering her apologies, a certain mulishness had overcome her spirit. She didn't want to apologize even though her conduct had been less than decorous or considerate. She was angry with him—angry that he had used Hetty to explain his dissatisfaction with her conduct and angry that later he felt it proper and right to come the crab with her over and over about the childlike parlor game.

Now, as she walked beside him, she felt not the smallest compunction to express regret over any of her conduct. She knew that he was nervous, for he had cleared his throat three times and otherwise could not seem to bring forward even a morsel of conversation to ease the tension between them, but her compassion for him was nonexistent at present. If she knew a nagging fear that her future was on a precipice of disaster as the maze drew nearer and nearer, she ignored it. Something far greater was at stake, something she had not quite identified as yet, but which seemed far more significant to her than whether or not she would be well settled by the end of the fortnight *fete*.

When she finally stepped into the first turn of the maze and began slowly wending her way toward the center, Freddy com-

menced a halting and quietly spoken speech. "I—I have come
to realize, my dearest Jane, that—that, I was completely beyond
the pale, earlier—before nuncheon today—when we were beside the lake. I fear that I . . ."

Jane turned to the left, then a quick turn to the right. He was
speaking in a low voice and she had lost the rest of his speech.
She stopped abruptly and turned around; he emerged into the
turn and bumped into her.

"Oh, I say!" he cried. "I am sorry." His hand was on her
arm. He let it rest there for a long moment.

He seems changed, Jane thought, surprised. "What did you
say? I mean, I didn't quite hear the last of your remarks."

He nodded slightly, and frowned. "I fear that I stepped far
beyond that which was proper. I . . ." His voice trailed off as
he held her gaze. His gold-green eyes wore a serious expression
she had never seen before. He let his hand drop.

Jane drew in a deep breath, feeling strangely confused. She
turned, the silk of her gown still in hand, and progressed more
deeply into the maze. She felt very odd, suddenly. Something
was happening between them. She could feel it as though it was
a tangible thing.

"Jane, I shouldn't have taken you to task as I did," he continued, close on her heels. "There. Do be careful, dearest. I see
a branch of yew that has not been trimmed."

"Yes, yes, thank you, Freddy," she said quietly as she pushed
the branch away from the delicate fabric of her pink and green
half-robe.

Another turn. His words were again lost to her. He stopped
speaking entirely until the final arch of the maze opened onto
the center of the maze.

Jane felt as though she was suffering a shock. Her cheeks
were tingling numbly. She didn't know whether she could speak,
and smiling was out of the question.

She sat down on the stone bench and he sat down beside her.
She released the silk of her demi-train and he gathered up her
hands in both of his. He kissed her fingers gently and began

offering his apologies in earnest. Though she was catching only one word in three, she realized he was humbling himself for his conduct earlier that day. She should have been *aux anges* at his shift in attitude toward her; instead she felt panicky. Her thoughts drifted back not more than a half-hour earlier when she had been alone with Thorpe in the library. She recalled vividly the touch of his fingers on her leg through the silk of her stockings. She remembered his passionately whispered speech as he begged her to come to Europe with him. Her desire to go with him, to be with him, rolled over her in a sudden wave of longing.

And all the while, Freddy kissed her fingers and spoke his apologies and regrets for having offended her.

She turned to look at him, wanting to beg him to stop and to insist that all had been a mistake between them, but the next moment he released her hands, caught her at the shoulders, drew her close to him, and placed a warm, moist kiss on her lips.

How different this kiss was, she thought, than the several he had given her in recent days. What had happened to him to have caused all his fears of her to evaporate so suddenly? She felt herself responding to the feel of his lips on hers. Hope trembled in her heart. Awareness swept over her that she had not been entirely mistaken in her choice of beau. She slipped her arm about his neck, he drew her more fully against him. Desire rushed over her in a wonderfully warm wave of sweet sensation.

After a long moment, he released her and looked wonderingly into her eyes. "Jane," he whispered. His breathing was shallow, he stared awestruck at her. "You squeeze the breath from me." Then he chuckled. "Not quite so poetically spoken, eh?"

Only then was Jane able to smile. Was love blossoming between them? Was it possible? Why had it suddenly bloomed?

"Freddy," she said softly, laying a hand on his coat of elegant black superfine, near the wide rolled and notched lapel. "I enjoyed winning the musical chairs. When you so heartily disapproved of my enjoyment and the expression of my enjoyment I was never more dismayed. I felt so hopeless that we could ever truly come to understand one another."

He drew her to him so that her curls and ostrich feather swept over his cheek and her head came to rest on his shoulder. "I daresay there will be many compromises one or the other of us will need to make over the years if we are both to be truly happy. I suppose I would only ask that you not engage in the game more than once a sennight."

Jane laughed. "I believe I could restrain myself for your sake," she responded, her heart lightening.

He hugged her. "My dearest Jane." She felt him shake his head as though trying to comprehend all that had happened, but one of her feathers must have tickled his nose for he suddenly sneezed violently and drew away from her. Jane watched him as he drew a kerchief from the pocket of his coat and blew his nose. "I say, not very romantic, is it?"

"I don't give a whit about that," she said, smiling softly. "I shan't wear feathers again if they disturb you this much."

He quickly took up his seat again beside her and possessed himself again of her hands. "You are very good, dear Jane." He kissed her fingers, each hand in turn. "When I saw you leap up beside Colonel Duffield, I was at first so much shocked that I must have appeared like a simpleton gaping after the pair of you as you galloped away. My mouth was agape and a gnat found his home on my tongue before I brought my senses to order. Had a dreadful time spitting the creature out."

Jane bit her lip. Sneezing was one thing, but spitting unfortunate insects out of one's mouth was another entirely. She swallowed and kept her countenance as he continued.

"I don't know what happened to me precisely after that, but after a few minutes, when you came galloping past the lake again and waved so happily to me, I felt as though I would swoon. You ripped my heart out of my breast when you burst past me on that wild horse. Only then did I realize that though I had thought we were in agreement about your conduct at the masquerade, I had been sadly mistaken. You were angry with me, weren't you, for speaking to you as I had—and perhaps a little for having had Hetty address you first?"

Jane was so relieved to have the whole of her sentiments laid out before her that she nodded immediately. "I was stunned. I didn't know what to say, and yes I was very angry. You ought never to feel there is anything you can't say directly to me, but at the same time, I'm not a child in need of a lecture."

"No, of course you are not. I was wrong, very wrong to have addressed you in such a manner. Forgive me?"

Jane nodded. Her thoughts ran like quicksilver over the forthcoming events. Saturday would see the end of the festivities. Five days only remained to bring her hopes to a fruitful conclusion. "Now that we understand one another better, I was wondering if you would care to ride with me to the caverns north of Wolfscar Ridge tomorrow morning. Lord Somercote has an excellent stable, the horses are of the finest blood, and I understand the caverns are but three miles distant and quite magnificent. We could go quite early and I believe the excursion would give us an opportunity to better know one another."

"I would like that," he said, very sincerely. "We have a great deal to discuss you and I, about the future. Do you intend to bring your maid?"

She shook her head. "I don't believe it to be necessary with you to protect me. I should like it very much if you alone had the responsibility for my protection, in every way, though generally only a husband bears such a responsibility."

There, she had said the words, she had brought forward the truth of her intentions toward him. Her hint lay heavily between them, his eyes grew misty as his gaze dropped to her lips. Instead of speaking, he leaned forward and his lips were again on hers, lazily, passionately.

Again, Jane felt desire ripple through her. She wondered how much more she could encourage him once they were at the caverns, and very much alone.

"I came to fetch you," a masculine voice erupted into the center of the maze. "They are all awaiting your arrival for dinner."

Jane flew back from her beau, stunned to have been caught

in such an indecorous *tête-à-tête* with Freddy. But she was further mortified to realize that it was Thorpe who had so abruptly disturbed their hugging and kissing.

Freddy rose to his feet, but Thorpe was ignoring him. The viscount had caught her gaze and was holding it firmly by the strength of his will. He was angry. She knew as much because she understood him, perhaps because she was so much like him.

Freddy was beckoning to her by holding his hand down to her. She rose from the stone bench, picked up her pink and green silk demi-train, and all the while Thorpe held her gaze, his thoughts punishing her, forcing her to admit to herself that she was a terrible hypocrite.

"Thank you, Lord Thorpe, for so kindly informing us," she breathed at last, the tension between them almost unbearable. "Will you lead the way?"

Only after a final, meaningful stare through narrowed eyelids, did Thorpe take his gaze from Jane's and dart a dissatisfied glance toward Freddy. He turned away abruptly after that and disappeared back into the maze.

Freddy entered the maze first, whispering to Jane that he would protect her from Thorpe by going first. Jane would have been gratified had his ability to protect her not been a complete absurdity. She sighed, knowing that though dinner would be an easy experience, and the enjoyment of hearing Hetty and Mrs. Newstead sing English and French ballads afterward, a delight, the very thought of facing Thorpe in the sword room nearly cast her into a fit of palpitations.

Her knees trembled at the mere thought of it.

Later that evening, Jane preceded Thorpe into the sword room, the train of her half-robe draped elegantly over her right wrist and the papers containing the outline of their vignette cradled in her left arm. She walked with her head high, knowing full well that Lord Thorpe meant to torment her.

"So Waingrove finally summoned enough courage to kiss you again, eh?"

Jane did not respond. Instead, she crossed to the round table, glaring at the spiked ball, and set the papers down. "I suggest," she began as she turned around to face the viscount, "that for tonight at least we forget about our ongoing quarrel and see what we might accomplish with regard to the vignette we will be expected to perform with some degree of polish in three days' time.

He did not answer her but instead joined her by the table and slapped the ink tray, silver pot of ink, and several stained pens down beside the stack of papers. Jane jumped slightly.

"What a witch you are," he murmured.

Jane gasped, frowned, and glared at him. "How unkind of you," she stated simply.

He returned her angry gaze, his nostrils flaring, the light from the candelabra near the spiked ball casting his handsome features in a reddish-gold glow. "You must be a witch," he continued, his voice low, his striking blue eyes narrowing. "How else can I explain my rage at seeing your lips touching that mealy-mouthed gudgeon." He flung his arm out and pointed toward the door as though Freddy was just beyond it.

Jane blinked, trying very quickly to comprehend precisely what he was saying to her.

He turned his back to her, stared hard in the direction of the fireplace, then took several steps away from her. "Did you enjoy kissing him?" he asked, crossing his arms over his chest.

Jane was stunned, not by the nature of the question but by what she believed lay beneath his brutal comments, and now by his abrupt searching of her sentiments. She slowly left the table and took several steps in a narrow berth around him in order that she might look into his face. He was enraged and something more she could not quite fathom. He would not meet her gaze directly. Yet she could see his eyes, that in them resided a cloaked expression she had never seen before, wary, deeply serious, intense. "You want to know if I enjoyed kissing Freddy Waingrove," she reiterated.

He nodded, his eyes narrowing to slits, but still he did not look at her.

She recalled the sensations she had experienced earlier in Freddy's arms, a birthing of desire and even of passion. "Yes," she responded simply. "Though I must confess that I was myself surprised. But then Freddy had just humbled himself to me and I found that his sincerity spoke to my heart."

The odd look in Thorpe's eyes seemed to deepen. His jaw worked strongly but she sensed that anger was not ruling him in this moment—but if not anger, then what?

"Then you mean to continue setting your cap for him?"

Jane nodded. "He is escorting me to the caverns tomorrow. I expect he will offer for me then. He hinted as much."

Thorpe turned around abruptly and moved back to the ink pot, pens, and papers. He was silent for a long moment, his neck, back, and shoulders tense. He picked up a pen and began slowly tapping the tip in a marked rhythm against the top paper.

Jane watched him, letting her gaze rove from his neatly brushed, thick black hair to the uppermost folds of his neck-cloth, to the high rise of his rolled coat collar, to the narrow line of his waist and the flare of coat-tails below. He wore black pantaloons and fine black leather slippers. Every line of his costume accentuated his strong, athletic body. His shoulders were broad. She knew an impulse to approach him, to run a hand across his shoulders, to feel the strength of him. Whatever newly birthed sensations had occurred between herself and Freddy earlier in the evening, they would never hold a candle to the way the mere physical presence of Thorpe made her feel. There had never been a single moment, even from that first day in Hyde Park, that she had not known an almost overpowering desire to be held in his arms, to be kissed by him, to be caressed by him. She could no more explain these extraordinary impulses than she could explain the presence of the man in the moon.

She reached a hand out toward him, her heart in her throat, strange tears in her eyes.

"I suppose then," he spoke at last, his shoulders drooping a little, the tone of his voice resigned, "we should proceed as you suggested, to complete our vignette that we might not disgrace ourselves come Thursday night."

Jane let her hand drop. "That would be best," she murmured.

He turned to look at her and what Jane saw on his face almost catapulted her into his arms. She saw longing, desire, everything that reflected her own feelings. She took in a breath and literally tore her gaze away from his. She felt the air crackle all about her. She swallowed hard and approached the table. Her hands trembled as she picked up the sheets.

His hand shot out and quickly covered hers. "Why are you trembling?" he asked in a hoarse whisper.

His touch was like molten metal on her skin. She wanted to cry out for the pain of it. She was in agony, wanting to tell him the truth, but not wanting him to know lest he take sore advantage of her—again. Today, she knew she had given part of her heart to Freddy. She could not then be so unfaithful, so disloyal, as to continue to permit Thorpe to touch her, to kiss her, and certainly not to make love to her.

With every ounce of strength she possessed, she drew her hand away from his, picked up the papers, and at the same time moved away from the table. Though her voice shook, she began to read aloud the parts of the vignette they had completed and the parts that yet remained to be written and orchestrated with fencing movements. She walked around the room, willing her voice to grow calm and her sentiments to dim sufficiently to progress in their vignette.

He followed her lead, a circumstance for which she found herself infinitely grateful. She began to write, to make corrections, to listen to his suggestions, to offer ideas of her own. He listened, he responded, they worked through every nuance of the vignette. He removed two swords from the wall and hour upon hour they rehearsed the scene, getting each word, each movement right. Always the scene ended the same way, he asked her to become his mistress and she responded, she could not because she was choosing not just for herself but for her children.

"Let's go through it one last time," he said. "Then I think we shall have mastered it."

"Yes," Jane said, aware that a seriousness now existed between them that had not existed before. She stood back to back with Thorpe. She bore a sword in hand and her arms were crossed over her chest as were his.

After a brief ten minutes and only a little stumbling, the rehearsal was complete and the vignette drew to a close as she said, "I choose not for myself, my lord, but for my children."

He let his sword fall and she held hers tightly across her chest. At this moment in the vignette, they faced one another. She smiled faintly. "Our audience will not know we are through until we link arms and turn to bow to them."

"Are we through, Jane?" he asked.

Jane looked into questioning eyes, but she couldn't bring herself to respond with the appropriate answer. Of course they were through. They had been finished before they had begun. He held her gaze firmly as he always did. He leaned down and retrieved his sword, he took back her gaze, he crossed his sword over hers and rasped steel against steel.

"I'm not finished with you yet," he whispered. "Our vignette may be complete, but you and I are not."

She gathered up her demi-train in her left hand. She took a step backward, he stepped toward her. Still he kept his sword pressed to hers. "What are you about, Thorpe?" she breathed. "Enough. Enough of this nonsense, I say."

"Never enough," he returned. She flicked her wrist and forced his sword off of hers.

He opened up his stance and thrust his sword at her, the point pressed into her stomach. She swatted it away with her hand.

"You are being absurd," she stated, fear and anger vying for supremacy within her. "Thorpe, do stop. You are making a cake of yourself." She was lying, she knew she was lying and in her heart rose the awful truth that she didn't want him to stop. Her breathing grew shallow and she felt dizzy. He kept pressing her, forcing her backward, step by step until he had backed her into a dark corner. His features were barely distinguishable as he removed the sword-tip from her stomach and moved to stand over her. Dropping his sword, he planted his hands on the wall behind her at each shoulder.

"Jane," he whispered, "there is nothing absurd about our being together."

Jane felt the breath desert her body. He leaned himself up against her and placed kisses at her temples. She closed her eyes, thrilling to the feel of his body touching hers along her thighs, her hips, her stomach, her breasts. Her sword slipped from her hand and clattered to the floor.

His lips drifted lower to cover her eyelids in a languorous sweep. She breathed in deeply, or at least tried to. "Thorpe," she murmured, gasping. He kissed her cheeks. Lower and lower he descended until he was barely brushing her lips. Over and over he kissed her lips until his tongue began to touch her and to tease her. She parted her lips and he ran his tongue over the sensitive inner rim until she was gasping with pleasure.

He moved his hips against hers and she arched her neck, barely stifling a groan. He crashed his mouth down on hers, thrusting his tongue deeply inside her mouth. She moaned, sliding her arms around his back and holding him fast. His hips rolled into her again, his tongue drove hard into her mouth. He moved her from against the wall and took her into his arms. His hand caressed her back, her waist, and her buttocks. He held her fast, pinning her into the roll of his hips until desire was flooding her. Only a thin layer of clothes separated the kiss from what it really was—Thorpe was making love to her, again.

She began clutching at his coat. The physical need he had aroused in her demanded release. "Please, Thorpe," she whispered, trying to pull him to the floor.

But instead of obliging her he grew strangely still. He stopped kissing her, he released her buttocks, he stared down at her. "You see," he whispered, "we are not through. We will never be through, Jane. Never. Not until you have become my mistress and we've had our day."

He let her go, he bowed to her. He picked up both swords, replaced them, and afterward quit the chamber.

Jane remained standing where she was, her entire body a hum of unfulfilled desire. Her heart felt numb as did her limbs. She couldn't seem to make her feet move, or her arms. Finally, she took a deep breath and set her slippers in motion. Perhaps she wasn't quite able to feel her feet as she walked but at least the round table was drawing closer and closer.

She picked up the vignette and stared at the opening words, *We are not three acts and a farce, but a vignette, two flames that come together and burn each other to cinders.* She may not have felt burned to cinders, of the moment, but as she clutched the pages to her breast and headed ever so slowly toward the door in order to return to her bedchamber, she decided she definitely felt singed, rather heavily singed if she was any judge of the way she felt.

On the following morning, Jane dressed in her very best riding costume of midnight-blue velvet bearing a long train of the same fabric to cover her ankles. On her head sat a charming black hat with black net over the forehead and a long, black ostrich feather streaming behind but curling around to touch her shoulder. She wore black leather gloves and black half-boots. Vangie smiled and exclaimed when the last ringlet on her forehead was set in place.

Jane, too, was quite content with her appearance as she regarded her reflection in the looking-glass. Freddy would approve, perhaps not of the audacious hat, but at least of the high-waisted gown that covered her modestly in yards and yards of blue velvet.

Thorpe would adore her hat.

Her heart grew very still as Lord Thorpe came to mind. She recalled in vivid detail how close she had come, yet again, to succumbing to his advances. Why had he let her go, she wondered, except that he had wanted to prove to her that she couldn't resist him. In that he had succeeded and he had left her feeling ill with desire for him.

Several times, as she dressed for bed last night and upon awakening this morning, she had reviewed all that had happened—both between her and Freddy and between her and Thorpe. She knew that she and Freddy were progressing in their love for one another. So how then was it possible that when Thorpe touched her, kissed her, held himself pinned against her, regardless of her feelings for Freddy, she was ready to give herself to Thorpe like a common tavern wench?

But then that had been perhaps the mystery from the beginning—her sheer physical desire for Lord Thorpe.

She smiled suddenly as she regarded her reflection. But her desire for Thorpe didn't have to dictate the course of her life, not by half. In all her ruminations, not once did she feel it to be a good and proper thing for her to finally acquiesce to Thorpe's schemes. On the contrary, even though he had all but made love to her last night, her conclusions had remained firm—she would marry Freddy.

And today, at the caverns, she meant to bring the whole of their relationship to its final, proper conclusion. By the time she left the caverns she would be betrothed to Freddy Waingrove.

Swinging the train of her habit up over her arm, she took her leather riding crop from her abigail and on a happy step left her bedchamber. She met no one on the stairs which she descended gleefully, running almost the entire way. She enjoyed running and riding and swimming. She could hardly wait to go to the caverns with Freddy, to enjoy his company, to see in what ways yesterday's kiss in the yew maze would now affect their future together. Everything had changed since yesterday.

But when she reached the entrance hall and found the butler waiting for her bearing a missive settled on an elegant silver salver, a sensation of foreboding turned her stomach upside down.

She recognized Freddy's handwriting at once. She took the brief letter, turned away from the butler, and began to read.

My dearest one, the missive began. *I fear I cannot go with you today to the caverns. I have the headache, a complaint which afflicts me more often than is at all reasonable, I know. Pray forgive me. Please don't stay your pleasant journey on my account. Miss Hartworth has sent for the physician and is presently searching for more laudanum for me, so you may be assured I will be well attended to. Perhaps we can go another time.*

It was all of a piece, Jane thought unhappily. She heard the butler's footsteps down the hall finally fade away to nothing. Freddy's pattern remained—he would make an effort, then somehow the next moment he would fail her completely. She had been depending on an excursion to the caverns to seal their lives together once and for all. She had meant for him to speak of his love for her. She had meant for him to kiss her again and again. She had meant for his growing passion to facilitate the words, *Jane, will you become my wife?*

Now she had but three days, three days to secure a proposal of marriage from him, for today was all but lost to her.

Three days! She groaned inwardly.

In only four days from now, on Saturday, when the recessional would take place, Freddy would be returning to his home in Shropshire. She had no invitation to visit him there—his overprotective mother would never allow an unknown female to attend her in her son's house!

Jane pressed a hand to her head, feeling her own temples begin to pulse with the dread of her situation. She had counted on a trip to the caverns to settle everything. Why had he failed her? The trouble was, she knew deep in her heart that if he did not come up to scratch by Friday, she would not see him again until the following spring, by which time she would be in debtors' prison—or worse, on the Continent travelling as Thorpe's mistress.

But why had Freddy failed her? It made no sense, no sense at all, especially after the wondrous kisses they had shared in the yew maze. So, what was it he feared so much that his headaches must rule his body and force her to wait in the wings like an understudy to a seasoned actress?

Second by second, she felt her spirits plummeting to a familiar place of despair, a place she did not want to be.

She took in a deep breath, and breathed out her horrid disappointment. She slapped her riding crop against her thigh twice, very hard, and bade herself not to sink into a fit of the sullens. She dropped her train and, glancing to the south, she turned on a determined foot and headed toward the music room from which vantage point she would make her way to the stables.

Freddy be hanged, then, she thought. The caverns north of Wolfscar were reputed to be fascinating and beautiful and she meant to see them. Besides, what she needed right now was a hard ride across the countryside.

Thorpe stood at the window of his bedchamber and watched the beautiful red deer mince their way down the slopes in the cool morning sunlight. Challeston had one of the finest aspects in all of England and a herd of deer that pleased the eye to the point of bliss.

He wondered, for the hundredth time, if he had erred in pressing Jane so hard last night, literally and figuratively. As he reviewed all of the twistings and turnings of his feelings from the time he had discovered her kissing Freddy until he had left her dazed in the sword room, he found himself bemused by what he was feeling. When he had seen her embracing Waingrove, her lips pressed to his, a bolt of sheer rage had passed through him, leaving his muscles tense with unreleased energy. He had wanted to march across the short square, pull Freddy up by the lapels, and plant him a facer for having kissed the woman he had made his object. The only thing that had prevented his doing so was the simple fact that he knew if he had, he would have destroyed all that he had been creating in his seduction of Jane. If he had never before known such a fit of jealousy, he carefully tucked away the nagging thought and concentrated instead on letting Jane know by his expression just how much he disapproved of her conduct.

As he thought of precisely that moment, however, his mind became fixed on one particular aspect of the event—the way Jane had looked while kissing Freddy, with her eyes closed and a sweetness in her expression that spoke to him of love.

A sharp pain ripped through his chest.

Good God, he thought. Was it possible Jane was actually falling in love with Freddy Waingrove? But that was impossible. Surely. Yet why would it be so impossible? Freddy treated Jane as though she was a rare jewel, to be treasured and adored. Forget that Jane preferred a rougher, more vital form of address, what woman would not be persuaded by adoration and respect?

He laughed bitterly at the thought. Why did he not adore and respect Jane? Or did he?

He felt so confused.

Though he believed Waingrove was far beyond being able to manage such a woman, certainly during the rough waters of the married state, what if Freddy actually summoned enough courage, enough spirit, to finally beg for her hand? What if in a moment of passion—conducted, for instance, at the caverns near Wolfscar—Freddy at last succumbed to the beauty of Jane's face, to the richness of her character, to the fire of her passions, and offered for her hand in marriage? What then? Jane would say yes and she would never jilt a man. Never. Not Jane. However ignoble her pursuit, she was a woman of honor and once her commitment was made, she would never leave a man at the altar.

Never before, during any of his previous pursuits, had he experienced such raw and quixotic changes in emotion as he had in this one with Jane Ambergate. Even now as he thought of her, his heart curled up in his chest, his stomach churned with excitement and every physical sensation became centered on just how soon, how quickly, he could again take her in his arms. The result was an ache so new to him and so thrilling that he was beginning to wonder if life would ever be the same again after Jane.

He touched the blue velvet drapes of his chamber, the soft fabric a delight to the tips of his fingers. Except for donning his coat, he was ready for the day, ready to see Jane again, to discover just how far the last kiss he had planted on her more than willing lips had turned her away from her present schemes.

Of course he would have to wait until she returned from her horseback ride to the caverns with Waingrove, but he was convinced he had initiated some good effect on her. He squeezed his eyes shut, remembering how fully aroused he had been while holding her in his arms and how badly he had wanted to oblige her by taking her to the floor and finishing what he had started. But however much he had ached to touch her more intimately, to enter her, to join with her, he knew he had been right in leaving her when he did. He wanted her to know the extent of her need of him and that he could fulfill her if she would only relent.

As he watched the deer beyond the yew maze and the formal French gardens, he was suddenly aware of two figures who entered the gardens from the rear stone terrace of the house. He watched disinterestedly until he realized that one of the figures was Freddy Waingrove. He glanced quickly to the bonneted woman beside him, thinking that for some reason Jane had cancelled the excursion to the caverns, until he saw a rather ugly yellow poke bonnet trimmed with an uninteresting bunch of something that looked like cherries. Jane would never wear a bonnet like that, he thought, disgusted.

A ripple of excitement coursed through him. Who was Freddy walking with at this hour of the morning when he was supposed to be at the caverns with Jane?

Miss Hartworth, of course.

He shook his head. Now that he thought on it, Miss Hartworth was always near Freddy when Jane was far away. Did the apparently docile and fragile young woman have designs of her own? Why not? In fact, the more he thought on it, the more they were suited. As though that mattered. All he cared about was the clear fact that Freddy was not with Jane.

He watched Freddy tilt his head down toward Henrietta. He

saw how languidly they moved through the French parquetry of the gardens toward the maze.

Another jolt of excitement struck him. He turned back into the room.

"Trimble," he called out curtly.

From across the elegant chamber, decorated in fine walnut woods, deep blue velvets, and a patterned Aubusson carpet, his valet emerged on a stately tread from the attached dressing room.

"Yes, m'lord," the valet stated, unperturbed at having been summoned so abruptly.

"I want my riding gear."

A faint lift of the brow was the only indication of surprise his longtime servant exhibited as he inclined his head and murmured a polite, "Yes, m'lord."

"Oh, and Trimble, there is one piece of discreet information I need, and I need it quickly."

Another faint lift of a dark brown brow. "Yes, m'lord?"

"I want you to discover if Mrs. Ambergate has mounted a horse and gone for a ride."

"Yes, m'lord."

Twenty minutes later, having learned that Freddy was suffering the headache again, and that Miss Hartworth was apparently conducting his recovery with her own peculiar methods of nursing, and satisfied that Jane had gone to the caverns despite Waingrove's cancellation of their plans, Thorpe was galloping down the lane toward the village of Ox Bow.

Jane dismounted her black gelding outside the caverns and tied the reins of her horse to a nearby tree. She had heard much about the beauty of the cave and though she still knew a nagging, unsettling disappointment that Freddy had forsaken her, she was looking forward to investigating the cavern for its own sake. After riding hard, her brow was touched with perspiration, her heart was beating strongly in her breast, and her sensibilities were greatly soothed.

The wide mouth of the cave beckoned her and, after folding back the black net of her veil onto the shallow brim of her hat, she entered the dank-smelling opening with anticipation. The light faded quickly, however, and she paused at the top of a flight of manmade stone stairs to descend into the first of what had been described to her as several rooms or chambers. When her eyes began to adjust to the dimness of the light, she descended the remaining stairs. When she reached the bottom and felt the sandy earth beneath her half-boots, she turned to look into the first chamber.

She caught her breath. The stalactites and stalagmites were enormous in size and the cavern seemed to extend far back into the recesses of the hill until the lack of light could no longer reveal the depth. A pocket of illumination came from a narrow crevice in the rock to her right and as she scanned the floor of the cave, she noted that a thin layer of water formed a pool along the bottom of the cave. To the left was a clearly marked pathway.

She began to move along the path, noting how close the pool frequently touched the edges of the path and once or twice actually swallowed up the path for a foot or two. She carefully traversed each section of water, skipping lightly across to carefully pick her way into another chamber. The direction of the path took her more deeply and farther down into the cavern, more so when another brief flight of stairs led to a place where she could fully view a third magnificent chamber.

Again, a shaft of light near the ceiling of the cave, perhaps also manmade, illuminated the cavern. She stood awestruck as she viewed the intricate, ancient shapes of the limestone stalactites. The silence of the cave soothed her. The beautiful light blue colorings along the rim of the pool sent a shiver of appreciation through her.

She still held her riding crop in her hand and she tapped it against her palm. Freddy would have liked the caverns, she realized unhappily. Almost at the same moment, she heard a voice call to her, a man's voice. Her heartbeat quickened.

Freddy had changed his mind. Surely he had realized that he had failed her and he had saddled a horse and come after her.

"Follow the path," she called back. "You must see this cave. There is a delightful blue color to the pool that—"

A man appeared at the top of the short flight of stone steps. How strange that though she was hoping and anticipating the arrival of Freddy Waingrove, the sight of Lord Thorpe in the aperture between the chambers did not in the least dismay her. Instead, she sighed and grimaced. "I suppose you somehow learned that my beau did not keep his assignation with me?"

Thorpe chuckled and descended lightly the few steps leading into the chamber. She watched him walk toward her with long, loose strides and felt his very presence give a hard tug on her heart. "Yes, I saw Mr. Waingrove walking toward the yew maze with Miss Hartworth and decided he must have once again broken a promise to you." When he reached her, a frown overtook his handsome features. "What is it?"

How could Jane possibly express what she was feeling? He had seen Freddy walking with Miss Hartworth. "Are you sure it was Freddy you saw?" she queried.

He nodded.

"But he told me he was too ill to escort me to the caverns."

"Apparently, Miss Hartworth cured him," he responded dryly. "She had certainly been seeking laudanum for some time. One of the footmen disturbed me in the middle of my morning cup of coffee requesting as much."

Quite absently, Jane let her gaze fall to the intricate folds of his cravat. She reached up and touched the folds with her finger. What had the design been called, *Thorpe's Revenge?* She wondered again at the name. The smell of his soap again touched her senses; she closed her eyes. So Freddy had been well enough to escort Miss Hartworth into the gardens. She wondered what Hetty would say this time. Probably something like, *I told him the fresh air would undoubtedly dispel the nagging pain in his head, and so it did. When you are betrothed, Jane, you will need to know precisely how to care for his delicate condition.*

Why was Freddy so deuced delicate!

"Don't look so downcast," he said.

Jane blinked and looked up at Thorpe. Now why couldn't Thorpe and Freddy have been one person, she wondered distractedly. The part of him that was Thorpe would never have failed to keep one of their assignations, and the part of him that was Freddy would have begged for her hand in marriage.

"I should go," she murmured, turning away from him. She felt inordinately vulnerable and not for the world did she want him to know as much.

He caught her arm and drew her toward him. "I can see that you're overset," he whispered softly.

"Yes," she said. "I am."

"He's not worthy of you. Take me, Jane. I'm here. I'm here now."

"I know," she murmured, her eyes cast down. She felt her spirit striving within her. All she had to do was take one step, then another, and she would be outside the caverns, she would be astride her horse, she would succeed in escaping Thorpe's devilish persuasions. Yet she did not move.

He took her chin in hand and forced her to look at him. The dim light of the caverns gave his face a dark, exotic appearance. Only his eyes were the same blue, piercing shards that had from the first had the ability to turn her knees to water. She was dizzy again as he leaned down to kiss her.

She was lost, completely lost. She knew as much the moment his lips touched hers. His lips moved lightly over hers, his tongue a feathery touch that caused her abdomen to tighten. She moaned faintly. His tongue flicked her lips until they parted naturally. As so many times before he began a gentle search of her mouth. She fell against him, a wave of pent-up desire cascading over her as he thrust his tongue against hers in quick, fluttery movements. He lightly touched her breast, teasing her. She moaned again.

He drew her gently to the sandy floor of the cavern, exploring her curves with wicked sensuality. Lost was her ability to reason; she could only feel and beg for release. He obliged her, working her clothing away, as well as his own, and in a careful, loving manner, he took possession of her, just as he had done twice before.

Jane wrapped her arms tightly about his neck as he fulfilled the promise he had been making to her since he first spoke with her at Challeston—that she would know great pleasure with him if she would but only let herself go. He drove her toward the edge of madness, claiming her lips again and again with hot, feverish kisses. Upward, he forced her, rising toward the pinnacle of passion only to fall back. Again he pressed her, his hips matching hers in a rhythm as perfect as it was ancient.

"Look at me, Jane," he commanded her.

She opened heavy eyelids and fell into the deep perfect blue of his eyes. Ecstasy swelled within her. She began to soar as he held her gaze, climbing with lightning speed to a place of infinite pleasure. "Thorpe," she breathed. Her back arched, her body shuddering with desire.

Only then did he ride her hard. She whimpered and called out his name again and again as together their passion roared to a wall of brilliant light and unextinguishable flames.

Jane disappeared, or at least that's what she felt happened. She was panting hard, trying to catch her breath, but her mind slipped into a place of perfect peace. After a few minutes, she lay still beneath Thorpe, whose own breathing had abated, as well.

"We must talk," he said after a long moment, rising up on his elbows to look down at her.

"No," she murmured. "Not now, not today. What I just did was wrong. I'm—I'm sorry." She felt tears sting her eyes.

"Why do you resist me so? You only torment yourself."

"I know. Thorpe, please leave me. I beg of you. We can talk of our circumstances later, tomorrow perhaps, but not now. I—I can't bear it now."

He allowed her to have her way. A few minutes later he was gone.

Ten

Jane walked down the path from the stables heading toward the music room. She wasn't certain what state her hair was in, though she knew that sand still fell from her tousled curls as she reached the door leading into the antechamber. Thorpe had already returned, the head groom had told her as much. She had just missed him by a matter of minutes. Her only concern now was to avoid seeing as many of Lady Somercote's guests as possible.

But the first sight that met her eyes as she crossed the antechamber and neared the music room was Hetty seated at the pianoforte and Freddy leaning over her. "No, no," he was saying kindly, but firmly. "There—the second measure. A half rest, not a quarter rest."

"Oh, how silly of me," Hetty replied. "No wonder we have stumbled time and again. Do forgive my stupidity. And I do think Jane will like your selection. What is it called again?"

"The Lucky Escape. I wonder what Charles Dibdin had in mind when he composed it?"

Hetty giggled. "Perhaps he was betrothed to a female whose mother he could not abide and the young lady eloped with another man. I should think any man would consider an obnoxious mother-in-law a fate to be escaped if at all possible."

He sighed suddenly. "You are referring to my mama, are you not—only in reverse?"

Hetty gasped. "Of course I am not!" she cried. "I would not be so cruel as to malign that good woman."

"You needn't spare my feelings," he said despondently. "I know what she is. Why the servants call her the Witch."

"They do?" Hetty breathed, shocked.

Freddy nodded. "But I refuse to be downcast by such unhappy thoughts of her. She loves me and in that I shall be content. Which brings to mind something I have been wishing to ask you, how fares your dear mother? Is her toe still swollen beyond measure?"

Hetty giggled again and pointed to the music. "Well, not beyond this measure."

Freddy chuckled along with Henrietta who then assured her duet partner that her mother fared very well. "But we ought to begin practicing again or you will only embarrass yourself in front of your beloved."

"You are goodness itself, Miss Hartworth. What would I have done without you this fortnight. Your support of my efforts in matters of the heart and the head—" They looked at one another and again began to giggle before he continued. "At any rate, I do thank you for all your kindnesses. My headache is gone!"

Hetty smiled up at him, her expression enrapt with delight at his expressions of gratitude. "We have been friends for so long that what else could I do but be of service to you."

Jane thought the whole of it a great deal of nonsense and then a little more. But as she watched the pair in front of her, she was a little astonished when Freddy's complexion became patched with red splotches as he looked deeply into Hetty's eyes.

Jane felt her own heart lurch a little. What did this mean?

Hetty's complexion grew quite pale and all the laughter died from her youthful features. She blinked up at Freddy and slowly began to shake her head. She blinked a little more, tilted her head as though to receive his lips, but then suddenly jerked herself back to her music and plunged into the piece settled before her on the fine rosewood pianoforte.

Freddy leaned back, placed a hand across his chest, and patted the place above his heart. He cleared his throat several times before beginning. *"I that once was a plough man—"*

Jane did not remain to listen further, but reversed her steps, left the antechamber, and circled the mansion to the back terrace where she mounted the steps and entered the house slowly, her long, dirty blue velvet train slung over her arm.

But as she crossed halfway to the hall leading to the circular entrance hall, Mr. Ullstree emerged from an antechamber that connected to a small, gold and red receiving room near the ballroom. She bowed slightly to him and would have passed on hurriedly, but he stopped her with an abruptly raised hand, a finger to his lips, and a quick, excited beckoning motion. He wanted to show her something. She stopped in mid-stride and found she could not keep from joining him by the half-open doors of the chamber.

Mr. Ullstree, his puffy face creased with a smile and covered in something of a flush, kept his finger to his lips as she tiptoed toward him. Her curiosity was now fully caught as she reached the doorway. She lifted inquiring brows to him and he jerked his head toward the parted door.

Jane listened and soon heard the undertones of a conversation. A moment later the words of the principals reached her. "Are you telling me, Sophia, that he has wagered his hand in marriage against succeeding at his schemes?" Jane could not mistake Colonel Duffield's voice.

"Yes," Mrs. Newstead replied brightly. "If he loses the wager, he must marry me."

"Marry you?"

"Why do you seem so surprised? You know that I have been in love with him forever and he is not entirely indifferent to me?"

"You don't *love* him, m'dear, you *want* him, you *desire* him, you *lust* for him, but you do not *love* him."

"Why do you quibble over words," she protested. A giggling

followed. "All I know is that being his mistress was not enough, not by half, and I mean to have him."

"You'll never succeed, for he is in *love* with Mrs. Ambergate."

"He does not *love* her. He *wants* her, he *desires* her, he *lusts* after her."

Jane heard the colonel chuckle. "You are mistaken, but you will never believe me were I to explain the difference."

Mrs. Newstead sighed. "I don't give a fig for any of it anyway. By the time I leave—and I have the means to achieve it—I intend to wed Lord Thorpe."

"Now what cobwebs have cluttered up that silly mind of yours, I wonder."

"How cruel you are." Jane heard the pout in her voice and even now could see the dimpling expression Mrs. Newstead used whenever she wished to appear adorable and irresistible— a tactic which seemed mysteriously never to fail.

A silence followed and Jane's gaze met Mr. Ullstree's wide open stare. They blinked together and Jane bit her lip. She should leave the doorway, she should not be eavesdropping in this truly reprehensible manner, but she couldn't seem to order her feet to move away from the door.

"There," Colonel Duffield said. "Tell me now that you insist on Thorpe."

A purring sound followed. "I insist on Thorpe."

Another long silence ensued.

"Tell me again," Colonel Duffield commanded.

"Don't be a goose," Mrs. Newstead said. "Stubble it and kiss me again."

At these words, Jane retreated and Mr. Ullstree quickly caught up with her. "There is more," he whispered. "All that I heard earlier. Do you wish to hear it?"

"No," Jane whispered, refusing to be drawn in further as she passed into the hallway leading toward the entrance hall and the staircase.

He dogged her heels. "You should hear me out," he whispered again, "for you figure largely in the conversation. There is something you ought to know."

Jane shook her head violently as she pressed two fingers to his chest. "No, I pray you, don't say another word."

He ceased following her at that moment and merely smiled upon her quite sympathetically. "As you wish, m'dear." He then turned around and began a quick progress to the back of the mansion. Jane had the truly wretched sense that he was returning to his former post for the strict and quite pleasurable business of listening to Colonel Duffield make pretty love to Mrs. Newstead.

Jane put a foot on the bottom step of the staircase, ready to flee to her bedchamber, when Freddy's voice stopped her.

"Jane," he called to her. "Whatever happened to you? Your gown is creased and covered with dirt of some kind."

Jane felt a blush creep up her cheek as she turned to greet her swain. "Oh, hallo, Freddy," she said, straightening her shoulders and trying to compose her ruffled sensibilities. She felt as though she had been caught tying her garter in public. "Hallo, Hetty. I see you have worked your wiles again and cured our dear Mr. Waingrove of another of his unfortunate headaches."

"Isn't it wonderful," she said, her smile thin and her complexion still quite pale. "For after only a drop of laudanum and a half-hour dabbing lavender water on his temples, he was strong enough to take a turn about the formal gardens. By then he professed the pain was gone."

Jane glanced at Freddy and saw that his expression was rather sheepish, just as it ought to be. She lifted a faint brow. "I congratulate you on your recovery, but truly I am presently unfit for company. I—I fell from my horse near Glapwich Stream—"

Freddy moved hurriedly toward her and took hold of her hand. "Are you all right, my pet?" he asked, his green-gold eyes filled with concern and anxiety. "You are not hurt? Should we not consult with a surgeon to make certain?"

Jane felt a rush of impatience strike her at his ridiculous

words. "Of course I am all right," she stated irritably. "If I weren't I would have been brought home in a cart by some poor farm laborer who chanced upon me. Please, do let me return to my bedchamber and tend to my, my bruises."

He let her hand go and she quickly mounted the stairs.

As she reached the first curve, she glanced down and saw that Hetty had moved to stand quite near him. She was holding his hand in a comforting manner and her whispers rose straight up the stairwell. "She seems very angry. You ought to have gone to the caverns with her."

"I know. I have used her ill."

"But your song this evening will please her and she will forgive you. Jane has the most forgiving of spirits. She is the kindest lady I know."

Jane watched them and wondered. She realized that they had forgotten all about her though their words remained fixed on her exclusively. How very odd. She thought it might be wise if, once she and Freddy were married, Miss Hartworth visited Swan Court only on the rarest of occasions.

Once they were married.

Jane slowed her steps as she reached the landing of the first floor. She didn't want to marry anyone. What she wanted was to go with Thorpe to Vienna, to Florence, to Rome, and to hire a yacht with which to sail about the Mediterranean and tempt the quick, light Corsairs to try to kidnap and ransom them both.

Lethargically she moved down the hall to her bedchamber. She needed a hot bath and the moment she entered her room, she rang for her maid.

A hot bath and a strong dose of common sense, that was what she needed.

She squeezed her eyes shut, waiting for Vangie to arrive. She had now made love with Thorpe three times, thoroughly, roughly, passionately. But there might easily be a most unwelcome, yet welcome result of such forbidden unions—a child. She pressed her hand against her abdomen, wondering if already such an eventuality had come to pass. How could she ever then marry Freddy or any man while carrying Thorpe's child? She was no chit out of the schoolroom that she would be unaware of the consequences of her conduct. The whole of what she had done today at the caverns, what she had intiated, was utterly reprehensible and done solely out of a childish pique because Freddy always seemed to develop the headache just when she needed him most.

She sank down into the light blue silk-damask chair by the door. She felt despondent.

Having learned that Thorpe had a wager going with the despicable Mrs. Newstead, who was herself conducting her own flirtations with two other men, all the while intending to marry her former lover—well, she was disgusted by the whole of it.

Not less so, however, than by her own conduct. How could she still be intent on wedding Freddy Waingrove when thrice she had allowed Thorpe to have his way with her?

Despicable. Truly. Her conduct was no different from Mrs. Newstead's, and Thorpe was right about one thing in particular—she was a hypocrite, wholly, unforgiveably, a hypocrite.

Later that afternoon, Jane was seated in a canal boat enjoying a scenic tour down a long, winding canal at the end of which the Challeston guests would enjoy a delightful *al fresco* nuncheon. She shifted her parasol of crimson red silk, adorned with long white fringe, to keep the sun from touching her cheek. She had been able to compose her spirits a little after having returned to Challeston, but her mind was in no way contented. She was as yet uncertain what she ought to do about either Thorpe or Freddy. Her future had never seemed so elusive.

At least she was gowned prettily in a half-robe of white muslin embroidered with cherries and dark green leaves. A pretty ensemble never failed to lighten her spirits. The sides of the gown were drawn up in enchanting billows of fabric to further enhance the daring red silk undergown. The low bodice was adorned by a red lace fichu, she wore fingerless red lace gloves, and in every respect appeared like a lady prepared to enjoy a summery outing on a pretty English canal. Over her dark brown curls she wore a small poke bonnet trimmed with gathers of white silk and adorned by a wreath of cherries. She was certainly dressed to perfection and the setting was lovely as the wide boat progressed down the canal.

She sighed, feeling as though she had lost her way. At least her present company was content, and for that she was grateful because the expression on Lady Somercote's face was helping to keep her own unhappy thoughts at bay. She couldn't be completely miserable when her hostess was clearly so happy.

Lady Somercote leaned slightly over the side of the boat and drifted her hand through the water. The refurbished barge had been neatly decorated with a dark green canvas roof and several rows of seats made comfortable with a range of cushions and pillows. The barge was drawn down the canal by horses who walked slowly along a path by the bank, creating a lazy ambience that perfectly reflected the countess's state of mind.

Lady Somercote wore an air of extreme contentment that flowed over Jane in a peaceful balm. She was presently smiling at secret thoughts. She delighted in the water rippling over her fingers. Jane wondered how Marc Antony, or perhaps Caesar, had enjoyed his Cleopatra of the night before.

She turned around and glanced at Lord Somercote who was seated opposite Mrs. Newstead and staring at her with the expression of a cat who had got the mouse. He frequently winked at her, and even once took her hand in his and placed a kiss on her fingers. Jane wondered if Mrs. Newstead even noticed that the earl was responding oddly to her, or if she had simply become puffed up in her belief in her abilities to bring a man to heel merely by her dimplings and simperings. Jane smiled, for Lord Somercote looked nearly as lazily content as his wife.

Behind the widow Newstead, Mrs. Ullstree left her place on the long, low boat and took up a seat beside Lady Somercote.

"What on earth is going forward?" Mrs. Ullstree whispered, giving her hostess a playful pinch on the arm. "I have never seen either you or your husband in such a deliciously amorous state and yet so far removed from one another. How is this possible?"

Mrs. Ullstree wore a gown of summery light blue muslin, her throat covered in folds of white muslin that rose to a pretty narrow ruff in a circle about her throat. Her dark brown hair, barely dotted with gray, was caught up in a shower of ringlets, covered with a small blue muslin mobcap trimmed with lace and ribbons in every color of the rainbow. She looked charming and youthful and her smile was wholly secretive as she waited for Lady Somercote to respond.

Lady Somercote fingered the fine white silk of her under-gown over which she wore a half-robe of pink cambric. A brooch of diamonds secured the half-robe just below her bosom. Over her peppered black curls she wore a turban of matching pink linen into which was secured a delicate white ostrich feather. She glanced at Jane and winked.

"Oh, now you must tell me," Mrs. Ullstree murmured in a low voice. "For I can see that the pair of you are full of secrets."

"Should I tell her?" Lady Somercote queried Jane.

Jane bit her lip, glanced at Mrs. Ullstree, and felt a blush burn her cheeks.

Mrs. Ullstree groaned. "Now Mrs. Ambergate is blushing." She returned her attention to Lady Somercote. "Miriam, if you do not tell me all, I shall start screeching."

Lady Somercote removed her hand from the water and shook off the few drops that clung to her fingers before turning to face her friend. She drew very close to Mrs. Ullstree. Jane leaned forward, expectantly, wanting to hear what she would say to her friend.

Lady Somercote took hold of a narrow violet ribbon dangling from Mrs. Ullstree's pretty lace cap and whispered, "Weren't you dressed as an East Indian Princess for the masquerade? You appeared quite exotic and certainly intriguing."

Mrs. Ullstree frowned and nodded.

"Would you mind then if I borrowed your costume, only

tomorrow you must promise to pretend you lost it somehow."
She stared at her friend meaningfully.

Mrs. Ullstree appeared bemused. "What riddles are you
speaking today?" She glanced at Jane, narrowing her eyes, then
returned her gaze to the countess. "Of course you may borrow—"

Her voice was too loud and Lady Somercote put her finger
against Mrs. Ullstree's lips.

Mrs. Ullstree's brows shot up in considerable surprise.
"Whatever is going forward?" she whispered, her eyes wide
with wonder.

Again Lady Somercote teased her friend by asking Jane, on
a whisper, whether she thought she ought to tell Mrs. Ullstree
the truth of her terrible deception.

Mrs. Ullstree finally took hold of a generous portion of the
tender skin just above the countess's elbow and leaned close to
her to whisper. "You know very well I always was a great
pincher, and if you don't wish me to return to my methods of
torture which I employed quite successfully at Mrs. Bartlowe's
Select Seminary for Young Ladies of Quality, then I would suggest you open your budget on the instant—and be quick about
it!"

Jane bit her lip and suppressed a fit of the whoops that nearly
escaped her. Lady Somercote was laughing and trying to slap
Mrs. Ullstree's hand away but she had successfully gotten hold
of Lady Somercote's arm and wouldn't let go. "Oh, do stop,
Venetia, or I vow I'll rip the brooch off my gown and stick you
through with it."

Mrs. Ullstree pinched her a little more. "Promise to tell and
I'll let you go."

Lady Somercote shrieked playfully which of course caused
all the guests to turn around, exclaim, and wonder. But the
countess promised, Mrs. Ullstree let go of her, and both ladies
fell to laughing and to telling the guests to mind their own
business.

Jane had never seen anything of the like before and found

herself both intrigued and delighted at the sight of the playful yet rather violent repartee between the two older women. She caught the barest glimpse of what each lady had been like in their respective youths and she hoped that when she gained a decade or two that not only might her wisdom grow but also her ability to retain the very best parts of each stage of her life, just as these ladies seemed to have done.

She watched as Lady Somercote leaned her head against the back of the seat and Mrs. Ullstree held her ear close to her friend's lips. Mrs. Ullstree began to blink rapidly as each revealing word succeeded the next. Jane could hear nothing of the discourse but Mrs. Ullstree's expression was sufficient to make the precise nature of the countess's speech clear.

Lady Somercote finished and Mrs. Ullstree moved back to stare at her friend in shock and amazement. She did not speak for a long moment, but when she did it was to say in a low voice, "Well it is no wonder there is a glow on your cheeks. But mind, I wish to have my costume returned to me before I leave—and perhaps a pattern of yours drawn up for my use as well, for I am beginning to be inspired. 'Pon my soul, inspired, I tell you! But you must tell me more, you must!"

· Jane envied the easy camaraderie that ensued, with heads bent together and caps and bonnets nearly touching, as a gentle murmur of conversation, quiet exclamations, and blushes were exchanged. She liked these women, she enjoyed their company, their manners, and the elegant style with which each tended to their wardrobes, the decor of their homes, and the well-turned-out equipages each sported during the Season in Hyde Park.

She suppressed a deep sigh. This was the society to which she wanted to belong so very badly, but not just as an insignificant, impoverished figure attached to this or that lady's train, but rather as an admired and respected hostess. Her spirits threatened to take an entirely downward spin as she realized that neither Thorpe nor Freddy Waingrove were likely to provide the sort of life she envisioned for herself. Thorpe wanted her for his mistress, and if she married Freddy she was likely to spend her days nursing his frequent headaches at Swan Court in Shropshire rather than tending to his children.

She let her gaze drift to the blinding reflections of the canal as the sunlight glazed the dark waters. She let her mind run away, into the sunlight, away from her difficulties. She was feeling far too sad given the beauty of the day and the sheer delight of travelling along a pretty canal and dining beneath a lovely tent on top of a grassy Derbyshire knoll. For the present, then, she would will herself to be content. For the present she would forget all that seemed to be heading for a spill. For the present she would try to enjoy the pleasures of the day.

Later, Jane watched as Lord Somercote handed each of the female guests from the long, canvas-covered boat. Lady Somercote preceded her, but before she had reached her husband, she turned back and in a whisper reminded Jane of her duty. "Now would be an excellent time to *wonder* about the loss of your costume, don't you think?"

"Indeed I do," Jane murmured in response.

Mrs. Ullstree squeaked her excitement behind Jane. "Is it really possible he doesn't know?"

The ladies all giggled together.

Lord Somercote graciously handed Mrs. Newstead from the boat, wriggling his gray brows meaningfully at the widow who returned his leer with one of what had been several bemused frowns of late. Jane again giggled at the sight of the onesided exchange, as did Mrs. Ullstree behind her. The earl handed his wife down, rather stiffly, Jane observed.

Then Jane took his hand, but quickly drew her free hand to her cheek. "Lady Somercote," she called to her hostess.

The countess turned around and at her most innocent queried, "What is it, Jane?"

Stepping away from Lord Somercote, Jane drew the countess close to her husband in a secretive manner so that he could overhear the conversation. "I do not want the others to know, because it is quite awkward. No, no, Mrs. Ullstree, I don't mind if you are informed, as well, but the truth of the matter is, I seem to have misplaced my Cleopatra costume—you know, the one I wore at the ball on Saturday night. My maid can find it nowhere, nor can the wig be found. Don't you think that odd?"

Jane heard Lord Somercote fall into a choking fit. His wife turned to him, "My dear, are you well? Whatever is the matter? Do you need a little lemonade or perhaps some champagne?"

"No! No!" the earl cried, his face scarlet from choking.

Lady Somercote patted his back. "But you are not well. Come. The gentlemen do not need you to see them safely off our barge. Come! A little lemonade." She turned to Jane and said in a whisper, "Don't worry or fret, my dear. I'll have one of the undermaids secretively search the rooms when we are at dinner tomorrow night. It must be somewhere. Perhaps someone is playing a little prank. But never mind. I'll see to it."

"Thank you," Jane murmured.

Again, Lord Somercote began to choke, but he permitted his wife to lead him toward the numerous servants who were situated on the banks of the canal and preparing a fine *al fresco* dinner for the Challeston guests.

For the picnic, Lady Somercote had chosen a beautiful aspect beside the canal near its intersection with the River Hart some two or three miles south of the village of Chadfield and Wolfscar Ridge. The canal had been built some thirty years earlier by a cotton-spinning mill owner who shipped his thread by way of barges along the canal and then by way of the River Hart to the southern Derbyshire towns. The canal also serviced several farmers in the area and was used for pleasure by those willing to pay for the hire of a boat or refurbished barge.

The Tuesday afternoon in July was quite brilliant, with a deep blue sky overhead. Lady Somercote had had her servants prepare for the canal-side event beforehand and by the time the pleasure seekers arrived, a large, open tent had been set up on a slight, treeless rise overlooking the river. A small village called Dove Hamlet was situated on the opposite side of the river at the base of a rounded hill. The hill was crisscrossed with numerous ancient dry-stone walls delineating the ownership and purpose of various enclosed fields.

The hamlet was of a lovely, warm brown stone and each cottage, scattered about in an almost haphazard manner to reflect the curves of the land and nearby streams, bore one and sometimes two chimneys, each three feet in height. A colorful sign, of painted wood, indicated the location of the tavern which Lord Somercote informed the party was known as The Mermaid.

Jane sat on a woolen blanket, her feet tucked to the side, as she listened to Mrs. Ullstree tell several anecdotes from her days at the Select Seminary. She listened attentively, intrigued to know how young ladies conducted themselves in bygone days, when tall, powdered wigs and wide paniers were the common apparel among the *haut ton*. If she had another motive for remaining close to Mrs. Ullstree—and when that lady was engaged elsewhere, to Lady Somercote—she did not fully reveal her purpose even to herself. All she knew was that she neither wanted to be near Freddy, who had earlier abandoned her to his headache, nor Thorpe, whose presence had become a complete and utter disaster for her.

The more that time separated her from their lovemaking in the caverns, the more distraught she became over her conduct. What had she been thinking, she wondered for the hundredth time, though very often she had only to look at Freddy Waingrove and know precisely how much her anger toward him had so foolishly plunged her into Thorpe's arms. Yet why?

Ordinarily she was the most sensible of women and she never, never, never let her emotions or her physical desires dictate her conduct. But so they had today, and for the past week or so, as well. She chewed on her lip as she watched Mrs. Ullstree signal to a footman to bring her a little more champagne.

What was she going to do now? She needed time away from both men to think, to ponder her future, to examine her motives as well as her horrendous conduct at the caverns. She felt as though she had lost her way entirely.

She blushed to think of it.

She glanced at Thorpe now and found that he was staring at her fixedly. He stood beside Colonel Duffield, who was engaged in chatting with Mrs. Newstead. Thorpe was ignoring the chatter of his companions and raised his goblet of bubbling champagne to her. He wore an assured, rather arrogant smile as he watched her. She remembered hearing of his wager with Mrs. Newstead, that if he lost the wager he must marry her. What were the remaining particulars of that wager, she wondered. Mr. Ullstree had certainly seemed to feel that she needed to know the details.

She recalled Colonel Duffield's comment about the wager—that Thorpe needed to succeed at something in order to win, but to succeed at what? His seduction of the widow Ambergate, she wondered. Was that what he needed to achieve in order to win his wager? But then he had already done as much, yet Mrs. Newstead still seemed so assured of success. Why would she be so assured?

She could neither smile at Thorpe nor even acknowledge his toast with a simple nod of her head. She felt numb and frightened.

Mrs. Ullstree broke into her reveries, leaning close and whispering, "He stares at you as though you haven't even a yard of silk to cover your legs, and your cheeks are so red that I'm beginning to wonder—oh, my."

Jane felt her blush deepen and she dragged her gaze from Thorpe's piercing stare. She didn't dare glance at Mrs. Ullstree but instead commented on the delightful sweetness of the champagne.

Mrs. Ullstree, to her credit, let the subject turn and did not bring it forward again. When Freddy approached, having finished his dinner, Jane spoke with polite indifference to him.

Freddy then asked Mrs. Ullstree quite directly if she would mind very much if he stole her companion from her side.

Mrs. Ullstree glanced at Jane, then at Thorpe, then back to

Jane. "Not at all. I have been thinking that both of us ought to move about a little, or our legs will go to sleep forever. Mr. Waingrove, will you please assist me to alight?"

Freddy quickly acquiesced, extending both hands to Mrs. Ullstree and drawing her up to her full height. As he turned to assist Jane, Mrs. Ullstree said, "I believe, Mr. Waingrove, that the view of the village yonder can be best observed from just a hundred yards or so down the incline toward the river. There." She pointed in the direction of the shimmering blue line of water where two children were launching large play boats attached to ropes. "Do you see? Where those boys are setting their toys in the water?"

"Yes, I see," he said. "Thank you. A most excellent suggestion." He quickly took up Jane's arm and began guiding her in the direction of the river.

Jane was angry as she moved beside him. At the last moment she had snatched up her parasol and now brandished it about, striking at the long grasses as she moved forward. But as soon as she was out of earshot of the other guests, she withdrew her arm from about his and stopped dead in her steps. "I don't wish to go with you, Mr. Waingrove," she said politely. "Please return to the others and leave me be."

"Jane, do come," he pleaded with her. "If we must quarrel, and I begin to think we must if we are to come to an understanding, then at least come to the river's edge with me."

Jane looked down at the long grasses climbing up about the red and white hems of her skirts. She didn't want to go. She didn't want him to speak reasonably to her and give her cause to hope yet again that all might be well between them, that love might spring up where none had existed before.

"Please, Jane," he said softly. "A few minutes, only. Let me have my say and then if you cannot change your mind, I will release you, forever."

Jane looked up at him and realized that she had been hoping for a natural separation at this juncture, that if she simply ignored Freddy, he would go away and not bother her anymore with his broken promises and his hateful headaches.

Instead, it would seem there was some sort of perversity in the goodness of his nature that demanded once he had offended her he must return once more to at least try to make amends. Her instincts warned her to send him about his business, but instead she acquiesced. "All right, but I promise you I'm in something of a temper," she said, raising her parasol upright and snapping it open. She held it in front and to the right of her in protection against the waning westerly sunlight.

He offered his arm to her again. She took it with a sigh and began descending the hill. "You have every right to be miffed with me," he said. "I know that I have disappointed you, I don't seem to be as strong as you, which is why, I suppose, that I am drawn to you as I am."

Jane looked up at him, surprised. Sincerity and humility shone in his gold-green eyes. Her heart softened toward him in quick stages. "I don't mean to be so harsh, either," she said. "So quick to fire up when I am annoyed or irritated."

"Don't forget the sullens," he said, casting a sidelong glance at her.

"Does it seem to you that I am pouting?" she asked, her mind troubled by all that was happening.

"When you ignore me, it does."

"I am usually not so blue-deviled, Freddy, over what must seem a trifle. The headache afterall is just a nuisance, not a broken leg or a horrible defect of character like pride or avarice." She sighed. For some reason she couldn't seem to shake the megrims that were settling into every particle of her being.

"You haven't seemed very happy while we've been here at Challeston," he remarked. "In London, or even at Mrs. Ullstree's home before we arrived here, you were smilingly content, or so I thought. I can't help but feel that you've changed or that something has changed."

"You've had more headaches," she offered, forcing him to

pause in his tracks and look at her. "Have you considered their source at all? For I have begun to think that I bring them on."

"No!" he exclaimed so forcefully that she was taken aback. He took up her hands in his and held them to his chest. Jane was amazed since she knew very well that all the guests as well as the servants at the top of the rise could see his conduct.

"Freddy," she whispered, "are you forgetting that we are in full view of the assemblage?"

"I don't give a fig for that," he murmured, his eyes misting over with tears. "Damne, Jane, I'm in love with you. I have been since I first met you in Lady Somercote's drawing room in Brook Street."

Jane felt her heart simply turn over in her breast. He had declared his love for her in such a manner as to leave her in no doubt of his true sentiments toward her. As never before, she sensed that a proposal of marriage would soon follow, if not in this moment, then at least before Lady Somercote's *fete* drew to a close.

"Freddy," she whispered. "I love you, as well. You have a good, noble spirit and an uprightness of character I value deeply."

"Jane," he breathed. "I—"

But he got no further as one of the two boys at the bank of the River Hart began to scream, a long high-pitched sound that obliterated everything else from Jane's senses. The boy's cries for help followed quickly afterward. "He's drownin'! M'brother is drownin'! Someone help me! Someone help me!"

Eleven

Thorpe stood deadly silent beside Colonel Duffield and Mrs. Newstead. His glass of champagne was poised to his lips. A strange, horrifying stillness had settled within him and all around him.

First, he had been struck dumb by the sight of Freddy Waingrove actually having the courage to take both of Jane's hands in his within sight of all of Lady Somercote's guests and servants. Only a nodcock could have mistaken his posture for anything other than what it was—a declaration.

When he had realized what was transpiring, he had felt as though lightning had suddenly fallen from the heavens, that Zeus had hefted a bolt in his mighty hand and with a yell, hurled the bolt straight through his heart.

I can't lose Jane, was the thought that accompanied the painful electrified strike.

I can't lose her, he thought now as one of the boys' voices rolled in a quick wave up the slopes of the grassy hill. Why was Jane tearing her bonnet from her head? He felt panicky and strange. Everyone around him grew restless. Mutterings and murmurings arose along with expressions of shock.

"Good God!" Duffield cried.

"She can't be serious!" Mrs. Newstead exclaimed in horrified disgust.

He watched, stupefied, as Jane began to run toward the river, her pretty half-robe of white muslin embroidered with cherries

being released into the wind and floating to the green grass behind her as she became a red blur. Only when she disappeared
into the river did Thorpe begin to run. The river appeared harmless and lazy, but the current was always faster than one supposed
it to be.

Jane felt an instant tingling and numbness as the cold water
flowed over her in a single shot of pain, a pain she ignored
completely. The current carried her swiftly as she set off in long
sweeps of her arms through the water. The boy was young,
perhaps only five, and had learned to swim that summer. But
swimming was one thing, the River Hart quite another.

He bobbed up and down in the water, his voice as he cried
for help mingling with coughs and sputterings as he dipped
below the surface with an open mouth. Jane stretched her arms,
kicked her feet, ground her teeth, and cursed the clinging, useless silk that trapped her legs in a narrow sheath. She felt the
sleeve seams give way as she fought a path to the child. A few
seconds more.

She caught him up with her left arm, swung him partially onto
her so that his head would be above the water, and struck toward
the shore with hard pulls of her right arm. The boy was coughing
and frightened, she not less so as she felt the current of the river
increase. Not far downstream was a ripple of frothy water indicating the presence of boulders. She couldn't allow herself, or
the boy, to get tangled up there, but the current was strong.

She fought toward the bank, but she realized she wasn't going
to make it. Even if she got close enough, the bank was steep.
There was nothing for her to take hold of. Panic poured a rush
of power through her, she surged and fought her way. She
couldn't give up. There must be some place of safety along the
edge of the river. Something hidden as yet from her eye.

A few feet more.

She heard her name called, she looked downsteam and saw
an arm clothed in white. Hope. She told the child to hold his

breath. She rolled the boy into the water and, with all the strength left in her legs, propelled herself to the bank, extending her arm upward at the same moment.

A powerful arm caught her, the current dragged her legs downstream, the boy came up gulping for air, coughing, and crying.

The saving arm held.

A moment later, she was dragged, along with the boy, onto the grassy riverbank. She fell on her stomach, gasping. The child coughed and cast up his accounts, then lay whimpering. She slid over to him and put her arm around him and held him close.

"You're all right," she murmured, her entire body trembling with exertion. "We made it." She laughed aloud, feeling hysterically joyous at having escaped death for herself and for the child. "We made it."

The boy continued to cry. She sat up and pulled him into her arms. She felt her half-robe fall about her shoulders and glancing up she saw that Freddy had brought the other part of her gown to her. She thanked him, then drew the garment about the boy's shaking body.

"But you need that," Freddy cried.

She shook her head. "Don't be ridiculous," she said, her teeth chattering in her head. "The child needs it more." Only then did she realize that Thorpe was sitting beside her in his waistcoat and shirt, his arm dripping, his clothes wet. She met his gaze, staring into light blue eyes that were lit with an unearthly fire. "You saved us," she murmured.

"You saved the child," he whispered, extending his hand to her.

She took it. He held her hand in a crushing grip.

"Thank you. A thousand times, thank you," she responded, rocking the boy in her arms. She closed her eyes and held the child tightly against her.

His brother arrived shortly afterward. "He's all right then?" he asked. "What a gudgeon. I told 'im he couldn't swim t' Hart, but he wouldn't listen t'me."

Jane looked at the older boy who couldn't have been more

than seven. "Why don't you fetch your mother," she suggested softly.

The boy, whose lips quivered and whose cornflower-blue eyes had suddenly filled with tears, nodded vigorously and took off running to the southeast as fast as his legs could carry him.

A half-hour later, Jane found herself sandwiched between Freddy Waingrove and Lord Thorpe as the latter drove one of the servants' carts back to Challeston Hall. She wore Thorpe's coat for warmth and a woollen blanket had been tucked about her legs.

The ordeal had left her feeling unsteady and ill. She wanted a warm bath, a glass of Madeira, and her bed. Somehow all of her emotions had risen within her the moment she had lain safely on the riverbank, not just her fear of almost having drowned, but also of her present difficulties and the sore limits of the alternatives before her. She felt a strong need to cry, something she had not done in years.

Occasionally, one or the other of the men spoke to her, but she couldn't respond except in monosyllables. In the end, they let her be and only blessed her with hopes God would keep her in good health as she slowly mounted the circular staircase. She wore Thorpe's coat about her shoulders. A red and green plaid blanket was wrapped about her waist and trailed her up each step like a demi-train of a fine gown.

Thorpe watched her go, his heart in his throat. She was a sight with his coat on her shoulders and the plaid blanket dragging behind her. Her hair was a wet tangle about her shoulders. When Freddy tried to put her hat on her head, she had taken it politely enough from his hands but afterward had thrown the bonnet a dozen feet into the air, though not because she was exhilarated. He sensed that there was enough frustration in that single movement to singe anyone who drew near. He recalled taking a step backward in that moment just as Freddy had wisely done.

He didn't know what to make of her.

He glanced at Waingrove, a roll of irritation forcing him to take a deep breath. He didn't know why it was, but the mere sight of the poet's noble brow and gold-green eyes was enough to make him want to plant a facer on his pretty face.

Freddy met his gaze, coldly, malevolently. "We can always finish what we started a few weeks ago," the poet suggested, an edge to his voice.

"You'd be unconscious within five minutes if I set at you, which is of the moment what I want to do."

"Don't hold back for such a paltry reason. I've seen the way you look at Jane, as though she's a worthless lightskirt with whom you mean to dally until you've had your fill. But I tell you, she's worth a hundred of you, a thousand, and I'll back up that opinion to my death if I have to." He stepped back, assumed a boxing pose, and lifted his fists menacingly. "Or are you man enough to accept my challenge this time?"

Thorpe looked into the poet's eyes and had a terrible sensation that the man, seven years his junior, was growing up, and more quickly than he would ever have expected. What he had always believed was Jane's choice of a pocketbook for a husband now began to look like more, and all his ire deserted him.

He released a sigh, lifting a hand in resignation. "You are right," he said at last. "I'm not worthy of her."

Waingrove's fists slowly lowered and he too released a heavy sigh. "Nor am I," he muttered.

At that moment, the front door opened and a servant passed through holding the door wide for Miss Hartworth. She glanced from one man to the other, her gaze fraught with concern. "I—I have come to lend my assistance," she said, swallowing hard. "Mrs. Ambergate has suffered so much. I thought she might want a female in attendance."

Thorpe narrowed his eyes at her and began summing up the waifish young lady. Her gown of gold and blue calico, which lent her complexion a yellowish, pasty tone, was as indifferent as was the girl's character. He knew instinctively there was only one reason she had returned to Challeston. He decided, quite selfishly, that he would make certain she was able to fulfill her purposes. Stepping forward he said, "You are kindness itself to have come to Mrs. Ambergate's assistance, but believe me when I say of the moment she will be better left in her maid's kind ministrations. Wouldn't you agree, Mr. Waingrove?" He glanced at Freddy and saw what he had expected to see—relief, pure and simple.

"Er, yes," he said with a slight bow of acknowledgement to Thorpe. He then turned his full attention upon Miss Hartworth and, moving forward, took her hand in his, "But you are to be greatly honored for having acted upon such a noble sentiment."

Thorpe saw in their easy and mutual affection how the future ought to be, but wondered cynically if Fate would intervene and toss everyone to the winds, just as Fate usually did. He left Freddy to tend to Miss Hartworth but snorted in disgust as he heard Henrietta say, "Are you feeling well, Fr—er, Mr. Waingrove. You appear so pale. Do you have another of your frightful head-aches?"

"As it happens, I fear I do."

"Perhaps a turn in the gardens would be of some use to you, then."

"Yes," he murmured. "I believe it would."

Jane cried herself to sleep once Vangie had her tucked be-tween the sheets and a warming pan placed at her feet. She had bathed, just as she had wanted to, and she had relieved some of her feelings by recounting to her maid all that had happened by the River Hart, but still the blue-devils would not depart.

She cried for herself and the life she had almost lost. She cried for the boy who might have died had she, and Thorpe, not been present to save him from his foolishness. She cried for the loss of her parents whose guidance she so badly needed, for her husband who had wasted both their fortunes before sticking his spoon in the wall, for Freddy who she realized had brought her half-robe to her not because he was concerned for her health but for her modesty, and for Thorpe who was everything she wanted in a man but who would never love her.

She cried and cried.

Though she was grateful to have been given her life back, she was utterly frustrated with the knowledge that having been given another chance, she didn't know what to do with it. She was hopelessly confused and the turmoil that kept her mind spinning only made her cry harder until her tears were spent and she finally fell asleep.

She did not awaken until the following morning, when sunlight shone through the underdrapes of sheer muslin setting in a pretty golden glow the chamber decorated *en suite* in a light blue silk. Jane's heart was not so heavy as it had been of the night before, probably because she had faced her deepest sorrows and had let her tears carry them out of her mind and body.

Still, a certain seriousness, perhaps even grimness, had settled into her spirit.

She heard a scratching on the door and drawing herself to a half-reclining position in her tall, four-poster bed, pulled the bedcovers up to her chin and bid her guest enter.

Lady Somercote's warm smile and affectionate countenance appeared in a crack in the doorway. "May I come in, my dear?" she asked softly.

Jane couldn't help but smile in the face of so much love and consideration. "Of course. You are always welcome."

Lady Somercote smiled more fully and entered the room followed by a serving maid who bore a tray that smelled delightfully of fresh, warm bread and hot, steaming chocolate.

"Oh," Jane sighed. "What a perfectly delightful way to have the day begin. I do thank you." She felt unwelcome tears well up in her throat and brim in her eyes. "Forgive me," she murmured, dragging the corner of her sheet to her face and dabbing away her tears. "I have become a ridiculous watering pot and for no good reason at all. So you will have to forgive me and you must tell me something absurd and ridiculous before I embarrass the both of us."

Lady Somercote nodded firmly and bid the maid settle the pretty wooden tray—bearing a fragrant, colorful array of sweet peas, on Jane's lap. Jane picked up the delicate cup and saucer, painted with matching sweet peas in pastel colors, and took a sip of chocolate. She felt her whole being relax in that moment.

Lady Somercote dismissed the maid and drew forward the chair covered in light blue silk damask in which she had sat ten days ago on Jane's arrival at Challeston Hall. "Well, I do have something to tell you that I believe you will find quite amusing."

Jane smiled, settling the saucer on the tray and holding the teacup with both hands. "Do tell me all," she said simply, prepared to listen joyfully to something her hostess clearly found a great delight.

"Well, earlier a breakfast was served in the morning room and only Mrs. Ullstree, my husband, and I were present. Duffield and Thorpe had gone angling, Mr. Waingrove had taken Miss Hartworth to see the bees in the flower garden, Mrs. Newstead was yet abed, and Mr. Ullstree was in the stables. Anyway, there we were and Mrs. Ullstree performed her much-needed role in my little charade to perfection. I'll try to recall her words, 'Miriam,' she said, wearing as true an expression of dumbfoundedness as I have ever seen on any of our fine London stages, 'Miriam, do you recall yesterday when Mrs. Ambergate said she had misplaced her Cleopatra costume?' 'Yes,' said I, frowning at her convincingly over my own cup of chocolate. 'What of it? Have you found it, perchance?' 'No, I have not. But this morning I noticed that while I was searching for my crocheted gloves—you know the pretty pink ones I embroidered with those tiny little pansies at the wrist—at any rate, I opened the bottom drawer of my chest of drawers and saw that my own East Indian Princess costume was gone. Don't you think it unbelievable? Have we a thief at Challeston?' " Lady Somercote drew up her shoulders in a gesture of childish mirth and trilled her laughter. "Poor Somercote," she said, laughing. "His face turned a violent shade of crimson and deepened to a burgundy when Miriam continued,

'I am beginning to wonder if these costumes are not being put to some sort of nefarious use. What do you think?' "

" 'I can't imagine what anyone would want with them,' I responded. Dear Jane, don't you think that was wicked of us?"

"Delightfully so. What happened then? Did your poor husband begin to choke again?"

"No. But there's more. I actually responded to Venetia's question further by saying suggestively, 'Unless someone is having a bit of sport by dressing up in these costumes. Is that someone you, Venetia?' Venetia looked properly shocked. 'No!' she cried vehemently. 'What manner of lady would don a costume merely to please a man, if that is, of course, to what you were referring.' I responded, 'I admit it was, and you are quite right. What manner of lady would gown herself as Cleopatra, or an Indian Princess, or Marie Antoinette. A strumpet, perhaps, but not a lady.' Mrs. Ullstree really is quite the good actress, which has given me an assurance that our vignettes tomorrow night will undoubtedly be the best ever."

"How did your husband respond?" Jane asked.

"He gave me a rather hard, penetrating glance after that, though his color had returned to its more normal hue, and then resumed reading his copy of the *Times*. Really, it was the most fun. Later, when Mrs. Newstead entered the chamber, he could hardly greet her. Then, when she had taken up her seat at the table, he rose from his chair, made his excuses, and left the room."

Jane smiled and nodded, pleased that Lady Somercote's schemes were faring so well. "Only tell me how the Indian Princess fared last night?" she asked, wondering if she should have posed such an intimate question. She set her empty cup of chocolate down on its companion saucer and lifted the cover off the bread. The smooth, soft butter flowed onto the slice of fine, aromatic white bread bearing a crunchy, golden crust about the edge.

But Lady Somercote was not at all shy about giving her answer. "I vow I've never known such pleasure. Isn't it odd. We are the same two people, but a little disguise and deception has changed the whole, er, event, until it has become a firework display of passion. Really, it is a complete mystery. I will only be sorry when my *fete* draws to a close in three days' time."

"What will you do?" she asked, setting her knife down. "Do you intend to tell him the truth?" She took a bite of the bread and sighed at the wondrous flavor.

Lady Somercote nodded. "Yes, but I think not until all the guests have departed. Once he gets over the shock, I think I might even suggest that Marie visit him again."

"Or Cleopatra," Jane suggested.

Lady Somercote giggled. "What fun this has been for me." She sighed happily, then leaned forward to place her hand gently on Jane's arm. "But not so happy for you. I can see that you must have spent the night shedding a few tears. Your eyes are rather puffy this morning."

Jane felt a lump in her throat again. "I don't know why precisely," she said. "I know I was overset at having nearly drowned myself yesterday—"

"What do you mean? I thought—"

"Thorpe saved me," she said. "I know that most of you weren't there, weren't close enough to know what really happened, but if Thorpe hadn't pulled both me and the child from the river, there would not have been a happy outcome."

"Oh, dear," Lady Somercote said, sitting back in her chair and letting her hand slide off Jane's arm, across her fingers, and onto the light blue silk counterpane on the bed. Her complexion had paled considerably. "Thorpe never said a word."

"And Freddy probably didn't comprehend what had happened."

"Well, it is no wonder then that you are not quite yourself."

Jane nodded, setting the bread down on the plate. "It isn't just that, however. The truth is, I don't know what to do anymore; I don't know what I want anymore. When I first arrived at Challeston, everything was so clear to me—I must somehow bring Freddy up to scratch, make him a good wife, and bear him a dozen or so children—"

"Oh, not a dozen, Jane, you don't know what you are saying. I bore five, and five is more than sufficient for any woman, for you must know it isn't just the bearing but the raising and training of each child that takes a certain toll. You must never leave all the instruction and care to a nurse or to your governesses. It won't do."

Jane lowered her head. "That's just it. I'm not sure children—at least in the usual manner—will be part of my future."

"Whatever do you mean? Now you are speaking nonsensically, or do you fear you are barren?"

Jane shook her head. "I may be. I did not give my poor major a child, but I wasn't thinking of that." She looked piercingly at Lady Somercote, willing her to understand her meaning.

Lady Somercote's mouth fell agape as her thoughts began running together in a quick series of knits and purls. "No," she said rising from her chair. "You are not thinking—Jane, tell me I am not to surmise what I believe you would have me surmise." She turned her back on Jane, then whirled around. "That day—when we viewed the well-dressings. You were distressed—you said you couldn't tell me why. Jane, you must tell me now."

Jane took a deep breath then began, "Thorpe made love to me. I thought he was Freddy. He stole the key I had placed in Freddy's bedchamber and he, he came into my room and he, well he made me feel like I was Marie or Cleopatra or an Indian Princess."

"Oh, dear God," Lady Somercote cried breathlessly, placing a hand at her stomach and sinking into the chair by the bed. "But you knew it was him, surely!"

Jane shook her head. "I had imbibed a great deal of champagne that night. I truly believed he was Freddy, though I must admit I kept thinking about Thorpe the entire time. Then the next day, I found Thorpe in the yew maze and he returned the key to me. I was never more shocked, more dismayed."

"But why? Jane, whyever did you—oh, dear, let me understand you. What made you think Freddy would come to you in the first place?"

Jane explained about Freddy's wish for a spiritual union, how she had bade Vangie take the key to his room, and how Thorpe had forced her maid to tell him what was going forward. "For I believe sometime earlier in the evening—when my tongue had been loosened by too much champagne—I dropped a hint about what was going to happen. Thorpe is quite perceptive and the following morning my key was in my hand and the truth of what had happened shocked my every sensibility."

Lady Somercote stared at her in disbelief. "It is so impossible. Wait a minute. This is very much like Somercote and me. Now who told me to do something like this, you know, put on a disguise—I believe it was Colonel Duffield. Is it possible he knows of Thorpe's escapade?"

"Of course not. I mean I can't imagine Thorpe telling him. But then, you and I are speaking of the same thing! Oh, Lord, what if everyone knows?"

Lady Somercote shook her head. "That is impossible or I would have heard it from my maid before now. No, this is not common knowledge."

"Well," Jane confessed. "Is it common knowledge that I have been with him twice since then?"

Lady Somercote's jaw dropped to her chest. "You have made love with Thorpe twice since the first time?"

"He is a very seductive, intriguing sort of man," Jane said, biting her lower lip and running her fingers nervously over the light blue counterpane.

"Yes, he is," Lady Somercote agreed. "But, Jane, more to the point, this is not at all like you. What is going on? When? Where? Why?"

Jane addressed her last query. "None of it will make sense to you, it doesn't make sense to me except that in some odious way I can't seem to resist Thorpe. But I fear I have gone to him when—that is, each time Freddy developed one of his monstrous headaches." She grimaced at her hostess, wondering what next she would say.

Lady Somercote again rose from her chair, an expression of

complete dismay and bewilderment on her face. She looked back at Jane and asked, "Did you wear a costume? Did you disguise yourself? Did he know who you were?"

At that Jane burst out laughing. "No, I did not disguise myself. That was your ploy, not mine. I had no ploy. I had only my desire, my lust. How is it possible I let my lust rule my conduct?" She groaned, squeezed her eyes shut, and rapped her forehead with her knuckles.

Lady Somercote moved to stand in front of Jane and clasped her hands tightly together against the pretty fawn-colored silk of her morning gown. "You cannot become his mistress."

"But doesn't it seem to you I already am?"

Lady Somercote shook her head briskly. "Not in the least. Not unless you begin meeting purposefully and regularly, and not unless he begins to pay your expenses. I would guess that is not the case, is it?"

"No," Jane said slowly. "But whenever we are together, without benefit of chaperone, I always end up in his arms. It is the most exasperating thing."

"But what of Freddy?" Lady Somercote asked despairingly.

"That's the rub," Jane responded, sighing. "When I came here, to your home, I thought he and I would progress in our affection to a degree that a betrothal would be a normal effect. Instead, his responses to me have been at best mercurial. One moment he appears utterly besotted, holding and kissing my fingers, calling me pet names, being as attentive as any moon-calf fellow can be. The next moment, however, one of his frightful headaches takes him off. He is nowhere to be found. He avoids my company. He even seeks comfort in Miss Hartworth's insipid ministrations."

"I have noticed as much," Lady Somercote offered with a frown between her brows. She resumed her seat beside the bed and leaned her elbow on the high mattress.

Jane had completely lost her appetite and set aside the tray of now cold bread and wilting sweet peas. She smoothed out the sheets, blankets, and counterpane, adjusted her mobcap, and settled back into the pillows. "The problem is," she mused, "that through all of Freddy's quixotic conduct, my fondness for him has grown instead of diminishing. I don't know that I can explain why, precisely, except that when we would brangle about his absences, he would always come forward afterward to humble himself and to beg forgiveness for having deserted me. Also, each time he did, much of his excessive display of sensibility evaporated. He became calmer and more rational. I began to feel there was some hope."

"But what happened to cause you to feel there was no hope for you and Freddy."

Jane felt the tears threatening to overtake her again. She bit them back. She wanted to find answers, not continue her career as a watering pot. Swallowing hard, she stared at the light blue silk counterpane and said, "When I was in the water, with that poor child balanced on my hip, and I took hold of Thorpe's arm, something inside me changed—forever, I think." She lifted her gaze to meet Lady Somercote's. Taking a deep breath, she confessed the unconfessable, "I fear I've fallen in love, deeply and irrevocably, with Lord Thorpe."

Jane spent the rest of the day closeted in her bedchamber. Lady Somercote had had no words with which to comfort her after she had admitted to being in love with a man who would never make her his wife. Lady Somercote had shared her misery and could offer her no hope whatsoever that Thorpe would suddenly leave off his libertine ways and marry her. She could only support Jane's conviction that if she could possibly see her way to doing so, she ought to make every effort to marry Freddy anyway, despite her sentiments, and especially in light of the fact that she was able to see progress in her feelings toward the budding poet.

Jane knew that the countess's advice was sensible, but there seemed to be little sense about her conduct these days. She had but to look at Thorpe and it was all hallow with her.

Dressing for dinner that evening, Jane donned a dark blue

silk gown patterned with a small gold diamond design and
trimmed with several rows of gold Brussels lace about the hem.
The bodice was cut in a severe decollete, setting off to advantage
the swell of her bosom. The puffed sleeves of the gown sat at
an angle across each shoulder so that the back of the gown
dipped down slightly instead of rising high to the neck. Her
hair was pulled up into a knot of curls that cascaded down the
back of her head and was wrapped in a spiral of gold bands
imitating the ancient Greek and Roman fashion. The waist was
very high and a small rolled bustle allowed the many gathers
of the fabric in back to billow slightly behind her. A necklet of
sapphires, made of paste, and matching ear-drops reflected the
beautiful silk of the gown. Over her elbows and draped in a
deep loop behind her, she carried a gold silk shawl edged with
a dark blue fringe. Long gloves of gold silk completed a toilette
that was as elegant as it was beautiful.

She began a slow descent of the circular staircase and somehow was not surprised that when she did so, Lord Thorpe
stepped into the entrance hall, pulling on his white gloves, almost as though he had divined she had finally emerged from
her bedchamber. He glanced up at her as she fingered the ban-
ister and progressed in halting steps toward him.

All had changed. She could feel it in the air as she watched
him. His visage lacked the arrogance he frequently displayed
and in its stead was an open expression that seemed to burn
itself into her heart. He didn't smile, but his light blue eyes
regarded her warmly. He didn't speak, but was that his heart
she heard speaking?

She loved him. Every nerve in her body spoke her love. He
moved closer to the bottom step, awaiting her. She couldn't take
her gaze from him. She felt as though she was seeing him,
meeting him for the first time all over again. He wore a coat
of black superfine molded to his broad, strong shoulders—
shoulders that had given him the strength to draw her single-
handedly from the river. Cutaway tails tapered away from his
narrow waist, revealing sinewy thighs and shapely legs. His

starched shirtpoints touched his handsome cheeks and his neck-cloth, *Thorpe's Revenge,* was arranged in immaculate folds. His thick black hair was brushed forward, *a la Brutus.*

When she reached the bottom step, he didn't move and she had the certain knowledge that, were there not several laughing voices sounding from the antechamber leading to the drawing room, he would have simply taken her in his arms and kissed her. Instead, he took her hand and, lifting her fingers to his lips, placed a warm kiss on each of them.

"I had prepared a speech," he murmured, holding her gaze steadfastly. "But I've forgotten it. I wanted to tell you how proud I am of you, of your courage and of your willingness to risk your life for that child, but instead all I can think is how pretty you are and how very much I long to be with you again."

Jane wanted to tell him that he must leave her alone now, that he must respect her need to live respectably, that he must permit her to continue her pursuit of Freddy. Instead she lifted her hand to his face and let the truth of her heart be known to him as she searched his eyes and memorized every feature.

She watched his lips part. He leaned toward her. He pressed her fingers. "Jane," he murmured. "Tell me what you are thinking."

She shook her head. "Perhaps when we practice our vignette tonight."

Desire rippled over his face. "I would that dinner and cards and music were all behind us and the swordroom had already swallowed us up."

She lowered her gaze, afraid that if the conversation continued, she would find herself in his arms regardless of convention, of every societal dictum, of common decency. She stepped off the bottom step and tried to pull her hand from his, but he wouldn't permit it. "Pray, allow me to escort you into the drawing room. Everyone is awaiting your arrival."

What did he mean by that?

She would have asked him, but there wouldn't have been sufficient time for an answer since they had but to cross the small antechamber before the dark green velvet drawing room opened up to her.

The moment she stepped over the threshold, the eight people in the chamber stopped speaking and broke into a round of applause. Both Lady Somercote and Mrs. Ullstree came forward on quick, pretty steps to take her from Thorpe to receive the congratulations and praise of her friends.

She was entirely overcome as Colonel Duffield bowed low over her hand and commended her courage. She was taken aback by the swell of pride in Freddy's chest as he, too, bent low over her hand. Henrietta cast herself into Jane's arms and hugged her, tears pouring from her eyes as she gushed her praise of Jane's fearlessness in diving into a veritable torrent of dangerous, rushing water. Mr. Ullstree clasped both warm, pudgy hands about her right hand and exclaimed over her virtues. Even Mrs. Newstead smiled somewhat kindly and admitted that Jane had acted bravely.

But as the praise died down and as it became clear that she must make a speech, she addressed the truth of the matter. "I fear you praise me overly much. I acted without thought of any kind except for the life of the child, and perhaps that demands laud and admiration. But I would have drowned and the child along with me, had not Lord Thorpe caught my arm as he did."

"How's this?" Mr. Ullstree exclaimed. "Thorpe, why did you say nothing?"

Duffield crossed the chamber to bring Thorpe forward and patted him on the back. "I had thought you merely assisted Mrs. Ambergate from the water. I did not know you had saved her life. We are all grateful, my good man."

Again praise flowed, but at least the attention was diverted from Jane entirely. She did not feel in the least heroic, although it was clear to her that the friends gathered about her and Lord Thorpe believed she was.

Later, after a delightful dinner had been enjoyed by all, and a brief musicale performed by Mrs. Ullstree and Lady Somercote, Jane was about to leave the drawing room to attend Thorpe in the swordroom for a final rehearsal of their vignette, when Mrs. Newstead approached Lady Somercote and said, "I have been given to understand that both Mrs. Ambergate and Mrs. Ullstree have mislaid their costumes. I found it very odd when I heard that such a disappearance had occurred until I began to search for my own costume. You see, your husband and I had decided to dress in costumes of thirty years ago for our vignette, a decision we had made at nuncheon. I have tried to ascertain the location of the gown, the mask, and the wig, but I can't seem to find any of them. Have you had any luck in locating either Mrs. Ambergate's costume or Mrs. Ullstree's?"

Jane glanced from Lady Somercote to Lord Somercote and knew her mouth had fallen agape, but she could not seem to close it. Lady Somercote did not at first speak, but exchanged a frightened dart of a look with Jane. She then turned to Mrs. Newstead and would have said something by way of explanation, but Lord Somercote, scowling, took a step forward and addressed Mrs. Newstead in a flat, demanding voice. "Whatever do you mean you cannot find your gown or your wig or your mask? I know you have it. I've seen you—that is, surely you still have your costume?"

Jane gasped as did Lady Somercote.

A shocked silence fell.

"To what are you referring?" Mrs. Newstead asked, clearly insulted by his form of address. "I cannot find any of these articles and I demand to know if perhaps there isn't a thief among the servants. I don't like to mention it, my lord, but it is rather peculiar that several of your guests would all be missing their masquerade costumes."

Lord Somercote appeared as though she had slapped him several times across the face. "I don't understand you at all, madame." He then bowed to her, pushed hastily by her, and quit the drawing room.

"Well, upon my soul," Mrs. Newstead remarked as she turned to watch Lord Somercote pass into the small antechamber beyond the drawing room. She then looked back at Lady Somercote and stated in some agitation, "Your husband is not at all well, madame. I know that I was intent upon flirting with him during your festivities, and perhaps that was very wrong of me, but I think you ought to know he is as mad as Bedlam. He has been winking at me for days now and I have become convinced he has a tic. He leers at me and makes comments about the very costumes I just mentioned as though I would know what he was talking about—and very suggestive comments, too, if I might add."

Lady Somercote lifted her chin. "You've done very right in bringing this matter to my attention. But would you mind telling me exactly what he has said to you—about the costumes, I mean?"

Mrs. Newstead lowered her chin and her voice slightly. "Only this morning, he whispered into my ear, 'I prefer Cleopatra to Marie Antoinette.' He then clicked his tongue several times. I told him he was speaking nonsense, but he merely gave me a quite familiar nod and a finger held to his lips, indicating he wished me to remain silent on the subject. I forgave him one or two such remarks, but only today he offered three, and I am out of all patience with him. I suggest you call your physician and see what ails the man."

"I will do that," Lady Somercote said. "And Mrs. Newstead, thank you so much for sharing your concerns with me. You've a large, generous heart. We should all be so virtuous as to follow your example."

Mrs. Newstead smiled appreciatively, at least at first. But after a moment's consideration, her smiles dimmed and with a petite, wondering frown marring her brow, she dipped a small curtsy and left the room.

When she was gone and Jane was left alone with Lady Somercote to wonder over the amusing exchange, she began to giggle, a giggle that soon infected Lady Somercote and after a few minutes, Jane let her restraint go and simply fell into whoops.

* * *

Lord Thorpe waited for Jane in the antechamber outside the drawing room. He heard the ladies giggling, whispering, and laughing and felt a deep contentment spreading through his chest. He enjoyed hearing Jane laugh, he especially liked how she delighted in the company of other women, and he most especially loved that whatever her purposes, she was respectful of everyone around her.

He paced across the green and gold Aubusson carpet, thinking and rethinking the events of the day. He was caught in an odd place of wonder, anxiety, and vacillation. He had always known what he would do, especially where the females of his acquaintance were concerned. But ever since he had leaned over the river's edge and had taken hold of Jane's firm, strong arm, his thoughts of her had been cloaked with a kind of fire hitherto unknown to him. His everpresent desire for her, to seduce and deflower her, had altered mysteriously. He wanted her more than ever, yet he did not.

Tonight, he had scarcely been able to keep his eyes from her—throughout the congratulations showered upon her by Lady Somercote's guests, through the fine repast beneath three glimmering chandeliers, through the brief musicale. No matter how hard he tried to keep his attention fixed on the conversation or duet at hand, his gaze had seemed to wander back to Jane as though he was a lode-stone seeking the north magnetic pole. Then, watching her, his heart would swell, smoke, and catch on fire, imploding, exploding, sending sparks of admiration and desire descending always into his loins. He wanted to make love to her tonight, but he didn't. He wanted to speak with her, yet he hated the thought of letting words speak for the flames burning his soul. He wanted to touch her, yet to stand apart from her, to watch and to admire seemed better still.

All had become a mystery the moment he had watched her tear her white bonnet from her dark curls and let her half-robe drift away into the wind behind her as she raced for the river's edge. For a moment, as he watched her in stunned silence, he had thought Freddy had spoken some injury to her. When she had cast her clothes from her back, he had thought perhaps she had gone mad, mad with her futile pursuit of a spineless man.

But when her body had disappeared in a long, sleek red arrow, into the blue, flowing waters, his feet had responded before his mind had ever acknowledged that she was in the act of saving the small boy. He closed his eyes, remembering the incident in every vivid detail, how his boots had half-slid, half-pounded down the grassy rise, how he had raced the current and her powerful strokes by running along the narrow path beside the river, the red silk of her gown easily spied in the water, the shock of realizing she would die if she and the boy were caught in the rapids ahead, and finally how he had willed her to come to him and to take hold of his arm.

He felt feverishly dizzy as he recalled the feel of her arm strapped to his. Pulling her from the water, the boy held fast to her side, had felt like nothing short of a miracle. Even then, she had had no thought but the child's comfort and had taken him up in her arms without a single word of reproach for his foolishness. Would he ever forget the sight of her, dripping wet from head to foot, holding the boy wrapped up in her white muslin half-robe, and rocking to and fro as though the child had been her own?

Therein lay the dilemma, he realized suddenly.

What was it Jane spoke of so frequently? The children of her body, the babes she longed to hold in her arms, the offspring for whom she wanted to provide the best of futures and lives.

As the ladies suddenly appeared in the antechamber, Jane's arm tightly and affectionately wrapped about Lady Somercote's, he took a startled step backward. They were both still giggling, though their amusement dimmed as each inclined their head to him.

"I was waiting for you, Jane," he said, sounding like a simpleton even to his own ears. Of course he was waiting for her, they were to rehearse their vignette for the last time and he had always escorted her to the swordroom.

Lady Somercote released Jane's arm and hurried away to the library where she was to practice with Mr. Ullstree.

When her footsteps had died away up the stairs, only then did Thorpe step forward to offer his arm to Jane. He lowered his gaze to receive her arm about his. He felt an odd vibration move through him, again of wonder and awe. He sighed deeply.

Good God, he thought with sudden amazement. *Have I tumbled in love at last?*

Twelve

Walking beside Thorpe on the way to the swordroom, Jane felt just as she had felt earlier while descending the staircase—her senses alive only to him, her love rising above every sensation. A warmth swam lazily about her heart in a gentle, pulsing ripple of affection.

She loved him.

He escorted her through the hallway to the back of the mansion, through an antechamber and into the magnificent tall-ceilinged swordroom. A fire had been lit and the glow of the flames danced on the polished wood floor. Silver implements of the muse rested on the round table, the vignette papers close by.

Jane was too full of what she was feeling to do more than smile faintly at him as he closed the door upon the world outside the swordroom. She watched him, wondering why he remained by the door holding her gaze intently but not moving his feet. He seemed almost paralyzed.

She closed her eyes and bade herself treasure the moment. They were alone. At last. But in two days she would see him no more.

Or would she?

She drew in a quick breath of indecision. She had wanted to keep the thought at bay for as long as possible but it was almost on her, she could feel it. Deep in her mind the question began to rise, of her future and of her love for Thorpe. She tried to keep the question from forming in her brain, but it came nevertheless. Would she become his mistress, afterall?

"No," he murmured.

She opened her eyes quickly and saw that his feet had found their step. He was crossing the room to her. "No," he reiterated. "I don't give a fig what your thoughts are, but you seem unhappy and there will be no unhappiness tonight."

He caught her up in his arms, but didn't kiss her.

"Did I appear to be unhappy?"

"Painfully so, but I tell you I won't allow it tonight."

She touched her gloved fingers to his face as she had done earlier in the evening. "Dearest one," she murmured, tears stinging her eyes. "So be it. There will be no unhappiness between us."

He smiled faintly as her glove slipped between the cleft of his chin. "No unhappiness, my love."

Jane heard his words and the tears that had been stinging her eyes birthed and slipped down her cheeks.

"You've broken my dictum already," he said, wiping at the tears with his gloved hands.

"But I am not unhappy," she said, letting her fingers drift over his cheeks to touch the edge of his eye, the ridge of his nose, the arch of his brow.

"Then why the tears?" he murmured.

"I don't know," she responded honestly. "I am overcome I think with all I feel for you tonight. Ever since the river—"

"Yes, ever since then," he interrupted softly.

A warmth flowed through her. He had felt something similar, then. "Ever since the river," she continued, "I have felt so very odd, as though all has changed, for me at least, though I couldn't tell you why or in what way. I believe it must be because I now owe my life to you and I feel in some magical, hidden, obscure way that I belong to you."

She watched him swallow as he took her a little more firmly into his arms. She felt his thighs touch her own and a wave of gooseflesh rippled up her legs and into her abdomen. She purposely breathed deeply, not wanting the sensation to obliterate the present perfection of her feelings.

He leaned forward and placed a soft, warm kiss on her lips. She closed her eyes. He was kissing her for the first time. She swore it. She heard a sound, a moaning. How odd to realize it came from her throat. She felt separated from what was happening yet more fully involved than she had ever been. She parted her lips and his tongue slowly entered her mouth, taking possession carefully and purposefully.

She opened her heart to the sensation, her thighs became liquid with desire, an intense heat moved upward through her abdomen to wash over her heart in a wave of molten bronze.

She loved him.

She needed him.

She slipped an arm up about his neck and encircled his back with the other. He tilted his head and kissed her more deeply, yet with a full, languid movement that took the slow, burning bronze and forced it into her veins, up her chest, into her shoulders, and down her arms until even the tips of her fingers were tingling with fire. She felt his hand slide to cradle her buttock. Again she breathed deeply, not wanting her longings for him to overtake and submerge the sweetness of her blossoming affection.

"Thorpe," she murmured. She liked the way his name sounded on her tongue.

He kissed her again, fully, deeply, slowly. She revelled in each languid swirl of his tongue. She let her tongue explore his in gentle sweeps. She heard another moaning, but this time his voice rippled through her. For a long time, she tasted of him and he of her. His hand on her buttock became an easy, gentle kneading. The fire within her, in her veins, in a wall about her heart and smoldering in the cradle of her abdomen, became a steady pulse of heat.

"Thorpe, I have something for you," she murmured, drawing back a little.

He seemed surprised. She searched the pocket of her gown and withdrew the brass key to her bedchamber, still decorated with a violet ribbon. She placed it in his hand. He seemed over-come for a long moment, staring at the key as though disbelieving she had given it to him.

"Come to me at midnight," she whispered.

He leaned down to take her shoulders in his hands, the key biting into the tender flesh. He slanted his lips across hers and kissed her hard on the mouth. The passion of his kiss made her feel as though all her bones might dissolve and she would remain crumpled at his feet forever.

He drew back and touched her breasts one last time. "Midnight," he murmured.

At midnight, Jane lay naked beneath the linen sheets of her bed. She wore no mobcap and her hair was unbraided. A branch of candles sat upon the table beside the bed. She had drawn the bedcurtains close about the bed except for the side which opened toward the door. In the truest sense she was bringing and allowing Thorpe into her bed for the first time. All that had gone on before was excitement and seduction, but this was more. Tonight was her offering to the man she loved. She had already spoken her love and symbolically surrendered to him. Now she would take him deeply into her and become one with him.

Only one thing was lacking, a document indicating that such a joining would be of a long-lasting nature. The pain that engulfed her at this thought was intense though shortlived because she willed it so. She was not a stupid chit of a girl who did not comprehend the consequences of her conduct. She knew full well that all that could come of such a complete surrendering tonight was a *carte blanche* and nothing more.

She sighed deeply, willing the hapless thoughts away.

Life held tremendous uncertainty, she thought. She had believed that her marriage to Edward would have lasted decades, instead of five short years. How much time would she and Thorpe have together? Fate was of a quixotic nature and she knew there was no use in either pining for what was or hoping that they would be together always. Even if they were married, death could separate them in a trice.

Regardless, tonight she belonged to Thorpe. She had given him her key and she had no regrets. Not one.

She heard the closing of a door in the hallway beyond and a few moments later, a key rasped in the lock. A click, a turn, a push, and Thorpe slipped into her bedchamber, gowned in a dark burgundy velvet dressing robe, open at the throat to reveal a fan of black hairs.

He looked down at her and smiled. "I want you to know how hard it was for me to wait for this, even for a scant few hours. I have been pacing my bedchamber since ten o'clock."

She smiled and stretched her arms out toward him. "Come to bed," she said quietly.

"Jane," he said, shaking his head slowly and untying the burgundy velvet rope from about his waist. "What have you done to me?"

She sighed more fully, then watched with great pleasure as he tossed the robe off his shoulders, shook himself out of the sleeves, and let the ankle-length dressing gown fall to the floor in a heap.

He was entirely unclothed.

Jane drew in a deep breath as she saw his body in the glow of the candlelight. He was strong, athletic, and it was reflected in every lean, muscled ripple of his frame. Black hair covered his lower arms, his legs, and his chest, descending down his abdomen to a dark, thick thatch.

As he slid into bed beside her, she pushed back the sheet to receive him next to her, a movement that gave him pause. His gaze roved her face, her neck, her bare breasts, the triangle guarding her femininity, her long silky legs. He leaned down toward her hips and pushed the sheet off of her completely. His hands ran along her hips since she was still lying on her side, and moved in a single, fluid motion.

* * *

Thorpe looked down at her body and sighed deeply.

He understood well the significance of the violet beribboned key. Surrender. Jane Ambergate had surrendered to him. Completely. At long last.

A sensation of exultation rose up in his chest and swelled over his heart and mind. He had conquered her, completely, utterly, just as he had said he would. He had only now to inform Mrs. Newstead of his conquest and their wager would be at an end. He smiled, placing a gentle kiss on Jane's lips as he thought with languid pleasure of just how grateful Colonel Duffield would be when he learned Mrs. Newstead was now obligated to become his wife.

He sighed with contentment.

A strange wriggle of anxiety however began to curl up all about the edges of his heart. Something about Mrs. Newstead. How exactly was he going to prove to her that he had vanquished the recalcitrant widow Ambergate, that he had succeeded in seducing her and that at this juncture Jane was his to bend to his will, whatever whim dictated his next course of action where she was concerned?

He felt his heart constrict, quite oddly, almost as though in guilt.

He frowned, drifting his cheek lightly over hers and enjoying the feel of her fingers tugging on his hair. He'd never known guilt before, of any kind. The ladies with whom he had dallied had always been easily conquered and easily relinquished.

Jane hadn't been so easily subdued. He kissed her ear, unhappy with the path of his thoughts.

What was wrong with him? Why was he suddenly feeling knots of anxiety twisting in his stomach? What the deuce was bothering him?

"I'll go wherever you want me to go," she murmured.

Her words seemed to send shards of ice skating through his veins. He felt cold and paralyzed suddenly as he realized she had spoken aloud her intention of becoming his mistress.

What the devil was happening to him?

"What's wrong?" Jane queried.

He felt her stomach rise and knew that she was lifting herself on her elbows to better see him. He met her gaze. "I don't know," he whispered. "Jane, I don't want you to go anywhere you don't want to go. Do you understand?"

Now, why had he said that? His mistresses always went where he dictated. He conquered them and then he ruled them. He always had, he always would.

She flopped back down on the bed. "There's only one place I want to go with you right now," he heard her say as he lifted himself up on one elbow. The peaks of her breasts were close and inviting. He slid down slightly and began drifting kisses over her breasts.

"So be it," he murmured as he took one nippled peak into his mouth and began a steady suckling. He watched her neck arch, her head digging backward into the pillows and soft cushion of the mattress. He slid an arm under her back and held her in an arched bow as his tongue glided over her smooth, inviting skin. His body hummed with growing pleasure as the softness of her breast played an erotic counterpoint to his hard masculinity.

Jane surrendered to the pleasure of his kisses and of his touch. A dance began, of slow languid movements, of unity of design, of increasingly heightened pleasure as he kissed her and stroked her with practiced movements.

"Thorpe," she murmured. She returned kiss for kiss, then teased him by touching her tongue to his lips, inviting him to receive what he was so ready to give.

His lips parted and she entered his mouth, driving deeply within. She placed her hand at the back of his neck and kissed him hard. He moaned, his arm sliding around her back, his hips beginning a forceful thrust against hers. She wanted him inside her. She slipped both her arms about his neck. "Take me," she murmured. "Now, my darling Thorpe."

He kissed her hard, forcing his tongue into her mouth this

time as he rolled her onto her back and spread her knees with his hands.

Time stopped in this moment. She didn't know why it was, but this was their first true joining. The rest had been teasing, haste, and ecstasy. But this was different. "Thorpe, I love you so much. I love you." She kissed his neck and his ear and held him tightly to her.

He drew back and began a second glide. "Why is this so different from anything I've known," he murmured into her hair.

Jane smiled faintly, letting the pleasure sweep toward her in a wave of desire. Her whole body was aware of only his body. She closed her eyes as a third thrust moved into her. She sighed deeply and for some reason released his neck to fling her arms wide. She arched her neck and he lifted himself off her chest, positioning his hands just above her shoulders. He began to move in slow, purposeful thrusts into her, over and over. She looked up at him, his gaze fixed on hers. She was one with him. He was one with her. She loved him. She always would. Tears formed in her eyes as he moved in the ancient way into her, pleasuring her, taking pleasure, loving her. She remembered being in the river, the child at her side, and catching hold of his arm.

Tears touched her eyes as she took hold of his arm again. "You saved me," she whispered. "I owe you my life."

"Oh, God," he murmured, his hips driving more powerfully against her. "I had only one chance. I willed you to come to me."

"I came to you," she whispered, gasping at the pleasure mounting within her. Her hand slid up his arm and touched his face. He kissed her fingers and drew one of them into his mouth. She moaned. Tears began to slide down her face.

He pressed himself harder into her. "Jane," he said, whispering her name. Again and again, he spoke her name. Faster he moved, and thrust and drove into her. He fell down on her chest and kissed her hard on the mouth.

Her back arched, she cried out, but his mouth took in her cry and he thrust his tongue into her. Desire began to flow and ebb in a steady rising whirlwind. She was crying and panting all at the same time. He spoke her name into her mouth, his tongue drove against hers. Desire spiked hard, refusing to ebb as ecstasy poured over in a wild wave of pleasure. She groaned loudly. His movements became erratic and demanding. Again pleasure spiked within her. She held him hard about his neck. He pounded into her, wildly, madly. She panted and once more pleasure tumbled through her. Only then did he release his seed, groaning deeply into her mouth, his hips tightening then releasing, tightening again and releasing, finally to settle against hers, his energy spent.

Jane let the tears flow. She couldn't stop them. Her life had been poised on a cliff for so long, she had picked her way so carefully along the edge for months, that giving voice to her willingness to go with him wherever he wished to go was a relief unparalleled. She was glad it was over. She belonged to Thorpe and whenever he next asked her to become his mistress, she would say yes.

Jane slept until late in the morning. Thorpe had finally left her bed when the grayness of dawn threatened to reveal the true nature of their relationship to the servants of Challeston as well as to the rest of the guests. She had not wanted him to go and even though she felt that her future had been settled, still the separation was painful, and very soon a type of anxiety began to work within her.

Even though he had not asked her outright, she knew that his interest in her did not extend beyond a *carte blanche*.

With her hand tucked beneath her cheek, she lay in bed staring at the full sunshine that glittered through the sheer muslin underdrapes. She could hear birds chirping and singing outside, evidence of summer's rich fruition in mid-July. She felt full and satiated, replete. Her body wanted for nothing. Her soul for even less.

She smiled.

Thorpe had made her happy. Purely and simply, he had made

her happy. They would enjoy their time together, prodigiously, and she would enjoy being free of financial cares. If she refused at the moment to think beyond these actualities, she forgave herself. Ever since her arrival at Challeston, she had been struggling with the dilemma before her—Freddy's affection, security, and respectablility or Thorpe's passionate love, security, and a lifetime of societal unknowns.

Neither choice was ideal. But after the rescuing at the river, she believed her choice had been made at the very moment when Thorpe had taken hold of her arm and dragged her and the child from the straining current of the River Hart. Had she ever truly had a choice, she wondered. Perhaps the real choice had been made when Thorpe tricked her on her first night at Challeston. She had allowed him to trick her. Champagne or no champagne, surely some part of her mind must have known Thorpe was making love to her and not Freddy. Surely. Or perhaps her decision had been made at Oak Cloud Spring, or perhaps at the caverns. Maybe altogether, each event had comprised the decision. Whatever the case, last night was not so much a decision as the moment of surrender.

But it was all settled in her mind, she thought, smiling drowsily. She belonged to Thorpe. She always would. Tonight they would perform their vignette, and he would come to her bedchamber again. On Saturday morning she would leave with him to enjoy the first day of their adventure alone together.

So be it.

Jane did not descend the stairs until half-past two o'clock, and then it was with the intention of taking up her bow and arrows. She wore a pink muslin frock over a white cambric undergown, white lace gloves, and white slippers. She wore a poke bonnet, trimmed with pink muslin and white, artificial lilies of the valley. In her arms she carried her bow and quiver as well as the long-legged target.

At the same time that she stepped off the bottom step onto

the black and white tiled entry floor, Freddy emerged from the gold and green antechamber that preceded the dark green velvet receiving room and stopped her from leaving the house.

He was dressed immaculately and quite stylishly in a burgundy velvet coat, a pale yellow waistcoat, and buckskin breeches tucked into glossy Hessian boots. He wore moderate but neatly starched shirtpoints and his neckcloth affected the simple style of arrangement know as *trone d'amour.* His blond hair was brushed in careful wisps about his temples and gleamed with Macassar oil.

He looked quite handsome. She smiled at him in a friendly manner and said, "Very fashionable, Freddy. I congratulate you. I've never seen you appear so dashing."

He seemed pleased, though nervous, as he moved into the entrance hall and took her proffered hand in his. He held her hand cloaked within both of his and lifted her fingers to his lips. He looked at her for a long moment before placing a passionate salute on her fingers.

Jane had an uneasy sensation as he did so. Oh, dear. What is the meaning of this, she wondered. His conduct, his clothes, bespoke purpose and objective. And he didn't seem in the least frightened of her.

"I see you mean to employ your bow and arrows this morning, dearest one," he offered hopefully.

Jane looked into expectant eyes and wondered what he was about. "Yes," she said, lifting her bow up slightly by way of answer. "You may come with me if you wish for it."

He seemed relieved. "I do wish for it," he responded with a smile. He took the target from beneath her arm, insisting he help her carry her equipment, then guided her out of doors toward the south lawn. "I was never more grateful than when I saw you just now, Jane," he began carefully. "For I have been wanting to speak with you since, well, ever since I awoke this morning."

"Indeed," Jane murmured, only half-listening to him. Her heart was light as she led the way toward the south lawn. She felt completely at peace with the world. They chatted as they walked along. She spoke of the weather and he made several comments on the beauty of the Derbyshire countryside.

When she reached her destination, she bid him set up her target at a distance of thirty yards.

It would seem however that he had an entirely different notion in mind than assisting her.

He let the target fall in the grass, then turned to her. He suddenly caught her up in his arms and before she could protest, her bow and arrows were lying about her feet, his arms were holding her fast, and his lips were pressed against her own.

The sensation was not wholly unpleasant, Jane thought absently as she permitted the kiss to continue, at least for a time. She didn't think it wise to rebuke a man who she had been pursuing so heatedly for the past four months, and who clearly had been lying in wait for her in the antechamber in order to steal a kiss from her.

After a moment, when some of his passion had abated, he drew back from her slightly and whispered, "I do love you, Jane. You know that, don't you?"

Jane looked into his eyes and felt a panic seize her. She knew what was about to transpire yet she could think of no way to prevent it. "You have said as much to me on other occasions," she answered, her mouth feeling dry.

He smiled faintly, searching her eyes. He laughed suddenly. "Why was I so afraid of this moment?" he wondered aloud. "So often I have imagined holding you and kissing you and speaking to you of the future, but in my imaginings my speech stuttered and my limbs shook. But here you are, your lovely brown eyes compassionate and kind, and I have no fear in me. None whatsoever. Only my love for you."

Jane could not believe what he was saying to her. She should have stopped him from saying more but she was in a state of shock, having come to understand that after all this time her schemes had finally borne fruit, but now the fruit had become rotten.

"My mind has never been more wholly fixed on one object," he continued, "to make you my wife. Will you do me the honor of becoming the next Mrs. Waingrove?"

He was beaming as he looked down upon her, his green-gold eyes lit in an unearthly glow. And not one pink patch marred his pretty complexion.

Thirteen

Jane tilted her head in dismay, unwilling to believe what was happening to her. Freddy, at long last, was actually begging for her hand in marriage.

How was this possible, after all this time, after having been kept in suspense week after week, and since her arrival in Derbyshire, day after day? How was it possible he was offering for her now? Now, when it was impossible for her to accept his offer?

"Speak your heart to me, my dearest Jane," he whispered, taking her hands in his, holding them to his chest and ever so gently leaning his head against her forehead.

"I—I don't know what to say," she murmured, blinking and wondering.

"I have been precipitous," he said, drawing back from her slightly. He released one of her hands that he might place a finger beneath her chin. He drew her chin upward so that she was forced to look at him. "I can see that I've given you a shock, but, but I had thought you were wishing to hear my proposal."

"I was," Jane answered truthfully. He leaned toward her. She could see that he meant to kiss her again. "Oh!" she squeaked and took a quick step backward. But her quiver was behind her left heel; she stumbled and fell lightly if indelicately to the ground. She giggled and felt a blush creeping up her cheeks. She was not used to feeling awkward and gangly. She wondered if this was how Freddy normally felt around her.

"Jane!" he cried. "Good heavens, what have I done?" He extended his hand down to her. "Do let me help you up, my pet. I vow I shall do myself some injury if I find I have wounded you in the slightest."

"I am unhurt," she said, taking Freddy's hand and allowing him to lift her to her feet. "Truly. Please do not fret and, oh, do stop feeling my arms for broken bones. I am completely unharmed, I promise you."

"Just as you say," he responded. "You are wearing a lovely frock, my dear. Pink suits you." He smiled and touched her cheek with the back of one gloved finger. "You're so very pretty. I've loved you so much and for so long. Now that I have asked for your hand in marriage and let all my sentiments burst forth, I feel as though my soul has wings. But I pray with all my heart that you in some measure return my regard."

Jane swallowed hard, guilt flooding her. She had worked tenaciously, especially since her arrival at Challeston, to exact just such words and expressions from her swain, that to express indifference at this juncture was to confess her hypocrisy.

"Freddy," she began haltingly. "For the present, I beg you will say no more. I must confess that because I saw your reluctance over the past several days and because you suffered from the headache so much, I began to believe you didn't love me afterall and that your headaches had become a symbol of your lack of true affection for me."

"I am a wretchedly weak sort of man in that regard," he murmured, taking a step toward her and slipping an arm about her shoulders. "It is no wonder that you are experiencing a certain ambivalence toward me."

"Perhaps it would be best then, if we did not—"

She felt his gloved finger on her lips. "I do not want an answer now," he whispered. "I beg only that you will consider my professions of love and my desire to wed you. Weigh the sweet growth of our mutual affection against the regrettable incidents of late, test the depths of your own sentiments. For I will not believe, given all your encouragement, especially since our arrival in Challeston, that you are indifferent to me. Besides, I wish you to see the vignette I created with Miss Hartworth's help and indulgence. Every word was written with you in mind, from my heart and through my pen. Will you at least ponder before answering?"

Jane could only nod. Guilt had taken hold of her mind, her heart, and her tongue. She had led Freddy down the garden path and to refuse his offer now was to behave like the worst sort of female who delighted only in conquests and cared not for how much pain she inflicted in the end.

He smiled at her silent acquiescence, placed a soft kiss on her lips, then bid her *adieu*. He would have stayed to watch her ply her bowstring, but he said he knew she needed time to think and to ponder his request that she become his wife.

Jane didn't have much to ponder, she realized as she placed an arrow tautly against the bowstring and with clear precision let the missile fly. She knew precisely the state of her heart. Her only concern now was how to tell Freddy that she loved another.

While Jane was practicing her archery, Mrs. Newstead sat by the window of her bedchamber, a room next door to Jane Ambergate's, and tapped her fingers on the window sill. She was in a state of acute anxiety. She had been awakened in the middle of the night by sounds as familiar to her as they were unwelcome. She had been utterly astounded, never having once truly believed that Jane Ambergate, once she knew of Thorpe's deception on the first night of the festivities, would ever invite him back into her bed.

But so she had.

She had covered her face and her ears with her pillows. She had screamed into her pillow, flopped over in bed, and screamed a little more.

So, Thorpe had succeeded. Never in a thousand years would she have believed it possible with such a prig as the widow Ambergate as his object. She was furious with them both and enraged that Colonel Duffield's predictions had come true, at least partially, that Jane was tumbling in love with Thorpe.

None of that mattered, of course. *Tap, tap, tap.*

All that mattered was that Jane refuse to agree to become his mistress. She could fall in love with him, she could sinfully take him into her bed, but all she had to do was to refuse to become his mistress.

Her thoughts were drawn sharply away from the elements of her wager with Thorpe by a scratching on the door. "Come," she called out.

The door opened and her abigail entered. Molly was a tall, thin female, as ambitious as her mistress. Her hair was covered by a nicely starched white mobcap trimmed with ribbon and lace, and wisps of blonde curls dangled beside each hidden ear. Her brown eyes glittered as she held up an object which brought a deep contentment to Mrs. Newstead's heart. "You got it!" she cried. "Good girl. You will be rewarded, Molly, make no mistake."

"Thank you, madame," the maid returned, dropping a curtsy.

When Molly made as if to cross the room and bring the object to her, Mrs. Newstead smiled. "Toss it to me!"

Molly lifted a surprised brow but with a gentle, upward motion she thrust the object into the air.

Mrs. Newstead watched the brass key shoot missile-like toward her as the violet ribbon extended itself behind. If Thorpe believed he had beaten her, he was greatly mistaken. She was not some green girl, wet behind the ears and untried in life, to be vanquished by something as absurd as his seduction of Mrs. Ambergate.

In the library before dinner, Colonel Duffield frowned as he watched his beloved Mrs. Newstead incline her head toward Lord Thorpe. What did the wench have brewing, he wondered with the first prickling of anxiety he had experienced since learning of her wager with Thorpe. He had inadvertently wit-

nessed Thorpe entering Mrs. Ambergate's bedchamber at midnight on the night before and he had summarily fallen asleep
in a deep state of glee because of it. Thorpe had clearly won
his victory over Mrs. Ambergate's reluctant heart and last night
had claimed his prize. Therefore, his own prize—wedding Mrs.
Newstead—was all but a matter of timing.

But now, as he saw the look of cunning and determination
in his beloved's eye, he felt completely uncertain. Mrs. Newstead was many things—she was avaricious, hypocritical to a
fault, and completely absorbed with only her own interests. But
she was also clever and intelligent, qualities when matched with
willfulness could result in the accomplishment of any objective
she sought. What was in her mind, he wondered, narrowing his
eyes at her. And how was he to prevent her from achieving her
purposes, for stop her he must, not only for his own happiness
but for the happiness of others.

Colonel Duffield had never married. He had never wanted to,
particularly. He had always viewed the marital condition as a
seedbed for every form of misery known to man. At least he had
believed as much until he had become fixed on the notion of
taking Mrs. Newstead to wife. He had been her lover since
Thorpe had abandoned her, a circumstance of which he believed
the *beau monde* was entirely ignorant. He wanted a home, he
wanted a ripe, warm woman in his bed, and if children should
follow, so much the better, though he found it exceedingly difficult to ascribe even the smallest maternal sentiment to his beloved.

Why Mrs. Newstead had become his object, he still did not
quite understand, except that he was not keen on many of the
regular virtues espoused but ignored by his peers. He admired
ruggedness of spirit and determination, qualities Mrs. Newstead
possessed in abundance. She would make an excellent army
wife and though he had not spoken of it to her, he had recently
received a commission for a post in India. He wanted her with
him, plain and simple, right or wrong. She would be devilishly
pricklish all the time, but then he never had cared too much for

evenness of temper. When he chose a horse from the stables, that horse had to have a mean eye to give him the kind of ride that suited him best.

Mrs. Newstead had a marvelously mean eye.

Well, well. If he was to travel to India with her at his side, he had best keep a watch of his own going.

He chuckled and lifted his glass of sherry to her. She returned the salute, then resumed staring at Thorpe hungrily and determinedly.

Henrietta Hartworth stared at Jane Ambergate's deep rose-colored silk gown, cut daringly low at the bosom. Lord Thorpe stood next to her, smiling down at her as though he knew a secret.

Secrets.

Freddy was telling her a secret.

"What did you say?" she asked. She had heard his secret whispered into her ear. His warm, beloved breath had sent a shivering of gooseflesh down her side, but his words had frozen her heart, yet she couldn't remember them.

Again his lips were poised near her ear. "I have asked Jane to become my wife. You told me to be bold and courageous and I was."

Hetty felt her limbs disappear from beneath her, the room spun once then twice all about her, she fell into a dark night sky.

"Hetty, dearest, do wake up?" Mrs. Ullstree petted the hand of the young lady who had become like a daughter to her. "Pray do not be ill."

"It is my fault!" Freddy cried out, pacing Hetty's bedchamber. When Henrietta swooned, he had sought Mrs. Ullstree's help. Together they had seen her removed to a place of quiet in order to help restore her to her senses.

"How was it your fault?" Mrs. Ullstree asked, placing a damp cloth on Hetty's forehead, then continuing to pet her hand.

"I gave her a shock. I thought she would be happy for me,

but then I have been in such turmoil and I have trespassed on her good heart for so long, that I should have given her a hint or two before telling her that I had finally summoned my courage and offered for Mrs. Ambergate."

At that, Mrs. Ullstree dropped Hetty's hand and turned to stare at the stripling still pacing the lavender bedroom. "You did what?" she asked, stunned.

Freddy turned to face the older woman, astonished by her tone of voice. "Well, that is," he stammered. "I—I thought you knew. I am in love with Mrs. Ambergate and I—I only needed the right moment, and I found it and I offered for her."

Mrs. Ullstree took her gaze from Freddy's countenance. She feared if she continued looking at him that the sheer force of her rage at his stupidity would kill him. "What a nodcock you are, Freddy Waingrove. Hetty is in love with you—she has been for years. Haven't you even a mite of sense in that poet's brain of yours?"

She heard an odd series of thumps and turned to find that Mr. Waingrove, for all his ten thousand a year, had swooned, as well.

Mr. Ullstree puffed out his cheeks and rocked on his heels as he listened to his wife's recounting of the nature of both Hetty's and Freddy's fainting spells. "Well, by God, if you aren't a damned shrewd woman."

He turned to admire his wife and saw that she was smiling at him. "I married you, didn't I?" she suggested softly.

He chuckled and slipped both hands into the pockets of his coat and rocked a little more. "Well, well. Harrumph. Isn't this a fine pickle. But I don't see what's to be done?"

"Nor do I, but if an opportunity should arise to give Fate a nudge, I trust you will do what needs to be done?"

"Now that I am armed with the proper information, of course."

* * *

Lord Somercote scowled at Mrs. Newstead, "What do you mean you never wore Mrs. Ambergate's Cleopatra costume? You had to. I wasn't imagining that you wore it or, or Mrs. Ullstree's Indian Princess costume, either."

Mrs. Newstead compressed her lips tightly together. "See here, my lord, I've had quite enough of your odd conduct. I've never known a man to be addled by so little. There was a time when I was enjoying our flirtation, but I don't anymore. You're a very queer man."

She moved as though to step past him, but he caught her by the arm. He was feeling very put-upon and finally asked her straight out, "Did you or did you not come to my bedchamber dressed as Marie Antoinette, as Cleopatra, and finally as an East Indian Princess? Do you deny it?"

Mrs. Newstead tilted her head, then shook it. "I suggest you consult with your physician, my lord. You are not well. I know that while we were practicing our vignette I permitted you to hug me and kiss me a little. But I don't hesitate now to say that you are caught up in great and absurd imaginings, of quite a perverse nature if I do not overstep my bounds in saying as much."

Lord Somercote blinked at the woman he had believed had been his lover for several nights over the fortnight *fete* and felt an odd sensation rip through him. When he had hinted to her of their affair, she had appeared confused and of late even irritated by his suggestive comments. But now, in the light of her complete denial of having engaged in a little costumed love-making, he could no longer believe her responses to his hints to be coyness or a wish to keep the matter secret.

But if she had not come to him as Marie or the others, then who had?

He glanced about the library. All of the ladies were present, except Henrietta, and he dismissed them all—Mrs. Ambergate, Mrs. Ullstree, his wife. No, impossible. One of the maids then, perhaps?

As the shock of having realized Mrs. Newstead had not shared his bed began to wear away, a new, rather dizzying sensation rose instead. Excitement coursed through him at the sheer mystery of it. What lady of his acquaintance or in his service had been so bold as to have assaulted him, disguised, in his own bed?

Such a woman he had to have again. And again.

Two of the maids had eyed him curiously of late. One of them, perhaps?

Oh, what fun he was going to have, once the festivities ended.

Lady Somercote had watched the many sentiments pass across her husband's face while he spoke to Mrs. Newstead—of anger, of bewilderment, of shock, and finally of delight. So, he had come to understand that Mrs. Newstead had not been his lover. What would he do next, she wondered. And just when ought she to next visit him in the guise of some historical character or other?

She glanced about the chamber and felt her heart soar. For all the sub-plots hatching around her, she still could not suppress the sheer enjoyment she always felt when the vignettes were almost ready to be performed.

The vignettes brought a kind of magical change to all who participated. In past summers, many lasting loves had been birthed by the scenes created by Fate and, this summer, though not directly through the vignette itself, her own marriage was undergoing a magical kind of transformation she had not expected at the outset of the festivities. She smiled and thought that she had even come to like her husband's black hair.

Jane knew she was ignoring everyone else present as she stood off to the side of the fireplace, behind a sofa, chatting in warm, semi-seclusion with Lord Thorpe. But she didn't care. She wanted to touch him. Over and over she had to repress an impulse to slide her hand over his arm, to reach up and touch his cheek with her fingers covered in a deep rose lace. Twice she had wanted to steal into his arms and embrace him.

Her heart was lit with a glow she had never believed possible. She loved him so very much. She could hardly wait for the vignettes to conclude after dinner so that she could make love with him again. He had already asked her to come to his room, stating that he would leave his door unlocked.

"Oh, that reminds me," she said quietly, leaning close to him and revelling in the smell of his shaving soap and the scent of his neatly starched neckcloth. "You ought to return my key because I will need to leave it in my room tomorrow night."

"Your key?" he queried. "But I don't have it.

"Yes you do," she said. "You took it with you when you left last night, don't you remember?"

He shook his head. "No, I left it on your bedside table. Wasn't it there this morning?"

Jane sought back in her mind and recalled that it had been. "Yes, it was," she said, surprised at herself. But when had it disappeared? "Later it was gone. How silly of me. I suppose Vangie must have put it somewhere."

"Have you seen the view from this window?" he said, changing the subject entirely. "The steeple of Bow Stones is visible from there."

Jane blinked, then realized he was offering a chance for them to engage in even more intimate conversation by drawing yet farther from the guests milling about the library and sipping sherry before dinner. "I have not done so, m'lord. Do lead me to it."

He grinned and took her arm. "Come, then."

Once by the window, with Thorpe gesturing in the distance toward the village of Bow Stones, he murmured, "I can scarcely keep my hands off you. And twice I've nearly dragged you into my arms and kissed you."

"That is nothing," she returned in a quiet murmur also gesturing into the distance. "Three times I have nearly thrown your arms wide that I might crawl into your embrace and fling my arms about your neck."

"I have stripped the gown from your body."

"I have popped every button from your cumbersome coat, waistcoat, and shirt."

"I have let my hands glide over your waist and back and downwards until—"

"Until I have kissed you thoroughly."

"Oh, Jane," he whispered.

She turned into him and noticed something odd from the corner of her eye. "They've all gone."

He shot a glance into the room. "You are mistaken," he whispered. "You have willed them to become invisible that I might feel free to kiss you."

Jane chuckled. "No, simpleton. They've gone in for dinner."

Thorpe laughed. Jane knew it was madness to do so, but before any other thought struck her she was in his arms and he was kissing her wildly, his tongue deeply within her mouth, his arms holding her waist fast. The moment couldn't last. Someone would surely notice their absence and come in search of them. But she didn't want to let him go, not just yet.

Henrietta placed a hand to her temple before she descended the tall, circular staircase. She felt much better and had come to accept the situation for what it was—Freddy was to marry Jane Ambergate. She had always known this would happen, but in her heart of hearts she had wanted Jane's schemes to fail. When all hope had deserted her, so had her senses and she had swooned. But how could she explain as much to Freddy?

"There you are, Hetty." A voice disturbed her, calling from the direction of the entrance hall.

She smiled faintly and waved at the man she loved, beginning her descent of the elegant staircase. "Oh, hallo, Freddy. Has everyone retired to the dining hall?"

"Nearly everyone. Lady Somercote bade me fetch you,

though, but she said not to hurry if you were still not feeling the thing."

"I am perfectly well," she returned, watching him mount the stairs quickly. He met her at the first landing and offered his arm to her. He seemed unusually sober as he watched her, eying her curiously for a long moment.

"Why do you look at me in that way, as though you've never seen me before?" she asked, setting them both in motion and beginning the final descent to the black and white tiled entrance floor.

"I'm not sure that I have," he murmured, a frown deepening between his brows.

"What nonsense, when we have known each other for years."

"We have, haven't we? In fact, I would guess you know more about me than any other lady of my acquaintance."

"Well, yes, I suppose I do," Hetty said.

"And, and you are never put off by headaches and the like, are you?"

"Of course not," she said, giving his arm a squeeze. "You are only human, my dearest Frederick. And illness of any sort is no respecter of persons." What an odd light he had in his eye suddenly. "Did I, did I give you a disgust of me when I swooned earlier?"

"Oh, no, Hetty!" he cried, also laying his hand on her arm and returning the squeeze. "I gave you a shock by blurting out my intentions toward Mrs. Ambergate." He sighed, letting his gaze drift away. "My intentions," he murmured almost sadly.

Hetty turned to look up at him. He seemed strangely distressed. "What's the matter, Freddy?" she queried gently.

He turned to look at her. "Mrs. Ullstree said something to me while you were deep in your swoon, something I have not been able to dismiss from my mind."

"What was that?"

"It was something about you, but I am afraid if I bring the subject forward I will cause you pain."

"Tell me anyway," Henrietta said, her heart picking up its

cadence. She sensed that her future was drawing very near to her and on no account did she intend to send it away merely by being frightened of a little pain. "You must tell me, for I can see that you need to speak."

He drew in a breath. "Mrs. Ullstree said you were in love with me," he stated in a quiet, gentle voice.

Hetty averted her gaze quickly. She felt a blush rise swiftly up her cheeks. She could not respond to his statement except to nod briskly several times and force her feet to continue their march down the stairs.

She heard him draw in his breath in a deep sigh. "Good God," he murmured. "Methinks I am too late."

Hetty knew, or thought she knew, or hoped she knew precisely what he meant.

What a dreadful coil!

At the close of dinner, Lady Somercote rose from her chair and gave the order of the performance of the vignettes. She and Mr. Ullstree would go first, followed by Mrs. Ullstree and Colonel Duffield. Jane and Thorpe would perform third, then Mr. Waingrove and Miss Hartworth, with her husband and Mrs. Newstead performing the final vignette. She trusted everyone had done their best to create amusing and enlightening scenes with which they would all be edified or, if not, then at least thoroughly entertained.

Jane walked beside Thorpe in the casual processional to the music room where the vignettes would be performed. She let her fingers touch his quite accidentally as now and then she would glide toward him. Once he even caught her fingers and gave them a squeeze. She wondered if either Freddy or Henrietta, following behind them, could see what mischief they were making. Jane had already decided that immediately following the vignettes she would take Freddy aside and have a long, serious discussion with him. For her own conscience's sake, she had to reveal the truth of her sentiments and the fact that she would not become his wife afterall.

Poor Freddy.

The music room was illuminated overhead by a dazzling chandelier. In addition, several branches of candles were lit all about the perimeter of the circular chamber. A small stage had been built in the center of the round carpet and a tall, box-like frame, draped with red velvet curtains, completed the theatrical setting. In order to diminish the loftiness of the chamber and lend a more intimate atmosphere to the music room, Lady Somercote had set up a myriad of potted shrubs, small trees, and numerous vases to either side of the red velvet stage. The effect was charming as well as fragrant since roses and sweet peas filled the vases.

Eight black lacquer Empire chairs had been arranged in a wide semi-circle before the stage and small serving tables set between. Champagne would be passed round, along with fruit, jellies, and creams to be enjoyed during the intermissions which would follow each vignette.

The first set of players, Lady Somercote and Mr. Ullstree, made their way to the antechamber connecting to the music room where all the various props and minor costume accessories were held for the performances. The trees and potted shrubs kept the antechamber from view. When they mounted the single step of the stage, Jane noted with a smile that Lady Somercote carried a riding whip and Mr. Ullstree a newspaper which he had rolled up tightly. The floor of the stage was covered in a small woven carpet of blues and red. Before beginning their vignette, Lady Somercote and Mr. Ullstree joined hands and bowed to the assembled guests. Jane could not keep from offering her applause, a signal picked up by the others. Because of the fine acoustics of the music room, the sound of eight gloved hands clapping gave the impression of a score of guests.

Lady Somercote took a step forward and said, "We have entitled our vignette, 'The Honeymoon.' "

Jane thought this should be intriguing.

Lady Somercote then took up her place opposite her fellow thespian and held her whip aloft in a commanding fashion. "We must have rules," she cried in a clear voice. "I shall begin—no reading of the newspaper at breakfast or nuncheon or dinner so long as I am present. I will not be surpassed by a paragraph about the horseflesh to be found at Tattersall's."

Mr. Ullstree stepped slightly in front of her and cast his newspaper, angling downward, across her white silk skirts. "Without my paper, without knowledge of the world, life loses its significance."

"But this is our honeymoon," the abused wife wailed.

Mr. Ullstree crossed his arms over his chest. "I will have my newspaper."

Lady Somercote affected an expression of willful determination. "Then I shall go riding."

He whirled on her, horrified. Lifting his newspaper aloft he commanded, "You cannot go riding on our honeymoon. Your attention should be settled exclusively upon me."

Lady Somercote planted her fists on each hip and turned to face him. "But your attention is fixed on your newspaper. So why then shouldn't I go riding while you gain your knowledge of the world?"

"So be it, madame."

"As you wish, my husband."

They turned their backs on one another. He ruffled open the newspaper and began to read, his head proud. She slapped her riding crop against her own leg, also proud of her decision to ride.

In stages, their expressions began to fall, to fail, to disintegrate. He let his paper drop to the floor. She tossed her riding crop aside. Slowly they turned to one another.

"You are come back early from your ride?"

"And you are not reading your paper."

"The world lost its savor without you."

"I did not care so much for the wind in my face without you by my side."

In a staged manner, they embraced.

"Oh, I forgot to tell you," he said, while holding her in his arms. "I invited Geoffrey to join us for a few days. He'll be arriving at noon."

Lady Somercote appeared shocked. "But I hate Geoffrey. You didn't give me enough time to prepare his rooms. He flirts with the upper maids. Besides, this is our honeymoon. How could you be so thoughtless?"

Mr. Ullstree placed a hand at his chest, feigning shock and pain. "I did not invite him with a design to hurt you. I did not know I was being thoughtless, but he's coming anyway."

"You are a cruel beast."

"I am but I won't do it again without consulting you."

Lady Somercote sighed deeply. "I forgive you." She paused while he placed a theatrical kiss on her cheek. "Oh, there is something I forgot to tell you," she said, clasping her hands together innocently beside her face.

"What is that my pet, my beloved, my dearest one?" he asked, pressing his cheek to hers.

"I invited Miss Smith to join us for a few days. Isn't it fortuitous that Geoffrey is coming afterall?"

"Miss Smith!" Mr. Ullstree exclaimed, appearing dumbfounded, drawing back from her. "Why I begin to believe, madame, that you knew all along Geoffrey was coming."

She shrugged prettily. "I did," she confessed.

"What a wicked minx you are!"

"But they would make a good match of it, don't you agree?"

"My pet," he said, shaking his head at her. "You are not going to be one of those females that engages in matchmaking, are you?"

"Of course not," she said, shaking her peppery curls earnestly. "It is silly to attempt to press Fate along in such a hopeless manner."

"Which brings me to a question I have been wanting to ask you for a long time."

"Yes, dearest one?"

"Did you know I was in attendance at Major Beverstock's honeymoon cottage, you know that day we first met? If I recall, you were visiting a neighbor of the major's, Mrs. Botherhead."

"I hadn't a notion you would be there. But wasn't it lucky for us."

He eyed her suspiciously. "Just as lucky for Geoffrey and Miss Smith no doubt."

She turned her cheek to him and he peaked it soundly. "No doubt." A long pause ensued, ending only with Lady Somercote's wink.

After a moment, they joined hands again, took a step forward and bowed to their audience.

The guests erupted into a round of enthusiastic applause. Colonel Duffield laughed soundly. Jane thought the whole of it as delightful as it was accurate.

Next to perform were Mrs. Ullstree and Colonel Duffield. They left their chairs to retrieve props from the antechamber. While they were gone, a servant offered glasses of champagne to the remaining guests. Jane took a small goblet in hand and sipped the bubbly wine.

After a few minutes, Mrs. Ullstree mounted the stage, wearing a white silk mask embroidered with gold thread. In her hand she carried a fan dressed in long white feathers. Because she wore an elegant white silk half-robe over gold velvet, the mask and the fan were enchanting accents. She stood quietly waiting, her gaze fixed upward. After a long moment, Jane realized that her pose was part of the vignette and the vignette had already begun.

She was intrigued.

When Colonel Duffield arrived, he wore his uniform, including a bicorn hat trailing with a long elegant black ostrich feather. "Oh," she murmured, the sound of her voice joined by Lady Somercote and Mrs. Newstead as they offered up in sequence a low, "Oh, my," and a "Duffield!" respectively. Even Henrietta was heard to choke on her champagne. What was it about a uniform that tended to unravel the feminine heart?

"I need my answer," he said, coming up behind Mrs. Ullstree

and removing his hat to hold it beneath his arm. "You promised me an answer. I have waited these many months and more. I leave tomorrow—for India. Will you marry me, or not?"

"I have already given my answer," Mrs. Ullstree said, bringing her fan to her lips. "I love another."

He took her by the elbow and turned her gently toward him. "You do not love him. You want only what he can give you. There is a difference."

"There is no difference. Besides, you speak as though you love me and I know that is not true."

"I have lied to you for weeks. I do love you. I have always loved you."

She lowered the fan away from her lips. "That is not possible. You do not have a heart."

"Every man has a heart."

"Then you pretended you did not."

"Yes, I pretended," the colonel said intensely. "I feared you would not love me in return."

"I do love you, but I don't want to give up the other one."

Colonel Duffield drew her into his arms and Mrs. Ullstree lifted her large fan to cover their faces. A silence ensued.

After a long moment, Mrs. Ullstree lowered her fan. "You shouldn't have kissed me."

"I couldn't help myself. You are so beautiful. I adore you. Please give up the other one and come with me. India will suit you, I am persuaded of it."

Mrs. Ullstree looked past his shoulder. "You must go. *He* is coming."

Colonel Duffield left the stage in the opposite direction. While he was gone, Mrs. Ullstree removed her mask and let it fall to the red and blue carpet at her feet. A moment later, Colonel Duffield returned, but now he wore an evening coat and a black mask. When he bounded onto the stage, Mrs. Ullstree lifted her fan and a silence ensued. She lowered her fan slowly, her expression frowning.

"What is it, my love?" the colonel queried.

"I—that is, I don't know precisely. But never mind that, you wrote in your missive that you wanted to see me, that you had something you wished to ask me?"

"I have the most delightful news. I have hired a yacht in the Mediterranean. If we leave tonight and travel posthaste we'll be in Italy Saturday next. You must come with me. The summer, and all its fruits, beckons us."

Jane felt strange suddenly. She realized that in part her own dilemma was being portrayed before her. She wondered what would happen next.

Mrs. Ullstree lifted her fan to cover her mouth for a moment, her expression downcast. When she lowered her fan, she asked, "But is that all? Are we only to enjoy the fruits of the summer?"

"Well, yes, of course. That is all I can offer. Do say you will come."

"I want more."

"I cannot give you more."

"But you pretended you could."

He slowly removed his mask and she appeared shocked. "Why didn't you tell me you were pretending that you were more than a summer's fleeting pleasure."

"I wanted you."

Mrs. Ullstree lifted her chin. "I will not go with you. As it happens, I have become betrothed. I leave for India tomorrow."

"You are to be married? But you were married once. I thought you'd had your fill?"

"I thought I had until I saw that all you could offer was the summertime."

The colonel left distraught. Mrs. Ullstree dabbed at her eyes for a long moment, then as the colonel returned with portmanteau in hand and wearing his bicorn hat and officer's coat of blue with red facings, Mrs. Ullstree exited. He stood as Mrs. Ullstree had posed at the outset of the vignette, with his face lifted upward, waiting.

After a moment, Mrs. Ullstree arrived on stage again, wearing a poke bonnet, a billowing cape, and bearing two bandboxes.

"I am coming with you," she said.

The colonel whirled around, ecstatic. But as he paused, he saw that she wasn't wearing her mask. "You look different; you've changed somehow."

"I've left behind all my pretensions, all my silly hopes that life was what it was not."

He took her hand in his and placed a fervent kiss on her fingers. "You will not regret coming with me."

"I know I will not," she responded, smiling. "Only tell me this, are there four seasons in India?"

Both players paused for a long moment, letting the meaning of her final words sink in fully. After a full minute, they relaxed their shoulders, joined hands, smiled at one another, and turned to bow to the audience.

Jane applauded briskly knowing that some of her own struggles with Thorpe were hidden within the body of Colonel Duffield's and Mrs. Ullstree's vignette. She turned to glance at Thorpe who sat to her right, but because the line of chairs was curved in a semi-circle, and Mrs. Newstead sat on the other side of Thorpe, her attention was caught by the sight of the widow looking up at Thorpe with a faint frown between her brow.

Jane looked away, reverting her gaze to the stage. She thought that for just a moment she had seen into Mrs. Newstead's mind and wondered if that was her flaw, that she believed life was what it was not—that she still believed somehow that within Thorpe resided more than one season of love. Her own spirits took a downturn as she realized part of her was holding onto the belief, as well.

She was drawn from her reverie by Thorpe's voice as he whispered into her ear from behind her, "It is our turn. Come. The stage awaits us."

Jane inclined her head and rose to her feet. Mrs. Ullstree and the colonel had not yet returned, so they had sufficient time to retrieve their swords without keeping the party waiting long. Besides, another servant was progressing down the row of chairs and pouring more champagne.

Her heart began to hammer gently against her ribs. She was used to performing publicly, on the pianoforte and in vocal duets, and she had never refused a request to dance or read aloud on a Sunday evening. But performing a vignette with Thorpe was a different matter altogether, especially since they were to use swords.

She was excited and distressed all at once, not less so than because the previous vignette had struck so close to home. Regardless, she gave herself a mental shake and walked into the antechamber with Thorpe. Retrieving her sword, she was about to return to the stage when Thorpe caught her by the elbow and whispered in her ear. "We are long past summer, Jane. Don't make too much of Duffield's vignette. His words were directed toward Mrs. Newstead, not you."

"I know," she said, still feeling troubled.

"I doubt that you will believe me," he said, looking deeply into her eyes. "But what you and I have is something I've never experienced before. Jane, I think I've—"

He got no further since Lady Somercote called to them in a stage whisper. "Come, Thorpe. We know of your flirtations, but you keep us all waiting."

He smiled at his hostess and with another smile touched Jane's cheek and said, "Shall we make them wonder whether we are not bound for a life of acting?"

At that Jane smiled, her nerves calming, her heart warming toward Thorpe. She could not be in doubt of just how he would have completed his sentence. *Jane, I think I've* can have only one possible ending.

Jane, I think I've tumbled in love with you.

She sighed deeply as she placed her hand on his arm and began to move on a steady tread toward the back of the stage.

Fourteen

"I will not be three acts and a farce," Thorpe insisted, lifting his sword and letting it press against Jane's throat.

Jane heard the gasp of the guests. Inwardly, she smiled. They would certainly enjoy this vignette, she thought. Using her hand, she slapped away the offending sword and lifted her own in a quick, orchestrated sweep to touch the viscount on his chest, where his heart was located. "What are we then?" she asked fiercely in response.

He took her sword and held it in his hand. "We are a vignette. Two flames that come together for a brief moment and burn each other to cinders."

"So you say!" she cried, stepping back from him and taking up the *en guard* position. She narrowed her eyes at him. "But I say we are even more than three acts and certainly more than a farce."

Thorpe smiled and narrowed his eyes at her, lifting his left hand aloft as he crossed their swords. "I've kissed you. You shouldn't have permitted it if you wanted more than a vignette."

"I permitted it because you stared at me as though you had already written an entire play."

Their swords rasped and clinked as they moved about in a circle on the stage.

Several times she heard gasps and exclamations erupt from the guests, as she thrust, he parried, and their swords scraped fire.

He caught her sword at the hilt with his own, then took strong hold of her arm. "You have deluded yourself, madame. I can barely write a sonnet, nonetheless a play as you suggest. I hold the line—we are a vignette."

With her free hand she pushed back his shoulder and he fell back theatrically. "You are mistaken in your abilities. The fire of your kisses and your words is more than even a play. Merely your perception is addled. You *see* a brief scene, but I see the whole of it."

Again their swords came together in a quick rasping, thrusting, lunging, and parrying. Again they came together and they met hilt to hilt, straining against one another. "It is your perception that is perverted," he responded coldly, his eyes again narrowing. "You speak like a woman."

"And you, sir, act like a man."

"Then why do you remain if you are so much in disgust of me?"

"I am not in disgust. I am in admiration and hope."

"You let the latter rule your senses. My offer stands, the enjoyment of a vignette that will be brief, fiery, but will one day end."

Jane suddenly stepped back and lowered her sword. She stared at Thorpe for a long, long moment. This was not a planned part of their vignette but somehow it seemed very right to her. She turned her sword in her hand and offered it to him. "Then do with me what you will. We cannot agree and I have not the ability to persuade you otherwise."

He lowered his sword and stared mutely at the handle of hers. After a long moment, he took it. "You force me to make the choice," he said, frowning at the sword.

"But what will you choose, I wonder," she said, "now that you are the one that must choose. You must search your own mind and see whether a vignette is all you are."

With that, she exited the stage. She heard him say to the guests. "How is it I feel that though I have won, I have lost?" When he left the stage the guests erupted into a burst of applause. Jane heard Colonel Duffield cry out, "Well done! Well done!"

Jane did not resume her seat immediately but returned to the antechamber. She was trembling from head to foot, a sensation she could not control. Thorpe followed closely on her heels and settled the swords on the table. He stared hard at her, his expression intense as he searched her face. She watched his piercing blue eyes cut a neat line through her mind and heart. She parted her lips, her breathing grew shallow. She let him into her mind and heart and allowed him to read every sentiment she possessed. His eyes glittered in the dimly lit chamber. He took a step toward her. She saw meaning and purpose in his countenance, in the fire on his face, in the glitter of his eyes.

"Jane, what have you done?" he murmured. He was very close to her and placed a hand on her arm.

She knew he meant to kiss her and even to speak the words she now realized she was longing to hear, of his love, his ardor, his devotion to her, of his wish to become more than a vignette.

But at that moment, Freddy and Henrietta arrived to retrieve their props. Jane stepped hastily away from Thorpe and after bowing to both players, she quickly returned to her seat. Thorpe sat down beside her and with the hum of a variety of conversations rising up about them, he said, "I must speak with you— tonight. We must settle this matter once and for all."

Jane looked at him and saw a light in his eye that had never been there before. "Yes," she whispered.

Applause resounded as Freddy and Henrietta took the stage.

Abruptly, Jane was drawn away from Thorpe and from his possible intentions toward her. Freddy was looking at her, holding her gaze steadily and forcing her to remember that in his declaration earlier that day he had pointedly told her that the body of the vignette he had created with Hetty was to hold some special meaning for her.

She felt her cheeks flush with the realization that though she was fully given to Thorpe, in nearly every possible way, Freddy believed she would soon become his wife. She felt mortified, ashamed of herself.

She glanced at Henrietta who was seating herself in a black lacquer chair that Freddy had placed on the stage for her. Her complexion was unusually pale, probably the aftermath of the swooning she had suffered earlier. Jane watched her for a long moment, thinking that something was wrong with Hetty. Her features bore a stiffness unusual for even her, and her eyes seemed almost glazed. She scarcely blinked.

She watched as Freddy knelt upon one knee before her, then murmured something to her. Hetty finally blinked and looked down upon him. She took a deep breath, "What is it you wish to say to me, my good man?" Her voice was breathless and trembled. Poor Hetty, so shy, so full of fears. She should not have been required to perform a vignette at all.

Before Freddy began his speech, he glanced at Jane, but an odd frown was between his brows. He turned back to Hetty and began, "Before ever there was a sun or moon, you lived. I am convinced of it. Having known you for such a brief earthly period, how else can I explain the celestial quality of your mind, your heart, the strength of your being. You cast the stars in a faint dimness unequalled. The moon is transparent next to you and the sun a hazy yellow orb of gleamless dullness. I am unworthy to stand next to such a glowing member of the heavenly expanse, nonetheless to kneel before you and beg for a union with you. But casting aside my unworthiness and summoning what little courage I possess, I beg you to consider my hand in marriage, to bless my existence with your halo of kindness, love, and brilliance, to bear my children in a pool of mercy and compassion. Will you, my dearest, accept of my hand in marriage?"

Jane felt a numbing sensation pour over her. If these truly were Freddy's sentiments toward her, then she had used him ill regardless of the nature of her feelings toward him. She could no longer look at him, but instead fixed her gaze on Hetty. Only as she watched the young woman, and her sensations of mortification diminished, only as she realized that there was a strange shifting of seats all about her, did she come to understand that something was amiss.

Hetty rose to her feet, and Freddy leaned back on his heels, his brows lifted in surprise. Jane found herself profoundly affected by the way Henrietta was glowing with some mysterious light as though the muse had just come over her. How surprising to find that Miss Hartworth could be an actress afterall.

"You do me far too much honor, Mr. Waingrove," she murmured. Jane was a little surprised that Hetty had used his real name. "I am no celestial creature, but I do love you. I have for a long, long time. The truth is, however, that I don't believe you've ever understood me—who I am, or what I could bring to your life if you would but let me. Your sentiments are blinded by your wish to see me as more than I am. I could only wish that you could see me for what I am truly worth. For that reason, I must refuse you. No woman can compete with the beauty of the sun, moon, or stars. She can only offer her willingness to walk beside a man while the heavens watch in splendor from above."

She placed a hand on his cheek and with tears brimming in her eyes, she quickly left the stage. Freddy blinked at the empty chair in front of him for some time, then rose at last to his feet. This time he did not look at Jane. He straightened his shoulders and stated, "This is our vignette. We are finished."

Jane glanced at Lady Somercote next to her and exchanged a look of surprise with her. The vignette had been lovely but the ending was so abrupt as to have seemed unplanned. A smattering of applause sounded as Freddy turned on his heel and quit the stage.

After several minutes, Freddy, his complexion exceedingly pale, rejoined the semi-circle of chairs. But only as Lord Somercote and Mrs. Newstead took the stage, did Jane become aware that Hetty had not returned to take up her own seat. She sensed that something was not right but she couldn't determine precisely what.

Her wonderings were interrupted, however, by Mrs. New-stead's commanding presence as she cried out, "But it cannot be!"

Lord Somercote came up behind Mrs. Newstead and whis-pered in a devilish manner. "But it is true. And pray don't keep pretending you believed otherwise, for I will not credit it for a moment."

Mrs. Newstead lifted her hand to her cheek and shaped her pretty lips into a round circle. "Oh," she cooed long and loud, her brow furrowed in stunned disbelief. "But you must be tell-ing me a dreadful whisker, you awful beast of a man! I have never trusted you above half, why should I believe you now?"

"Why should you disbelieve me?" he returned, placing an arm about her waist and turning her to face him. "You have already admitted the truth of my character. I am a beast of a man, a rogue, a libertine, I am all of this—and more."

Jane heard Thorpe murmur, a string of words that sounded like, "The devil!"

She had an uneasy sensation herself, as though the vignette in front of her was strangely familiar.

"Besides," Lord Somercote said, "I have proof of my mis-conduct."

Again, Mrs. Newstead turned to the audience and cried out a long, "Oh." She blinked and appeared so delightfully dis-tressed that Colonel Duffield laughed aloud and even Lady Somercote chuckled beside her. Mrs. Newstead continued, "What proof could you possibly have that you visited my room last night instead of my husband?"

At that, the guests all murmured their astonishment at the true meaning of the vignette and the conflict between the players on the stage. But Jane felt something entirely different as she turned slowly to look up at Thorpe. He did not turn to meet her gaze. Instead, he glared at the lady on the stage, a glare that confirmed her suspicions—he had told the widow Newstead of his trickery in coming to her chamber the first night of the festivities in lieu of Freddy.

She was dumbfounded.

How could Thorpe have revealed so intimate an experience?

His nostrils flared, he ground his teeth, he crossed his arms over his chest.

As Jane watched his ire rise, she thought that however much his nose might flare and his jaw work strongly, he wasn't experiencing even a particle of the rage that flowed through her in this moment.

Mrs. Newstead repeated her question, "What proof, my lord?"

Lord Somercote then reached into the pocket of his coat, visible from the audience, and Jane watched in horror as the brass key and violet ribbon belonging exclusively to her bedchamber came into view. He let the key dangle from the long ribbon and held it up to the nose of the lady next to him.

The audience gasped as one.

Jane felt the warmth drain from her face. She wanted to scream, to bolt, to strike the man next to her, for there was her key—the one that was missing. Mrs. Newstead had stolen it from her chamber!

"You have my key!" Mrs. Newstead cried. "But how did you get it?"

"I threatened your maid and she happily gave it to me. It would seem she has been flirting with one of the stablehands of late and feared you would punish her were you to know the truth of her misdeeds."

"What a beast of a man you are!" Mrs. Newstead cried, taking the ribbon and the key from his hand. "I am undone. What if my husband learns of your heinous conduct?"

"He will not learn of it if you return the key to me."

Mrs. Newstead feigned shock and dismay. "Will you then leave me in peace?" she asked.

Lord Somercote, affecting a seductive expression as he lifted one of his eyebrows. "Yes," he responded, accepting the key back from her. "But only if you wish me to."

"Oh," Mrs. Newstead again exclaimed, turning to engage the

audience before her. Her expression was naughty beyond words and Jane might have been amused by it, except that the vignette struck too close to home for her to be anything other than horrified.

So, this was the extent of Thorpe's character and sense of decency, to baudily reveal to his former mistress his own triumph early in the summer *fete*. She despised him thoroughly.

The rogue!

The beast!

The beast of a man!

He would never change!

Close on the heels of this realization was the truly reprehensible knowledge that he had almost succeeded in seducing her completely and wholly. She had all but agreed to go with him to Europe for a long, sensual holiday from which she would return forever marred in the eyes of the *ton* and with the sure knowledge that his interest in her would have waned entirely.

What a foolish woman she was and had been for the past twelve days—as foolish as any romantic chit weaving her daydreams in the schoolroom of love and of lust, as though the two could ever be successfully united.

She was angry with herself and applauded the last vignette with blind rage. She felt numb to her toes and wondered if she would even be able to stand. She stopped clapping and turned to stare at Thorpe. She rose to her feet, as did he, a string of reproaches readied on her tongue.

"I can explain," he whispered. "Don't judge me on this, I beg of you, Jane. Not now. Not after last night."

Jane felt Lady Somercote's arm beneath her own. "I forgot!" her ladyship cried, disrupting Jane's intention of giving Thorpe the dressing down he so badly deserved. "But I have a little present for you. Will you come to my bedchamber at once and accept of it? Your birthday is next month and since you will have returned to Kent by then, I did so want to give you something. Come!"

Jane turned slowly to look at Lady Somercote, wanting to

rebuke her for preventing her from speaking. Instead, the countess stared at her meaningfully and tugged at her arm. Jane blinked several times as again Lady Somercote tugged on her arm. At last comprehension dawned within her enraged mind. She could hardly come the crab in the midst of the countess's guests.

"A gift?" Jane murmured. "But how lovely."

Lady Somercote breathed a sigh of relief, smiled, then drew her away even as she seemed to be waving awkwardly to Thorpe behind her. "Not now," she whispered urgently.

Jane knew that the countess was protecting her, leading her from the music room and away from the scrutiny of the other guests. Her mind was reeling as she walked swiftly beside her friend down the long hallway and up the circular stairs.

Only one thought ran through her mind, over and over, as she walked—how could Thorpe have used her so cruelly?

When she found herself in her bedchamber with Lady Somercote frowning worriedly upon her, she finally gave vent to her anger and her frustration.

"Oh!" she squealed in a loud, unforgiving voice. "The beast! The cruel, horrible, detestable beast who will never change, who will always be seeking only his own pleasure and never have the smallest interest in love or in learning to love or in valuing what is given to him."

"A terrible. cruel beast," Lady Somercote agreed. "He should be hung at Tyburn Tree."

"No, hanging is far too good for him. I have read of much better tortures. His fingernails should be stripped from his hands and hot oil poured on the bare flesh."

"Oh, dear," Lady Somercote murmured. Jane turned to her hostess and watched as that dear lady placed a hand over her mouth and sank into the light blue silk damask chair near the door. "You may hold such happy thoughts in your mind, dear Jane, but I beg for my sake you will not repeat them aloud."

"I am sorry," Jane said, crossing to the chair and sinking down beside her hostess. "It was rather macabre, wasn't it?"

"Yes," Lady Somercote said, staring at Jane in horror.

Suddenly, however, a smile peeped at the countess's lips and Jane bit her own lip in response. "Good God," she murmured. "How could I have even thought such a dreadful thing?"

Lady Somercote began to laugh and Jane joined her, tears of mirth springing to her eyes and cascading down her cheeks. But just as quickly as the unexpected laughter had engulfed her, so did a deep, overwhelming sadness. She buried her face in the skirts of Lady Somercote's gown and began to sob. She felt the countess's hand upon her back and more than once felt a teardrop, not her own, fall on her bare neck.

"These men," Lady Somercote whispered. "Whatever are we to do with them? They cause us such grief, all in the pursuit of their pleasure, the form of which can never bring them even a mite of true and abiding happiness. Why do we love them so?"

"I don't know," Jane wailed, her heart breaking. "It was my key and ribbon. She must have stolen it."

"She must have. How I despise her and I can't understand why such a good man as Colonel Duffield should wish to marry her when she is full of such vile mischief as she is."

Jane felt the initial pain of the situation begin to subside. She leaned back on her heels and Lady Somercote rose from the chair to find her a kerchief. When Jane heard the sliding and slamming shut of several drawers, she finally called to her, "In the dressing table, on the right."

A pause, a few footsteps, another sliding of a drawer. "Found them," Lady Somercote called back to her.

Jane took the two her friend proffered to her and with her knees on the wood floor and her feet scrunched up behind her, she let one of the kerchiefs drop into her lap and the other she used to blow her nose soundly.

"I am such a fool," she whispered. "I had almost surrendered even my life to him."

Lady Somercote took up her seat. "You would not be the first to have done so," she said, still patting Jane's head. "Only tell me now what I can do for you? Shall I send up your maid with a tray of hot chocolate or tea or something?"

"Chocolate," Jane said with a sigh as she again blew her nose. "And an apricot tart. Laudanum. A pint of it. I shall drink it all and not awaken for a year."

"Jane," Lady Somercote said, "I don't like to mention it, but if you imbibed a pint of laudanum, you'd be asleep for longer than a year."

Jane laughed. "Chocolate and a tart, then. And a small glass of port wine."

Lady Somercote rose from her chair, turning to smile encouragingly at Jane as she opened the door. "Tomorrow, all of this won't seem quite so odious."

"I know," Jane said rising to her feet. "I have endured worse, but I suffer because my hopes were so stupidly misplaced."

"Just so," Lady Somercote returned kindly. Then she was gone.

On the following morning, Jane stayed in bed for hours, refusing a tray of food or the ministrations of her maid. The apricot tart she had ordered of the night before was uneaten and now crusted over though the cup of chocolate was empty.

The night and a few more tears had given her counsel. She thanked God she was no longer young and innocent. She was able to quickly find fault with her own conduct sufficiently to place only the proper blame on Thorpe's wicked betrayal. No one had forced her to allow his seductions. She had drawn them to herself with her own desire for love and perhaps to even a larger degree with her lust for sensual pleasure. That she had tricked herself into believing all was well and could be well with such an arrangement as Thorpe had dictated, was foolish beyond permission.

So, here she was, cloistered in her bedchamber, confessing her sins to her own uneasy conscience, and trying to decide what she needed to do next. She was surprised, however, that not all was confusion in her mind. On the contrary, never before, since her arrival at Challeston Hall, had her life and her choices been clearer to her. She had married Edward for love and for lust. As she reviewed her stormy courtship with Captain Edward Ambergate, later to become major, she realized that he hadn't been a much different fellow from Lord Thorpe. He had been dashing and exciting and had kissed her as though raining fire from heaven. She had delighted in all the excitement, the turmoil, the sense that she was poised on the very edge of the universe ready to be propelled into the unknown six minutes of seven.

When his gaming had become a fixed part of their lives, only then had the passion diminished. The greater the gaming, the less the passion. The equation had remained steady until his demise when even the equation itself had been blotted out.

Thorpe, it would seem—though not a gamester—was even a step removed in character from Edward. For while Edward had married her, Thorpe's only intention was to make use of his passionate feelings toward her until, as he had said often, they burnt one another to cinders.

But it wasn't until she saw her brass key, strung with pretty violet ribbon, emerge from Somercote's coat pocket, that the truth of her decisions had crashed down on her. What had she been thinking? That a man who purposely pursued female after female actually had a particle of a conscience? That such a man could possibly respect a woman who succumbed to his advances? That such a man would suddenly alter the patterns of his life simply because *she* was Jane Ambergate?

Foolishness. Monstrous, conceited, wretched foolishness!

She was in this moment the perfect example of feminine stupidity.

But she needn't remain so heinous a model. Thorpe had sent her a missive begging her to meet him in the yew maze at noon and she simply wouldn't go, nor would she respond in any other manner to his request. From now on, Thorpe no longer existed.

Such was her conviction that a great peace descended over

her. She turned her thoughts away from the past and with a smile embraced the future—a future that would include the Honorable Frederick Waingrove.

Later, long past nuncheon but an hour before tea was to be served, Jane emerged from her bedchamber wearing a half-robe bearing a slight demi-train of fine Indian calico in faint patterns of brown and cornflower blue over a soft white lawn undergown. Her dark brown curls remained unbonneted. From her blue-gloved hands dangled a poke bonnet dressed with matching blue and brown calico and trimmed with artificial forget-me-nots. Her brown leather slippers could easily manage the many paths about the exquisite grounds of the house. Her sole intention in finally leaving her bedchamber was to find Freddy and beg him to escort her on a long stroll about the prettiest of the gravel paths. She had a great many things she wanted to say to him and she knew now the answer she would give to his offer of the day before.

But as she closed the door behind her, Henrietta emerged from her bedchamber directly opposite her own. Jane smiled at the young lady who started at the sight of her.

"Oh!" Hetty exclaimed, pressing a hand to her heart. "You gave me a fright, though I know very well you did not mean to."

"Of course I did not," Jane responded kindly. She then approached her friend and begged to know if she had seen Freddy this morning and whether or not he had made plans for the afternoon since she was desirous of speaking with him.

Henrietta colored up, a deep blush burning her neck, her cheek, and spreading up and outward to encompass her entire face. "Yes!" she cried. "That is, no! At least, I'm not certain."

Hetty's mouth was agape as though Jane had indeed given her a shock.

Jane smiled and patted her shoulder. "Never mind, dearest. You are not his keeper. You are not obligated to know where he is every minute of every day. But rest assured I will find him, for I have news that I believe shall make him the happiest of men."

Henrietta's eyes took on a tortured appearance. She blinked, she swallowed, she drew in a deep breath. "I—that is, I've little doubt he will be gratified to see you and to, to hear your most excellent tidings. However—that is, Jane—" Hetty swallowed again and blinked and drew in another breath.

Jane found herself becoming impatient. "For heaven's sake, Hetty, what is troubling you? Speak. You have nothing to fear from me." She huffed a sigh.

Hetty closed her mouth but only with a strong effort. At last she waved a hand down the hall. "Now that I think on it, I believe you will be able to find Mr. Waingrove in the library."

Jane was pleased. "Oh, then you've made my task much easier than I expected it to be. Thank you and don't worry. All will be settled and then I daresay you may be easy again."

"Yes," Hetty answered, almost sadly. "I suppose so."

Jane was a little surprised when Henrietta turned around and slowly opened the door of her bedchamber, then disappeared inside.

Poor little thing, Jane mused. The vignette of the night before, being so shy and of having to perform in a theatrical manner, had clearly taken a toll on the frail, waifish young lady.

Well, she was sorry for Hetty. Indeed, she felt great compassion for the poor young woman who had no voice with which to speak. But if that was Hetty's cross to bear, then her own was her tendency to let her heart and the passions of her body run away with her.

Jane turned away from Hetty's door and made her way on a steady, nearly spritely tread, toward the library. She swung her bonnet on its blue ribbons and smiled. She felt deeply at ease in her heart, as she had not felt even from the day of the processional beginning in Chadfield. Now that she recalled that day, she remembered that before she had descended from her room at the inn, she had been staring at Lord Thorpe from the window and lusting after him. Even from the first, her foolishness had ruled every ounce of common sense she possessed, and that in abundance! Never again, she promised herself, would she underestimate the powers of a man of libertine propensities.

The rogue!

The beast!

When she entered the library, she found it to be deserted except for Freddy who rose immediately upon her entrance, a joy beaming from his pale complexion, gold-green eyes, and fine, even white teeth.

"Hallo, Freddy," she called to him lightly.

But even as she advanced into the chamber she was stunned to watch as his face fell. The joy in his eyes grew oddly dim, his complexion turned ashen and then began to be dotted with familiar pink patches as his lips closed firmly over his pretty white teeth.

She blinked at him as she crossed the room. "Whatever is the matter? Were you expecting someone else? Hetty only just now informed me of your whereabouts."

"I was expecting no one," he responded, the pink patches joining together into a solid blush of embarrassment. "Truly. I—I was, that is, Jane, how lovely to see you. When I did not find you at breakfast or nuncheon I had supposed that you had taken ill."

"I was ill," Jane said, moving past him to seat herself on the sofa opposite his chair. Freddy followed her lead and took up his seat again. "But not as anyone would suppose I had been. My illness was more an affliction of the mind and of the heart."

Freddy opened his eyes wide and crossed his knee over his leg. "What—what do you mean?"

"Only that after seeing your delightful and heartfelt vignette, I was consumed with every manner of turmoil. You see, earlier I had decided we should not suit, so you can imagine what a shock your proposals of yesterday brought to me. But you asked me to stay an answer until I had seen your vignette, and so I did. Freddy, I have come to tell you that after much searching through every corner of my mind and heart I wish above all things to become your wife, to make you the very best helpmeet of which I am capable, and, God-willing, to bear you a host of children."

His mouth had fallen agape as each word dropped from her lips. He appeared much as Hetty had appeared earlier—almost pained, certainly embarrassed, and oddly quiet. She had stunned him. Clearly, she had confounded him and stunned him.

She knew what she needed to do. She rose from her seat on the sofa and dropped to her knees beside the man she had chosen to become her next husband. She laid her head on his knee. "I can see that you weren't expecting me to accept of your hand in marriage and that I have given you a shock. But I trust it will be a shock of a short-lived nature and that before evening has fallen upon the countryside we will be able to share our delightful tidings with all who I know will wish us well."

She felt Freddy's hand lightly upon her neck. "Just as you wish," he said quietly.

Was there a resigned note in his voice?

Jane looked up at him quickly. "Freddy, you do still wish to marry me, don't you?" she asked.

He blinked rapidly several times. "Marry you?" he queried, then laughed brightly. "I have wanted nothing else for the past several months. You have made me the happiest of men."

Jane smiled and sighed, returning her cheek to his knee. "I am so glad," she said, contentment pouring through her. "And I intend to continue to see that you remain the happiest of men."

Before dinner, Thorpe stood in mute, shocked silence beside Mrs. Ullstree and watched a veritable glow of happiness shine from Jane's face. Freddy had just made the announcement of their betrothal. He felt as though a bolt of lightning had entered his head and exited through every nerve that jerked and vibrated over his arms, chest, back, and legs.

"What the devil," he muttered.

"Isn't it extraordinary," Mrs. Ullstree said, sounding stunned. "I knew she wished for a marriage with him, but I had supposed he would wed Miss Hartworth."

Thorpe only half-listened to her. He didn't give a fig for who Freddy did or did not marry. What he cared about was that Jane had actually agreed to wed him. She can't have taken Mrs. Newstead's silly vignette to heart! She can't have! Though now, as he watched how tightly Jane clung to Freddy Waingrove's rather stiff arm, he realized she must have.

He should have known something was amiss when she did not respond to his missive to meet him in the yew maze at noon, that they had to talk, that he had something of a particular nature to say to her. He had intended to use his every ability of persuasion to force her to forget about the brass key and the violet ribbon and to convince her to become his mistress. The key wasn't important, all that mattered was that they be together, for a long time, for a long, delicious, sensual time—especially since his feelings for her had grown powerful enough that he had admitted to himself that somewhere over the past weeks or months he had tumbled in love with her. He knew Jane loved him, that she wanted to be with him; there could be no two opinions on that score. But why had she gone and accepted Freddy's offer at this eleventh hour? Surely she was not such a simpleton as to choose to ruin their happiness by placing too much stock in Mrs. Newstead's vindictiveness. Surely not!

But here she was glowing and smiling and accepting the well wishes of Lady Somercote and the rest of the guests, and here he was feeling as though lightning had pinned him permanently to the floor next to the fireplace and Mrs. Ullstree.

"You see, the truth is," Mrs. Ullstree said in a whisper, leaning close to him. "I always thought you and Mrs. Ambergate would make a match of it. Never have I seen two persons so beautifully suited to one another as you and our arrow-shooting, hard-riding, quick-dancing, sword-fencing Jane Ambergate. But it would seem you're a whisper too late. I pity you, Thorpe, indeed, I do."

Thorpe turned to her and frowned. "Make a match of it?" he queried, a slight edge to his voice. Had the woman no sense at all? He would never make one of his mistresses his wife.

But Mrs. Ullstree sent a rush of hot oil over his already prickly nerves by staring at him pointedly, smiling in a reprehensibly knowing fashion, then walking past him to offer up her felicitations for Jane's and Freddy's happiness.

He lost all sense of time at that moment. He couldn't even see his surroundings for the mist that had rolled into the forest-green drawing room and obliterated everything except Jane holding tightly to Freddy's arm.

She seemed so happy, he realized.

But how could that be? How could she be happy with anyone but him?

Jane, to be married.

Jane, not to go with him to the Continent, not to travel in easy stages through Europe, not to sail about the Mediterranean and fend off the quick, ransom-seeking corsairs.

Jane.

Thunder rattled through the drawing room, rolling over his chest in a hard, brutal wave of power and pain.

Jane.

He began to feel light-headed and nauseous. He couldn't breathe precisely. The summer storm was breaking within his heart and tearing his clever, self-absorbed schemes all to flinders.

Jane.

Good God, what had he done?

He felt an arm slip about his and he looked down to his left to find a peach-glinted complexion, round, shining blue eyes, and a smile full of summery dimples smiling up at him. "You are mine," Mrs. Newstead whispered, sighing deeply. She then trilled her laughter, released his arm, and moved away.

Thorpe didn't know what she meant by it, at least somewhere deep in his brain he knew, but he couldn't quite make it out. Afterall, a violent storm was raging all about him and in him.

A wind had come up and was whipping rain onto his face and obscuring his vision.

"We're in the basket now," a man's voice said, somehow breaking through the noise of the storm swirling about him.

"What do you mean, Duffield?" he heard himself say.

"If what Mrs. Newstead told me is correct, you promised to marry her if you didn't make Mrs. Ambergate your mistress by tomorrow's recessional."

Thorpe stared at him, horrified at what he was saying.

"You didn't forget, man!" Duffield cried. His expression was both mocking and dumbfounded at the same time. "Surely you knew what she was and that she wouldn't have hesitated playing her last card to her advantage, even at the expense of your love for Mrs. Ambergate? Surely you weren't that green, Thorpe?"

"I didn't expect it," he said numbly. The rain had settled into a steady drone on his face and over his head and on his shoulders and chest. "I should have. Good God, what a stripling I've been!"

"The only question now is what do you mean to do about it?"

"I don't know," he said, shaking his head. "I still can't credit she actually agreed to marry him?"

"A little puffed up in your own conceit, eh?" Duffield asked provokingly.

Thorpe felt a quick whip of rage crack in him. "If you don't care to receive a little of the home-brewed, I suggest you retract that remark at once."

"Shan't do it, old fellow. The way I see it, you're in need of a bit of a dressing down. What did you think? That there wasn't a lady born who found being in your bed sufficient solace, comfort, and security to last her a lifetime? Hah!"

Thorpe was shaking as he turned toward Duffield. "I've never been so insulted."

"I'm only holding up a looking-glass. I've no intention of picking up your gauntlet, not when right now you need your

wits about you more than ever—just as I need mine, or neither
of us shall win the day. Can you understand that, *my lord?*"

Duffield held his gaze so piercingly that Thorpe finally felt
the rain on his face begin to diminish. He drew in a deep breath.
A kind of calm after the storm begin to sweep over his shoulders
and invade his head. "My wits," he murmured. "By God, you've
the right of it," he responded at last in a whisper. "I've been
puffed up, I've misjudged the woman you love, and I don't think
I ever understood myself so well before."

"A woman always looks different when she's on the arm of
another man," he said cryptically in response.

Thorpe turned to look at Jane and saw that her fingers were
splayed across Freddy's arm. She had a tight hold on the man
she was to marry, as though if she let him go, she would spin
away from him and never stop spinning.

What a coil! What a deuce of a coil!

"You must let up a little, Jane," Freddy whispered, leaning
slightly down to her.

Jane looked up at her betrothed and smiled brightly. "Whatever do you mean?"

"My arm. You're gripping me just a little too, er, firmly."

Jane looked down at her hand and with a jerk, released her
talon-like fingers. "I do beg your pardon. I am just so excited
of the moment. And a little nervous."

Freddy looked down at her and smiled. Jane saw the com-
pression of his lips and as she had for the past hour or so,
wondered why his smiles seemed so stiff, almost forced. At
least his fear of her was entirely gone. He moved next to her
with great confidence, and all his silly, agitated movements
which had previously characterized his conduct with her had
disappeared.

As Mrs. Ullstree approached her and offered her best wishes
for her happiness, all the while regarding her with an oddly
quizzical expression, she noted that Freddy had grown very still.

The hum of conversation all about her, as Mrs. Ullstree moved away, gave her a moment of respite. All was settled, she felt more content than ever, her heart was at ease.

She was about to give Freddy's arm a squeeze, when she suddenly saw Henrietta, situated across the room, seated on the sofa near the fireplace. Because Mr. Ullstree was standing near Lord Somercote, and both of the men were several feet in front of the sofa, she saw Miss Hartworth through a narrow aperture between the shoulders of the two men.

On instinct, she knew she was not supposed to be a witness to what was occurring, that Miss Hartworth had believed herself to be concealed by the two men. Her expression was fraught with pain and longing, her hazel eyes brimmed with tears. She was miserable, and in her misery she was letting her pain be known, but to whom?

She glanced up at Freddy and saw that since Lord Somercote had bent his head toward Mr. Ullstree, ostensibly to hear a joke, Freddy had a plain view of the young woman. She had never seen such a look on Freddy's face before—of anguish, of pain, of need, even of desire.

She gasped at what she saw, and in her gasping Freddy turned to look down at her. Tears rimmed his eyes as well as he blinked at her. Silently, he began to speak to her, straight from the desolation of his heart.

She thought back in quick, painful stages to the moment she had surprised Hetty while leaving her bedchamber. How deeply Hetty had blushed when she had asked her if perchance she knew where Freddy was. First she had insisted she did not know, then she had revealed the truth—in the library.

She blinked at Freddy now, her entire body growing chilled as she recalled the moment she entered the library. He had risen swiftly to his feet, his expression enrapt, his heart on every familiar feature. She also recalled how quickly the loving expression had faded.

How stupid she had been not to realize he was shocked to see her at that moment, and no doubt utterly disappointed.

"Oh, Freddy." she murmured. "Why didn't you tell me?"

"I—I didn't know," he said quietly. "But it doesn't matter. I know my duty to you and I will do it."

Jane laughed aloud at the irony of it. "Oh, my dearest one," she said, lifting a hand to his face with the deepest affection. "Just as I have promised myself, over and over, that I would do my duty by you."

He frowned. She knew he hadn't even the smallest notion what she meant by it. But it hardly mattered. She laughed again as dinner was announced and begged him to enjoy his meal since she was persuaded it would be very close to his last supper as a bachelor.

"You wish to be wed so quickly?" he asked, taking up her arm again, his expression acutely anxious.

Jane chuckled again. "Not precisely."

Perhaps she should have released him instantly from his obligations to her, but she didn't. Maybe it was a certain perversity in her nature, or maybe she was just irritated that Freddy was such a fool, but she thought that for at least one night he was going to have to bear being betrothed to her.

Tomorrow, sometime before the recessional, when all the guests would depart Challeston Hall, she would inform him of her decision. But for now, she would enjoy the irony and stupidity of the moment.

Fifteen

On the following morning, Jane moved about her bedchamber in preparation for her departure from Challeston Hall with something of a light heart. She chuckled at all the ironies that had beset her since her arrival, she sang ballads that had been performed over and over during the past fortnight, she refused to acknowledge that in leaving she was returning to Kent where she would have to face the sale of Woodcock Hill Manor, the confiscation of all property belonging to her of even the smallest value, even the surrendering of her beloved gelding, the only beast to have survived Edward's penchant for the vice of chance.

Her schemes had failed, one and all, and she realized she was glad of it. She knew now for a certainty that though she had revelled in Thorpe's embraces and come to love him with all her heart, she could not live as he insisted they live. It was all or nothing with her, even though her heart and her passions willed it otherwise. She was simply not of a mind to become his mistress, or any man's mistress. She would rather muck stables to earn her keep.

She supposed it could be argued that she had been his mistress for a fortnight. But in her opinion, he had only been her lover, and that because she had accepted none of his bounty—she had not truly surrendered herself to him in that hated role.

Of course, she had Mrs. Newstead to thank for opening her eyes to the precise nature of the life she had been on the brink of choosing. The vignette she had performed on Thursday night had proven Thorpe's character to her beyond regression. Never again would she trust him to be other than what he was, never again would she succumb to his seductions that she might become one of several conquests.

So be it!

Two of her portmanteaux were lying wide-mouthed on her bed, receiving her numerous garments—dozens of thin linen shifts, silk stockings, and hand-embroidered garters, slippers of every color, of leather and of silk, gloves in a rainbow of colors, knit, crocheted, formed of hand-woven lace, silk, fine linen, several bustles and corsets that had displayed her charms to great advantage over the past two weeks.

Ordinarily, Vangie would have performed these services, but today she needed the experience of bringing her adventure to an end by herself, if for no other reason than to straighten her thoughts into a clean line of purpose so that when she finally descended the stairs she could leave Challeston with no regrets.

She rolled one last pair of stockings, settled them next to one of her finely crafted corsets of whalebone, and moved to the window. On the drive below, she saw that four travelling coaches had been drawn up and were even now being decorated with long vines of ivy, white, pink, and red roses bound into lovely, looping festoons, and braids of pretty green ferns.

The moment of the recessional had arrived.

Jane pressed a hand to her stomach, trying to hold back the sudden sadness that moved through her.

An ending to everything.

Even to her societal pleasures, since she thought she must now become a governess or perhaps a companion to an elderly resident of one of the watering holes—Bath, for instance, or perhaps Brighton—in order to sustain her existence.

She closed her eyes, refusing to let her spirits falter. She had only one object now; to make certain that her friend and confidant, Lady Somercote, would not worry about her. She also needed to speak with Freddy in order to inform him that their betrothal was at an end.

Having completed most of the packing of her portmanteaux, she decided Vangie could now finish the task for her. She crossed the room to ring for her abigail. When she had given her instructions to the maid she left her bedchamber and made a slow descent down the circular staircase and headed toward the back gardens. She wanted to be among the flowers for a time, perhaps with the hope that the sweetness of their fragrances would return some of the sweetness to her life.

She wore a travelling gown of dark green silk, high at the neck though with lovely puffed sleeves trimmed with light pink point lace, and long pink linen gloves. Over her dark curls, she wore a straw bonnet, covered over the brim with matching green silk ruching and a fall of pink lace from beneath the brim touching her dark brown curls arranged in a fluff on her forehead. A shawl of patterned yellow, pink, and green silk accented her gown in a loop behind her as she carried it elegantly over her elbows.

She made her way slowly toward the beehives, and the closer she drew to the coiled basket houses, the stronger the drone of the contentedly busy creatures. She passed by them, walking to the far end of the garden, a hedge separating the pretty red deer, still grazing on the slopes of Windy Knowl, and the flower garden. When she turned toward the house on the far side of the luxuriantly crowded flower beds, she noticed with a start that Thorpe had entered the garden and was wending his way diagonally through the beds toward her.

Her heart turned over in her breast; her breath was squeezed from her lungs by the shock of seeing him as well as by the sure knowledge he meant to dissuade her again in her refusals, and her knees began to tremble. She walked quickly down the path nearest the hedge, making a straight line toward the house. She didn't want to speak to him. There was a part of her that hated him, hated him for not having loved her enough to offer her his name instead of just his body.

He began to break up the diagonal of his path and moved to intercept her. She walked faster. If she hurried she could elude him completely, for once she returned to the house she defied him to set up a caterwaul.

Again he altered his course; she began to run. He turned toward the back of the house. She moved back up the path. He drew within ten feet of her.

"Oh, do stop!" she cried suddenly, whirling in her flight to face him. "Can't you leave me in peace? There's nothing you can say to me that will change my mind. I shan't forgive you for having revealed your treachery to Mrs. Newstead and I certainly shan't join you on a love-journey through the Continent."

He smiled crookedly. "A love-journey?" he queried. "Jane, please stop. Please let me speak with you. Please try to find it in your heart to forgive me. A few days ago you said you loved me."

"I was deluded with a belief that you could love me in return. But you can't. Deny that you can't! Even then, I wouldn't believe you. How I despise you! You've no idea!" It was then that she burst into tears. Hated, dreaded tears! She had not wanted to succumb to the misery of her disappointment but there it was, streaming down her cheeks. She turned away from him, ripped a kerchief from the pocket of her pretty green silk gown, swiped at her cheeks, and blew her nose in unladylike sound.

She felt his hands on her arms first, his gloves placed no doubt purposefully on the small space of flesh between the hem of her sleeve and the top of her long light pink glove. "I never meant to cause you such pain," he whispered.

"Well, you have, but I know I am not the first—or do you suppose that all the women you have pursued and snagged have been truly indifferent to you?"

"Yes," he responded baldly. "I am convinced I was never loved before and I refuse to believe that you have stopped loving me."

"My more tender sentiments for you are now so mixed up with my hatred for you that I can promise only this—I can be of no use to you now. Mrs. Newstead's vignette showed me my future with a man who has no respect for the women he seduces, and I refuse to embrace such a future."

He turned her gently and drew her into his arms. "Look at me, Jane," he murmured. She lifted her head to meet his gaze. "What a pretty bonnet," he sighed, letting his gaze drift over her face. "What a beautiful woman." His lips touched her cheeks, her nose, and began a light, delicate caress of her lips.

Jane felt more tears begin rushing to her eyes and pouring past her eyelids. He was so well suited to her physically, why then couldn't he simply love her? The knowledge that love, marriage, and family were an impossibility with him caused a strange frigidity to flow through her. His kisses no longer teased and tantalized her. She felt dull, empty, and drained. The tears stopped flowing.

After a moment he drew back from her and searched her face. "What is it?" he murmured.

She didn't respond. Instead, she slipped out of his arms and walked away from him, wiping the last remnant of her tears from her cheeks.

"Jane," he called to her. But she knew now that he had no power over her, and with her head high she returned to the house.

In the green velvet drawing room, Jane began to bid her *adieus* to her fellow guests. Freddy and Henrietta had not yet descended to the receiving room, otherwise everyone was present. She ignored Thorpe though she did notice that upon his arrival after her in the beautifully appointed chamber he seemed oddly somber, so much unlike him. She also noticed that the first person to greet him and begin her farewells was Mrs. Newstead.

The widow was dressed jauntily in a gown of embroidered white muslin, gathered about a high waistline into a frothy morning gown bearing dozens of little cupids all about the skirts. The gown had long, sheer sleeves and she wore light blue lace gloves. About her neck was a blue ribbon and a cameo worn tightly at the throat of ivory and peach silhouette. Her bonnet was trimmed with rosettes of a matching light blue lace. Her expression was triumphant, due no doubt to her knowledge that she had effectively separated Lord Thorpe from his latest object. Her blue eyes glittered and a fine orange blush seemed fixed permanently to her ivory cheeks.

Jane wanted to turn away from the sight of her having engaged Thorpe intensely in conversation until she noted that the viscount had a scowl on his face. Whatever was being said between them turned swiftly to a quarrel into which Mrs. Newstead quickly drew a passing Colonel Duffield.

The murmur of their voices began to draw notice.

Lady Somercote moved to stand next to Jane. "Whatever is going forward?" Her dear friend sported a striped lavender silk gown, rather decollete for the morning hour, but which displayed her charms to delightful advantage. She wore no bonnet, only a fall of lace tucked into a pretty wreath of peppery curls.

Jane shook her head. "I can't imagine but I daresay though they brangle, they at least deserve one another."

She looked into Lady Somercote's compassionate eyes and gave herself a mental shake. "How bitter I sound," she said, reproaching herself. "But I shan't be, I promise you that."

"You are speaking quite oddly for a lady about to be married."

Jane chuckled slightly. "Freddy and I are not to be wed," she confessed. "He is in love with Henrietta."

"You know this to be true?" she asked, startled.

"Very much so. I should have ended our betrothal last night when I discovered the truth of his sentiments, but I was so stunned that I decided to wait until this morning. By the way, have you seen Freddy? I have been wanting to speak with him in order to finally release him from his duty."

Lady Somercote shook her head. "I'm sure he'll be along presently. But, oh, Jane, I am so very sorry."

Jane shrugged her shoulders slightly. "Pray forgive me for cutting up your peace on this last day of your *fete*. I want you to know, I've had a marvelous time and I am so grateful for everything you've done for me."

Lady Somercote slipped her arm about Jane's and drew her near the fireplace, away from the quarrelsome threesome near the door and from her husband and the Ullstrees watching in shocked silence by the pianoforte.

Lady Somercote turned her shoulder away from the rest of her guests and whispered, "You don't need to leave Challeston. You can remain my guest, forever, if you wish for it."

"What nonsense," Jane returned in a warm murmur. "You've done enough for me. You gave me all the opportunities I required, I simply misjudged everything."

"But Freddy would still have you—he is obligated."

"I wouldn't subject him to a marriage to me when I know for a certainty his heart is engaged elsewhere. I am not so base."

"Of course you are not. Dear Jane."

Jane peeked past her shoulder and saw that Mrs. Newstead appeared peculiarly triumphant now as she slipped her hand into the pocket of Thorpe's coat and whispered something in his ear. Lord Thorpe appeared outraged as he found her hand and threw it away from him. He then turned on his heel and left the drawing room. As Mrs. Newstead's laughter flowed after him, Jane could only surmise that the widow had somehow managed to win her wager with Thorpe and now he had to marry her. So there was justice afterall, Jane thought maliciously.

Remembering that Lady Somercote had schemes of her own in progress, she addressed the matter with her. "Enough of my troubles," she whispered, smiling and realizing she was feeling better minute by minute. "Only tell me if Somercote has discovered your identity."

"Not yet," she whispered. "But I intend to tell him very soon. In fact, the moment all our guests are fixed in their carriages, I mean to ask him which costume he would prefer I wear tonight."

Jane gasped then giggled. "I count the minutes, then," she whispered. "He will be ever so shocked."

"He will likely faint."

"He will be very happy."

Lady Somercote turned to regard her mate, who was watching

her askance as though a mysterious notion had just occurred to him. The countess blew her husband a kiss, he lifted his brows in response and smiled faintly, curiosity rampant on his features. He touched his black hair at the temple, then turned to address something Mr. Ullstree was saying to him.

Mrs. Ullstree excused herself and joined Jane and the countess by the fireplace. She wore a loose gown of cherry-red silk, a white silk spencer, and a matching red silk bonnet over her brown curls. Her spirits were diminished by the fact that she was leaving. Mrs. Ullstree suffered terribly from carriage-sickness and though she managed to pretend all was well, even Jane could see she was dreading the forthcoming journey to her home in Hampshire.

"What are these two discussing?" Mrs. Ullstree whispered, gesturing with a roll of her eyes toward Mrs. Newstead and the colonel who were now moving slowly toward the window overlooking the drive where the carriages stood in readiness.

Mrs. Newstead's eyes were narrowed and her head lowered as she listened mulishly to the colonel.

Mrs. Ullstree clicked her tongue. "She would be a fool not to accept his offer."

"Has he offered for her then?" Jane queried in a whisper.

Mrs. Ullstree nodded. "He has loved her—or what was it he said, oh, yes, *desired* her forever. Curious he did not use the word lust."

Mrs. Newstead's voice was heard across the room. "India?" she was heard to cry out.

Jane lifted her brows. India had been mentioned in his vignette with Mrs. Ullstree. The latter explained, "He has received a commission with The Company there."

"The East India Company?" Lady Somercote remarked.

Mrs. Ullstree nodded.

"Mrs. Newstead will not go," Jane said. "I have heard her say that London is the only place that suits her."

"I think she would do well in India," Lady Somercote remarked.

"I would not be sorry to see her go," Mrs. Ullstree added, tilting her head. "She is amusing in her own way and certainly I enjoyed her engaging and quite provocative performance during her vignette on Thursday night, but she is a hopeless mischief-maker. I hear it is so hot in India that one does not care about making mischief so much as keeping one's servants employed in the use of palm fronds."

Jane smiled and Lady Somercote chuckled.

When Mrs. Newstead fell silent, Jane thought it would not be a bad time to bid farewell to both a woman who had proved her enemy and to a man she had come to admire if not understand precisely. She excused herself to her hostess and Mrs. Ullstree then moved to bow to Mrs. Newstead and to offer her hand to Colonel Duffield.

Mrs. Newstead offered a deep curtsy in response, a gesture full of irony and triumph. Jane merely lifted a brow and addressed the colonel. "I was very glad to have furthered my acquaintance with you. You were a constant delight during the festivities and I wish you every happiness and future success."

Mrs. Newstead rolled her eyes and moved away impolitely.

Duffield cocked his head at her and with an odd smile twisting his lips, he said, "A word with you, Mrs. Ambergate, if you please?"

Jane was surprised. But when he turned his back toward the other guests and lifted his arm to her with the intention of escorting her from the drawing room, she hesitated only slightly before accepting his escort. He drew her across the black and white tiled entrance hall and walked her slowly down the long hall connecting with the music room.

"I have only one thing I must beg of you, my dear," he said in an oddly fatherly manner, "and you must trust me wholly when I tell you what it is you must now do."

"Why, Colonel Duffield," Jane said, slightly amused since he seemed so serious. "If it is within my power, of course I will most happily oblige you. Whatever is it you wish me to do?"

"You won't like it, not above half, but you must trust me.

Tell me first—before I reveal the nature of my command—that
you trust me."

Jane swallowed. "I fear to give you offense, but given the
circumstances I can't help but tell you the truth. I trust you—but
only in part."

He seemed a little shocked.

"You must admit you are not on ordinary fellow."

"I suppose I am not," he responded a little uneasily. "Only
do you trust me enough to know that what I ask you to do next
will be for your good, truly for your good?"

Jane sighed. "Tell me what it is you wish me to do and then
I can give you an answer."

He stopped walking and turned to face her, holding her gaze
squarely. "Lord Thorpe will be asking you to become his mistress and you must, you absolutely must, agree to it."

"What?" Jane responded, dumbfounded. "Are none of my
affairs kept secret from anyone?" She supposed by his odious
words that he had been informed of her relationship with Thorpe
from the beginning.

"Come! Come!" Colonel Duffield cried. "Missishness will
not serve you at this eleventh hour. Only trust and a little courage will win the day. Your cheeks have worn the glow of a lady
in love for this past fortnight, so I refuse to listen to any of your
outraged protests."

Brought down from her high ropes by his sensible retort, she
responded, "But I can't do as you ask. I refuse to become his
mistress. I refuse to allow him the pleasure of seeing me humble
myself to him when he has used me so ill."

"He did not use you ill—well perhaps a little. It was Mrs.
Newstead who betrayed a confidence she should not have—
that's all. Don't make too much of it."

"You are clearly not a woman or you would never have said
to me, *do not make too much of it!* A man can boast of such
activities but a woman can only be shamed by admitting to
them. I'm sorry, everything in my heart tells me not to comply
with your request."

He shook his head violently. "Get over this rough ground lightly or else you will fall."

"What are you not telling me?" she asked, suddenly suspicious.

"If I tell you, all hope is lost before it is begun."

Jane turned away from him impatiently and began moving back toward the entrance hall. "You are speaking in mysteries and riddles and I won't listen. I won't cast myself at his feet. Now, no more!"

She heard the colonel sigh. "As you wish," he said, taking up his place beside her as she moved swiftly down the hall. She realized she was ready to go, to be done with the whole of it, to be as far from Thorpe as possible.

As she drew near the doorway opening onto the entrance hall, however, she watched Freddy pass through to the front door on a hurried, almost anxious step. "I must speak with my betrothed," she said. "I must release him from his obligations."

"Well at least you are showing some sense."

"And you have offended me enough today, Duffield!"

She cast him an arch look, but he merely burst out laughing. "I have, haven't I? Forgive me, Mrs. Ambergate. I promise you that whatever happens, I shall always remain your most obedient servant."

Jane slowed her step a little and again took up his arm. "You are being posted to India, aren't you?"

He nodded.

"You will do wonderfully well there, I am persuaded. I am only sorry that Mrs. Newstead will not be accompanying you."

"I haven't lost hope, yet," he said. "But my ship leaves in two days' time, so . . ."

He let the words trail off as Henrietta arrived at the entrance hall. Her complexion was a pasty white and she had a bandbox dangling from each hand. Her bonnet of rust-colored silk was slightly askew and the curls which trailed from the back of it were unkempt.

"What the deuce!" the colonel cried.

Jane moved into the entrance hall and from the opposite side, through the antechamber connecting to the drawing room, the remaining guests emerged. Thorpe arrived at the exact same moment as though following a stage cue, entering from the direction of the terrace.

"Oh," Hetty exclaimed as she rushed across the entrance hall and disappeared through the doorway in Freddy's wake.

"Whatever is going forward?" Jane cried, moving quickly to the doorway where the butler, his complexion high, held the door wide.

Colonel Duffield was not far behind her and she heard his voice shoot over the top of her head, "By God, it's an elopement!"

Jane drew in her breath sharply, moving onto the drive.

"Oh, Jane," Mrs. Ullstree cried, clapping her hands together. "Your betrothed has jilted you!"

Jane only laughed. "Just as he should when his heart is given elsewhere."

A fine series of murmurs, exclamations, and wonderments followed her pronouncement. Laughter then rippled through the crowd as Freddy, in his haste, pushed his beloved into the travelling chariot and she fell on her face. The hem of her rust silk travelling gown became caught in the carriage steps and Freddy tore the silk while trying to disengage the fabric.

"My pet! My dearest one!" Freddy exclaimed. "Are you all right?" Pink patches covered his complexion. He turned to look at Jane, his face a mass of worried lines, as he bowed to her. How comical he looked with his black beaver hat askew. "I'm sorry, Mrs. Ambergate—Jane. But I cannot marry you."

She took a step toward him and felt the crowd of guests move as one behind her. She waved at him and smiled. "I wish you joy, Freddy Waingrove, intense, long-lasting, wondrous joy!"

His chest collapsed slightly with relief and once he saw Henrietta settled within the travelling chariot, he turned toward her. She moved forward on a quick step, then ran toward him. He took up her hint, walking briskly in her direction. He caught

her up in his arms. "I release you from our betrothal," Jane
said. "I had meant to earlier, but I couldn't find you."

"Dearest Jane," he murmured. She heard a sob in his throat.

She drew back to look up into his misty gold-green eyes.
"You don't have to run away," she assured him.

"Oh, yes I do," he responded anxiously, withdrawing a letter
from his coat pocket. He held it up and crushed it in his fist.
"It's from my mother. Somehow she has deduced my true feelings for Hetty and has forbidden such an alliance. She knew of
my love for her before even I did. As much as I dote on my
dear mother, she is . . . she is a deuced termagent!"

"But I thought she adored Hetty," Jane cried, astonished.

He compressed his lips. "Hetty has only three thousand
pounds. Mama would never forgive my having wed such a paltry sum."

"But Freddy," Jane said, again dumbfounded. "You courted
me, you begged for my hand, but I was destitute!"

She watched Freddy's complexion pale, "Yes. That was one
of the reasons I found it so difficult to bring myself up to scratch
where you were concerned. But, all's well that ends well, eh?"

Jane again embraced him, chuckling all the while. "Yes,
Freddy, all's well."

He turned to look back at the carriage. Hetty's frightened
gaze was visible peeping around the corner of the window. A
slight breeze ruffled the light brown curls on her forehead.

Jane smiled and waved to her, but instead of responding to
her gentle overture, Hetty drew her head quickly back inside
the coach like a frightened tortoise.

"Well, we'd best be going," Freddy said. "I'll write to you."

"You must do that, and tell me about all your children."

Freddy blushed and she gave him a shove toward the carriage.
He stumbled awkwardly, blushed more deeply still, then
climbed aboard the travelling chariot. Once the door was shut,
he leaned his head out to give the postboy the office to start,
then looked back at Jane and with his gloved fingers blew her
a kiss. Of course, the horses jerked the carriage forward at just

that moment, and her former swain smashed his nose on the edge of the window frame. He cried out and Jane was sure he had earned himself a bloody nose.

She couldn't help herself as she burst out laughing as did most of the guests now drawing up next to her. Freddy, for all his budding poetic genius, could be such a nodcock.

"What a simpleton," Mr. Ullstree commented, drawing up beside her.

"Very much so," Jane responded. "But a loving one, so all is forgiven."

Lady Somercote's voice rose above the ongoing, astonished din of remarks about the elopement. "The time has come—of course prompted by a most appropriate flight undoubtedly to Gretna Green—to say *adieu*. All your chariots have been supplied with a basket of food and a bottle of wine for the commencement of your journeys. Thank you ever so much for gracing my house and for participating so enthusiastically in every element of my *fete*."

A round of huzzas went up about Lady Somercote in appreciation for her efforts. Jane, standing at the edge of the crowd, looked back over her shoulder at Freddy's and Hetty's carriage turning into the lane and disappearing from sight behind the long hedgerow. She sighed deeply and turned around more fully to discover which of the chariots would be escorting her home to Kent.

She walked toward the first coach, but did not recognize her portmanteaux, then the second, the third, and found that the fourth, covered with red roses and ferns, was hers. She was about to climb aboard when a commotion was heard behind her.

"I don't believe you, Thorpe!" Mrs. Newstead cried. "You are telling a whisker merely to avoid the entrapment of our wager!"

Jane turned around, curious as to why the widow had set up a caterwaul, and saw that Lord Thorpe was trying to disengage Mrs. Newstead's arm from about his. "She agreed and now we will ask her."

Colonel Duffield drew up sharply beside Thorpe. "It's true, Sophie," the colonel said. "I heard her agree to it m'self."

"You are both telling whiskers," Mrs. Newstead insisted, finally relinquishing her hold on Thorpe's arm. "And I shall prove it at once."

Jane watched in some surprise as Mrs. Newstead turned to look at her, set her chin determinedly, and headed straight for her. Thorpe and the colonel were not far behind.

How pretty and how vixenish Mrs. Newstead appeared in the July sunshine, the soft breeze gently swirling the gauzy muslin of her richly gathered gown.

Jane placed a hand protectively against her bosom. Her heart began to beat unsteadily in her breast. She felt strange, almost dizzy as the three of them descended upon her. She took a step backward and felt the door of the coach, opened wide to receive her, press into her upper back. "Whatever is going forward?" she asked politely.

Beyond Mrs. Newstead's shoulder, she noted that Mr. Ullstree began a quick, rolling amble toward her, as well. His hand was lifted up, a finger pointing into the sky, as though he wished to gain her attention. But why?

Mrs. Newstead smiled wickedly, "So tell us, Mrs. Ambergate, are you or are you not Lord Thorpe's mistress?"

"I most certainly—"

"Mrs. Ambergate," Mr. Ullstree called to her, cutting her words off abruptly. "You have not bid your farewells to me and I take it most unkindly in you not to have done so." He pushed his way forward, between Mrs. Newstead and Lord Thorpe, and caught up Jane's hand in his. She was never more astonished in her life. "I thought we had become great friends. Have I in some way offended you?"

Jane lifted her brows in stupefaction. "No, of course not," she said, staring at Mr. Ullstree dumbly. "Though I promise you I have already bid farewell to your lovely wife."

"However polite that may be," he said. "I should never have forgiven you had you not at least kissed my cheek and promised to return to London next spring." He smiled at her so sweetly and his obvious affection for her was so genuine, that she did the only thing she could and leaned forward to place a kiss on his cheek.

"Say yes," he whispered into her ear.

"What?" she queried, uncertain she had heard him and yet wondering what he meant by it.

He drew back from her slightly, stared at her meaningfully, his bushy brows lifting in alternate musical beats to some message he was trying to convey to her. "Say yes," he mouthed.

"Yes?"

Mr. Ullstree took her hand and whirled her about to face Mrs. Newstead squarely. "You have your answer, Mrs. Newstead. Mrs. Ambergate said *yes,* she is Thorpe's mistress. She will tell you so herself this very moment."

Jane was shocked, mortified, and undone all at the same time. She stared mutely at Mr. Ullstree. She tried to wriggle her hand from his grasp but he caught it up securely beneath his arm, then drew her close to him.

"Tell her, Jane," Mr. Ullstree stated, squeezing her hand again in a marked manner as his brows had done earlier. Whatever did he mean by it? And why would he insist she admit to something she had no intention of admitting to?

At that moment, Mrs. Ullstree, seeing the commotion and that her husband had some sort of hold on her, came round Mrs. Newstead's right side and said, "Whatever are you doing to poor Mrs. Ambergate?" she asked, an amused smile on her lips. "Do not tell me you have taken to flirting with her when we are just now about to leave Challeston? I don't like to mention it, m'dear, but you've quite missed your opportunity. We are not likely to see Jane until the spring."

Jane turned to blink at Mrs. Ullstree and then to smile gratefully for her arrival. Perhaps the good woman could lend some manner of sense and logic to the odd, hysterical quality of the moment. For the life of her, as she again glanced at Mr. Ullstree's round cheeks, she could not conceive of why he was insisting she tell Mrs. Newstead she was Thorpe's mistress.

"Mrs. Ullstree, would you please explain to your good husband that I am not—"

She got no further as Mr. Ullstree again cut her off. "Mrs. Ambergate was just explaining to Mrs. Newstead that she has agreed to become Thorpe's mistress and will be so for a very long time to come."

"Well, of course she has," Mrs. Ullstree agreed, also taking up Jane's free arm, thereby effectively pinning her between the pair of them. Mrs. Ullstree continued, "However, can't you see that you are putting Mrs. Ambergate in an intolerable position? How can any woman claim such a position when to do so generally means social ruin. A woman can be any man's mistress and have her name bandied about all the drawing rooms of London, but she cannot confess to the deed. What I begin to wonder is who precisely has put Mrs. Ambergate in such a wretched place of mortification? Not you, Charles, surely!"

Mr. Ullstree shook his head. "Mrs. Newstead asked her directly if it was true."

Mrs. Ullstree turned a shocked, disgusted visage to Mrs. Newstead. Her nostrils flared, her eyes narrowed. Mrs. Newstead took a step backward. "It—it is of the utmost importance that the truth be known," Mrs. Newstead cried.

"If I recall correctly," Mrs. Ullstree said in a coldly soft voice, "when you were sharing Thorpe's bed, no woman of quality ever confronted you about your activities, now did they?"

"Well," Mrs. Newstead responded breathlessly. She took several shallow breaths, her cheeks flaming. After a long moment, she lifted her chin, "I—I begin to see what this is. You are all against me." She glared at Colonel Duffield. "I suppose this is your doing?"

He shook his head, smiling crookedly. "No, though I begin to be grateful for the intervention of friends."

Mrs. Newstead compressed her lips and stamped her foot and

turned to Thorpe. "I will have an answer, from her own mouth, or I shan't relinquish my prize!"

Jane turned to Thorpe and blinked at him. She saw in his face a measure of reserve and regret that gave her pause more than Mr. and Mrs. Ullstree's strange support of her during an even stranger confrontation with the widow Newstead.

His expression softened in quick stages as he returned her gaze. She saw love, love for her, reflected in his blue eyes for the first time. Her heartbeat quickened. He drew in a deep breath and said, "I would never sully Mrs. Ambergate's name or her fine reputation by suggesting anything so beneath her dignity, her character, or her delicacy of mind. I would only beg her forgiveness for having permitted the wretched subject to have been brought forward at all."

Jane was never more astounded. A silence fell upon the small group clustered near the rose-strewn carriage. Only the breeze, rustling the ladies' gowns, disturbed the flow and sweetness of Thorpe's words. She smiled gratefully at him, then glanced at Duffield whose brown eyes watched her intently. She recalled her conversation with him earlier in the long hall, his insistence she must agree to become Thorpe's mistress, for reasons he could not explain. She felt Mr. Ullstree pinch her arm. She remembered the night, a few days past, when they had listened to stolen kisses and a secretive conversation between Colonel Duffield and Mrs. Newstead. She knew of Colonel Duffield's wish to wed Mrs. Newstead, she remembered that there was some sort of wager Mrs. Newstead had with Thorpe and that Mr. Ullstree had wanted to tell her more of the particulars—that the particulars involved her.

Lord and Lady Somercote, who had drawn near the group, begged to know what was going forward, but no one could speak.

Jane however finally began to piece together all the mysteries. As her brain made one connection upon the other, ending with the fact that Mrs. Newstead had used her violet-beribboned brass key during her vignette with Lord Somercote, she finally understood that she had been the object of the wager. Or more specifically, Thorpe's ability to make her his mistress. Perhaps she should have been outraged, but seeing that Thorpe's expression had not changed and that he would not press her further about the matter, she finally drew in a deep breath and began, "You don't need to protect my reputation further, Thorpe. Of what use would that be? When we travel through Paris or Salzburg or Venice do you really suppose that we will meet with no one with whom either you or I are acquainted? For whatever reason, Mrs. Newstead seems to require my admission to our plans, and though I am loath to admit the whole of it, I will. I am intent on becoming your mistress as I have been for the past fortnight."

She then held Mrs. Newstead's gaze firmly and had the satisfaction of watching the color drain from the pretty widow's face. She was not surprised when Mrs. Newstead's knees crumpled and she tumbled onto the gravel of the drive in a deep swoon.

The group gathered about Jane, dropped their heads, almost as one, to stare at the widow Newstead. No one moved to assist her. The July sunshine continued to flow in a steady, warm beam. A breeze, fragrant of roses, tugged at the muslin of Mrs. Newstead's skirts.

Mrs. Ullstree lifted her gaze from the widow's prostrate form and smiled at Jane. "You've done well," she said, patting Jane's arm and speaking as though Mrs. Newstead did not even exist. "They had a wager, you know—Thorpe and Mrs. Newstead. He had agreed to marry her if he couldn't make you his mistress by the end of the *fete*." Mrs. Ullstree then frowned accusingly at Thorpe. "You don't deserve Mrs. Ambergate's kindnesses toward you, my lord, and as for your conduct, I consider it of libertine proportions. I would give you the cut direct except that my dear Charles has already told me he believes you might just have learned your lessons during this fortnight and that the whole of it will have made a man of you."

"I would like to think so," Thorpe said humbly. "And I do beg your pardon for my conduct. It was wholly ungentlemanly and unforgivable."

"Yes, yes, you look very handsome when you make your

speeches but you know very well what I expect you to do next."
She stepped indifferently over Mrs. Newstead's sprawling legs
and embraced Thorpe, placing a kiss on his cheek. "But now
we must go. I have every hope of seeing you both in the spring.
Come, Charles, I think we've done all we can of the moment."

Mr. Ullstree chuckled, finally released his stranglehold on
Jane's arm, but turned to embrace her warmly. He bid her good-
bye, then rounded one of Mrs. Newstead's feet to take his wife's
arm and escort her to her carriage.

Lady Somercote stared down at the widow, shook her head,
and clucked her tongue. "What a disgraceful female," she murmured. "I suppose I should render her some assistance."

She was about to call for a footman, when the colonel stepped
forward and said, "Don't bother any of your servants," he said.
He leaned down, gathered up his beloved in his arms, and while
holding her somewhat triumphantly, said, "We will be married,
my love and I. She will reign like a princess in India." With
that, he carried her to his coach and gave instructions to the
postillion with regard to the disposition of Mrs. Newstead's travelling chariot. He gently placed his bride-to-be on the squabs
of the coach, following quickly after her to take up his place
beside her. A moment later, he stuck his head out the window,
gave a single, sharp, soldierly wave good-bye to his fellow
guests, then gave the postillions the office to start.

His coach, followed by Mrs. Newstead's, began bowling
down the lane. Soon afterward, the Ullstree coach—last in
line—rumbled by. Mr. Ullstree waved, but Mrs. Ullstree already
had lost a great deal of the bloom on her cheeks and was settling
herself into her husband's gentle embrace, a kerchief to her lips.

"Poor Mrs. Ullstree," Jane murmured as the coach passed by.

"Are you ever ill when you travel, Mrs. Ambergate?" Thorpe
asked.

Jane looked up at him and shrugged. "Never. I was granted
a strong constitution and rarely ever falter no matter what the
mode of transport. Even sailing, my stomach seemed to delight
in the roll of the sea beneath the hull."

"Will you travel with me, then?" he queried. "I am never ill myself and I believe we would do prodigiously together."

"I believe we should," Jane responded, drawing close to him and slipping her arm about his.

Lady Somercote drew in a sharp breath. "But I thought—I mean surely, Thorpe, you don't intend—"

Lord Somercote took hold of his wife's hand and gave it a forceful squeeze. "None of our concern, m'dear."

Lady Somercote bit her lip and sighed deeply. "No, of course not." She then gave Jane a final embrace and tears suddenly flooded her eyes. "I'm sorry," she whispered. "I should have protected you from his advances, only I didn't know."

Thorpe whipped his hat off his head in a long-suffering manner and offered Lady Somercote his kerchief. "Dry your eyes, madame," he stated flatly. He then astonished Jane by dropping on one knee at her feet and wincing as the gravel bit into his buckskin breeches at the knees. "The devil take it," he muttered.

He took hold of Jane's hand and she bit her lip at the sight of his unromantic expression. "I suppose there is nothing for it," he began as though wretchedly pressed beyond his desires, "but the fact is that neither Mrs. Ullstree nor Lady Somercote will be willing to acknowledge me during the next Season if I do not do right by you. So I ask you now, Mrs. Ambergate, are you willing to tolerate me for the next forty or fifty years?"

Lady Somercote was heard to catch her voice on a sob as she turned to bury her face in her husband's shoulder.

"I must have one or two assurances," Jane responded.

Thorpe glared up at her. "I suppose you wish for a settlement?"

"Something far worse than that, and you may not be able to comply with my requests, in which case I will have to refuse you."

He eyed her suspiciously from between narrowed lids. "And what might these *requests* be?"

Jane kept a smile from her lips as she began, "Firstly, are you willing to leave off reading your newspaper until you have exchanged at least three pleasantries with me during the course of each morning?"

"I knew you would be a taskmaster," he retorted as he flared his nostrils purposely, his blue eyes twinkling. "Good God! So it begins already, even before the banns have been read."

"Will you or will you not?" she asked firmly.

"I consent," he said, stiff-lipped.

"Very well. Secondly, for each of our daughters, will you promise to guide them in their choice of a husband without behaving like a brute or a beast?"

"You go too far, madame," he cried, shifting his pained knee to make the poor joint a little more comfortable. "A father always reserves the right to conduct himself as crudely as possible in front of his daughters' *beaux*. It is the true mark of civilization."

Jane shrugged. "Then there can be no marriage."

"Oh, very well," he muttered, his lips twitching. "If you insist on it, I suppose I must consent."

"Excellent. I'm proud of you. Finally," and here she glanced askance at him. "Will you promise to frequent White's only once or twice per week during the Season and the rest of the time to make certain that I am not neglected?"

Lord Thorpe growled. "You push me too hard, my good woman."

Jane withdrew her hand from his and crossed her arms over her chest. "Mrs. Ullstree said she permits her dear Charles to attend Brook's only once per week, so I feel that I am being lenient beyond permission."

Thorpe again narrowed his eyes, grumbled a little more, and in the end nodded.

Jane again shrugged her shoulders. "I suppose I will marry you, then, if I must."

He rose from his knee and turned toward Lord Somercote. "You will have to congratulate me right now, else I will not feel my promises in any way valid within the context of our gentlemanly vows, or in any manner subject to the Laws of England."

Lord Somercote burst out laughing. "I congratulate you,

Thorpe. Yes, you are doomed, but there it is, so we all are. But you will be happy." He glanced at Jane and smiled crookedly. "Very much so, if I don't miss my mark."

"Well, of course he will," Lady Somercote said. "I have already instructed Jane about the use of costumes to create all manner of diversion, though she is permitting me to keep her Cleopatra creation. She said she could have another one made up without too much fuss."

Lord Somercote's mouth fell agape as he turned to stare at his wife. "Damne, I was right!" he cried. "I admit once or twice I suspected, but Miriam—!"

Lady Somercote ignored him and instead embraced Jane. "All's well," she said, intoning Freddy's earlier remark.

"Indeed," she murmured. "Thank you for everything. You've been a most excellent friend to me."

"I wish you every happiness, my dear."

Jane released her friend and took up Thorpe's proffered arm. He drew her toward his coach but she stayed him from opening the door. "I prefer that we travel in mine," she said provokingly.

He turned to look at her, his blue eyes wide with surprise.

Jane merely laughed at him and opened the door to his coach. "Just don't push me inside," she cried, as she lifted the green silk skirts of her travelling gown.

He seemed to realize she had been teasing him, and he relaxed visibly. "I am not so hamhanded," he responded, holding the door wide and letting down the steps for her.

Jane was about to mount the steps when she turned to look back at Lord and Lady Somercote. "Oh, dear!" she cried.

Thorpe glanced in the direction of her gaze as well and chuckled at the sight of Lord Somercote kissing his wife quite passionately in front of two postillions, three footmen, the butler, and two of their guests. After a moment, he released his wife and with his hand at the small of her back began guiding her quickly into the house. The footmen and the butler followed suit, the door closed, and Jane had an odd sense of finality as she looked up at the sparkling gray-white stone.

So much had happened in the fortnight visit that she knew she had only begun to assimilate it all. But above everything, she marvelled at the fact that here she was alighting Thorpe's travelling coach and preparing to enter a new life with him—not as his mistress but as his wife.

With a sigh, she climbed aboard the coach and took up her place on the seat, pushing the basket of food and wine a little out of the way of her leather half-boots. The fragrance of a bounty of sweet peas with which Thorpe's coach was decorated along with the bitter-sweet redolence of ferns flowed through the open windows of the carriage. The exquisite, warm, rich summer day, laden with the bounty of life, surrounded her as Thorpe took up his place beside her and shut the door with a firm snap. He called to the postillion sharply from his window. The horses strained in their harnesses and finally brought the coach moving at a gentle pace.

"What a nicely sprung town chariot," she said.

"Yes, it is," he agreed, turning toward her and possessing himself of her hand. "Jane," he began quietly as the coach rumbled across one of the small stone bridges scattered about the rolling lawns. "I want you to know that I do indeed wish for you to become my wife."

"I know that," she said, smiling shyly up at him.

"You do?" he queried. "Are you sure?"

"Thorpe," she responded firmly. "I have not known you these many months and more without having come to understand you a little." She chuckled and lifted her pink-gloved fingers to touch his cheek. "You would have eaten me for breakfast rather than married me if the former had been your true pleasure. If I understand you at all, you could never have been forced down such a path unless your heart was fully engaged. Besides, you redeemed yourself with me when you risked taking Mrs. Newstead to wife in order to protect the few remaining shreds of my reputation."

"So I did," he responded, smiling at her softly. "I love you, Jane Ambergate. I believe I have from the first, only having been so inexperienced in matters of the heart, I mistook my sentiments for something transient. For that I do apologize most sincerely."

"I accept your apology." She leaned up to him and placed a kiss on his lips, sliding her hand to his ear and into his hair behind.

"Oh, Jane," he murmured, his tongue beginning to play wickedly on her lips. She parted her lips and let him explore the moist depths of her mouth. His hand drifted onto her waist and in slow circles began a fiery progress upward until he was caressing her breast.

She felt desire flow into her abdomen and she gasped. He kissed her harder still. She moaned and drew back from him. "We don't have to marry today, do we?" she asked breathlessly. "I mean, just for a time, wouldn't it be something of a delight if we could—"

His groans stopped her words as he drove his tongue again into her mouth and his hand slipped from her breast down to her waist, over her hip to slide beneath her buttock. He kissed her long and hard, his fingers kneading the flesh of her buttock until she was moaning with her need for him.

She drew back from him and stared hungrily into his face. "The chamber I enjoyed at Chadfield had a most delightful bed," she offered hopefully.

"Are you suggesting—?"

She nodded.

He pulled back from her and leaned his head out the window. "To the Peacock at Chadfield, my good man, and be quick about it!"

ROMANCE FROM FERN MICHAELS

DEAR EMILY   (0-8217-4952-8, $5.99)

WISH LIST   (0-8217-5228-6, $6.99)

AND IN HARDCOVER:

VEGAS RICH   (1-57566-057-1, $25.00)